THE

TRAILING
SPOUSE

THE
TRAILING
SPOUSE

JO FURNISS

Text copyright © 2018 by Jo Furniss
All rights reserved.

Published by Lake Union Publishing, Seattle

www.apub.com

Amazon, the Amazon logo, and Lake Union Publishing are trademarks of Amazon.com, Inc., or its affiliates.

ISBN-13: 9781503949218
ISBN-10: 1503949214

Cover design by David Drummond

Printed in the United States of America

For Mark

I will always be haunted by thoughts of a sun-drenched elsewhere.

—Isabelle Eberhardt

Chapter 1

Amanda Bonham watched an infinite number of Edward Bonhams shrink to the depths of the mirrored walls in the elevator. She jabbed the button and the lift rose with a shudder. When the doors opened, she followed a single Edward Bonham into their apartment, and the elevator made a silent retreat like a well-trained servant.

Ed weaved toward the bedroom, shunting a console table with his hip as he steered himself into his en suite. Amanda hurried to catch a teetering ginger jar, her heels squeezing mewls of pain out of the marble floor. She straightened the display and turned into her own bathroom. Jasmine scented the air from a sprig of cuttings by the sink. For the first time that evening, she broke a genuine smile; Awmi, their maid, always brought flowers from her evening walk in the condo gardens.

After washing, Amanda sat on the bed to undo the ribbons of her shoes. With no curtains to obscure the view of Singapore, copper light lapped the walls, swelling with the same perpetual motion as its source—hundreds of container ships moored off the island. The boats lolled in the dark waters, lit up like jovial taverns, as though a ghostly vision of the raucous old port rose from the waves every night and burned itself out again by morning.

Ed's bathroom door opened. The bed rolled beneath his weight. If she let him, he would start singing "When My Ship Comes In."

"There's an art exhibition coming up at the Sentosa Club." She glanced over as she spoke and saw him grimace while swallowing a sleeping pill. "Breakout painters from Southeast Asia."

He settled against the pillows; his crisp profile caught the light, creating a high ridge amid a valley of shadows. "I like the apartment minimalist," he said, with the verbal precision of a drunk man, then scowled at a portrait of Chairman Mao rendered in pixels made of painted fingernails, which hung beside the doorway. "Are they human nails?"

"Acrylic."

"Human nails might justify the price tag."

"He watches me when I undress," Amanda said. "I hate the thing."

"So why did we buy it?" Ed asked.

"You bought it. You were hammered at a charity auction and got into a bidding war with another dad—"

"Who called Josie a prick-tease."

"He didn't say that—"

"He said she'd been leading his son on. Like a seventeen-year-old boy ever needs leading on. I won't let some limp-dicked kid talk about Josie like that."

"So you defended your daughter's honor by outbidding his father for artwork? Every day I'm with you, Ed, I learn vital lessons in parenthood." Amanda slapped his bare thigh and held up her palm to display the red oblivion of a mosquito.

But Ed was still trying to stare down Mao. "Josie went on and on about this picture. The fingernails represent the eternal spirit of humanity."

"Why?"

"Because your fingernails never stop growing, do they? Even after death."

"That's a bit literal," Amanda said.

"Yeah, well, that was before she decided it was creepy and we got lumbered with it. But at least I got to show that dad who has the bigger dick."

"It was pretty clear to everyone who was the bigger dick."

A slow smile pushed aside Ed's scowl. "What's got Mrs. Bonham so crabby? Is Mr. Bonham less attentive than Mr. Mao?" He rolled toward her, but she slid out of his grasp and off the bed. His attempt at a light touch chafed her raw feelings. Any reasonable person would have smelled the acrid perfume of hurt and anger that she'd worn all evening. In her dressing room, she struggled with a zipper, then gave up and tried to pull the dress over her head, ending up with a tight bundle around her face.

"Stay exactly like that." Ed's knees buckled hers from behind. "I'm going to fuck you in the closet."

"For God's sake, Ed. Who wants to do it in a wardrobe?" His hand wrenched her bra so that one breast stuck out, treacherously responding to the chilly air con.

"All tied up for me." The other hand enclosed her wrists in the air above her head.

"Since when have you tied me up?" She bucked him away with her haunches and tugged at the fabric until the dress landed on the floor with a huff. Ed had retreated with his hands raised in submission. Warm light from the bedroom cast him in copper. He invested an hour a day in the pool or gym because "no one wants to be the clichéd *ang moh*" — the overweight, sweaty white guy. Normally, she delighted in his efforts. Even now, through her indignation, she detected his resinous scent of whisky and amber, a strumming base note that reminded her of the first time they'd met, on New Year's Eve in Switzerland, three years earlier.

Of course, Ed had been fully dressed then, wearing an open-necked shirt when everyone else was trussed up in black tie. He'd made eye contact from his high stool at the bar, and she'd let herself rise the length of the room like a bubble in her champagne glass, carried by an inevitability that relaxed her, made her feel that what was happening was as natural as gravity. Other women approached him—but it was Amanda he watched over their naked shoulders.

"Since when have you been into bondage?" she asked.

"It was a joke. I thought everyone tied each other up these days. And you've been wearing those hooker shoes all night, with the ties—"

"Ribbons." She slid her feet into the shoes again, wrapping the black silk up around one calf and then the other, before facing him again, hands on bare hips. "You like the shoes?"

"Of course I like the shoes. And the underwear."

"You like this?" She turned her back to him and bent over to lay her palms on the seat of an upholstered chair.

"Of course."

She hooked her thumbs in her knickers. "What makes you want to fuck someone, Ed?"

"Not someone—you."

"So prove it's me that you want."

As soon as skin touched skin, she tugged down the front of his boxer shorts.

"Give me a minute," he said. "I've taken a sleeping pill—"

"You won't last a minute."

Ed gave a pant of laughter and took hold of her hips, and Amanda had to lay her palms on the seat for support. When they parted, a minute or so later, he dropped his underpants into her linen basket while she punched her arms into a bathrobe.

"What was that about?" he said.

"I'll be ovulating soon. Just getting the party started."

"You're angry."

"I'm speeding things up. Milking the cow."

"Charming." He walked into the bedroom. "I'm off to Manila tomorrow with Bernardo, did I tell you?"

4

"So that's another month down the drain." Amanda undid the shoes' ribbons and they tumbled to her ankles.

"I thought we agreed to take a break, give you time to recover from the IVF and the rest of it."

"The *rest of it?* We can say the word out loud; it was a miscarriage, not the return of Voldemort. And anyway, you agreed, not me." She kicked the shoes into the bottom of her wardrobe and threw the dress on top. "Will you be back in time to take Josie to the Cold Sister gig? She's been looking forward to it." She didn't remind him that she was the one who'd made an early-morning dash halfway across the island to queue at the venue for tickets that sold out in record time. Because it was her husband and her stepdaughter's favorite band.

"Can you take her?" Ed said. "I can't leave Bernardo to close this deal. You know what happened last time. I can't lose another client."

Amanda heard the bedsheet brush his body. A gig might be fun, but Josie should go with a friend. Or a date. Like a normal teenager. Ed's daughter was pretty and droll and cool in an unplucked-eyebrows kind of way. Not passive enough for boys her own age, that was the problem. Amanda would never say it to Ed because he would huff and puff, but Josie needed an older boyfriend—not weird older, just a handful of years. Like her and Ed.

She went through her bathroom to the hallway, listened for a moment at Josie's door, then continued on to the curio shelf in the living room. Shrouded in a pocket of shadow amid the ambient light, she lifted the lid of a blue-and-white urn and felt around its copious belly. After she counted three fat bundles of plasticized bills held tight by hair bands, she replaced the ceramic lid with a low chime. She glanced over both shoulders, first along the hallway toward the family bedrooms and then to the maid's quarters beyond the kitchen. Then she picked up a much smaller ginger jar from the shelf, cupping it in one palm as she adjusted her wedding photo: a candid shot of her and Ed beside a London cab, the flash picking out Josie's pale face and chalky gown in the interior. They'd married just six months after that New Year's Eve party; not, as some people said, because Ed planned a move to Singapore—although a marriage certificate did make their paperwork easier—but because they knew it was right. *Sometimes,* Amanda thought, *you just know when something is right.*

Or wrong. She bounced the ginger jar, hearing its contents bristle. *Sometimes you know when something is wrong.*

She felt all *Blade Runner*, beautiful and tragic. The mood made her wish she could smoke while looking at the view, but none of their huge windows opened. Instead, she went to the deep-red kitchen and put the ginger jar on the island counter. There was no movement in the apartment. Only the ceaseless expiration of the AC, as familiar as her own breath. Her thumb and middle finger encircled the lid of the pot, and she lifted it away. Turning the jar upside down, she shook out a stiff strip of packets, neat rubber rings visible through the transparent squares.

Amanda ripped one square off at the perforation. The packet opened easily. She supposed it would be a design fault otherwise; no one wants a delay while opening a condom. The rubber ring slopped onto her palm. A tart smell hit the back of her throat and she remembered the taste of lubricant. It had been years since she'd encountered a condom. They didn't use them anymore, she and Ed.

Well, she didn't.

As she held the teat aloft, the condom unraveled to the shape of a dead squid, as sticky and wrinkled as an empty scrotum. Amanda dropped it into a paper towel and poked it to the bottom of the waste bin. She washed her fingers. The remaining condom packets she pushed back into the ginger jar, wondering when Ed would miss them from the travel bag where she'd found them hidden inside a pocket. Once he noticed, would he worry that she knew? Would she be able to tell when he realized? Would either of them show their hand at the marital poker table?

His sleeping pill must have kicked in by now. She should go to bed too. But her intoxicated blood hummed through her veins. Her mind also hummed with the effort of not freaking out about the condoms and the encounter in the wardrobe, Ed grabbing her bound wrists. *I'm going to fuck you in the closet.* Since when did he talk like that?

Don't rush to conclusions, she told herself.

So she focused on the sound, the external hum she heard. Not the perpetual whine of the fridge, air con, lights: their life-support system. Something else. She swung around and saw that the glass door leading to the rear balcony was ajar. The maid's quarters lay at the end of the balcony, and although Awmi would be asleep and the streets below would be quiet at such a late hour, the open door broke the seal on the sterile vacuum that passed for her home.

Amanda got up to close the glass door. But as she gripped the handle, she saw that the door to Awmi's bedroom was also open.

Amanda called out to her. She hesitated on the threshold of another woman's territory; what little privacy Awmi had she tried to respect. "Awmi? Are you awake?" She pushed the balcony door wider; night air, as dank as a wet towel, engulfed her.

Her shadow stretched away, a path leading to darkness and a black shape on the floor. The humid air clotted with the brute fumes of bleach, making her eyes tear up. A rattle from Awmi's room told her the air con was switched on, melting through the open door into the heat of the night. It made no sense: Awmi was frugal with everything but especially air con, which was a luxury for a Singapore maid. Amanda took baby steps toward the black shape. Something warm mashed between her toes. The bleach clutched her lungs and a scream scorched her throat.

Stumbling backward over the threshold into the kitchen, she slammed the door shut with both hands flat on the cold glass while she gasped for breath. She had almost touched the black shape before it registered as Awmi. Her broken body lay in a puddle of blood and vomit that crept like a living organism, reaching out to touch the polished tips of Amanda's toenails.

Chapter 2

Camille Kemble walked to the bus stop under rain trees, their limbs flexed in a centuries-long dance. Hot mist shrouded the leaves and lampposts. These city streets were carved from the jungle, and the jungle raised ghosts every morning so it would never be forgotten.

She stuck out her arm at lights coming through the gloom, and the bus snapped open its doors before it even came to a halt. Since she returned to Singapore a year ago, she'd noticed that everything ran faster here than it did back in London. Public transport in general, elevators and escalators in particular, and even urban planning: entire new districts had evolved in the fifteen years since she'd set foot on the island.

Stretching to hold the leather strap that stopped her from bowling down the aisle as the bus sped on, Camille returned the greeting of a man who wished her a good morning. Maybe he'd singled her out because she had her head up and alert, like a scrappy little terrier that enjoys getting its ears rubbed. Or maybe it was because her red hair and freckles marked her as a foreigner—a guest in a country she'd once thought of as home. Even if Singapore was printed on her passport under place of birth, she was legally and culturally and indelibly an outsider now.

Everyone stumbled as the bus braked. Camille jumped off, then followed the shaded walkway to the British High Commission. At the gatehouse, a guard swabbed her handbag with a cloth-tipped wand before buzzing her inside the compound. As she strode up the path toward the embassy offices, a buzz inside her bag made her pull out her cell phone.

"Good morning, this is the British High Commission press office, Camille Kemble speaking."

"Camille, it's Ruth." The little-girl voice of Ruth Chin from Reuters News Agency always pleased Camille, although a press officer had to keep her guard up: Ruth's forthright reporting was a stark contrast to her timid delivery.

"What can I do for you today, Ruth?"

The journalist had emailed the previous day asking questions about the British High Commission's influence on Singaporean domestic politics. Now she was calling to raise the issue again. As Camille made her way into the building, Ruth's questions circled the same ground like a tiger waiting for a glimpse of soft underbelly. Camille kept her responses brief and bland until Ruth gave a sigh of exasperation.

"Come on, Camille, I know you have a personal interest in the welfare of maids."

"Maids?" Camille managed not to show her surprise at the conversational about-turn. "I thought we had to say 'helper' these days."

"Helper, so *cute*"—she made the word last a long time—"but so *expat*. We call a maid a maid. In any case, the parliamentary debate on the working conditions of foreign domestic workers—if you prefer the official name—is coming up."

"You're covering it?" Camille glanced toward her boss's office, but it was still early; his door remained closed. She pulled open the bottom drawer of her desk and slipped a file from beneath a stack of brown envelopes. It was a document she had stayed late the previous evening compiling—long after the rest of the BHC staff had left—because it had nothing to do with her day job. She slid down the corridor to the staff kitchen and closed the door behind her. "I'm speaking as me, not the BHC, and I'm off the record."

"Okay."

"Since when does the world care about the rights of poor migrant women?" Camille asked.

"The world doesn't care. Parliament will discuss the issue and probably decide that nothing can change without inconveniencing voters. Or maybe a new law gets passed that appears to protect maids but with a loophole wide enough for all the usual problems to slip through."

"You're preaching to the converted, Ruth."

"So, let's be evangelical. The rest of the world pretends not to see the exploitation because Singapore is rich and stable, and the government has a calming influence over its troublesome neighbors. But I've got a bee in my bonnet about women's rights, and I know you have too."

Camille pressed her hand over the mouthpiece as though the journalist might hear her thoughts. A few months ago, she'd let slip to Ruth that she volunteered at HELP, an NGO that campaigned for the rights of foreign domestic workers. She'd set up an interview between Ruth and Sharmila Menon, a hotshot lawyer who'd offered her services pro bono to HELP. *Bloody journalists,* Camille thought, *they never forget.* "But what can I do? The BHC can't comment."

"I need an angle," the journalist said.

"You won't get one from us."

"Maybe a quote? A teensy-weensy one?"

"Nope. But HELP is lobbying members of Parliament ahead of the debate. Sharmila's outspoken, no holds barred. Very, very scary woman, as you may have noticed. But lovely too."

"She's a lawyer." Ruth spoke in the bored tone that journalists get when dealing with talking heads. "What does the BHC in Singapore do to promote human rights?"

Camille closed the file on Sharmila's number. "As I said before, the UK urges all countries to uphold fundamental human rights. But we don't interfere in the democratic process of a foreign nation."

"And the colonies breathe a sigh of relief," Ruth said sweetly. "We're back on the record, right?"

"If you speak to Sharmila, she'll be more forthcoming and relevant."

"Sure, sure."

After the journalist hung up, Camille opened the briefing she'd pulled together for Sharmila. The welfare of a quarter of a million maids would be affected by this debate. Camille scanned her report and concluded that she'd done as good a job volunteering for HELP as she did for the BHC. She treated herself to an espresso from the machine. With both hands full, she shouldered her way through the door and came face-to-face with a security tag hanging over a chest that retained its military bearing.

"Glad you're in early," Joshua MacAlpine said. "A call just came through on the bat phone. Thought you should know the details in case it makes the news." A British woman had requested consular assistance. Her apartment was full of police, she was freaking out, and Josh thought he might pay her a little visit.

"Do we do house calls?" Camille asked.

"Mrs. Bonham found the body of her helper late last night. Suicide. And cases like this can be complicated if the press get wind of it. Another suicide just as the foreign domestic worker debate comes to Parliament—"

"I'll come with you."

"I'm not sure that's necessary . . ." Josh walked away, but then came right back around to face her again. Camille waited. Her boss was not an indecisive man. He was a trained diplomat, for goodness' sake, smooth enough to tell you to get lost in a way that made you look forward to the trip. "Not necessary" wasn't the same as "not invited." He wanted her there for some reason.

Camille shrugged one shoulder. "I could advise her on how to handle unwanted media attention."

Josh rubbed his chin, and finally nodded. "Come on, then, Batwoman. Get your cape."

The taxi reached the turn for Sentosa—a leisure island off the mainland of Singapore—and pulled free of the traffic knotted around the port. Camille drummed a finger on the pleather armrest as they drove over the causeway, past container ships on one side and superyachts on the other. She considered how Singapore trades in superlatives: the largest port, the biggest boats, the richest people. The recreation island of Sentosa—home to theme parks, man-made beaches, and golf courses— was one of its weirdest residential areas.

A Merlion rose up behind trees. The creature had bewildered Camille even as a child. A ten-story-high mythical creature, a fish with the head of a lion, rendered in concrete. The time her parents brought her and her brother, Collin, to climb the Merlion was one of her few focused memories of the Singapore years, beyond a vague sense of heat and happiness.

She must have been about five. Collin raced up the steps inside, darting between plodding adult legs. Camille gave chase. Somewhere amid the saris and chinos, she gained momentum and beat him to the top, where she could look out from the lion's mouth, between its four teeth. Down below, tiny people circled a mosaic fountain as though moving to the music of the water. She thought her parents must be there too. Camille inched forward on her belly to see them, the concrete scraping her skin. But then Collin dragged her away from the edge, and however much Camille shouted that she wanted to see what Mum and Dad were up to, he wouldn't let her go. They'd been playing the same roles ever since.

The taxi jerked to a halt outside a waterfront condo, and the Merlion was replaced by a much taller structure, an apartment block fronted with black glass and marble. Someone had tried to soften the effect with fountains and orchids, but there was only so much yin an herbaceous border could bring to the yang of a forty-story phallus. Camille and Josh negotiated stepping-stones over running water to reach the lobby, where a concierge dipped his head at their introductions and waved them to the lift. As they stepped out seconds later into the Bonhams' apartment, Camille held her nose to regulate the pressure in her ears, and had the fleeting thought that she was jumping in at the deep end.

She slid her shoes into the cubby beside the lift, noting the wealth of the furnishings, the enormous square meterage of the space, the expansive view over the Straits of Singapore. She itched to take a peek through a telescope that stood astride its own oriental rug. Josh was already in conversation with a neat woman perched on the edge of a rock-hard sofa. She was attractive. Tie a little scarf around her neck and she'd make a fantastic air hostess. But Camille suspected this woman had never had a job that required long hours on her feet: they stretched out from her yoga pants, too slender and creamy to have spent time pounding the aisles in shoes that pinch. Josh asked for her husband's travel schedule.

"I've lost track. He's away a lot . . ."

Camille wondered how a wife could *lose track* of her husband. She marked Amanda down as a trailing spouse, a career wife, a professional expat. And Josh seemed content to put his straight back into attending to this high-maintenance woman. Despite a year of eight-hour days, Camille had rarely seen Josh's private alter ego. He hid behind the anonymity of a tailored suit and the kind of banter that created a lighthearted atmosphere but forbade real intimacy. But now he was drawing on all his charm to put an attractive woman at ease. Frankly, he was a dark horse. Camille wondered if he already knew Mrs. Bonham and meant to impress her—they would be around the same age, midthirties. But she didn't seem to know Josh, so Camille shook the thought away.

Her bare feet were silent on the marble. A hallway stretched away to her right, lined with bedroom doors and a home office at the far end, facing the corridor. *Bad feng shui,* she thought. The kitchen lay on the opposite side, beyond the vast living space. In pride of place opposite the lift, a Chinese cabinet of rounded shelves held a display of blue-and-white ceramics. There were more ginger jars perched on a console table farther along the hallway.

Camille glanced at a wedding photo of the couple lounging against a black cab. London. She bent closer. The bride was Mrs. Bonham, but the groom . . . Behind her, the elevator doors shivered as the lift passed. Camille focused on Mr. Bonham, who looked so famil—

"Camille?" Josh's voice snapped her to attention. She hurried across a dense rug to shake the hand that Mrs. Bonham offered, surprised to find it feverishly warm despite the chill of the apartment. Her eyes were tinged pink, and Camille felt a kick of guilt as she wondered if everyone Mrs. Bonham met was so quick to judge her by her trappings.

She introduced herself and, at Josh's prompt, explained why there might be media interest in the suicide of another helper. The woman listened until Camille finished and then said simply, "I have some experience with media intrusion."

Josh segued seamlessly into paperwork while Camille made a mental note to google Amanda Bonham's past. Meanwhile, she took surreptitious glances around the apartment. Aside from the ceramics, everything was sleek and neutral, the television sunk into the wall. And that reminded her: in the police procedural shows she loved to watch, detectives always found an excuse to nose around.

"Could I make you a cup of tea, Mrs. Bonham?" she asked.

"Well, the police are in the kitchen . . ."

"Let me check," said Josh, and guided Camille with one hand floating under her elbow. Clearly, he wanted to nose around too. In the kitchen, he peeped through a glass door that led to a balcony and the maid's quarters. Outside, a policeman in a white jumpsuit was packing up his gear.

"Mrs. Bonham found her helper out there. The girl drank a bottle of bleach. No cry for help, this one, she really meant it. The husband, Edward Bonham, left this morning for Manila."

"He left?"

"Urgent business, he said." Josh gave a flick of his hand but made no comment. "There's a stepdaughter too, Josie Bonham, but she went to school. Exams. Mrs. Bonham is holding up well in the circumstances, and the condo manager will arrange a cleaner once the police leave." He handed over the paperwork he'd taken from Mrs. Bonham, which included important phone numbers and the family schedule for the day. Camille offered to make herself useful by following up on the cleaner, and Josh returned to the living room.

Camille put her bag on the countertop, then picked it up again. This was a crime scene. Forensics. On the floor by the door, she could see red circles marking little half footprints, yellow stains on the white tiles from the toes and pads of a foot. Amanda Bonham's feet, Camille supposed, after she'd found the body. As though on cue, an officer stepped through the door, pulling a white hood back from his face and dumping his kit on the counter. The smell of bleach that came off his clothes encircled Camille. His phone beeped and he answered, identifying himself as Officer Pang.

He turned his back, resting his free hand on the counter. He gripped two ziplock evidence bags that must have come from the helper's room: the first contained two stocky bottles with printed labels while the second held flimsy foil packets of tiny pills. Side by side, little and large, they looked to Camille oddly male and female. She slid one foot forward and leaned in. The bottles were in the name of Edward Bonham but had been prescribed by different doctors in Manila. The other pills were contraceptives: long, thin strips marked with days of the week and wrapped together with an elastic band.

How did the helper get such a stash? The more conservative doctors refused to prescribe contraceptives to maids, so they weren't easy to come by except under the counter. Maybe Edward Bonham got them from the same place as his medication. With a quick glance to check that the police officer was still focused on his call, Camille flicked her phone onto silent and snapped a photograph of the two evidence bags full of drugs. Just as she slipped her phone back into her pocket, the officer hung up and started to leave the kitchen.

"Officer Pang?" she said.

He stopped with his hand on the sliding door. "Who are you?"

"British High Commission. I wanted to ask if cases like this are prosecuted. Suicide is illegal, correct?"

"Who can we prosecute? The woman is dead."

Camille felt herself pink up. "Sorry, I wasn't clear. I mean, if you find contributory factors—abuse and the like—could there be a prosecution of the employer?"

Pang showed no reaction. "I can't say."

"I'm asking generally. Not about this case."

"I can't say." He slid aside the door.

She couldn't help herself. "What nationality was the helper? Do you think she was underage?"

Pang stepped through the door, and Camille had to move closer to ensure she wasn't overheard by Josh and Mrs. Bonham in the living area.

"There have been a number of recent suicides by helpers from Burma, and some of them turned out to be underage," Camille explained.

Pang leaned back through the door. "I can't tell a person's age or nationality by looking at them." Then he was gone.

She picked up the paperwork to find the number for the condo management. But her mind drifted. The contraceptives made sense; pregnancy was a deportation offense for maids. But why did she have Mr. Bonham's medication in her room?

Camille considered why a helper who had a good job in a prestigious apartment might kill herself; at what point did the girl decide that her dream of a better life had become a nightmare? She glanced again at Mrs. Bonham's footsteps, yellow smears on the white floor. Maybe the wife's feet weren't the only ones creeping through the door to the young maid's room late at night.

Chapter 3

As the taxi crossed the causeway to the main island of Singapore, the driver swerved between lanes, throwing Amanda sideways so that her cheekbone bumped the window.

"Sorry, ma'am."

The police and the pair from the British High Commission had wrapped up that morning, leaving her alone with the absence of Awmi. The apartment was always quiet in the middle of the day, the period when the two women usually went about their domestic lives in companionable peace, but now the hush took on a malignant quality. The space whispered with fleeting sounds that Amanda found herself straining to identify. A scrape that might be a footstep. A click that might be a door. A hiss that might be air sucked through gritted teeth. It reminded her of when she was a little girl, alone in a vast bedroom at the top of a town house, holding her breath to check if the breathing she could hear was her own or—

It's just the shock, Amanda had told herself. *There's nobody in the apartment but me.*

She had taken her laptop down the hallway to the office, as far from the rear balcony as she could get, away from the smell of bleach that triggered thoughts of Awmi's pain—not just her final moments but the months the girl must have spent smiling through her despair. Because however hard Amanda tried, she couldn't recall a single inkling that

Awmi was unhappy. Homesick, yes; they had discussed many times how Awmi missed her sisters—one working in Hong Kong and one in Dubai. But suicidal? Amanda hadn't had a clue. Had Ed? She'd tried to ask him before he left for the airport, but he only held her while she cried, saying that he hardly knew the girl, not really, and she felt him check his watch behind her head.

And so, when she'd received an email reminder about that afternoon's book club, she'd made a quick decision to go; anything was better than sitting alone in the apartment, wondering what else she was oblivious to.

Her greasy makeup on the taxi window smeared into a flesh-colored fingerprint that she couldn't erase however much she rubbed. Book club was populated by vibrant women with vibrant opinions based on vibrant careers—some present, some past. The group made Amanda feel drab, as neutral and featureless as her apartment. If it weren't for the permanent record maintained by the Internet, she could've invented a new version of herself: someone who belonged. If only former school friends who knew her past—it was an old classmate who'd introduced her to book club—didn't keep turning up in Singapore like bad pennies circulating the banking capitals of the world.

With a tissue, she wiped the smudge off the window as the taxi took the ramp onto the highway. *Having a child might help me belong,* she thought, not for the first time. Maybe alchemy was at work inside her now, unfelt, unseen, brightening the darkness of her fallopian tubes. She pressed her belly with both hands, but she knew the magic wouldn't happen this month, not with Ed traveling. The more she understood the nuts and bolts of fertility, the more improbable it seemed that it could happen to her; the precise timing and intricate sequence of steps seemed like a Japanese puzzle box. Everyone else seemed to have the knack—especially those who didn't want a child or those who would squander it or lumber it with a ridiculous name. Even her gynecologist had apologized for the "clumsiness" of human fertility—making Amanda feel like a giant panda—while simultaneously pushing a needle through the wall of her vagina to extract ripe follicles. *The science is potent,* Dr. Chan had said when the procedure was done, *though the final step requires nature's intervention; its*—what did she call it?—*thaumaturgy.* The spark of life. What were her and Ed's chances of a miracle? Diminishing further with every month he spent overseas.

Well, Amanda concluded, the benefit of fertility treatment was that she didn't have to take it lying down. She should make that joke at book club. The women might find it funny, laugh off some tension. Stress didn't help fertility. She had to stop obsessing and think about something else. So she got out her phone and tapped on Facebook, where she typed in a username and password: Annaliese Del Rey / identity1. She ignored the timeline with its scant handful of friends and clicked through to a private page: Singapore Overseas Wives, known to expats on the island as SOWs. The group had a membership of tens of thousands of women like herself—overpaid, overwhelmed, and over here.

She navigated to the classifieds. Good: people were queuing to buy a pair of Louboutins that Ed had brought back from Shanghai a few weeks before. The style reminded her of those little booties for women with bound feet. Ed always returned with expensive, impersonal gifts from his trips, and she never asked why. She'd even felt sheepish when she started flogging them, as though it were a betrayal. But then she found his condoms and began imagining hotel hookups based on alcohol and anonymity. The morning after: a guilty headache assuaged by an expensive trip to the hotel shop. *Look, darling, I was thinking of you.*

Amanda marked the shoes as sold. She logged out and logged in again, this time as Jacaranda Mitchell / identity2. Here she was selling a Prada purse, another surprise gift from Ed. It had rarely been out of its dustcover. "Jacaranda" ignored the first name in the queue—Amanda knew the woman from the Sentosa Club and couldn't risk being recognized—and messaged the second. Her buyers would meet her in some mundane location where the stardust of the original designer packaging would shine. Thousands of dollars would slide across a Starbucks table, sticky with frothed milk, and Amanda would take it home to hide in the expectant belly of one of her ornamental ginger jars.

The taxi veered to the exit and turned almost immediately onto a narrow lane flanked by jungle.

"Haunted!" The taxi driver shifted in his seat.

The meeting was at the home of a woman Amanda thought of as "Hostess with the Mostess." She lived in a Black and White, one of Singapore's colonial-era mansions named for their distinctive dark timber beams and whitewashed walls, located in jungle locations that meant they were overrun with snakes, monkeys, and maintenance bills. Beautiful as they were, Black and Whites appealed mainly to expats who were willing to pay for a romantic slice of history. And who weren't as superstitious as taxi drivers.

"*Pontianak*, you know? They live in the trees."

"I don't believe in ghosts."

"Not ghosts. Vampires. Angry women who lost their babies."

"Angry women I do believe in."

"Ah!" The taxi uncle was pleased that she agreed.

Amanda pointed out the house and paid the driver, then pushed through the iron gate. Heat swarmed inside her clothes, and even in the shade of the tembusu trees, her skin prickled and started to seep. She reached the cool of the carriage porch—they knew how to build for the climate in those days—and realized she'd left her expensive gift of moon cakes in the cab. Now she was empty-handed.

Inside the dim interior, voices were muted. Usually, they were as sharp as elbows in a crowd. She followed a mahogany staircase to the upstairs living area, where the ladies hunched over chips and dips. Mostess charged across the rug to scoop her into the group, which barely greeted her before turning back to a woman Amanda knew as Crazy Antic—because of her infamous holiday disasters—who was simultaneously crying, talking, and gesticulating with a hummus-loaded tortilla chip. All the women lowed in sympathy except Mostess, whose eyes traced the flight path of the chip above her antique carpet.

"And she WhatsApped me this morning—totally jet-lagged, hasn't slept in a week—and poor little Livvy can't even put on her own panty hose. She's literally never worn a pair in her life. And suddenly, boom, she has to get up on Monday morning in freezing-cold London and go to a new school wearing panty hose." Crazy Antic finished by pushing the whole chip into her mouth with her palm. Mostess sat back on her planter's chair, turned her head to Amanda, and stage-whispered: "Ann's talking about Melissa Hodge—plays tennis at the British Club, three kids at the British Overseas School?"

Amanda shook her head.

"Ran the Great Wall marathon with Ann? You remember the time Ann fell off the wall?"

"Oh, Melissa!" Clearly, *everybody* knew Melissa, so Amanda figured she should too.

"Lovely, lovely woman. Husband was killed last month. Light aircraft came down in Indonesia—"

"Microlight," Crazy Antic corrected, spitting baba ghanoush.

"Microlight came down in Indonesia. Broke his neck. As if that isn't bad enough, the policeman who informed Melissa of the death mentions in passing, 'By the way, you know you have thirty days to leave Singapore?' And Melissa's like, 'I've lived here for thirteen years and you're giving me a month?' And the officer's sympathetic, but them's the rules."

"She could have appealed," said Crazy Antic, "but she couldn't afford to stay."

The trailing spouses murmured about rental prices.

Someone said, "You never know how long you've got, do you? Ticktock . . ."

The fragility of life and lifestyle circled book club on the syrupy afternoon breeze. It drew the conversation into a spiral of competitive woe that covered homesickness, a marriage on the rocks, postnatal depression. The horror of what had happened to Awmi the previous night was a burning coal in Amanda's stomach, but she held it inside. She wasn't sure how these women would react. And her anger at Ed's decision to go to Manila—even if it was for a make-or-break meeting—was still raw. A single verbal sideswipe from one of these strident women would bruise her thin skin. Instead, she thought of Melissa Hodge's child, whatever her name was, wrenched out of the Singaporean sun into an inhospitable London winter. There was something Dickensian about the rapid change in fortune, the death of the patriarch plunging his family into the cold. It was self-absorbed, Amanda knew, to feel a chilly blast of recognition, but her eyes filled at the thought of losing Ed. Those condoms suggested it was a possibility.

She felt a squeeze on her bicep and turned to see moist eyes looking into her own.

"The shock's hitting you, isn't it?" Mostess said. "Melissa would be touched to know she's so well loved."

Amanda excused herself and roamed acres of polished parquet toward a bathroom. A sideboard stocked with family photos and enigmatic curios was laid out like a finger buffet of fulfillment. She pushed herself past it into a covered veranda, past the kids' rooms: a pink bed and a blue bed.

In the bathroom, she closed the door and stood before the sink. The romantic house, the perfect children, the solid husband. She really was the Mostess. Amanda picked up two Disney-character toothbrushes and took a moment to decide which was her favorite.

On her way back to the fray, she fell into step behind a helper carrying a tray of white wine spritzers. Book club eyed the arrival of the drinks like sailors in a brothel. Amanda took her seat and watched the maid clear the table. At last month's meeting, it never occurred to her to consider the helper, but now she wondered what the woman was thinking. Was she full of envy? Or resentment? Or was she simply content to do a job—as billions of people around the world do every day—and see money in the bank at the end of the month? Amanda had a sudden urge to question the woman, as though she might have insight into whatever Awmi had been thinking, but of course that was ridiculous; they were different people, from different backgrounds, with different experiences.

The women toasted their host, who then turned to Amanda. "I've been thinking about you since last meeting. I meant to drop you a line, but we had half-term and then I was organizing table decorations for the gala ball . . . How is your health?" Such a carefully chosen phrase; she'd clearly planned it. Amanda couldn't remember how much she'd told them the previous month. She'd drank too much at that meeting—no reason not to anymore—and recalling her exact words was like looking for a coin in the deep end of a swimming pool.

They'd read a memoir about infertility and adoption; all the women cried, except Amanda. At the mention of a miscarriage, someone commented that "everything happens for a reason" and all the women mooed in agreement. Amanda's throat lumped with ripostes that she knew would be social suicide if she let them come out: for what *reason* have I lost my baby again, for what *reason* has your particular celestial being decided that I deserve this, what possible *reason* could justify your bad philosophy, bad theology, bad advice? *You're basically saying,* Amanda had wanted to spit out, *that what happened to me—what has happened to me three times now—is right, fair, benign. But you know what—you smug, fertile creature—to me, these miscarriages feel wrong, unfair, cruel. Unreasonable.* She'd chewed that anger back and felt it scrape down her throat like a broken tortilla chip, until right at the end of book club, when that thoughtless woman left, and Amanda blurted out the news of her most recent loss.

The women who'd been heading out the door with purses over their shoulders came back to the sofa. Several had had miscarriages too, including Mostess. Someone said, "It's okay to be angry," and Amanda cried in relief. Mostess said, "Even if it was early days, it was still your baby," and Amanda hugged her. But then someone else said, "At least you know you can get pregnant," and the tortilla chip of anger threatened to make a reappearance. Mostess wrapped it up by saying, "We don't talk openly enough about miscarriage," and the women agreed and apologized because they had to rush home before school buses delivered their children, who—judging by the put-upon tones—were tiny vampires who terrorized their mothers for snacks and cuddles.

Now Amanda's eyes filled again. Mostess topped up her wine and gripped Amanda's arm. Strangely, the hand steadied her. Kindness spread like the warmth that follows an electric shock.

"My husband wanted to stop the fertility treatment. 'Just for a while,' he said, though I've never fully understood why. So I've been doing it on my own. Paying for it myself. After all, he's made his contribution and we have two frozen embryos left. I can't just leave them in the freezer, can I? And if I get pregnant and it sticks this time, I'm sure he won't care how it came about."

She thought she detected a sourness spreading through the air like a dash of lime cordial. She took a shot of wine and felt alcohol rush into her veins to form a moat between herself and their opinions.

What if he finds out?

Are you sure he's ready for a child?

Doesn't he have a right to know?

Afternoon sunlight streamed through the wooden shutters, creating leaden shadows. She felt cloaked in wine while the women talked, supporting her or Ed's case. They took sides, as black and white as the house they sat in.

She remembered how, at her last gynecologist appointment, she'd explained to the doctor that she felt guilty about leaving her babies—blastocysts, Dr. Chan gently corrected her—suspended on ice, not allowed to live and yet very much in existence, like tiny prisoners on death row. Unless she went back for them one day, they would eventually be destroyed. They had a life span before they were even alive. Dr. Chan suggested that she might consider a mild antidepressant.

Someone passed Amanda the tortilla chips and told her to hang in there. She took one and snapped it into the shape of a flint head. "You know, 6 percent of couples never get pregnant. Someone has to be the statistic. I'm blonde and rich and healthy, so I don't *look* like a statistic, but what if I'm the unlucky one? What if being blonde and rich and healthy used up all my luck?" The woman who passed the chips raised her eyebrows. Mostess cleared her throat, and Amanda decided not to mention that her unborn embryos cried out to her in the night.

Instead she ate the tortilla chip in silence. Outside the window, a bird launched into an urgent song, as luscious and hard as the sunlight.

"I wish I'd never had children," Mostess said.

Someone agreed: "We all have those days."

"No, it's every single day. I regret having children every single day. I love them—I do—but I wish I'd never started a family." Mostess laughed harshly, like a dog's strangled bark when it ran to the end of its chain. "Regretting having your children. Now there's a taboo."

Amanda glanced around the group; the women's faces had turned as pink as a raw nerve.

Mostess carried on. "I don't know what's wrong with me, really. I thought it was postnatal depression, but it's different. My husband feels it too; says he's become a machine. It's like . . ." She nodded out through the window to the tropical garden. "There's a kind of ficus in the rain forest that clings to a healthy tree and grows all around it, blocking the sunlight and hogging the nutrients, until the original tree rots from the inside and disappears, and the ficus is all that's left, wound around a void." Mostess threw her glass up toward her mouth and noticed halfway that it was empty. "I used to buy ficus plants when I was a student but couldn't keep the bloody things alive. Now they're everywhere." She stopped herself, pulling up with a jerk. "I'm sorry, Amanda. I don't mean to downplay what you're going through."

"It's okay, really it is," Amanda said. And it was. The honesty was refreshing. In that moment, Amanda decided that she too hated the jungle. Its fecundity was a slap in the face. She nodded at a display of stylized family photos and squeezed Mostess's arm. "Your children look happy. You're doing a great job."

Mostess gripped her hand in return. "But I'm afraid they'll find out."

Amanda took a taxi with two other women. She scrunched down in the front seat, using her compact to replace foundation that had sweated off. The conversation in the back returned to Melissa Hodge's dead husband and the impact on the daughter.

"Do you ever wonder what your husband gets up to when he travels?"

"I assumed his midlife crisis might involve backstreet bars in Bangkok. But thrill-seeking? Microlights? That's new."

The taxi's jerky progress made Amanda nauseous. When a station for the underground MRT train appeared, she signaled to the driver, and he swerved across two lanes to drop her at the curbside. As she clambered out, her bag fell open and the contents scattered on the grass verge: phone, purse, Little Mermaid toothbrush. She snatched it all up and hid from the gossiping mothers as the taxi lurched into the traffic.

Chapter 4

Camille opened her mouth to ask what the difference was between *kopi O* and *kopi C*, but the elderly woman behind the counter slammed down a glass and said, *"Kopi peng."* Camille paid and picked up the iced coffee. The café was packed with office workers grabbing lunch; she headed for the only free seat under a fan.

It was worth two dollars to gain entry to this *kopitiam*, one of Singapore's original coffee houses. She placed her drink—the color of carrot soup—on the far side of the marble table, leaving space for her Filofax, which was as outmoded and as well loved as this café. Her finger tapped the cover with the relentless rhythm of a dripping tap while she surveyed the scene. But nothing triggered memories, not even the saccharine smell of Carnation milk in her *kopi peng*. Across the road was a branch of Starbucks, the logo flouncing its long hair to call Camille hither. Its familiarity was tempting, but she resisted.

It had taken over an hour to find the Filofax in the cartons she'd shipped from London a year ago. When Collin helped her pack, he'd sardonically marked the boxes as "childhood treasures." He'd scoff if he knew they clogged up her wardrobe, growing silverfish and mildew. He wouldn't understand that they didn't need to be unpacked: their proximity was enough.

The Filofax opened to photographs that had faded to the color of boat varnish. She hesitated over a picture of her parents on a hospital bed hugging a newborn who must be either Camille or Collin. There was no one who could confirm which sibling, no date scribbled on the print, no clue whispered through time. With no one to recount her early years, Camille felt she had simply floated down to earth as a fully formed child around the time her memory became more or less reliable.

She flipped to another photo, which she slipped from its plastic sheath. Her eyes lingered on her parents in a *kopitiam* like the one where she sat now. The tiles on the wall were different, but they could have been replaced. In the picture, there was a poster in Tamil script. She brought the photo almost to her nose, eyes moving more quickly from the image to the street outside. Then she slid it back inside the Filofax and clipped the organizer shut. Her chair made a sharp complaint as she stood up to leave.

This was not the same coffee shop; she wouldn't find out any more about her parents here. Nothing to do with the tiles, but—idiotic not to have noticed it before—the arched doorway to this *kopitiam* was obscured by a pillar belonging to the covered walkway outside. In the photo, her parents were framed in a perfect arch, and she could glimpse the shape of a pagoda across the street. After such a long time, she had a fresh clue, and she filed it in a clandestine folder in her mind.

Whereas most people rely on memories to keep loved ones alive, Camille suppressed hers in order to make her parents dead. Dead rather than "missing." Not better, but simpler. "Dead" was final. "Missing" was an unintelligible whisper, a shadow disappearing around a corner, the incessant flapping of a door in the wind. An earworm. An itch. It drove her mad. It had *almost* driven her mad.

When she left London for Singapore, she'd promised Collin that she wouldn't start asking questions again. Questions like: Why? Why would two perfectly normal people vanish? With no definitive answer, there was only one explanation on which Collin and Camille could agree: they didn't know all the facts. But whereas Collin was content with that, the mystery gnawed at her, a constant scratching as though she lived in a house with rats in the wall cavities. And she started to wonder: perhaps they weren't *perfectly normal people* . . . Her madness had developed its own buoyant logic. And here she was again, pursuing memories dredged up by the Bonhams' helper. She'd grown up with a helper—Collin had too, but Camille was younger, more dependent on the stability Lani offered when their parents were away doing . . . whatever they had really been doing.

But why now? Camille thought. Why had this case opened up her curiosity about the past? It had started with the maid's belongings in those cold evidence bags. The intimacy of the woman's contraceptives. In her volunteer work for HELP, Camille crafted women's stories into press releases; they were case studies, kept at arm's length. But at the Bonhams' apartment, she had stood in Awmi's home and workplace, seen where a woman chose to die. It felt personal.

And it had something to do with Edward Bonham. The photo of him beside a black cab. She knew him; she just had to figure out how.

Camille snatched up her phone. She found the photo she'd taken that morning and zoomed in on Edward Bonham's medicine bottles. Then she navigated to her browser and typed in *clonazepam.*

Clonazepam: Medication for seizures and anxiety disorders with the common side effect of sleepiness. Dependence occurs in one-third of people. Also commonly used as a recreational drug. Increased potency when mixed with alcohol. Clonazepam may be prescribed for social phobia, restless leg syndrome, alcohol withdrawal syndrome, and many forms of parasomnia.

Parasomnia: a sleep disorder that may include sleepwalking, night terrors, and sleep sex.

She navigated back to the previous page, then tapped the hyperlink on "recreational drug."

Clonazepam is from the same drug family as Rohypnol (roh-HIP-nol—street name: roofies) and has a similar sedative effect. It can induce muscle relaxation, memory loss, or—when mixed with alcohol—blackouts. However, clonazepam is not a common date-rape drug in Singapore, as it is only available on prescription.

She set down her phone. So . . . Edward Bonham could be taking clonazepam because he was stressed—not surprising, given the cost of running that apartment. But surely if he suffered from anxiety disorder, or restless leg syndrome, or weird sleep sex, or any other credible reason to take clonazepam, he'd simply get a prescription from a doctor in Singapore. Instead, he'd obtained it from doctors outside the country. He might keep a large stash to take alongside alcohol or drugs for kicks. Or even because the pills make an efficient date-rape drug.

She picked up her phone again, and this time she wrote an email to Sharmila Menon at HELP, asking if they might meet to discuss a case of a young—possibly underage—helper who committed suicide. Hit "Send." Her attention returned to the *kopitiam*, and she became aware of icy condensation from her glass dripping off the table and into her toe cleavage.

This case was a wake-up call. She had left the memories of her parents—and Lani—languishing in a box for too long. Maybe Collin was right, and they'd never know what happened to their parents. But she thought she knew what happened to Awmi; Camille couldn't bring this poor woman back, but if she could prevent one more needless suicide, it might feel like closure.

Chapter 5

Amanda perched on the sofa while waiting to be connected to Officer Pang. Whether it was the afternoon spritzers at book club or the emotional outpouring about her infertility or the sober chill of her apartment, she felt light-headed.

When Pang answered, Amanda inquired about the death certificate for Awmi. The one instruction she could remember from this morning's meeting with Joshua MacAlpine was that she had to send the document to the Ministry of Manpower right away.

"We sent the death certificate to the MOM today, Mrs. Bonham."

"I understood that as Awmi's employer I had to do it?"

"We sent it along with some other paperwork. The autopsy will take more time, but we were obliged to alert the MOM to the maid's condition."

Condition? "I'm sorry, I don't . . ."

"Your maid was pregnant."

Amanda sprang to her feet and went to the window, focusing on the horizon as though carsick. "She couldn't be. Helpers aren't allowed to get pregnant."

Officer Pang gave a huff of laughter and made no comment.

"If you don't have the autopsy result, how do you know?"

"She looked pregnant, so we ran a test. I guess with loose clothing she hid it, but it was pretty obvious once she was on the slab."

She winced at his choice of words.

Pang picked up on her silence. "I'm sorry to inform you."

"How far gone was she?"

"Her last medical examination was in June, so less than five months."

"I guess it's possible that she didn't know?"

"It's probable," said Pang, "that she knew she would be sent home."

After they rang off, Amanda went to the fridge and accidentally dispensed ice cubes over her feet. She got down onto her bony knees to dry the tiles before the floor turned into an ice rink. Only twenty-four hours ago, her toe prints had been exactly here: dried smears of bile. Everything had been washed away, leaving no trace except the smell of bleach. A vision filled Amanda's mind of a woman standing against the glass, black hair spread into drowning tendrils. *There's nothing there,* she told herself, *it's just shock.* She wadded the soggy paper into a dripping ball. When she stood, she turned to confront the door, and the wet clump fell through her fingers.

There *was* something there. A face.

A barstool teetered as she slipped on the wet tiles and grabbed for the counter.

No, not a face. She righted the stool. It was a moth. Huge: the size of a girl's face.

Amanda sucked on a fingernail that had ripped to the quick.

The moth flattened itself on the glass. Legs as thin as thread held up scalloped wings that ended in a swallowtail. Her mouth filled with the earthy taste of blood and bleach from her fingertip. She banged a palm on the glass, but the moth didn't fly away, just lifted up its flimsy wings to protect itself. Like Awmi.

Why hadn't she said something? Amanda had always been friendly, inquiring each morning about her well-being, encouraging her to spend time outside the apartment, to visit Peninsula Plaza—Singapore's Little Burma, where maids hung out and the shops sold special items that reminded them of home. She knew the girl was vulnerable, that Awmi was away from home for the first time and needed support, and she thought she had anticipated her needs because they were similar to her own: the homesickness, the challenge of making new friends, the kick in the teeth when old friends at home manage perfectly well without you. She convinced herself that she understood, one migrant to another. But in reality, Amanda saw now, all that she and Awmi had in common was proximity: her helper was a pilot fish swimming beneath a shark, earning protection by cleaning up after its powerful ally. But the fact remained that the shark was king of the ocean. And the expat was king of the migrants.

And Awmi had been *pregnant*. Deep water, indeed. No one could protect her there, not even Amanda. The choice would have been abortion or repatriation. No third option. But Amanda would have helped her through it.

Wouldn't she?

She spun away. Nausea rose from her stomach, and she needed to wash it back down. She flung open the fridge. Inside, held upright in the egg rack, were glass vials of leftover IVF meds, rattling like the test tubes holding her embryos on ice. Frozen. Cold. Waiting for her to collect them.

How could Awmi be so selfish? Amanda thought. *How could she kill herself when she was carrying a life? How could she waste something so precious, so hard to come by?* Awmi, who made Amanda feel guilty if she threw away so much as a ham sandwich. Somebody wanted that child; somebody would have loved it. How dare she be so profligate!

"It's not fair," Amanda said out loud. She kneaded the fat of her belly, the least painful spot for injecting herself. It was ridiculous that she'd held on to these bottles; they were mostly empty. As empty as herself. It was ridiculous that she held on to everything for so long.

She bustled through the motions of clearing the vials out, throwing them in the trash. As she went outside to the chute, the moth watched, flattened against the glass. "I would have helped you, Awmi," Amanda whispered. She put her hand out to the animal, but it took flight and careened over the edge of the balcony. *I didn't mean it when I said you were selfish.*

She went to her curio shelf. The biggest Chinese urn opened without a sound, and she found the rolls of notes. Three thousand dollars. It wasn't enough. She'd had to pay the latest bill for embryo storage, leaving her short of the funds to pay for another procedure. She pulled out her phone. On the Singapore Overseas Wives Facebook page, the usual heated discussion was in full flow.

> Jemima Sassoon *I need some advice, ladies. Our maid is with us 5 years. Yesterday I put cotton threads between the doors of my wardrobe (she is not aloud to look at my clothes). Now threads are gone! She is checking out my clothes!!! Do you think she is wearing them? Don't judge me—I have rights to know!!!*

> Jennifer Moran *I hope you don't leave your children with her?*

> Fionna Stone *My one did this—I saw her on Facebook dressed in my bikini, made me vomit.*

> Allison Ghosh *You say "don't judge" because you know this "test" is wrong. Poor girl, living for 5 years under suspicion.*

> Florence Breeze *Hear, hear!*

> Tara Hussein *This is called "entrapment."*

<u>Nina James</u> *My helper never cleans my wardrobe.*
Should I send her back to the Philippines? ;-)

<u>Gayle Cocktail</u> *ROFL!*

Imagine if she posted about Awmi. *Need some advice, ladies! I found my helper dead in a puddle of bleach!!! What to do?!* Half of them would launch a fund-raising campaign for the maid's family while the others would suggest having the tiles steam cleaned. There was something pornographic about the forum—womankind exposing itself, red in tooth and claw—and yet she couldn't resist the titillation. Or the income.

In the classifieds section, she posted a picture of her ribboned shoes. She liked them—they were Jimmy Choo—but now they would always remind her of the run-in with Ed in the closet. *All tied up for me.* The condoms in his travel bag. His guilt gifts; he'd brought the Jimmy Choos from Zurich. Amanda priced them to sell and pressed "Post."

Another $250: enough to preserve her babies for six months. Some women might use their escape fund to leave a cheating husband. *But I'm not wasting my war chest on a battle with Ed*, Amanda thought. *I'll come out of this marriage with something I value more than dignity.*

Chapter 6

Camille observed the receptionist from behind the glass wall of the press office; when the woman went to fetch her afternoon tea, as she always did at this time, Camille seized her chance. Josh was at an off-site meeting. When she lowered the handle of his office door, it gave a squeak that made her wince, but she darted inside. His desk was neat, documents arranged into piles at both ends of the work space, as though two armies awaited battle. She thumbed through manila files until she found one marked "Bonham."

Back in the main office—the reception counter still unmanned—Camille placed the entire stack of paperwork from the file into the copier and pressed "Scan." The white-green beam slid back and forth. As the final sheet emerged from the machine, she slid into Josh's office with the manila folder just as the receptionist came back up the corridor. She waited until the woman leaned down behind the counter to answer the phone, then slipped out, closing the door behind her, pressing her thumb to her wrist to find her pulse racing.

The digitized documents were waiting on her computer in the downloads folder. She skimmed the Bonhams' identification papers and Josh's handwritten notes. The latter were sparse. In his elegant scrawl, he'd noted significant dates and the details of the maid agency that had brought Awmi over from Burma. She scrolled down the sheet, and there was a copy of the police statement. She zoomed in to read Officer Pang's blocky handwriting.

At 0130 hours on 29 October at unit #30-01 The Attica I met with Mrs. Amanda Bonham regarding the death of a foreign domestic worker "Awmi." Mrs. Bonham confirmed that she discovered a body at approximately 0045 hours on the rear balcony of the property and confirmed it to be her employee. Officers confirmed that the maid was deceased and detected no signs of foul play. The cause of death appears to be chemical poisoning from ingesting domestic cleaning products.

At 0800 hours I obtained a sworn state-ment from Mrs. Amanda Bonham: the registered employer of the deceased, as confirmed by the Ministry of Manpower. Mrs. Bonham confirmed that the maid had made no previous attempts to harm herself. Mrs. Bonham had no cause for concern about her behavior or mental health prior to death.

After conducting routine procedures and removing personal items belonging to the deceased, I provided Mrs. Bonham with a case number and copy of the statement. I also gave her a copy of Leaflet 99/17, "What to Do If Your Foreign Domestic Worker Dies." I entered the case into the police database as a suspected suicide.

Camille watched the cursor blink. Pang seemed to have assumed it was suicide. She remembered an ex-boyfriend, a trainee policeman, saying that when a case was first reported as a suicide, officers often made assumptions that led them to miss signs of foul play. But she had to admit that suicide looked likely. Even considering Edward Bonham's date-rape drugs, it was hard to imagine that someone would kill a person in their own apartment. And by making them drink bleach? Messy method. If Bonham had killed the helper by accident, for example, with an overdose of clonazepam, there had to be easier ways to cover it up. The most common method of suicide in helpers was jumping from a balcony, which would be easy enough to fake when you lived on a high floor.

No, murder didn't look likely. But something had driven the girl to suicide. Maybe the unwanted attentions of her employer? If so, imagine the pressure of keeping Edward Bonham at bay while also hiding it from his wife, who was her legal employer and had the power to deport her at a moment's notice. What a hothouse up there in the penthouse.

She would show these documents to Sharmila Menon during their meeting; maybe the HELP lawyer could give Ruth Chin an "angle." The media would sit up and notice a wealthy expat who preyed on his young maid and drove her to suicide. That reminded her . . .

Camille googled Amanda Bonham but got only a few hits on social media. Nothing to explain her comments about being on the receiving end of paparazzi interest; maybe something had occurred before she married? She googled Edward Bonham too. For several minutes she read about his business, GetSetJet. From the minimal text amid blue-sky shots of aircraft, she worked out that Bonham brokered sales of private jets. A glamorous lifestyle would play well in the press.

She clicked on an image of Edward Bonham, studied it for a moment, and flicked her thumbnails together while her brain realigned its assumptions. Amanda Bonham so fit the mold of the trailing spouse that Camille had anticipated Edward Bonham to be a typical fat cat. She hadn't noticed on the small wedding photo, but in the pictures online he appeared more fit than fat. She clicked on a snap taken recently on a runway in China, where Edward had delivered a Gulfstream to a billionaire. He was a pilot too. What a guy. Camille zoomed in on the picture. She tapped the screen with her fingertip. Right on his handsome face.

The Bonham smile drifted in and out of her mind as the afternoon wore on, Camille watching the clock until she could wish her boss a good evening and head out into the ebbing heat. Finally, she set off down a side street and picked up the pace. Two Filipino helpers, chatting at machine-gun speed, were tugged past by panting dogs. Camille didn't understand Tagalog, but its pattern was as familiar as a lullaby. Lani used to sing to her as a child; the words had long since slipped away, but the cozy feeling remained.

Camille thought of her memory as one of those kitchen drawers where you throw odd bits that don't have a rightful place. Every so often, she opened it up and something glinted, but it was only a broken thing, a fragment, a useless recollection without context or meaning. Lani's face, her voice, even her full name: that knowledge was as faded as the colors of a photo left in the sunlight. Like the items in the kitchen drawer—a single cuff link or a stopped watch or an obsolete cable—her memories were incomplete. But she hoarded them nonetheless, hoping that one day someone might put them in order.

As she pushed herself up the hill, the high-rise condos retreated, and the houses grew larger and more private. The soundtrack of traffic turned into the tune of cicadas. After a few minutes, she reached a long metal fence and stopped. Behind the cracked and peeling posts was Tanglin Green, where she had lived until the age of ten. The jumbled drawer of her memory didn't seem deep enough to account for that length of time. Her hands slipped through the fence and gripped the metal. Rust pierced her skin, but she squeezed tighter. The former army barracks, which had been converted to private homes long ago, was arranged in rows of squat terraces like a small village. Everywhere were the lipstick palms and rain trees and dangling epiphytes that she loved. One tree had a long rope swing hanging from a vast bough, just like they'd had in their garden. The climate would have eaten away her rope swing by now; it was fifteen years since she'd lived here.

She released the fence and brushed metallic flakes from her hands.

Tanglin Green drew her back time and again. Sweaty walks that necessitated cooling herself under the air-con vent when she got back to the office. Sometimes, as today, she walked here after work and stood outside, watching through the bars. Smelling leaf mold and jungle pepper, and listening to maids sing power ballads while baking cookies. The place hadn't changed since Camille had raced up this road, knowing that Lani would have fresh gingerbread waiting for her. Poor Lani, who got sent away not long after Camille and Collin got sent away.

The image of Edward Bonham surfaced. She could imagine Collin mocking her—she'd call him later to give him the chance to do so for real: *So what was it, Camille, that first attracted you to the handsome millionaire?* Would Collin understand that something about Edward Bonham chimed, faint but distinct, like a harbor bell through the fog? She didn't know why, but her pulse beat with a nagging insistence that was impossible to ignore.

Edward Bonham might be out of the country, but there were other Bonhams who were available. And while Amanda had "lost track" of her husband, the daughter might be more attentive. Josie's school resembled the headquarters of the United Nations, impressive and forbidding with its array of national flags. Of course, Josie was only seventeen; Camille wondered if she needed parental permission to interview her. Probably. Technically. But she shook off the qualm. She only wanted a chat. She came in peace. Besides, she was closer to Josie's age than to her parents', a fact that was underlined by the ease with which she strolled onto campus amid the end-of-the-day throng. It helped that she was smaller than the oldest kids, and her freckles gave her a youthful air.

Camille knew, because she'd related the Bonham family schedule to the cleaners earlier, that Josie attended an after-school class in advanced coding. She asked a boy for directions, and he pointed to where "Geek Club," as he called it, met in the senior library. She took the stairs and came to a room that resembled a groovy bookstore, with librarians' suggestions laid out in piles on tables and a coffee bar at one end. A group of students occupied a work space in the center, attended by a teacher. After a few minutes, they packed up and exited in a gaggle, and Camille stepped into their path and asked for Josie. One girl jabbed a thumb backward over her shoulder without breaking stride. Camille wondered how much of a misfit you had to be to get rejected by the geeks.

Inside the library, a girl remained at the central work space, hammering at her laptop, a textbook open by her side. A long sweep of dark hair obscured her face. Camille watched her brush it over a shoulder and noticed that her face was pale, her skin sallow in a country where people literally glowed with sunshine. The teacher held the door open as he called out, "Home time, Josie." The girl said something Camille couldn't hear, and the teacher's reply was brusque: "Security will chuck you out." When she carried on typing, he let the door drop and jogged down the stairs.

Camille went inside just as Josie stood, carefully placing her belongings inside a backpack and fixing it shut with a neat bow.

"Josie Bonham?"

The girl's head snapped up, revealing extreme cat-eye makeup. She swung the bag defensively onto one shoulder, which she kept turned to the newcomer. She carried melancholy like the placard of a lone protester, but Camille pressed on, introducing herself as a volunteer for HELP, an organization that protected the rights of foreign domestic workers.

"Our helper died," Josie said, pulling lush hair off her face into a band. "She was only eighteen. Is that why you're here?"

Camille explained that Awmi was the latest in a spate of suicides. "At HELP, we campaign to highlight the mental health challenges faced by helpers."

Josie turned to face Camille. "It's important what you're doing because some of them have a rough time."

"They do. Did you say your helper was eighteen?" Camille asked.

"She liked to call herself Auntie, but it was a joke because we're basically the same age. We made the same joke over and over because her English wasn't very good, but she found it really funny. I'm sure she said she was eighteen. Is that okay?"

"The minimum age for helpers in Singapore is twenty-three. But a lot of girls from Burma get false passports and lie about their age."

"Will Amanda get in trouble? It's not fair if she does because she paid an agency to do the paperwork, so it's not her fault if they got the age wrong. Maybe Awmi didn't know her real age because in some countries they don't have proper documents or even know their date of birth. Awmi said a woman came to her village to recruit girls and took her away the next day, and they came straight to Singapore. She hadn't even seen a washing machine before she got to our apartment." Josie stopped and licked the corners of her lips. "She was quite bad at laundry, actually, so I started handwashing my stuff in the bathroom sink." She glanced up from under her thick fringe, and Camille saw that her wide-set eyes were swimming. "Not that that's important now."

Camille touched her lightly on the arm. "It sounds as though you listened to her."

Josie ground the toe of her Converse against a crack in the wooden flooring, working off a sliver of oak. She wore socks and full-length leggings; even her sleeves were long, layered under a school shirt. Apart from being inappropriate for the climate, her dress was a contrast to the usual expat-brat uniform of as much bare skin as possible.

"So is this your job?" Josie asked.

"I work at the British High Commission as a press officer. But I studied human rights law. Some people don't have a voice, so I donate my skills to let them be heard."

"Why didn't you become a lawyer?"

"So many questions!" Camille glanced around as though someone might rescue her, but Josie didn't flinch. "Too impatient, I suppose. I wanted to get a job. Get to Singapore."

"Is it bad to have a helper? Is it like modern slavery?"

"No, I don't think that at all. But it's wrong that helpers are dependent on the goodwill of their employers. All workers—including migrants—should be protected by law."

"But why do you care?" Josie bent down to pick up the splinter and turned it in her thin fingers. "The world is full of refugees. Child soldiers. Prisoners on death row. Why helpers?"

"I've been thinking about that recently. I grew up in Singapore with a helper. My parents took me to boarding school in the UK, and I thought I would see her when I came back, but . . ." Camille wanted to reach out and take the shard of wood from Josie's hands before she cut herself on the sharp edge. "But I didn't get to come back. So I don't know what happened to her."

"You never saw her again?"

"She was too old to apply for another job in Singapore, so she was sent home. And I didn't know her surname—I just called her Lani—so I could never find her."

"Didn't your parents know her name?"

Camille gave a tight shake of her head. Josie turned the splinter one last time and flicked it with a deadeye shot into the wastepaper bin. "Awmi asked my dad for help."

"Oh?" Camille's pulse picked up.

"She needed an advance on her salary."

"Did he give her the money?"

"Said he would transfer it to her account." Josie's eyes sought hers, eager for approval. "Do you think the reason she needed money had something to do with it?"

"Do you know how much?"

"You'd have to ask him." The girl's eyes darted away now, worried she had said too much.

Camille smiled reassuringly and explained that maids often requested advances for perfectly legitimate reasons, such as sending presents for a child's birthday.

"Awmi didn't have children; she was only eighteen."

"Well, I suppose it can be a sign of trouble," Camille went on. "Moneylenders—they call them *ah longs* in Singapore—take advantage of helpers. They give the women contracts in a language they don't understand. But the helpers do it because agencies deduct their salary for months to recoup the cost of bringing them to Singapore, leaving them with nothing."

"Amanda paid Awmi direct. We didn't treat her like a slave."

"Of course not." Camille's mouth was moving, forming words, telling Josie about the problems that helpers face when they first arrive and don't have anyone to turn to, but her brain was spinning counterclockwise, scrolling back through the conversation. Why had Awmi gone to Edward Bonham for an advance when Amanda paid the girl's salary? "But"—she had to be careful now—"it sounds as though your helper did have someone to turn to?"

"My dad speaks Burmese. Only ten words or so, but Awmi found it a-maze-ing." Josie flicked her fringe aside to give her eyes more room to roll. "I think she was a little bit in love with him. She did this giggle . . ." Josie placed the back of her hand over her lips and kicked one heel out behind. "Dad found it embarrassing. Who knows, maybe her crush had something to do with what happened? Unrequited love? It's not like he would be interested in a girl like her, is it?" She swung her backpack onto her shoulder, her arms ending in a defensive knot across her breasts. Camille was considering Josie's last comment as a janitor clattered a bucket and mop into the library.

"Time to go home sweet home," Josie sighed. Camille watched the girl leave, wondering which one of them Josie's statement about her father's innocence was designed to convince.

Chapter 7

Cash made Amanda nervous. Especially the plasticized Singapore dollars that slid around in her hand like toy money. She lifted the lid of a ginger jar and dropped in a wad: $600 from selling her Louboutins at Starbucks to a woman with fingers still greasy from a muffin. The roll of notes hit the bottom, and she heard it unfurl with a shrug. If only she could shrug off the sense that she too was unraveling. Ed and his furtive activities, Awmi and her secret life. The apartment was so bright and so quiet, you wouldn't think so much could remain in the dark and hush-hush.

She lifted a small jar and assessed its weight. Maybe there was an innocent reason why Ed had condoms. His leather travel bag predated Amanda; he'd had it for years. The condoms hadn't expired, but she had no clue when he might have purchased them. She would ask him straight out, get it off her mind . . . once he came home . . . once she came up with an excuse for why she had been snooping in the first place.

The lift gave a dull chime, and Amanda put the lid on the ginger jar just as the mirrored doors slid aside and Josie stepped into the hallway.

"Oh, hey."

As Josie shed her rucksack, Amanda stretched her hand toward her stepdaughter's arm, hovering an inch above the sleeve. "Are you feeling okay?"

"Well, a woman died in our kitchen, but apart from that . . ." Josie picked up the bag again, as though realizing that no one was going to clean up after her now.

Amanda forced a calm expression onto her face. "Are you hungry? You've had a long day."

Josie walked a few steps toward the now-inappropriately red kitchen. Her giraffe legs crossed as she stopped and hugged herself, pulling her school shirt tight, the logo of a dragon stretching across her shoulder blades. "I don't feel like eating."

Amanda took the rucksack out of her hand. "Freshen up and I'll bring you a snack. Maybe we'll go for a swim before dinner?"

"How can you act normal when we don't know what happened?" said Josie.

"We know what happened. The police said it was suicide. It's horrible; I feel sick thinking about it." Amanda busied herself by dragging out a water bottle strangled by a damp swimming kit. She handed back the empty bag. Josie waited, eyeing the kitchen. The silence seemed to squeeze Amanda until more words were forced out. "We bought her an iPad and you set up Skype so she could speak to her sisters. Do you remember?"

Josie shook her head, her wide eyes scrunched under messy brows. "Something must have pushed her. No one gets that homesick." She shifted the bag onto her other shoulder. "I'm leaving home soon."

"Next year. And it's different—you're going to university, you'll make friends, start a career." Amanda gestured toward the huge windows, as though Josie's bright future was out there, ready to come flooding in.

"Wasn't this Awmi's career? Just because I'm destined for a profession and she cleaned floors doesn't make her life any less valid."

"I wasn't saying that—"

"Do you think it had something to do with the *ah longs*?" Josie said.

"What are *ah longs*?"

"Moneylenders."

"Awmi was involved with moneylenders?" Amanda moved around to face Josie, and the gesture seemed to trigger a switch that shut off the conversation. The girl pressed her lips together and then licked the corners of her mouth like a cat. "Josie?"

"She asked dad for money."

"Why?"

Josie wiped her mouth with a fist. "I thought he told you. He gave her an advance. That's all I know."

"When was this?"

"A couple of weeks ago."

"Why would she borrow from moneylenders?" Amanda didn't ask the other question that leaped to mind: *Why didn't he tell me?*

"We should have told the police," Josie said.

"We don't even know it *was* moneylenders."

"Well, there must be something that pushed her over the edge, because she was totally fine, full of beans, and then—boom—she's dead on the floor. It doesn't make sense."

"I don't think suicide makes sense to anyone except the person doing it."

"Don't lecture me about suicide." Josie wheeled off toward her room. She stopped with her fingertips on the door handle and spoke without turning back. "Sometimes, Amanda, you could just . . ."

"What?"

"Stop talking a bit sooner. While it's going well." She slammed into the bedroom, leaving Amanda alone in the hallway. The elevator doors trembled as the lift navigated its empty void. She lifted one foot off the cold tile as though she were literally going to kick herself. *If I had any maternal skills, I would know when to stop talking.* She turned toward the kitchen. *If I had any maternal skills, every fetus wouldn't bail out of my womb.*

She bustled through the motions of pouring a glass of water, went to the cupboard, and forgot why she'd come to that side of the room. Josie's revelation echoed back to her. She grabbed her phone from its charger, navigated to online banking, and logged in. The balance of their joint account had miraculously topped itself up, as it did every month, its rise and fall like a tide, out of her control. Scrolling back through transactions, she spotted a payment of $2,500 into an unidentified account. Almost two weeks ago. Ed's loan to Awmi? With only an account number listed, there was no way to tell. She called the bank and verified that she was the account holder.

"Are you on an Employment Pass, ma'am?"

"I have a Dependant's Pass. My husband holds the Employment Pass. But the account is registered in both our names."

"Mr. Bonham is the account holder; only he can request more information about this transaction."

"I just want to know the name of the account that received this $2,500 payment."

"Mr. Bonham is welcome to request that information."

"But the account is in both our names." Amanda said this last part very slowly.

"Yes, ma'am. But he has the Employment Pass."

There was a long silence. In the background, she could hear the hubbub of a call center, the soundtrack of working life.

"Is there anything else I can do for you today, Mrs. Bonham?"

Amanda drew in a long breath. "I understand that in your eyes a Dependant's Pass means I am a second-class citizen and must be treated like a child." Her lips trembled with the effort not to spit. "But I am a joint holder of this account, it is my money, and I have a right to know where the payment has gone."

"The Employment Pass holder can make a request for additional information. If Mr. Bonham could instruct us—"

"Mr. Bonham is out of the country. Aren't you concerned that money is being fraudulently removed from our account?"

"We are very concerned about fraud, ma'am. And Mr. Bonham is welcome to contact our twenty-four-hour customer service at any time to request further assistance." The voice was triumphant, beatific, with the air of a cult member. Amanda paused to settle her flailing mind. No doubt this corporate automaton would think her rich. Rich and angry, like all the female *ang mohs*, these high-maintenance Western women.

"Can you see the balance of this account?" Amanda asked in a low tone.

"Yes, ma'am. You have more than a million dollars." She gave a two-syllable laugh.

"Where do you think that money came from?"

"I can't say."

"Do you assume that Mr. Bonham earns the money and Mrs. Bonham spends it?"

"Ma'am, I—"

"I may be a dependent in Singapore, but back in England I had a life. I owned property. A house. Half the balance of this account is the profit I made when I sold *my* house. Mine, bought and paid for by *me* long before Mr. Bonham came along. And now you're telling me I don't have the right to inquire about payments made with my own money because I only have a Dependant's Pass?"

"The Employment Pass holder can make a request for additional information. If Mr. Bonham could instruct us—"

Amanda jabbed her finger on the red button, longing for an old-fashioned phone that she could rip out of the wall and fling across the room, where it would curl up in a corner like a vanquished snake. Instead, she flung open a cupboard door and clattered out Josie's favorite bowl—kid's melamine so faded she could barely make out the shadow of Eeyore.

She'd behaved like a typical *ang moh* on the phone: arrogant, angry, aggressive. *But the rules are so unfair; why do women accept it?* She slashed a banana into slices while her breathing slowed. *Because in so many areas of life—fertility, aging, love—choice is an illusion.*

She turned to the fridge to get yogurt. That moth was back, flattened on the balcony door, its ugly face leering. She strode over and flicked the glass. The moth shuddered. Why had Ed given money to Awmi? Why keep it secret? Did he simply forget? But $2,500—such a substantial amount. Why did Awmi need—?

Ah. Pregnant Awmi. Facing deportation or abortion. But if she'd wanted money for a termination, why not ask Amanda—woman to woman?

She tried to halt her mind. Tried not to think the next thought, one that connected an unwanted pregnancy to the condoms in Ed's travel bag. *Unless Awmi couldn't tell me. Because I would ask after the father.*

Her heart stumbled in her chest. This was even worse than the anonymous encounters on far-flung continents that she'd imagined. Her husband taking advantage of a vulnerable woman—in their own home. The implications made her light-headed. She slopped yogurt into Josie's bowl and steadied herself before snatching up the tray. The living area was still scented from the jasmine Awmi had picked the night she died, but now Amanda wished she could open a window and air the place. At Josie's room, she kicked the base of the door and it swung open. "Can I come in?" At her desk under the window, Josie snapped her laptop shut like a clam.

Amanda looked around for somewhere to deposit the tray, but every surface was covered with Josie's childhood ephemera. A museum of herself. The only space was on the bedside table, so she set the tray atop a journal, beside a framed photo of Josie, still a plump-faced toddler, holding a rainbow lollipop the size of her own head. Next to it, a teenage Josie and her mother, ruddy-cheeked on an English cliff. Ed must have taken this photo; it was so intimate. Josie looked as though she'd just plunged a foot into an icy puddle, but the woman was all white teeth and sparkling eyes despite the winter wind. Despite knowing—as she must have done even while smiling into the camera—that at the top of these several hundred feet of shale and sheep shit she would take her own life. Amanda winced, remembering the lecture she'd doled out to Josie about suicide.

"I'm sorry about before." Josie's voice was little.

"We're all upset."

"It's not your fault, though, is it?"

"I hope not." The TARDIS-blue walls, paint she'd sourced at Josie's request, felt oppressive. If only the rules of stepmotherhood could be defined as easily as Pantone numbers. Josie took the snack and dallied a spoon in the yogurt.

"I need to ask you about the money your father gave to Awmi."

"If I tell you something, do you promise not to be upset?"

Amanda tried to smile, but her lips stuck to her teeth. "Go on."

"A lawyer came to school asking questions about Awmi and Dad. She's doing a media campaign about helpers who commit suicide."

"What lawyer?"

"She said she met you? Camille Kemble? From the British High Commission? And HELP—she volunteers for them. Is she going to publish Dad's name or something?"

"She's not a lawyer. She's some kind of assistant. When was this?"

"Just now, after school."

"What did she want to know?"

Josie shrugged. "About Awmi. Just the details. About the money. She was the one who said it might be *ah longs* and—"

"Wait. Did you tell her about the money?"

"I didn't think. I'm sorry—"

Amanda rubbed her temples. "They can't name and shame us when we did nothing wrong!"

"Maybe we did do something wrong."

"Like what?"

"Like not upholding Awmi's human rights." Josie got up to put her bowl back on the tray and took the water to her desk.

"It'll be humiliating if this gets in the newspaper. Everyone will hear about it. Your dad's clients even. I'll call her boss, what's-his-name, Joshua MacAlpine. How did she even get on campus without a security pass?" Josie shrugged helplessly, and Amanda cut short her rant. She snatched up the tray from the bedside table and nearly trod on a vinyl record on the floor. Cold Sister's most famous album, its cover as iconic as Nirvana's swimming baby. The woodcut image was like something slashed and shredded until you looked closer and saw a bird's nest with a single sparrow inside. "I forgot about your concert tonight."

"I gave the tickets to Willow." Willow lived upstairs; the girls hung out by the pool, pretending they weren't on Tinder. Amanda didn't have the mental bandwidth to worry about why Josie wasn't going to see her favorite band with her friend—probably she was just upset over Awmi. Instead, she went to her own room, sitting on the edge of the bed to face the window, while she reached down and put the snack tray on the floor. But she kept hold of Josie's journal, which she'd held, hidden, underneath the tray.

Josie knew more than she was telling. Amanda was sure of it. She was smart enough to know what was going on with her father and smart enough to keep it hidden from his wife.

The cover of the journal was a hand-drawn copy of the Cold Sister artwork, the sparrow in its nest. Amanda folded her legs beneath herself and opened Josie's journal. In Amanda's day, a child might have written a warning for adults to keep out. But Josie had a list of Internet log-ins. It was an active list: passwords struck through or whited out, each replacement scribbled in increasingly tiny letters. Josie obviously updated her passwords more frequently than Amanda did, which was, admittedly, never. The inside cover of the journal had only one note.

There, Josie had written "a-scribble-of-a-girl.com" with a fluorescent heart encircling it.

She flicked through the journal, finding it filled with dense, anxious pencil drawings. Self-portraits and depictions of Josie's mother, obviously copied from the windswept photo beside her bed. That flailing hair, as though she were already falling. And there were pages and pages of Ed's long fingers, the tiny curling hairs so detailed Amanda felt she could touch the paper and feel warmth. But she didn't touch them; she didn't know where those hands had been. At the turn of a leaf, the journal went blank and the starkness of the white pages was like the houselights coming on at the end of a movie.

She'd had no idea that Josie was such an accomplished artist. She stowed the journal under her pillow and left the bedroom, traversing the marble hallway as quietly as the whispering air con. In the kitchen, she got her phone and tapped in the website address: a-scribble-of-a-girl. When it loaded, Amanda turned the phone lengthways. There was a photo of a stormy sky, but that wasn't what caught her attention.

Layered over the image was a black box containing a retro-style timer, numbers ticking in a countdown: 15 days, 03 hours, 36 minutes, and 15 seconds. The microseconds were a blur.

Amanda scrolled up and down, but there was no indication of what the timer was counting down to. She tried clicking on the numbers, but a text box popped up to tell her it was a private blog. Password required. She watched microseconds pass. Then she scrolled up to the photo of the stormy sky. That sky, the sea, those ships scattered like devil's playthings. This was Singapore: the straits off Sentosa. It was the view from Amanda's bedroom.

Chapter 8

Camille arrived early at the BHC, itching to go over the scanned Bonham file again, but Josh was already in his office. He appeared in the doorway. "Early again, Camille? Anyone would think you have a guilty conscience."

She tried to stop her eyes from darting to the pile of manila folders on the desk behind him.

"Come into my office for a moment, would you?"

Josh went to perch on the edge of his desk. Camille took her cue and remained standing.

"Amanda Bonham," he said.

"Yes, sir." Her mind went again to the file; how could he possibly know she had copied his notes?

"Why is she phoning me to complain about her stepdaughter being doorstepped over the death of their helper?"

"By the press?"

"No, Camille, by you."

"Ah."

"Why?"

"I wanted background information on the case."

"Unless you're moonlighting for the Singapore Police, there is no 'case.'"

"It was for HELP, sir. In my own time. I'm preparing documents for their pro bono lawyer, who is going to lobby MPs before the parliamentary debate on—"

"Do you understand the word *confidential*, Camille?"

"Yes, sir. I do."

"Our meeting with the Bonhams was confidential. Leaking confidential information to an external organization puts you in breach of your employment contract."

"Sir, I—" Camille tried to swallow whatever had lodged in her throat. She couldn't lose her job, not after she had arranged her whole life so she could get back to Singapore. "It won't happen again, sir."

"Kindly close the file on the Bonham case. We've done our bit, and if there is any further call for assistance, I will deal with it personally."

"I've finished my report."

"Then you can print a hard copy for my attention, but don't put it through the system." Josh glanced toward the high commissioner's office. Camille waited for an explanation of this breach of protocol; all files went through the system. His gaze returned to hers, and his shoulders gave a faint roll that he only just prevented from reaching his eyes. "Truth be told, I only made that house call because I was curious. I knew Edward Bonham a long time ago—at least, I knew *of* him—and I was intrigued to learn that he's back in Singapore. Surprised I missed that. So when the wife called in a tizzy about death certificates and having police officers in her home, I decided to pay a visit. But I should have stuck to protocol and advised her over the phone. As there's nothing doing, we can quietly let it drop."

"Of course, sir."

"Excellent." He pushed himself off the desk, back to full height.

"There was one thing?" Camille said.

Josh pulled the elastic of his security tag to full stretch. The metallic zip as it wound back in set her teeth on edge.

"Edward Bonham's medication was found in the helper's bedroom," she said.

"Oh?"

"When I was in the kitchen, an officer came in with a stash of pills he'd taken from the maid's room. Some were contraceptives, but there were also bottles of clonazepam, in Bonham's name, from different doctors. They're sedatives that can be used as date-rape drugs."

Josh narrowed his eyes and gave a single shake of the head. "If Edward Bonham was secretly drugging the helper, why would the drugs be in her room?"

Camille faltered. "Yes, but . . . it might explain why she killed herself. Maybe she put them there for the police to find?"

"That sounds a little fanciful. Please do not get involved with Edward Bonham."

"But what if he was abusing his helper?"

Josh pushed his fists into his trouser pockets and rocked back and forth. His security card tut-tutted against a shirt button. "You have to understand that detective work is not our job. We do not have the power—or the inclination—to protect British nationals from the law of the host country—"

"But—"

"—nor do we have the power to investigate them of our own accord."

"So what is the protocol if we suspect a UK citizen of committing a crime?"

"All residents of Singapore are subject to its laws."

"So we should inform the police?"

"Didn't you say a police officer found the drugs in the helper's room?" he asked.

Camille looked down to see the toe of her shoe twisting into the carpet, trying to bury itself.

"So the police are already informed, am I correct?" said Josh.

When she looked back up, her boss indicated with one flat hand that he wished to exit his office. "I've always found the police here to be thorough and fair. You will not plunder this case for information to feed to HELP. I support their cause, I do, but you have to keep it separate from your day job if you wish to remain in gainful employment." He ushered her out. "Is this matter closed?"

"It's closed."

Josh stalked away with his trousers snapping like flags around a pole. She sat at her desk, forwarding the Bonham file to her personal mail. Better to print it at home and delete all trace from her work computer. If Josh found out she had taken notes from his office and copied them . . . Phrases from his dressing down blurred through her brain. *Do you understand the word* confidential? She felt her cheeks burn. *Breach of your employment contract.* She had let Josh down. It went beyond a simple pride in her job—she liked to please him.

What had he said? *I knew Edward Bonham a long time ago.* That gave Camille pause. *I was intrigued to learn that he's back in Singapore.*

Back in Singapore.

She picked up her phone and downloaded the case file from her personal email. In the identity documents, she found Edward Bonham's Employment Pass. It was current, but his ID number linked to a previous work permit, which had been canceled in 1999. So he had lived in Singapore at the same time as her parents. In fact, he'd left in the same year as Camille. She swore under her breath.

She'd known there was something about Edward Bonham. He wasn't just a pretty face; she recognized him, and there was every chance this was a real recollection.

Do not get involved with Edward Bonham.

If Josh knew she intended to speak to Bonham about his maid, he would fire her. He'd made that clear. So she wouldn't talk to him about the maid. This was personal: a link to her childhood. If Josh could drop into the Bonhams' lives because of curiosity about the past, then so could she.

Chapter 9

Amanda got back to the apartment after making an emergency dash to the condo shop for dinner essentials—she had always appreciated Awmi, but now she realized how much work she had delegated to the helper and how seamlessly the young woman had run the household. As soon as Amanda stepped out of the lift, she heard Ed's shower hammering. It was his habit to clean up right after a flight—the sort of thing that wasn't suspicious until she had reason to wonder what made him feel quite so dirty.

Outside the cavernous living room, the volcanic colors of the sunset made lava of the sea. She felt intimately acquainted with this view after a long day watching it ebb and flow with her mood, the forgiving morning light giving way to a ferociously hot afternoon that broke in a storm. Three times she had dialed Ed's phone, vowing to confront him. Three times she'd pressed the red button before it connected. His shower stopped abruptly. As she moved to take the shopping to the kitchen, she noticed on the coffee table a black box wrapped up with an enormous bow.

"Amanda?"

Ed came down the hallway still damp in a towel. He leaned down to kiss her on the forehead while tapping a message into his phone, and she let her hand trail across a long scratch on his hip.

"What happened to you?"

"Caught myself getting out of the pool."

"I thought you were staying in Manila another night?"

"Wrapped up quicker than I thought. And I'm going to Tokyo tomorrow so I needed to pick up my winter suit. Open it," he said with a nod to the black box.

"What's that for?" she asked.

"Just to show I was thinking about you."

She lowered herself onto the sofa and placed the gift on the dais of her crossed legs. The white bow loosened with a satisfying tumble, the lid came away, then the dustcover, layers of anticipation until she finally revealed the gift: a black leather wallet printed with a doll-like face. She ran her fingertips over a girl's downcast eyes. The leather was soft and smelled floral with an undertone of flesh.

Ed had his back to her, fiddling with his phone. She wondered if another woman had held him last night. Given him that long scratch. Maybe Ed had washed her off his body in the shower and off his conscience in duty-free. Maybe he was texting her now, right in front of Amanda. Brazen. Then music burst through wireless speakers, and Ed slid his phone onto the coffee table. He came toward her, performing a little shuffle to the tracks of his youth. She wanted to ask him right then about Awmi, but the words roared in her head. If she tried to articulate it, she might scream. Keep screaming.

Ed sat next to her on the sofa. "There's something else inside the bag."

She clicked open the clasp and peered into the satin interior. Tucked between the red folds was what looked like a scrunched piece of paper. Amanda lifted it out between thumb and forefinger and held it up to the light. "Is this . . . ?" She smelled the thin tube to confirm that it was, as she suspected, a joint.

Ed circled one arm around her butt and pulled her in close. "You look like you need it, Mrs. Bonham. Put some color in your cheeks." He ran a fingertip under the curve of her cheekbone. "I thought we could smoke it and, you know, like that time in New York."

"You smell of whisky," she told him.

"Ed on the rocks. Your favorite."

"You're playful tonight."

"Well, I sold a plane and I'm about to fuck my wife." Ed dropped onto his knees on the rug, uncrossing Amanda's legs as he went.

"Josie's here."

"She's at Willow's." He pushed her skirt up, revealing neon-yellow panties. He ran the tip of his tongue along the edge of the lace.

"She could come home any minute," Amanda said.

"Okay."

"I'm worried about her, Ed."

He came up from between her knees and slumped back onto the sofa. "I'll need another drink if we're going to talk."

"Wine?" Amanda escaped to the kitchen with the shopping bag and heard a crunch as he got off the sofa to follow her.

"I want a Bloody Mary. Do you want a Bloody Mary?"

"Not really." She poured herself a glass of red.

"Why are you so worried about Josie?" Ed ground a solid layer of black pepper that floated on the tomato juice like ash.

"She's got a secret website. And it's counting down to something, but I don't know what."

"Probably her birthday. Blogs are like teenage diaries these days. Just read it."

"It's password-protected. And she doesn't have any friends; that's the other thing that bothers me. Apart from Willow, and they didn't go to the Cold Sister gig together last night."

"Josie said she didn't feel like it after Awmi."

"When did she say this?"

"I called her earlier. Willow has a crush on this Rafferty boy, so Josie let her take him to the gig. And anyway, she's got about three hundred friends on Facebook."

"You're on Facebook?" Amanda held up her wineglass, and Ed clanked it with his own.

"I joined to keep tabs on Josie. Don't see the attraction myself."

"That's what I mean. Apart from Willow, how many real friends do you know about?"

"It's expat life: friends come and go. It seems normal to me, but maybe I'm not qualified to understand teenage girls' friendships."

"Being her father qualifies you."

"Being her stepmother and a former teenage girl qualifies you more."

"Don't be an arsehole."

Ed stepped forward and gathered her around the waist, hands sliding to her buttocks. "Being an arsehole is part of my manly essence."

Over his shoulder, Amanda sucked red wine through clenched teeth. "This spliff, Ed?"

"Shall we smoke it on the balcony?"

"Since when are you that reckless?" She wriggled out of his hold and pushed him to arm's length. "What were you thinking, bringing drugs into Singapore? Have you never noticed the 'Death to Drug Traffickers' signs all over the airport?"

"It's one spliff. You don't get hanged for one spliff."

He moved to top up her wine, but she laid a palm over her empty glass.

"But you do get deported. Employment Pass revoked. No appeal. Out of the country within weeks. Josie yanked out of school. All this, gone." She waved her hand around their apartment and the sea view and the swimming pool glowing from thirty stories below. "Where did you hide it, anyway? Not inside the Prada wallet, surely? That's the first thing customs would have opened if they'd picked you out."

"I'm not stupid, Amanda." Ed knocked back the dregs of the Bloody Mary. "It was up my bum." He burst into a cough, either laughing or choking on pepper. She handed him the wine bottle, and he took a swig to clear his throat before slapping himself on the chest. "It wasn't up my bum. Honest. Bernardo brought a couple back in his shoe."

"I've never trusted that guy."

"He's too well connected for his own good. Thinks there are no consequences; for him there probably aren't. But he also knows a lot of people with the cash to buy private jets."

"Please don't come through the airport with him if he's going to pull that kind of stunt."

"Shall we get rid of the evidence then?" Ed held out the joint and a plastic lighter, grinning. The full beam of her husband's attention landed a spark in her kindling. Giggling and flirting—this is how they were once. Before infertility sucked the joy out of intimacy, turning each encounter into a test fraught with failure. If Ed had been seeking cheap thrills elsewhere, then Amanda could understand the need for escape, levity, a chance to act without thought of the consequences. Except—unlike that spoiled brat, Bernardo—there were consequences for the less privileged. Awmi, for example, left holding a baby.

She took the joint out of his fingers and laid it on the counter. "I need to talk to you about Awmi."

Ed refilled his glass with wine. "What about?"

"Did you give her money last month?"

He sipped his drink, eyes locked on hers over the rim. Although she was watching for his reaction, she somehow felt that she was the one being sized up. "How did you know?"

Amanda's heart faltered. "Josie. And the payment on the bank statement. Was it for *ah longs*?"

"What are *ah longs*?"

Not moneylenders then. She gulped her wine. "Was it because she was pregnant?"

Ed's gaze dropped for the first time, and he turned the wheel of the lighter. "I didn't want to upset you. You seem so brittle after the last miscarriage. And she was frightened of going home after her family scrimped and saved to send her here, so I paid for an abortion—"

"Who was the father, Ed?"

He picked up the joint, turning the delicate parcel in his fingers. "Not my place to ask."

"Why did she go to you and not me?"

Ed flicked the lighter into flame. "She knew what you'd been through. She was young and naive, but not stupid. Women lose babies in Burma too. We agreed it was best you didn't know." He pulled Amanda close and kissed her forehead. She laid her hands flat on his chest. "We'll get there one day. I can already see them running about, our kids. Reckon we'll have twins. One little arsehole like me and a beauty called Edwina. Look, there they go now." He held up her wrist and made her hand crazy wave so that their distorted reflections crazy waved back from the window. "It'll happen, Amanda. We have to hold our nerve."

"And if it doesn't?" She glanced again at the window, but the twins had turned away, dejected.

"Then we pick ourselves up and dust ourselves off, and lead a full life of decadence and freedom and long lie-ins."

"But what if it doesn't feel like a full life? What if I never get past it? What if I lead half a life? Because I've only lived half a life so far, and it's not been very satisfying." In response to a look that suggested he was about to mansplain her feelings, she pushed on. "It's true, Ed. I've got no siblings, no career, no friends in Singapore, and my old schoolmates lost interest once my parents were too broke for me to keep up with them. I'm not a sister and hardly even a daughter. I'll never be an aunt or a bridesmaid. I'm no one's best friend, no one's confidant, no one's colleague or mentor. I'm never the go-to girl or someone who gets a phone call in the middle of the night when the shit hits the fan. I will never be any of these things. But I thought that one day I might be a mother. Because right now, I feel like a ghost. I need flesh and blood to bring me to life."

"But you are a mother, aren't you? A stepmother to Josie. And you're a wife. My wife." Ed caught both her hands. "So I'm your flesh and blood." Cordite from the lighter lingered in the air, reminding Amanda of the New Year's Eve fireworks the night they met. She took the joint from his hand.

"Switch on the extractor fan then."

Ed lit the spliff, holding it to her lips. She hesitated and took a nip, then when the warmth swaddled her, pressing the creases out of her thoughts, she inhaled again. After a few shared drags, the haze of smoke swirled into a galaxy of white wisps and floating black orbs. Amanda reached out a hand to touch her—"Eggs." She said it out loud.

Ed bent double into silent laughter: "What the hell does that mean?"

She waited for him to stop laughing and when he didn't, she took hold of the whorl of his hair and tipped his head back to look her in the face. "I don't want to stop fertility treatment, not even for a rest. I want to transfer the last two embryos. Did you know I can hear them, sometimes, jostling together in the cold? You think I'm nuts, but it's real. It's instinct. They're alive, or at least they're . . . dormant. They need me." There was a pause that may have been a beat or an entire drumroll. "And if I'm not pregnant soon, I want to file adoption papers."

Ed curved his head out of her grip and straightened, moving his body as though slotting bones back into place. He sucked the spliff down to his fingertips and offered a last drag to Amanda, but she shook her head and let him stub it out in a teacup. His last swirl of breath enchanted her for a few seconds before being sucked away into the fan.

"No adoption." His words were as light but as lingering as the smoke.

She shook her head again, and its contents took a moment to catch up. "Can't we at least discuss it?"

"It's not the same, loving another person's child," he said.

"I love Josie, don't I? Like you just said. And a new baby wouldn't be another person's. It would be ours."

"We're not up to it." Ed threw back the remains of the wine. "The pressure could break us."

"A child would bring us together."

"No adoption. And no treatment for a while, please? If we get pregnant naturally, then great, but take a break. You treat it like you're in training for an Iron Man competition."

"But we don't get pregnant naturally—"

"We're good at trying." He put his wineglass to Amanda's lips, holding her chin steady like the priest at her convent school mass. She drank up, her tongue scraping the caustic tannin that coated the back of her teeth, and let him take her hand and lead her out of the kitchen, leaving the extractor fan on full blast. In the chill of the bedroom, she sank into the mattress with her arm and her gaze flung toward the heaving boats, while the other palm rested on the nape of Ed's neck, grazed by his velveteen hairline. His tongue etched her surface, and she closed her eyes, following his progress from beneath her skin as though she were trapped under a sheet of ice. It deadened the sound of his breathing, blurred the light, narrowed her focus to a sharp point of sensation until she herself was drowned out. Time ducked and dived and she became conscious of floating, alone now, and pulled the duvet over her chilled torso and sat up and focused on the offshore ships, wavering spots of light like deep-sea creatures. She unraveled her wrist from the bedsheet, got up, and found her bathrobe on the floor.

Ed was flat out, her neon panties crumpled beneath his long thigh. Time returned like a camera flash, and she recalled the noise they'd made. God, what if Josie had come home? Her hand pressed down on her mouth as she remembered that even Ed had laughed at one point and shushed into her ear. And had they left the spliff in a teacup in the kitchen?

She opened the bedroom door and peeped down the hallway. Josie's door was closed. The roar of the extractor fan blasted down the hallway. Her bare feet squeaked on the marble as she scuttled to the kitchen, pocketed the butt of the spliff, and clicked off the din. She washed the smell of cannabis off her fingers at the kitchen sink. In the living room, Ed's music was still playing. "Chocolate Girl" by Deacon Blue, one of the old bands that made him maudlin. Amanda heard how his chocolate girl was sheathed in silver, snapped in two, and swallowed. She turned off the speaker.

Her mobile phone was on the coffee table, next to the new leather wallet. A text blinked. Josie: Gone to a late movie. At least she hadn't heard her stepmother squealing. Amanda sent a reply to say that Ed was home but they'd turned in for the night. She sat on the sofa and slipped the Prada into its dustcover. She would sell it on SOWs. In its original wrapping, it should fetch $2,000. The price of an embryo transfer.

She clicked through to the Facebook page. Even late at night, SOWs were out in force. Someone had a cobra on their patio. Someone sought a piano tuner. Someone needed to seal her teenager's bedroom window for fear of exam-time suicide.

Her thumb was hovering over the "Logout" button when her eyes focused on a new post. It was a fuzzy photo taken in dim disco lights of a man with one arm raised over his head, dancing groin-first against a scantily clad girl.

> Is this your husband?! Ladies, I spotted this loser with a wedding ring and a stripper at Orchard Towers. Does this man belong to you? #PublicServiceAnnouncement

Orchard Towers: a building full of bars offering ladyboys and cheap girls. In just a few minutes, the post had attracted a shitstorm of comments, from "poor wife" to "poor guy" to "this is like watching puritans with pitchforks pushing adulterers onto the scaffold in the town square." The post was irresponsible, no question. But Amanda double-clicked the image.

The guy was a tall Caucasian, with long limbs and dark hair. Jeans and a blue shirt. His face was partially hidden behind the raised arm. As she zoomed in closer, the picture grew as fuzzy as her mind, pixelated by the spliff. There was something about his posture . . . Her breathing shallowed as she saw the way he had the dancer's long hair wrapped in one hand, exactly the way Ed had just held her down in their marital bed. But surely not. The joint had made her paranoid. Running around the flat worrying about a stepdaughter who wasn't even there.

But the man in the picture did look a lot like Ed. Holding that woman's hair.

Was it so unbelievable? You heard it all the time: the magnetism between beautiful Asian women and rich *ang mohs*. Why should Ed be any different? What made him so special that he wouldn't stray? *No,* nagged a nasty voice in her head, *what makes* you *so special that he wouldn't stray?* Amanda put her hand to her mouth and smelled a sharp tang of bleach. *And what makes you so sure he's telling the truth about Awmi?*

Chapter 10

After a night disturbed by dreams of Ed with his hands twined in dark hair, Amanda was woken by his predawn alarm. She feigned sleep until he left for the airport. Feeling heavy and sluggish, she stayed in bed until a surprise phone call cleared her head. She barely had time to shower and dress before her mother arrived, striding into the apartment without preamble as though it was normal to turn up in Singapore on a whim.

"Edward not here?" said Laura. "He certainly gets around."

A picture of Ed's hands flashed into her mind again, and she wondered if the image came from her dream or the photo posted on SOWs. "He took the early flight to Tokyo." Her mother could hardly criticize, considering her own nomadic lifestyle. "He's traveling more than usual at the moment. Nature of his business, I suppose."

"It's not good for a marriage. You start living separate lives."

"He only goes away for a night or two."

"It adds up."

Laura always blew in like a tropical storm, a tussle between hot and cold. Her ship, the MV *Guanyin*, had docked at neighboring Batam Island for repairs—an unexpected pit stop en route to Thailand—and Laura decided she had time to make the short ferry ride to pay her daughter a visit. And go to Marks and Spencer. She fished a compact out of her handbag and swiped powder across her forehead and down her nose. "Men are good at compartmentalizing," she said and closed the compact with a click. Amanda plunged the cafetière and muttered that she didn't know what her mother was getting at. "I mean, Amanda, they're like babies; women grow sentimental about them, but the reality is, they'll suck on any old tit."

Amanda placed a cup on the low table in front of Laura and turned the handle to make it easier for her to pick up. Both women watched the coffee steam.

"Mother . . ."

"I know. I'm bitter." ·

"Which is not surprising in the circumstances. But Ed is no baby."

"That's what worries me."

"You hardly know him. Maybe if you'd come to the wedding—"

"What did you expect at such short notice?" Laura got up and went over to the ginger jars, toyed with a few lids, producing a short melody of porcelain chimes. A dud note sounded from the pot stuffed with condoms, but luckily she didn't investigate further.

"How is Dad?" Amanda asked.

Laura came back to the sofa and picked up her cup. "He's basing himself in Sri Lanka. For this women's clinic project. Not a chance of getting the funding, but it's become quite the obsession."

"How is he?"

"Happy as a pig in muck. He's in love. Thinks I don't know. And she thinks there's money. I should show her the state of my underwear. But it's not my business anymore, is it?"

"That's not a healthy situation."

Laura eyed the sea. She might be the first person to enter the apartment without praising the view.

"How long are you sailing this time?" Amanda asked.

"I'll give it a year to let her star fade. I can stay out of his way on the ship, cover as many ports as we can reach in Southeast Asia. So long as he doesn't aggravate my donors." Laura spoke to the horizon, replaying an argument she'd obviously had many times before. "The American church groups are too conservative to fund his clinic. I told him this. They support my library ship because of the Christian literature we carry. If we slip in a few women's health pamphlets along the way, no one needs to know. But this clinic in Colombo—a family planning center by any other name—it's too much. He's promised not to target my donors again, but woe betide him if he brings down my ship."

It's all I've got left, Amanda thought.

"After all," said her mother, "it's all I've got left."

You've got me. I'm left.

But instead she said, "Marks and Sparks? Shall we cheer ourselves up with some new knickers?" The first sip of coffee felt like it would sear a hole in her gut, so she took the cup through to the kitchen and poured it away. Breakfast dishes were still in the sink, and a line of ants formed a highway along the counter. Awmi would throw her hands up in despair at the state of her kitchen. Amanda's mobile rang. The screen read "SCHOOL."

"This is Kelvin Milne. Josie's head of year? I haven't been able to reach your husband, so I wondered if you might be able to pop in for a chat today?"

"My mother is visiting—"

"It's serious, I'm afraid. It's about Josie's online activities. She breached our code of conduct, and we have issued a suspension. But this conversation would be better in person . . ."

Suspension? "Please just tell me what happened."

He paused, and Amanda heard running feet, shrill voices, the hub-bub of school life. "It came to our attention that Josie invited fellow students to a forum hosted on a website concealed inside the dark web."

"Oh," Amanda said, relieved. "Is this her blog? A-scribble-of-a-girl? I looked it up on my phone, but I can't read it—it needs a password to enter."

"If you looked it up on your phone, then no, it's not the same website. The site I'm talking about is called Sexteen. I've been unable to visit it myself because our devices on campus are blocked from accessing that part of the Internet. Are you aware of the dark web, Mrs. Bonham?"

"I've heard of it."

"It's the Wild West of the cyber world. It's accessible only with the appropriate software and know-how—or should I say inappropriate software and know-how. We're talking hackers, drug dealers, criminals, plus of course pedophiles."

"What was Josie doing there?"

"As I say, I haven't been able to see for myself. The students who reported her activities—and there have been several—tell me it's a discussion forum where they talk about exam stress, bullying, peer pressure. Innocent in itself, but the content isn't the problem; it's the fact that Josie has recruited students onto the dark web and exposed them to . . . well, goodness knows who or what she's exposed them to. We requested she shut down the forum or move it to a safe location, and when she refused, we felt a one-week suspension, starting today, was the best course of action. We've already sent her home."

Amanda started to pace. "She's got exams."

"She's an exceptional student. She can study at home and contact her teachers by email if necessary. The intention is to minimize contact with other students—"

That made her scoff. "How can you minimize contact if they're chatting on the dark web?"

"Cyber risk is a challenge, but . . . ," he droned on.

"She's had a difficult time recently, Kelvin. We had a shock this week because our helper died—"

"Oh, I'm sorry!"

"—and Josie is particularly sensitive after losing her mother a few years ago."

"I understand, and we'll take it into account, but she needs to recognize the danger she's posed to students who are less savvy." He offered to set up a session with the school counselor, and once that was arranged, he rang off. There was a whisper as the kitchen door slid open: she'd forgotten about her mother.

"How old is she?" Laura asked.

"Seventeen."

"Oh, well then . . ." She looked away, matter closed. "I took myself to London at the age of sixteen."

The school of hard knocks, Amanda thought. Laura's ingenue mistakes, the sweat and tears—whispered hints that there may have been *blood*, sweat, and tears. But those dark times were overshadowed by the bright lights of her sparkling rise as she turned model, turned muse, turned socialite, turned lady of the manor, turned bankrupt, turned full circle. At no point, judging by the autobiography published a decade ago to the delight of the gutter press but to little acclaim or financial return, did she turn into a mother.

"I'll call us a cab then, shall I?" Amanda asked.

"Can't we save the money and walk?"

"It's the other side of the causeway. And it's pissing down."

She left her mother to disapprove of the kitchen as well as her language, and went to change her shoes. On the way, she opened Josie's bedroom door. The bed was made. The air con was running (she switched it off—not as profligate as her mother seemed to think). The laptop was gone, but Josie often took it to school. Amanda called Josie's cell phone, which went to voice mail, and sent a careful text asking where she planned to spend the day, considering they both knew she wasn't in school.

In her own bathroom, she studied her face in a magnifying mirror, compartmentalizing herself to a sculpted eyebrow, a teardrop earlobe, the kind of philtrum that a face reader in Chinatown once said signified a deep imagination. She resembled her mother very closely if you took it feature by feature. Gullible eyes, prim nose, mouth tapering to arrow slits. But, somehow, the sum of Amanda's parts added up to less than her mother's. A spark shone in Laura so that she seemed permanently backlit; it was beyond beauty. It was the glow of the fire that drove her to London at the age of sixteen to seize her fortune. Losing it was Amanda's father's fault; everyone agreed on that, even her father.

Amanda didn't have her mother's spark. Instead she was a mirror image—a reverse life story: childhood riches to rabbit-in-headlights poverty when the parental funds dried up, and back to riches when a husband came along. Her life achievements amounted to being born lucky and marrying well. Even the profit she'd made on her Camden house had disappeared into the ether of their joint bank account because she made the stupid decision (against Ed's advice, in fact) to transfer her funds to Singapore, back when she felt she could better assert her independence by having her own money. Maybe her mother was self-absorbed and remote and circumnavigated the globe on a leaking ship that peddled Christian propaganda to the poor, but at least she lived.

"I thought you'd forgotten about me," Laura said, when Amanda returned. She had forgiven the elegant sofa enough to sit on it. But she kept her back to the extravagant view.

"I was trying to reach Josie. She's been thrown out of school."

"Happens to the best of us. Surely it's not your problem to deal with?"

"I'm her stepmother."

"Exactly."

Amanda fiddled with the awkward clasp on her least expensive sandals. "She's vulnerable after everything that happened—what she saw her mother do." She didn't mention that their helper had died, didn't want to endure her mother's scrutiny on that matter too. "I think Josie might be depressed, actually," she said instead.

"Well, of course she is. You were dreadfully moody at seventeen."

"How would you know? I was at boarding school."

Laura gave a high laugh, like someone dinging a glass to prompt silence. She picked up the Prada box from the coffee table and inspected it from all sides. "I knew Miuccia and Patrizio when they first took over at Prada. They were radical then, can you believe it? No logo. Ahead of the times."

"Ed bought it. He brings me presents from all his trips."

"Men do that. Cats too. Do you remember Bluebeard?"

Amanda watched her mother's hands, the color of papyrus, curling the pristine ribbon. "Haven't thought about him in years."

"Well, you were still young when he died. Disgusting animal, really—filthy manners—but I was fond of him. Big handsome tomcat. Used to leave birds' wings on my pillow. Only the wings. Mostly sparrows and starlings. Though the first time your father went off, Bluebeard brought me a dove." Laura tugged the bow. Taut silk slipped through her fingers. She peeled away crackling layers of tissue until the girl's painted face peeped out. Laura smiled a little and hummed through her nose.

"Why don't you keep it?" Amanda said suddenly. "It's your birthday at the end of the month. I can never send you anything on the ship. Let me give you a present."

Laura pressed the paper back over the wallet and jammed the lid on top.

"What on earth would I do with it? Give it to charity, if you don't want it." She glared at her watch. "Where's this taxi?"

Amanda snatched up her phone and checked the taxi app. "Can we have lunch?" she said. *I need to talk to someone, anyone. Even you.*

"I don't want to intrude. You're so busy."

"I haven't seen you in eighteen months. And now you're sailing for another year. Normal people don't turn up unannounced—in Singapore—as though they've popped around for a cup of tea. Can't you stay for lunch?"

"Is that what normal people do?"

"Yes, it is." Amanda wanted to tell her mother that these expensive trinkets meant nothing. She wasn't that kind of woman. But she needed to sell them to get money for treatment because otherwise she would be left as hollow and disappointing as an empty Prada box. All wrapping, that's what Amanda would become: as flimsy as tissue and held together by ribbon.

But her mother moved to the elevator. "You go to lunch if you like," she said. "I have a ship to run."

Chapter 11

Sharmila Menon's office boasted a view of the Supreme Court, a glass structure shaped exactly like a flying saucer that hovered over the surrounding buildings. When the lawyer bustled in and caught Camille snapping a photo of the surreal design, she loosed her distinctive chesty laugh. "People say that if we get invaded, it will take off and carry the government to safety." She dropped an armload of files onto an otherwise pristine desk. "We love conspiracy theories."

"People are always telling me there are plainclothes police on every street corner."

"Oh, that one's true." She said this with the kind of straight face that left Camille wondering whether or not she was joking. "Seriously, there's no need, we have CCTV. Much cheaper." The lawyer squeezed past bookshelves to take her seat. Her office was well located but tiny, its walls lined with files labeled by the same looping cursive. Some of the case names Camille recognized from her work with HELP. Sharmila had attractive writing, baroque but legible. Distinctly female. Bold.

"I have a client at one o'clock . . ." She waved Camille into a seat.

"Thanks for seeing me. Something came up at the British High Commission, a helper who committed suicide at a British couple's apartment. I think she was underage, and I'm suspicious about the husband. But I can't work on it myself." Camille laid out the details, including the trouble it had caused with Josh. Sharmila made notes and then clicked her pen three times.

"So what can we do with this information? We have three options. Number one: we pass it to HELP and they add her name to their statistics. The fifth Burmese helper to commit suicide in Singapore this year. Number two: we pass it to Ruth Chin at Reuters—"

"She was looking for an angle to run a story about the parliamentary debate."

"Yes, but I am not too hopeful she'd find it here. No evidence. She can't print suspicions. Of course, if this maid had killed the husband—"

"Edward Bonham."

"If she had killed him, then the press might be interested." Sharmila reached for a bulging file and spun it around on the desk for Camille to see. "This is a case I defended last year. A maid who killed her employer and tried to make it look like she fell down the stairs. The girl pleaded guilty, but I managed to commute her sentence from the death penalty to life imprisonment because of a history of abuse. No rest day for eighteen months and hadn't left the employer's premises for six months. In her statement she said—where is it?" Sharmila flipped a page. "Here: 'I only see daylight when I hang clothes on the washing line.'" The lawyer paused for a moment to let that statement sink in; Camille could imagine how impressive she would be in court. "The maid was diagnosed with acute stress. I likened her experience to false imprisonment, like someone kept in a cellar by a madman."

Camille felt her throat thicken, partly in disgust at the treatment the maid had received and partly in awe of Sharmila's command of the facts.

"Another one. Indonesian girl convicted of harming an elderly woman in her care. I got her sentence reduced on medical grounds because she was severely malnourished: her employer only gave her leftovers." She flipped a page. "I got this couple jailed for abusing two maids—they made them whip each other with bamboo canes."

"So you're saying that what happened to the Bonhams' helper is nothing special?"

Sharmila closed the file and put it back on the shelf. She clicked her pen three times before continuing. "No, I'm saying that some days I feel like I'm bailing out a flood with a teacup. The media is only interested in the most extreme cases—the nutjobs on both sides: evil employers, crazed maids. Ideally, both in one story. But most of us don't live at the extremes. It is quite possible for this system to work—I myself employ someone to care for my toddler, and between us we make a happy household—but not if the law continues to abdicate responsibility. At the moment, we rely on market forces and the goodwill of the employer. I want to raise the standard of living for all maids via legislation."

"And how do we do that?"

"We play the long game. We show that the law is not working. Which brings me to option three: investigate further. You said she was underage?"

Camille related the conversation with Josie. When she mentioned the agency, Sharmila gave a snort. "Not the first time that name has come up in this office. Okay, so this is what we do." She clicked her pen once and put it down. "I'm going to dig into the background of the girl and see if I can't skewer this agency once and for all. There's not much we can do about Bonham unless a postmortem shows the helper was full of this drug—"

"Clonazepam. But—"

"We can't go after him out of vengeance or because he seems shifty or loose with the truth. We only have the law. Has he broken the law? Even if he was sleeping with his maid, has he broken the law? Maybe she was too young to work in Singapore as a maid, but she wasn't under the age of consent."

"No, he hasn't broken the law—as far as we know."

"So we don't waste our time. And you don't lose your job."

"Okay, so when will you—" Camille was interrupted by a shrill ring of Sharmila's phone.

"My one o'clock is here. Keep in touch, Camille. I like your verve."

Camille stepped out of the office into a wallop of sunshine that burned off her verve. As she walked to the taxi stand, she thought how it was true that Edward Bonham might not have broken the law—but what about morality? Even assuming Josie was right, and Awmi had been attracted to her employer, his behavior put the young woman in an impossible situation, one that could only end badly for her. Surely, as her senior in age and status, he should have had the maturity to resist?

She'd leave it to Sharmila to focus on Awmi's background. Meanwhile, Camille was free to scrutinize Bonham about his connection to her parents. During the taxi ride, she opened the email she'd drafted to him the day before. As the taxi reached the BHC, she hit "Send" before echoes of Josh's voice could talk her out of it.

Chapter 12

Amanda scratched a mosquito bite on her elbow while she waited for the bank assistant to exit through the privacy door. As it clicked shut, she turned the key in the safety-deposit box. Her phone flashed a text from her mother, who was back on the library ship. Her three-hour visit to Singapore must be a new first for efficiency. Delightful as always, happy to see you doing well, with love Laura. What constituted "doing well" in her mother's mind?

Amanda removed her school reports from the safety-deposit box. Her teacher's heavy calligraphy conveyed faint praise. She didn't need to open the envelope; her fingers traced the surface as though she were reading its contents as braille. She could still hear her fluty voice: "Don't worry about the results, dear, you're pretty." At least she never got suspended. She checked her phone; no response from Josie. But this was Singapore, one of the safest cities in the world. She was probably drowning her sorrows with ten-dollar lattes in a hipster coffee shop.

Amanda put her school reports aside. There was a parcel of Polaroid pictures from a period when she had embraced the prettiness that her form mistress prized so highly. At least these amateurish nude shots had been taken pre–social media. Nowadays, Snapchat snapped up girls like her and snapped them in half. Or worse: their images circulated forever in dark corners of the web. Kelvin had said Josie's forum was innocent chatter, but was that all? By comparison, Amanda's sordid envelope of snaps seemed quaintly old-school. As she moved it aside, a Yale key landed in her lap. All she had left of the Camden terrace house, which she'd bought in a hurry when she realized her father was plundering her trust fund. By dumb luck, she'd bought well. It was ridiculous; the Dependant's Pass meant she couldn't control her own money, and a grown woman should be able to control her money. The Yale key clattered back into the box.

She picked up her mother's engagement ring. A massive emerald in a halo of diamonds. Amanda forced it over the knuckle of her ring finger and spread her hand to admire it. Then she lifted from the box a powder puff, as mottled as aged hands. She slipped the finger ribbon on next to the emerald and pressed the puff to her nose, breathing in her mother's scent. Violets and rancid oil and something metallic, redolent of old coins. She wiped the powder puff across her forehead and swept it down each cheek before dropping these treasures back into the box.

From her handbag she pulled out a ziplock bag. Her bare nails prized open the plastic zipper, and she slid out a key card printed with the logo of the MV *Guanyin*. Her mother had left her bag wide open on the console table. Too easy to pluck out a trophy and drop it into a nearby ginger jar.

Amanda watched the card drop into the box. She rooted in her bag and found the Little Mermaid toothbrush. And, finally, Josie's journal. She flipped to the scribbled Internet log-ins. Did one of these enable the girl to access the dark web? The fact was, Amanda had no clue. Maybe it was better to keep hold of the journal for the time being? She dropped it into her bag to take home, even though she cringed to have her *things* in the house. A glimpse of them, when she wasn't prepared, turned her stomach.

She dropped the lid of the safety-deposit box. The key turned with gossamer ease, and she felt a corresponding release in her skin, like undoing a pinching bra. She slid her secrets into the wall along with her shame.

As soon as she got home, the solidity of the air revealed that Josie wasn't there. The apartment had the aura of a dead thing—a rat or a mouse—as though death had left a stain. Josie couldn't be at school because of the suspension, and she wasn't answering her phone, so where was she? As a formality, Amanda rapped on her bedroom door before going inside. A citrus smell from the en suite almost covered the gamey undertone of pheromones. It took Amanda back to the shower room at boarding school. Dressing under a towel, while her "friends" singled her out for unremitting compliments involving the word *skinny* closely followed by the word *bitch*. Her permanent state of contrition, as though slenderness were a sin against the sisterhood, meant she wore her skin and bones heavily. Twenty years later, all the girls in Singapore were coltish. It was like evolution had succumbed to public demand.

The room was cluttered, but neat. Without the laptop, the desk was clear apart from a mug of pens and a block of Post-it notes. Maybe this mysterious scribble-of-a-girl blog might give a clue to Josie's where-abouts. She'd already tried all the passwords from the journal; surely Josie had written this one down somewhere?

Under the desk was a trash can, full to the brim. Hourglass remains of apple cores and snowballs of paper. She pulled one open and found the same style of anxious sketches that featured in the journal, this time depicting girls—girls running, girls cowering, girls falling—scribbled with dense strokes that matted the pages. Her stomach lurched to think that the disappearance of the journal might have distressed Josie enough to produce these jittery drawings.

Amanda sat cross-legged on the floor with the waste paper. Most had been ripped to shreds and twirled through the air, flicking around like destinations on a departures board. One scrap came to rest beside her foot, a note in marker pen: WhoIsShe2000? Amanda picked up another fragment and read again: Who Is She? Each sliver of paper had the same scribbled words. And then there was one that broke the pattern; on the reverse was a scrawled address: www.a-scribble-of-a-girl.com. Josie's blog, the one with the timer.

Amanda pulled her phone out. The site loaded and the timer read: 13 days, 01 hours, 51 minutes. It could be counting down to Josie's birthday, as Ed suggested. She worked it out on her fingers, but no: it was much longer than that until Josie's birthday. She tried "WhoIsShe2000?" in the password box and the page reloaded.

The website had a header of Singapore's concrete skyline against cement clouds. Its mood was melancholy, not in a teenage way—the online equivalent of dressing as a goth—but something deeper. Whoever had designed this page wasn't celebrating, not a birthday or anything else. Below the banner, there was a GIF, an image of Amy Winehouse silently mouthing her song "Stronger Than Me." Amanda recognized the video; Josie often played it. Alongside that she had posted a drawing of a woman and a caption reading, "Who Is She?" The face looked a lot like Josie—a self-portrait, perhaps?—but the dense scribble that made up the hair echoed a picture that sat next to the bed: Josie's mother looking out from her gilt frame, squinting through a squalling wind on a cliff top.

Below the drawing was a blog post, dated that morning. Amanda turned her phone to let text fill the screen.

> Hello World! This is your first post! Edit it or delete it, then start writing!
> OK, then, here goes :)
> Hello Inner World! This is my private diary! One post per day, unless I lose the will to live!
>
> In the future: Thirteen Days Until D-Day
> In the past: Thirteen Days That Made Me Me
> Post 1 of 13: My Earliest Memory

The frosted grass crackles under my boots like spilled sugar. The cold shatters when I run through it. He snatches me up in the crook of one arm and holds me against his chest and laughs that I'm full of beans. Smoke comes out of his mouth when he says it. I say *Beans—Beans!*—and smoke comes out of my mouth. He holds up his cup of coffee and smoke is coming out of its little mouth too, like a tiny volcano about to go off.

Take me on the slide, Teddy? I ask him.

Come on then, Jo-Jo Sparrow, race you!

When we get to the playground, Chloe from playgroup is there at the top, too frightened to slide. I climb the steps and she sees me and knows she has to get out of the way, so she slides and tumbles onto the wood chips and starts wailing like she always does. I slide and the cold rushes inside my ears and tugs my sleeves, but then I realize that Teddy's hands are the ones tugging me; he is dragging me from the slide and all I can see is wood chips scattering under his boots. When we reach a bench on the path, my mother forces me to sit next to her on the burning-cold metal. She smells of smoke and her cigarette is still alight on the broken paving stone.

Oh my God, it's horrible! Teddy says.

She splays her fingers over my eyes. I scrunch my nose up so I can see. Chloe under the slide. A black and brown dog on top of her. Chloe is staring up at the marshmallow sky, but down on the ground her mummy is pulling her one way and the dog is pulling her the other and a man is pulling the dog. Everyone is screaming.

Do something, Teddy! my mother says.

Her fingers slide from my face as my daddy runs and leaps over the slide and throws his coffee into the dog's face. The dog jumps back and the man gets him around the neck and drags him away. Teddy stands with the cup in his hand, dripping. We run over. He helps Chloe's mum get her up, and they sit on the end of the slide. There are two black holes in Chloe's face and even when her crying washes away the blood, more wells up out of the holes. We stroke the mummy's arm, but we don't touch Chloe.

Later, when the ambulance slams its doors and drives away across the thawed grass, we go back to the cold bench and hug. *Thank God,* she says, *it wasn't Jo-Jo Sparrow;* she thanks God again and again, and I wonder why she doesn't thank Teddy— he was the one who saved Chloe from that dog.

Amanda had never heard Ed tell a story about a dog. Maybe it was just a writing exercise . . . something for English class. The seconds on the timer landed with the sting of sharp slaps designed to rouse her. Outside in the hallway, the lift chimed and she darted from Josie's room, ready to greet the girl. But the elevator bustled past. The gong sounded a floor above, and Amanda realized that she'd only heard it because the slightest sound echoed through her hollow home, and she faced another evening with only suspicion for company.

Chapter 13

The electric peal of a kingfisher signaled Amanda's early-morning presence on the balcony, the first time she'd stepped through the glass door since finding Awmi's body. She wrinkled her nose at the garbage smell that had seeped through the apartment overnight, as rancid as the mood that pervaded her home. When Josie had sneaked in late the previous night, she refused to offer any explanation for her whereabouts, saying she would discuss the suspension with her father—if he deigned to return her calls. Amanda cursed Ed; what after-hours activity in Tokyo had sucked him in this time?

Amanda was determined to clear up the mess contaminating her household, starting with the garbage smell. But Josie entered the kitchen and Amanda watched from outside the girl's nimble movements, her fastidious way of laying out cutlery and arranging breakfast into a bowl: a layer of M&M's hidden beneath healthy fruit, yogurt, and honey. Her eyes flicked up and locked onto Amanda's, widening to see her stepmother on the balcony. She recovered quickly, gathering her breakfast onto a tray, making to leave. Amanda stepped into the kitchen and closed the door on the smell.

"Can we eat together, Josie? I'd like to clear the air."

"The air stinks."

"It's coming from out there." Amanda nodded to the balcony. "I'm on it."

Josie grunted, but slid her tray onto the counter and her behind onto a stool.

Amanda tipped the dregs of Awmi's homemade muesli into a bowl and added milk.

"Did you manage to speak to your father last night?"

Josie skimmed banana into her mouth and shook her head. Amanda crunched on nuts. Once upon a time, he jumped through hoops to avoid his working week spilling over into the weekend. And yet here they were on a Saturday morning, one man down.

"Do you mind me asking where you went yesterday after you were told to come home from school?"

"Central Library. Downtown." Josie's spoon clattered as she reached for her phone, jabbing at the screen while she spoke. "I can prove it. I have a check-in at the Starbucks next door and the books are in my room—"

"You don't need to prove it. But when your father is traveling, I'm responsible—"

She put the phone down on the counter. "So you can report back to him."

"So I can protect you."

"From what?" Josie threw her hands open.

From yourself. From your father. Amanda stirred her muesli to mush. *But let's go with from the dark web.* "Mr. Milne couldn't tell me much detail about your forum. Except the name—Sixteen—which does sound provocative."

"That's because he doesn't even know how to access the site."

"The school computers are blocked from the dark web—for good reason."

Josie's spoon screeched against the bottom of her bowl. "What *good reason* is there for censorship? School is dominated by the thought police. And then I come home to the Taliban."

The exchange reminded Amanda of the first weeks after she moved in with Ed, when Josie unleashed histrionic tirades on a daily basis. Ed had responded to the melodrama with indulgent smiles or teasing, which only infuriated the teenager, an anger she laid down like a layer of fat for the cold winter that raged between the two females. Eventually, things seemed to thaw. But then, as now, Josie's mood could change with the unpredictability of the wind. She got up and blasted her bowl clean under the tap.

"I did it for Willow, if you must know. Everyone at school is shit-scared of messing up. We know how much the parents have spent on our education. We've been given everything on a plate, but—" Josie let the crockery drop onto the drainer.

"You're under pressure, I get that. But how does this forum help?"

"You know what Willow said? 'I'm ready to cut myself.' The forum was a place to blow off steam while remaining invisible."

"It was a mistake to put it on the dark web—"

"It was a mistake to think adults have the requisite technical skills to appreciate that the dark web offers anonymity. That's the whole point."

"But you only drew more attention to yourself. Couldn't you have given people fake names?"

"Fake names. Yeah, genius." Josie made eye contact with Amanda as she moved toward the door, giggling as though her stepmother was an amusing child. "I'll see what Dad thinks. When he surfaces. And FYI: I'm going to the library again. I'll check in on Facebook so you can track me."

I could track you on Find My iPhone if I wanted to; I'm no Luddite. But remembering Josie's previous comment about knowing when to stop talking, Amanda let her go. In any case, she didn't know how to ask about the scribble-of-a-girl blog and its puzzling countdown without revealing that she'd stolen Josie's journal and rooted through her bin. She'd have to confront that little mystery another time.

After stacking the dishwasher, Amanda returned to the balcony to tackle the smell. She peered over the balustrade into the muggy air. A cobalt kingfisher flitted through rain trees that never wilted. They were as stoic as the trailing spouses who insisted this city was a marvel, despite the heat. A wonderful place to raise children. Once Amanda had some, maybe she'd acclimatize.

She opened the rubbish chute to a belch of sticky air. Rancid, but not strong enough to account for the stench that circulated the whole apartment. She cracked the door of Awmi's room, and her throat closed up as though someone had grabbed it. Two bulging black sacks sat inside. She let the door swing wide and turned away to gulp air as thick as molasses.

The bags must have been there since Awmi last emptied the kitchen bins. Why the condo cleaners had left them, she didn't understand; they'd probably assumed a new helper would arrive right away and deal with them. After five days in tropical temperatures, the trash could almost walk itself to the dumpster. One bag sat in a mucous puddle. The other looked dry, so she decided to carry that one onto the balcony to tackle first. She opened the sack and receipts from Ed's credit card tumbled onto the tiles along with reams of tissues used to blot her red lipstick, images of her mouth printed over and over again in a dumb ring of shock. For a moment, she watched the slips blow about the floor.

Does this man belong to you?

She sat down and gathered the receipts into a pile between her outstretched legs. Taxis, meals, currency exchanges. For the first time in weeks, she had an insight into his working day. He used to write his itinerary on the family calendar. Now: *What's the point when a flight might change at the last minute?* It was true that he often switched flights, but it was also . . . convenient. Furtive, even.

Josie's blog came to mind. Maybe Ed had forgotten the incident with the dog, though it clearly made an impression on his daughter: "my earliest memory," she wrote. But Amanda hardly recognized the man Josie described. Of course, when two people meet in their thirties, there is history. The past is unveiled in snippets, a radio broadcast of your life constantly playing in the background; sometimes you tune in and pay close attention to an intriguing segment, but mostly your focus is required in the here and now. For the first time in three years—with their intimacy breaking up like a bad signal—Amanda was all ears.

She got to work. Via taxi chits, she followed Ed from Sentosa Island to Changi Airport, across the South China Sea to the Philippines. He'd withdrawn a modest amount of pesos at an ATM in downtown Manila and then bought a solitary lunch of a BLT and an avocado smoothie. Back at the hotel, he'd purchased the *Economist*. She scrunched this evidence of Ed's unimpeachable behavior into a tight ball and tossed it down the chute.

What was she doing? Snooping around because of some dingy photo posted by a pissed-up expat. It was certainly true that Ed was traveling more (a nasty voice in her head chipped in: Does he relish the freedom?) and he brings too many presents (guilty conscience?), but there could be a perfectly simple explanation for the condoms in his travel bag (oh, *come on!*). Real evidence, not just her gut instinct, would be useful . . .

Arranging the receipts chronologically, she pursued Ed around the globe, and soon she had a trail of question marks. It started in Manila, a few hours after the BLT. In the hotel bar: beers and a Cosmopolitan. A drinks bill from Kuala Lumpur included a vodka and lime. In Zurich, an Aperol Spritz. Ed drank Bloody Marys, beer, wine, whisky—sometimes in that order.

So who'd ordered the girlie drinks?

Amanda went through the whole sack, collecting five instances of Ed buying drinks for women in hotel bars. She laid them onto the tiles between her feet, photographing the offending checks with her phone. The images blurred, lost to a haze of tears, like Ed's features when they kissed. Too close to see him clearly.

She had to find out more about this stranger who stood at the epicenter of a perfect storm of other women. Josie's blog would show her the kind of man he had once been. But while Amanda waited for the past to be revealed, she needed to focus on the present. And evidence. Hard evidence. The travel receipts tumbled down the chute, her husband's trash murmuring on its way to the incinerator.

Chapter 14

The revelry of the bars along Boat Quay struck Camille as a kind of mass hysteria. Each raised toast, each swell of laughter, each friend welcomed with bear hugs and air kisses pounded her chest like an oncoming wave, grinding her down to a lonely grain of sand, one insignificant fragment among the millions. Her fingers pinched the skin between her eyes. A walk had done nothing to relieve her headache, but at least it got her out of the apartment, away from the brand-new filing cabinet that she'd spent the day buying and then filling with documents about her parents. She wondered what Collin was doing with his Saturday night, and what level of exasperation he might reach if she told him how she'd spent hers. At the crest of a bridge above pewter-colored water, she found a calm spot and pulled out her phone: still no reply from Edward Bonham.

"Hello, Camille."

A voice behind her: Josh. Out of context—dressed in running gear, his shirt marked with a heart of perspiration—he seemed like a different person, his own younger brother, maybe. Camille almost introduced herself. But as the moment passed, she dropped her phone deep inside her pocket and hoped her freckles would hide her flush as well. He apologized for being sweaty and she managed to joke that those might be the most commonly uttered words in Singapore.

"Waiting to hear from a friend?" he said. Josh didn't miss much.

"Just taking advantage of a cool evening."

"I managed to squeeze in 10K before the rain. But I need to keep walking or I'll seize up like the Tin Man."

They dropped down onto the promenade, heading away from the hustle. A catamaran bustled through the slick water beyond the mouth of the Singapore River, distorted party music and garish lights churning in its wake.

"My dad would have called that a 'cattle-maran,'" she said.

"A sailor, wasn't he?" Her boss knew the basics of her family history from her background checks. Though Camille wondered how much more he might know, given the proximity of the Foreign Office to the Secret Service, the very reason she'd gone for the job in the first place.

"He ran a yacht charter."

"Nice life."

"He said you had to be a saint or a schmuck. And Mum said she was a saint *and* a schmuck because she was the one who mucked the boat out on turnaround day."

Josh stopped at a drinks stall to buy calamansi juice and handed one to Camille. The tart flavor of lime took her right back to Tanglin Green. They strolled on, and Josh left a stillness between them that she wanted to jump into with a splash.

"I've been thinking a lot about my parents since I got back to Singapore."

"You know what they say: neurons that fire together wire together."

"Meaning?"

"I read it in a magazine on a plane. If I remember the article correctly, when you repeat an experience over and over, the brain triggers the same neurons each time until they're permanently wired together. So if your mother makes you cocoa each night, after a while the smell of cocoa makes you sleepy. Or if you practice your golf swing, the moves become instinctive. Or if you return to the place where you grew up after being away for a long time, the sights and sounds and smells fire neurons that are hardwired to memories."

Camille finished her juice with an ungraceful slurp of the straw. "My neurons don't fire or wire. I don't remember much at all."

"There's a theory that we store everything. Forgetting is simply an information retrieval issue. It's in there somewhere. After all, you can ride a bike, can't you?"

"Yes."

"You can tie your shoelaces?"

"I can."

"And who taught you that?"

"My parents. Or more likely our maid, when my parents were on their . . . assignments."

"And you remember your father's sayings."

Camille was impressed by Josh's willingness to speak about her parents. People weren't usually so comfortable. They tended to think on it more than she did, as though it were a scar on her face that she forgot but they could see. What she'd endured was indefinable to them, not grief and yet—realistically—not hope. It was a lonely limbo that daunted some people, an evil twin who scared away outsiders. But maybe Josh was older, wiser, bolder.

"But those skills—the cycling and shoelaces—have been reinforced since I was ten; they've taken on a life of their own. How can I find memories of my childhood when there's been no one to tend the fire between neurons over the years? Maybe the connections can fizzle out?"

"Good point. The article didn't tell me that. Your experience is somewhat unique."

They reached a dessert stall, and Camille realized that she'd skipped dinner. Sticky rice wrapped in a pyramid of pandan leaf called to her. They found a bench, and she pulled her parcel apart to get a fragrant mouthful of sugared coconut.

"So you grew up at Tanglin Green," Josh said. "I've noticed that you often walk that way."

She nodded, relieved that the glutinous rice gave her no chance to elaborate. She didn't want to blurt out that her most recent memories of that place involved Edward Bonham.

"It seems you have good associations with your childhood home. You're drawn back there. You must have been happy."

Camille used the chewing time to organize her thoughts. "There's a thin line," she said, "between nostalgia and mawkishness." She told Josh that her brother had accused her of wallowing. And then she segued from unreliable memories to hard facts—the police report into her parents' disappearance. A week after they delivered her to school in the UK and flew back to Singapore, her parents took a taxi from Tanglin Green. They left before dawn at 5:00 a.m., which the guard noted in a logbook. But he failed to record the license plate of the taxi, which was never traced, or the destination, which was never established. Lani told the police that the couple left in a hurry, but their schedule was always unpredictable: she used the word *secretive*. The case remained unsolved, and Lani was sent back to the Philippines. Camille never saw her parents or Lani or her home again.

Sharing the story made her feel light, giddy almost, and she took another bite of sticky rice, craving its density to fill the space that had opened up. Neon lights picked out the muscles of Josh's face as he turned morsels of coconut in his mouth. He didn't patronize or pity or pooh-pooh her belief that she might one day explain her parents' disappearance. When they walked on along the riverside, Camille felt she had left something indefinable behind, like a balloon tied to the back of a chair.

A storm was blowing in from the sea, firecrackers of lightning amid the clouds. Beads of windblown spray advanced up Camille's bare arm.

"Does Singapore feel like home?" Weekend stubble softened Josh's jawline and the edge of his formality.

Jo Furniss

"In a way. But I've done my reading too; detailed memory is an active process. You have to kind of . . . lay down a store of memories. Harvest them."

"Like putting apples in the cellar for the winter."

That made her smile. "Exactly. I recall moments, places, images. But I feel like I'm visiting film locations. One of those old cine films, you know when it gets to the end and it's still whirring but the screen's gone black?"

She noticed his arm swinging in the space between them, his fingers curled up as though cradling a mouse.

"But it would be good to know what happened. Just to stop it whirring in my head." She saw his fist close. The first rain fell, and they jogged to reach the cover of a communal area under an overpass where buskers played and lovers mooned. Camille waved her hand at the water coming under heavy fire from the sky. "I love Singapore rain."

Josh was quiet for a long time. Camille knew that they lived on opposite sides of the river. This was the obvious place to part. They turned to face each other.

"I have a child back in England," Josh said. "A son from a brief relationship. He's almost ten. What you said made me wonder"—he looked over the water and then back at her—"if I do enough to lay down memories. I'm so far away."

She looked into Josh's eyes, the color of an old bronze statue. "Does Singapore feel like home to you?" she asked.

"I love it here, but I would happily move back to the UK if I thought he needed me . . ." He shrugged. "He's happy. She married and had more kids. They're a family. By the time I worked out what was important, the ship had sailed."

A blast of K-pop from a nearby bar seemed to taunt him with its exhaustingly upbeat energy.

"We could stop for a drink," Camille said in a rush.

Josh indicated the lack of pockets in his running gear. "I blew my emergency dollars on lime juice."

"I'll shout you a beer," she said.

The party catamaran heaved into view, pulsing with dirty beats, rocking beneath glistening girls in bikinis. Josh glanced it over. "I enjoyed our stroll down memory lane, but I should do my stretches."

"I wouldn't want you to stiffen up." She felt her freckles burn as she realized what she'd said. "Like the Tin Man. After your run." *Stop talking, just stop talking.* She saw him suppress a smile, trying to spare her blushes, though it was too late for that, and she stepped backward into the shadows thrown by the bridge.

"Good night, Camille. See you Monday."

She set off to retrace her steps, wishing she could backtrack on that last comment too; what a thing to say to your boss! He was still on the promenade, arms braced on a handrail, stretching his calves. The existence of a son was news to Camille, but somehow she wasn't surprised that he had his own intrigue. As he jogged off, she thought again that Josh was a dark horse. The kind of person who kept secrets, personal and official. And if he'd known Edward Bonham, maybe once the neurons fired he'd remember something about her parents too.

Chapter 15

When Amanda returned from a sunset run to find Ed's travel bag in the hallway, her stomach shriveled. Voices came from behind Josie's door. She wiped pearls of sweat from her hairline, as her trainers made silent progress over the marble.

"So move the forum to the normal web. Whatever you call it—the webby web. Then it'll all blow over." Ed's voice sounded tight, his levity squeezed out through frustration. The door handle dipped; he must be standing on the other side, poised to leave.

Keen to get into the shower after Tokyo.

Josie's response was indistinct.

Ed again: "The surface web. Put it there. Problem solved." The door opened a crack, and Amanda backed up.

"If it's no big deal, why ground me? That's antiquated; I can Skype whoever I want."

"I'm grounding you tonight because I want to take my wife out for a meal and I need to know where you are." The door swung wide, and Amanda retreated almost to the lift.

"You know where I am." Josie's wail tore the air. "I'm here, waiting for you." Her door closed. Amanda crept forward again, but the voices inside were too low to hear. When the handle dipped again, Amanda rushed past into her bathroom.

They met in the bedroom ten minutes later, both immaculate from the shower. He suggested an impromptu date night and Amanda agreed; not that she was in the mood for romance, but—she realized with a spark of shock—going out seemed less alarming than sitting with him in an apartment that echoed with the rustle of receipts going down the chute. How long until their gossiping voices filled her head and she couldn't resist asking him, *Who ordered a Cosmopolitan in Manila, Ed, an Aperol in Zurich?* Questions that could tear her world apart.

So she put on a dress and makeup, papering over the cracks for another night. An hour later, they were beside the Singapore River. Ed turned his back on the restaurant, facing the steps that led down to the promenade. He seemed mesmerized by the water that ran as smooth and slick as fleeing rats. When a waiter arrived with the cocktail menu, Amanda took it.

"Do you fancy a Cosmopolitan?" she asked.

"No."

"Aperol?"

"God, no. Bloody Mary, no celery."

"And a gin and tonic for me," she said to the waiter, snapping the leather cover closed. "Don't you like Aperol?"

"Tastes of mothballs. Why?"

She was saved from answering by the arrival of a huge man who took the steps from the promenade two at a time. His arm was decorated by a tribal tattoo of an octopus, its tentacles bulging around his bicep and tapering to the wrist. He shielded himself behind a pinboard that jangled with key rings.

"I'm sorry, gentleman, lady, a moment of your time." He spat the words without making eye contact, as though he might gag if he didn't let them out. "I must be honest, I am an ex-convict, sir. I served my time and want to improve."

Ed fingered a key ring—decorated with a yellow smiley face—and tapped a handwritten sign saying $10. "Price is criminal, mate."

The grinning key rings clattered as the guy shifted from foot to foot, his octopus pulsating when he snatched up the pinboard. Before he could speak again, the waiter arrived and the hawker vanished into the crowd below. The waiter muttered as he set down their glasses. Ed slopped the celery onto his tray and chinked the glass against Amanda's.

"To my favorite wife."

"To my faithful husband."

She held Ed's blue gaze over the rim.

"You all right?" Ed spoke once he was a quarter of the way down the glass.

"Yep."

"You seem a bit—"

"Nope."

"Okay. Glad we cleared that up. Look, here's a welcome distraction." He pointed the base of his glass down the steps to the riverside.

A crowd had formed around a street performer. He stood in a dramatic pose side-on to the audience, red cloak raised to cover his face. He held the position for several minutes until the crowd settled and music crackled from a speaker. Then he sprang around, face tilted up to reveal a green grimacing mask. The audience rippled.

"I love this," said Ed.

Amanda glanced at his rapt face. "What is it?"

"*Bian Lian*. Chinese opera."

The dancer lunged at the crowd, swirling the cape. He mock charged the audience, until the soundtrack reached a crescendo and he stopped, a hand glanced across his face, and—Amanda gasped in time with the crowd—the mask flipped from green to red.

Again, the dancer reached toward onlookers and then—with a flick of the chin—his mask flipped red to black. As the music pounded on, his masks scrolled through emotions. From anger, to fury, to death, and back to light. So many changing faces. When the red cloak sailed off his shoulders and he faced the audience full-on, the music built to a climax and his hand made one last sweep. The dancer's own smiling face was revealed before a final snap of his chin left the audience staring at a bony death mask.

Ed slapped one palm on the table, sending their cutlery and glasses dancing. "'The Man with Fifteen Faces.' Haven't seen that for years."

"How did he do it?"

"Sleight of hand. They pass the skills down from father to son. It's a secret art."

"It's dark, though. That death mask—"

"Opera, isn't it? Star-crossed lovers." Ed reached a hand across the table, and the tenderness of his palm made her want to throw off her own cloak and confront him, force them back to normality—

"Hello!"

Over his shoulder, Amanda saw a woman on the promenade waving her arms like she was bringing in an aircraft. Ed frowned, and Amanda hissed through her smile that it was Willow's mother, Erin, from upstairs. She bounced toward them, her husband a few steps behind. "Fancy running into you two. We're not even supposed to be here. Arnault fucked up the Uber booking, and we're so late we lost our table."

"You told me it was the other side of the river, Erin."

"Let's leave the domestic argument at home with the helper. Shit, I've said the wrong thing already!"

Arnault shook hands with Ed and came toward Amanda with his arms out. "My wife means to say we're sorry to hear what happened." His lips caught the corner of hers and peeled away. "She's rabid for details."

"I am not!" But as the subject was hanging over the table, Erin decided to make a centerpiece of it. "Willow tells me there's an investigation? The case is going to be featured in a media campaign?"

Her barely concealed glee stuck in Amanda's craw.

"Won't happen," Ed said.

"How can you be so sure?" Erin voiced a question that Amanda wanted to ask herself.

"Let me ask you something." Ed turned a wineglass in his fingers. "Why is it we can sit here, in the tropics, and not get a single mosquito bite? Not one fly on our food? No bugs swarming the lanterns?"

"Pest control," said Arnault.

Ed bowed his head in agreement. "If someone makes a pest of themselves, we control them."

Amanda looked at him, startled. A cannonade rumbled through her bones, and she glanced up to see the peaks of the downtown skyscrapers swamped in storm clouds.

"What about Josie?" Erin was saying. "I heard about her suspension. You've had it all going on."

Arnault rolled his eyes from Ed to Amanda. "Thinks she's Oprah."

"After raising three teenagers, I know *a little bit* about how girls think." Erin closed one eye, like a photographer trying to get something huge into shot. She preached while Ed knocked back his drink. When Arnault's phone glowed in his palm, Erin stopped abruptly, glaring at her husband as he took the call to the river.

Out of embarrassment, Amanda invited her to join them. Ed's eyebrows shot up as quickly as Erin snatched a spare chair. By the time her husband returned, she had drained a cocktail and ordered wine. Arnault held a closed fist across the table toward his wife: "Don't say I never bring you anything." A key ring clattered into her palm. "That was New York. I have to go to the office."

"Now?" Erin held the smiley face aloft and it swung on its chain. There was no tell in her poker face as Arnault made a swift exit. Ed also got up, saying, "Little boys' room," and leaned down to kiss Amanda's cheek, the grip of his fingernails on her wrist as tight as his voice: "Get rid of her"—the pinch got harder—"before I wring her neck." He set off and she saw a row of notches indented in her skin.

Amanda tuned out Erin's monologue and rubbed the marks left by Ed's fingernails. He had a temper but had never once turned physical. Yes, she had seen his irritation building, but—her fingertips traced upside-down smiles—he'd shown no flicker of this level of anger. It gave her the sense of being inside a magician's box with an up-close view of the trickery, his emotional sleight of hand, while she waited to be sawed in half.

He returned one step ahead of the waiter, who laid down a burrata the size of a pert breast. Amanda cut the cheese and watched it deflate, figuring she had nothing more to lose on this disastrous evening; Erin could surely be relied upon to show off her superior knowledge of the risks that girls face online. Maybe enough to put a seed in Ed's mind that Josie needed more help than just a pep talk and grounding for a night.

"Erin," Amanda said. "Could I ask your advice?"

Erin ducked forward as though presenting herself for a medal. Amanda ignored Ed's look.

"Does Willow use the dark web?" Amanda said.

Erin picked up the topic without breaking stride. "Willow's very tech-savvy"—*she's certainly Tinder-savvy,* thought Amanda—"but she wouldn't go onto the dark web."

"She didn't visit Josie's site?"

"Josie showed it to her. Said it was a discussion forum for kids struggling with exams. Of course, Willow has a tutor."

Amanda reached to top up Erin's wine.

"You have to remember"—Erin's eyelids fluttered as she continued—"they're the digital generation. Here's a funny story: Willow follows a girl on Instagram who posts pictures of owls. Just owls. I asked what she would do if this girl wanted to meet in person. And you know what Willow said?" Erin swirled her glass, and the wine circled like her punch line. "'Mummy! It's probably an obese man in a tracksuit.'" Erin widened her eyes at Amanda over the rim of the glass.

"Josie's business is a family matter," Ed said tightly.

"I'm trying to help," Amanda said. "I know she's upset about Awmi, but—"

"If there's one thing I've learned from living in Asia"—Erin dug her fingers into her fringe as though straightening a halo—"don't let your children grow attached to the help."

Sod it, Amanda thought. She got to her feet and set a course for the ladies' room. *Let Ed deal with his daughter and her best friend's mother.* She dodged waiters until she reached the bathroom, where the door closed with a soft suck that inhaled the din. In the sudden hush, Amanda's ears rang with a heartbeat as unruly as the Singapore River.

She went into a stall and sat on the lid. Why was she the only one worried by Josie's need to hide—on the dark web, on her secret blog? She navigated to the site on her phone: the timer showed twelve days. Twelve days until *what?*

Ed was Janus-faced: overprotective and careless at the same time. She recalled how her own mother had been erratic, her father distracted by affairs—business or otherwise. Who did Josie have on her side? Luckily, Amanda's skin had been cured by a lifetime of her mother's vinegar. It was thick enough to endure as many knock-backs as Josie needed to dole out before she could let down her defenses.

She tapped the timer and entered the password. The previous blog post had been replaced by a new pencil drawing: a man's hand reaching out. Amanda touched his palm and text filled the screen.

> In the future: Twelve Days Until D-Day
> In the past: Thirteen Days That Made Me Me
> Post 2 of 13: Summer Daze
>
> When we get to the park, the ice cream van is driving away but stops to give me a cone. My mother lays down our red tartan picnic blanket, and Chloe

is there on the playground, watching my every lick. Then I'm told to go play for a while, because Daddy will arrive "in his own sweet time." I like this phrase even though my mother says it through hard lips; I'm looking forward to sweet time with Teddy.

From the water pipes comes a burp like the sound of bath taps when you first turn them on. I grab my boat, beating Chloe to the top of the chute because, like always, she starts crying. Chloe is spoiled because of her face where the dog bit her—my mother says that all the time to Teddy, but I'm not allowed to repeat it because it's not kind.

She comes up and lifts me into the chute. Underwater, our hands are gray and flat. Up high now, I see Teddy coming over the grass with his tennis bag across his chest and I think of a knight with his shield. But he walks to Chloe's mummy. His fingers slide over her shoulder like the cold water running over our hands. Chloe's mummy pops her head up just how our rabbit does. She looks up at us and then Teddy looks up at us. He waves the hand that was on her shoulder and jogs to the top of the water chute. His hair is wet and smells of orange when he hugs me.

"I didn't spot you up here," he says.

My mother tells him, "That much was obvious." Teddy pushes his fists into his hair and says he was only asking Chloe's mum about Chloe's treatment. She flicks cold water off her hands and the drops spatter his shirt. He says, "Are you hungry, Jo-Jo Sparrow?" So we go to our blanket.

On her side of the rubbish bin, Chloe's mummy is packing their bag. Chloe comes over with my boat in her hand. She stands on our blanket with her dirty shoes and says: "S'your boat."

My mother tuts and says, "No manners. We're in the middle of lunch."

Chloe hands the boat to Teddy. "S'her boat."

Now I'm getting up. Chloe has no manners—

Chloe says, "Here you are, Teddy."

—and there is blood on her lip.

Teddy grabs my arms, squashing my shoulders so hard his fingernails plough my skin. "Josie! You knocked the boat right into Chloe's face!"

Chloe cries out—"Teddy!"—and he lets go of me and picks her up. Chloe's mummy walks onto our blanket and takes Chloe from Teddy and for a few seconds they're both holding her. "Sorry," Teddy says to Chloe's mummy, "we're overtired."

We're not overtired. We're wide awake. And we're angry because his name is Edward.

Not Teddy.

He's not hers, he's ours.

Only we call him Teddy.

Chapter 16

The door to the balcony was cracked open again; Amanda felt it as soon as she stepped into the kitchen to make her morning tea. Perhaps her brief proximity to death had triggered primal instincts that never troubled her before, because the fine hairs of her arm had started rising and falling like a barometer of her alarm. An animal adapting to its environment. She'd had the same feeling the previous evening at the restaurant, as she came back from the restroom to see Ed and Erin nestled together at the table. Erin's hand flitted between her hair and the neckline of her dress. Ed was laughing, even though he'd been ready to throttle her.

Ed. Edward. *Teddy.*

If he wasn't consistent for the duration of a meal, how could Amanda judge his presence across the years of Josie's life? Her mind slipped to the *Bian Lian* dancer, how his sleight of hand revealed, for a split second, a handsome face behind the silk mask.

A lasso of wind swung the balcony door inward and sucked it shut with a bang that lifted the skin off her bones. Outside, Ed stepped into the frame. Amanda felt the hairs on her arms ripple. He waved at her to let him in.

"What were you doing out there?" she asked as she opened the door.

Positioning himself directly under the air-conditioning vent, he peeled his shirt off his back. "I was looking for my passport, the second one." He picked up a tea towel and mopped a trickle of sweat from his cheekbones.

"Why would it be on the balcony?"

Ed sniffed the towel and threw it onto the counter. "That's filthy. When are we going to get another maid?" He went to the sink and drank straight from the tap, sucking in water while glaring out the window at the sun. When he was done, he bunched up his shirt and used that to wipe his armpits. "I thought it might be in the rubbish."

"I threw the bags down the chute."

Ed swore. "It's the one with my Philippines visa."

"I could phone the British High Commission? They could rush through a replacement."

Ed stopped in the doorway. "They let you have a duplicate if you're traveling a lot, but they don't hand them out like flyers."

You're not the first klutz to lose his passport. She heard the sarcastic retort in her head, but didn't let it out. Normally, she would pull him up, put a stop to such self-importance. But she recalled his fingernail dents in her skin the night before. *Since when do I tiptoe around my own husband?*

"Get another helper." He waved his arms as he walked away, drawing two circles that took in ants—back already—smears on the massive windows, coffee-cup rings on the white counter. "Domestic goddess martyrdom doesn't suit you."

Amanda picked up a dishcloth from the sink, and more ants streamed out from the folds. She opened the cupboard to get bleach, then remembered why there wasn't any.

"What's eating him?" Josie slid into the kitchen and went to the fridge.

"Lost his passport."

"It'll be in his office downtown." She went out with a carton of milk.

Amanda found detergent and sprayed the surfaces. The white floor was streaked with stains as though creatures were burrowing beneath their feet. She passed a wad of paper towel between her palms like a bowler limbering up. Why had Ed been outside on the balcony? How had he known there were bin bags out there?

She dropped the paper towel and went outside. First she pulled open the chute, wrinkling her nose against the smell. There was nothing out here worth searching. The door to the helper's room was ajar. She pushed it open. She'd taken Awmi to IKEA once and, when the girl was too shy to state any kind of preference, Amanda had picked out a bed, a lamp, a blind. Compared to the opulence of her own living space, it felt like handing out spare change. She opened the closet door, found it empty. Even the clothes rail had gone. Had the police taken that? The metal bed frame held an uncovered mattress. She pressed it down with both hands. Under the bed, the bare tiles were peppered with white-tipped gecko droppings. Nothing that Ed could have been looking for.

Amanda took hold of the stiff mattress, but it slipped from her grip and dropped, making the headboard clatter against the wall. She tensed, her attention snatched to the kitchen, but there was no response from the apartment. Then she heard a slap, a single handclap. A silver rectangle the size of her palm lay under the bed.

She had to lie amid the gecko muck to reach it. It was a smartphone, fatter than her current one, an older model. It must have slipped from a hiding place between the mattress and the bed frame. Was it Awmi's? The police paperwork, Amanda seemed to remember, listed a phone among the items removed. And if they'd been thorough enough to remove a wardrobe rail, would they have missed this? She pressed the button and it came to life, showing a screen saver of a sunrise with a blurred propeller in the foreground. She knew this picture: Ed had taken it from the cockpit on his first-ever solo flight. He had a copy in his office downtown.

Ed's taut voice called her name through the apartment.

She slipped the phone into her pocket and darted to the kitchen, pulling the glass door closed behind her, dropping to the floor to scrub the stains. Ed came in, groaning when he saw her on the tiles.

"Ah, come on. I didn't mean it. About the domestic goddess. I was hot and pissed off."

"Did you find your passport?"

"Must be in the office. I'm going to nip downtown to check." He came over and lifted Amanda to her feet. "You are a goddess, honestly. Just not a domestic one. Can we please get another helper? The apartment is starting to look like people live here."

He wants to live in a showroom. What else is just for show? She took a deep breath. "I don't want another helper, Ed. I don't want to feel responsible for someone's entire life."

He rolled his head on his shoulders. "One minute you're desperate for kids, the next you don't want responsibility . . ."

She frowned at that. "It's a totally different issue. I don't want a stranger in the house. I don't want to deal with another adult's emotional baggage, feeling guilty that she sleeps in a room smaller than our bed, worrying that she's going to get pregnant or mixed up with loan sharks or suicidal. It's like being a boss, mother, coworker, and prison guard all rolled into one."

"It's also a privilege that frees you from the shackles. Isn't that what women want?" He waved a hand at their domestic realm. "You talk about independence, Amanda, but you don't want the responsibility that comes with it."

Feminism mansplained as one woman profiting from another. Ed put her in her place, which was, at the precise moment the line was delivered, a blood-red kitchen. "I'm going to stage an intervention," he said, "and phone the maid agency. And I'm going out for a drink tonight."

"On a Sunday? Must be someone nice."

"No rest for the wicked. It's only Bernardo, so you're not missing much." He leaned in to kiss her goodbye, and she turned one cheek to receive it. When the lift chimed and she heard Ed slide into the void, she pulled the phone from her pocket. It opened to a number pad superimposed on the sunrise. She punched in the code they used for Apple TV, but the screen shuddered. She tapped in Josie's date of birth. No. She tapped in Ed's date of birth. The screen cleared to icons. Inside Messages, no conversations were listed. The music folder was empty. She tapped on Photos as she slid herself onto a high stool.

The first image on the camera roll was blurred, but it appeared to be a woman's leg from the knee down. The next was a focused version of the same: a high-heeled shoe hooked on a barstool. Peep toe. She scrolled on. Full lips around the rim of a cocktail glass. A manuka-colored clavicle. Cleavage.

The phone contained no mail, no apps, no contacts. Only photographs: images of women or—more specifically—parts of women. Mouths, feet, breasts, legs, hands. Never a face. Never a full body. Mostly blurred in the dark of a bar or nightclub. They must have been shot without the women's knowledge. Voyeuristically. Like a boy rolling on the floor to look up women's skirts. A digital Peeping Tom.

Was that what Ed did with dodgy Bernardo? Or did he use his business partner as a cover story and sneak off alone to nasty bars? She'd only met Bernardo once, back when they first arrived in Singapore. The company of an overt man's man didn't appeal, but now she wondered if Ed kept them apart so Bernardo didn't blow his cover.

She let the phone rest in her lap, her fingers twitching as though she'd gripped an electric wire and couldn't let go. She put one hand to her head and pressed, trying to push back the high whine that carried one word like a live current: *pervert*. She selected an image at random and clicked on "Details" to check the location: Orchard Towers, Singapore.

Does this man belong to you?

Turned out Josie wasn't the only Bonham hiding in dark places.

Amanda went to put the phone back in the maid's room—otherwise Ed would know she was onto him. But before she slid it under the mattress, she opened the web browser and the last page visited loaded. It wasn't what she was expecting: a personnel page for the British High Commission. She scrolled down and another image of a woman appeared. Amanda recognized the crisp gaze from the consular visit after Awmi died. Alongside his perverse collection of photos, Ed had saved a picture of the young woman she'd invited into her home. Camille Kemble.

Chapter 17

Camille took a Sunday-morning run down memory lane. No rose-tinted path, no nostalgic stroll. Instead, she was slip-sliding over mulch on a boardwalk alongside a mangrove swamp. In the gray mud, crabs shoveled dirt from their holes. Out in the straits, a schooner scudded by on its motor, sails wrapped up tight.

She had often heard her father joke to customers inquiring about a yacht charter: *The best time to visit Singapore? Well, we have four seasons—hot and hotter, wet and wetter.* Josh was right: she remembered his sayings. There would be laughter; the caller would book. Looking back with adult eyes, Camille recognized it was an act. She remembered him saying that foreign clients expected an Englishman to be half Hugh Grant, half James Bond so he played the part. Half charmer, half secret agent. The former came naturally and, if Camille's theory was correct, the latter was no act either.

Her trainers slapped the boardwalk to the beat of her heart. She ran without headphones, no distractions, her rhythm making medita-tive music that drowned out the inner monologue. Today, though, one image nagged her: London, on the silver-frosted morning her parents delivered her to boarding school, her breath forming visible gasps as they waved goodbye with incongruously tanned hands before heading back to the airport.

Rounding a curve on the boardwalk, she saw a forest of white masts inside a small harbor. The squat lighthouse looked familiar. She picked up her pace to sprint off the end of the boardwalk onto land, but a sinuous motion below a broken slat made her jump just as a black snake twisted from where it had been basking in the morning sun. She landed heavily and spun around to see its tail slip between mangrove roots. A nervous laugh escaped along with a deep shudder as she turned to face the marina.

The schooner had found its berth. Her bicep buzzed as a call came in on her mobile phone. She wrestled it out of the running holster and noted the blocked number before answering. Her greeting came out breathy.

"Have I called at a bad time?"

She didn't recognize the voice. "Who's calling, please?"

"This is Ed Bonham. I'm looking at your profile picture on the High Commission website."

Camille spun away from the boats, her gaze seeing but not registering the gray waters of the strait.

"Mr. Bonham."

"Just Ed. Otherwise you sound like a police officer." His voice was low, as though he were accustomed to people making the effort to hear him.

Her thoughts rushed in like the small waves that made up an incoming tide. "My parents . . ." she said. But now that she had him on the line, her questions sunk out of sight.

"Your parents. I don't know if I'll be a help or a hindrance."

"That's okay." She wondered why she was reassuring him.

"I'm free tonight. A drink might lubricate my memory."

"I don't want to take up too much of your time."

"To be honest"—the line was quiet enough to hear the breath catch on his tongue—"I'm intrigued." Edward Bonham was not afraid of letting the silence gape. It felt like a passive engagement; *en garde,* thought Camille. She suggested meeting in a coffee shop, a hipster place downtown.

"I know a bar. Not far from there. I'll email you the address." He rang off.

Inside the marina, the yachts nodded in their moorings. Camille followed the perimeter fence to the main entrance. Staff wearing matching polo shirts were laying tables in the restaurant, setting up for brunch. She walked onto a wide balcony overlooking the water, feeling at home among sea gypsies and charterers. This had been her playground once.

"Do you need a launch, ma'am?" A guy wearing a yacht club shirt leaned out of the management office, hanging on to the doorframe.

"No need."

He didn't flex his pecs, but he might as well have. Camille wandered over, wishing she wasn't meeting him for the first time when she was sweaty. She picked off strands of hair that were stuck to her cheekbones while he told her about the year he'd spent training with a crew on the south coast of England. Camille pretended to know Southampton better than she did. She told him she'd lived in Singapore until the age of ten and her parents had been yacht charterers.

"So you know this place?" he said.

"I remember the lighthouse. Not so much the clubhouse."

"It was rebuilt in the last few years. After a fire." He laughed. "Actually, they shifted the lighthouse too. Extended the marina and rebuilt the breakwater."

"Huh! I was sure I could remember running along it with my brother."

"There are a few in Singapore. Same style."

She stared at the lighthouse as though it might move again right in front of her eyes. "So if there was a fire, does that mean the records are gone? I was wondering if the yacht club might have some paperwork about my parents. Or photos."

"We have old photos framed around the place; you can take a look. Paperwork, I'm not too sure."

"I'm interested in records of their trips in the last few months of their business."

"Float plans and outward clearances?"

"That's it!" She smiled at the familiar phrase.

"How long ago? Ten years?"

"Fifteen, actually."

"No, then, sorry. Even before the fire, we don't keep documents that long."

"Never mind." She watched a family arrive from the car park, a young couple with two toddlers who made a break for the water and had to be steered to safety. An old familiar feeling surfaced, making her feel like one of the overexcited kids, chasing every whim and half-baked idea. For years, she had wasted time and emotion and money trying to uncover her parents' movements on the day they disappeared. Like the toddlers, running headlong toward the sea, she didn't know what she was looking for; she only knew she was compelled to keep going. She even wondered if she wanted it so badly because everyone told her to stop. Her friends, her brother, even a private detective who she funded by working an entire summer vacation while at law school. He found nothing and concluded that the original police investigation was sound. *Some cases are simply never solved,* he said.

"Well, it was nice meeting you," she said. "I'm going to finish my run."

"You should come sailing sometime." He gave an exaggerated stretch that involved his biceps. Camille saluted him goodbye. It was tempting to invite herself for coffee, but she needed to get back to dry land. She ran into the heat of the car park and stopped when she heard a shout. The guy stood on the steps, framed in the yacht club entrance. "You could try the port authority. For the float plans? They digitized a lot of historical records. It could be there, what you're looking for?"

It could be there. Indeed, the truth must be somewhere. Whether she liked it or not, the past had cracked open, awakened by the smells and sounds of a childhood that wasn't entirely lost even though it had been forgotten. First Edward Bonham, then the photo in the *kopitiam*, and now the float plans. As if on cue, her phone shuddered: an email with the address of a waterfront bar. She set off alongside the choppy straits. Information was coming up like sediment in a bottle that had been tossed overboard and finally drifted to shore. All she had to do was seize the day, and give it a good shake.

Chapter 18

Amanda watched on the security camera as a woman buzzed from the lift lobby for a second time. The maid agency had sent a candidate straight around—only an hour after Ed staged his "intervention." Amanda hauled on a smile as the lift arrived.

Magdalene introduced herself, her intricately painted fingernails clutching a schedule of interviews. They both knew good help was hard to find. Amanda wondered who was interviewing whom. Magdalene was two decades older than Awmi and a Filipina: likely part of an established community of maids who supported one another, the lore of their unique lifestyle passing down the female line the way other women's crafts—midwifery, natural remedies, ceremonial rites—were once inherited. Her gaze was steel, forged by hard knocks.

"You have nice home, ma'am. Not too bad."

"And you have great references."

Magdalene proved to be pleasant company, but throughout their conversation, Amanda was distracted by images popping into her head as though downloading from the phone hidden under the helper's mattress and merging with real life. She saw Magdalene's lips closing around the rim of a cocktail glass, her nails scratching the elm-wood table that was the same tan color as Ed's skin, her toes massaging the marble—a foot as petite as Camille Kemble's. Amanda couldn't focus on a single question about cooking or laundry. Instead, the maid chatted about former employers, American *ang mohs* who were overly generous and British ones who weren't. Spoiled children. Hard-drinking women. The family who broke her heart when they left Singapore with kids she helped raise for twelve years. And a wife who offered "headache money."

"Headache money?"

"You know"—Magdalene covered her mouth with her hand as she spoke—"to be with the husband."

"I don't understand . . ."

"When the wife has headache and the husband needs special attention, she pays me to go to him."

"The wife paid you to have sex with her husband?"

"Stop him taking a mistress."

"How old were you?"

"Very young. But not dumb. One time, I told her I'm pregnant and need to go to Philippines to lose the baby. So she took my passport from the safe and I go to the agency instead. They find me longtime family, good employer."

Nice bluff, thought Amanda. She detailed the duties, salary, and benefits, and gave an assurance that there would be no headache money. Magdalene asked to see the living quarters. Images from the phone filled Amanda's head again, so she left her to go alone.

If she *had* to take someone on, this woman seemed like she could shoulder her own baggage. But Josie should meet her first. Amanda called the girl's number, which went to voice mail. While the phone was still in her hand, an alert popped up from the SOWs Facebook page.

From the administrators: Please share this appeal from one of our members. Her 18-year-old niece is missing in Tokyo. Laureline Mackenzie was working as a hostess, but hasn't been seen for two days.

Yesterday she missed her scheduled flight home to Australia. Her family are flying to Tokyo. Please read the details in the attached police statement and SHARE!!!

Amanda clicked through and scanned the statement. Star student. Multilingual. Blonde beauty. Last seen at the Golden Girl, an upscale hostess bar in the Roppongi district specializing in Western women. No contact with family or friends for two days. And she missed a flight home for her mother's fiftieth birthday.

When Amanda looked up from the screen, she found that she had walked through to her bedroom. *Why am I here?* After a second's hesitation, she knew the answer. She dropped the phone onto the bed and went into Ed's bathroom. In the trash can, as expected, were his credit-card receipts from Tokyo. Taxis. A bottle of water and the *Financial Times*. A thick envelope containing his hotel bill—the Grand Hyatt in Roppongi.

Amanda kneeled at Ed's side of the bed to spread out the papers. She grabbed her phone and went to Maps, plotting the hotel with a pin. Then she typed in "Golden Girl." The second pin overlapped the first. Amanda finger-pinched the map to zoom in. The unfamiliar streets jigsawed into place. But the pins pressed together like an amorous couple. The Golden Girl was located one block from the hotel where Ed had stayed on the night Laureline Mackenzie was last seen.

"I'm finish, ma'am." Magdalene's voice came from the hallway.

Amanda stuffed the Grand Hyatt bill into its envelope. *I'm not bringing another woman into this house,* she thought, *however hard Ed pushes for it. Get out,* she thought, *get out while you can.*

Chapter 19

Camille strolled along the waterfront, which was busy with tourists and locals on a Sunday evening, to meet Edward Bonham. Night fell with equatorial haste, and then, like a current through a string of fairy lights wrapped around the bay, the city sparked back to life one blazing tower at a time. As she left the throng, the promenade turned to a secluded boardwalk, and she reached a half flight of steps that led to a terrace atop an old jetty. She stopped at the top of the stairs. The lighting in the café was low, both literally and figuratively: avenues of glowing ice cubes illuminated her ankles and little else.

"Do you have a reservation?" came a voice from the dark. Female. Young. Camille blinked a waitress into focus.

"I'm meeting Mr. Bonham?"

"He's not here, but we have the reservation. Please mind the step." The waitress produced a tiny torch and showed Camille to a table overlooking the water. Camille chose to face the bar. The Old Quay Cafe had no more than twenty seats and was attached to the most prestigious hotel on the island. One of those in-the-know places. Every table was occupied, and the unobtrusive music was just loud enough to cover clients' discreet mutterings. The air swelled with intrigue: a dodgy business deal, a spot of espionage, an illicit affair. She thought of the white bottles of clonazepam. This was a perfect place to slip someone a roofie, wait a few minutes for it to take effect, and then direct the victim's unsteady legs—*Oops, get the door please, waitress, one too many*—into a lift toward a hotel room . . .

"Camille Kemble, I presume?"

She recognized his voice from the phone: London, with a well-traveled hint of mid-Atlantic.

"Don't get up," he said. "I'm just checking I'm not accosting some poor woman in the dark." As he sat down, Edward Bonham's face entered the glowing orb of light that hung over the table. His wedding ring glinted as he gave his thick hair a ruffle and hunched forward in an exaggerated attempt to see her.

She held out a hand. "Hello, Ed. I appreciate you agreeing to meet like this. Especially on a Sunday."

They shook. Cool palm. Firm grip. One pump. Their hands retreated to the darkness, but she still felt his imprint. She had the same feeling as when she'd seen his photos: a tinge of recognition that translated into familiarity.

"Drink?"

It wouldn't be wise to get overfamiliar. "I'm fine with water."

"Unless you're a recovering alcoholic—you're not a recovering alcoholic, are you, Camille? At your tender age?"

"No . . ."

"Well, then, will you have a drink with me? I have a policy never to drink alone." He unleashed a smile that popped like a flashbulb. The waitress reappeared, and he turned away to order, his smile burning an afterimage onto the night.

"So." Ed rearranged his chair closer. "Needless to say, I'm intrigued. Did I understand right? You're looking for your parents?"

She nodded. "It's a long story, but in a nutshell . . . we lived in Singapore in the '90s. My parents took me to boarding school in the UK in September 1999. My brother too. They said they needed to travel for business; they ran a yacht charter."

"Tough times. The Asian financial crisis was, what, '97?"

"Exactly. They didn't say much about it—not that I remember anyway, I was only ten when they disappeared—but I sensed there was trouble."

Two drinks slid into the spotlight. Ed pulled celery from his Bloody Mary and clinked his glass against hers without interrupting.

"So Collin and I started our respective schools on September 5, 1999. And then . . . we never heard from them again."

"They disappeared?"

"They were never reported missing. As far as I know, my headmistress alerted the police. She called Interpol, which I think was probably the most exciting thing that ever happened to her." Camille reached for the Bloody Mary. The cold drink was shot through with fiery spice, a startling blend of opposites.

"And you were ten?"

"I was ten."

"So what next?"

"They must have taken the yacht—"

"I meant for you. What happened to you?"

"Me? Stayed at school. After a year, my parents were pronounced dead, so we could claim a trust fund and pay the fees. My mother was estranged from her family. The grandparents on my father's side were elderly and died within six months of each other. We bounced around friends and relatives. Went to university. Grew up."

"And now you think you can find them?" He drained his glass.

"I'm a realist." She tipped her drink and ice slammed into her teeth. "But I'd love to know what happened."

"You think there's such a thing as closure?"

"Do you?" she asked.

Ed picked up the celery stick, snapped it in two. Camille realized she'd said too much, alluding to his own recent experience with death. But he stroked his lips with a thumb. "I think the concept is used too lightly." He gestured at the dark water below. "You can't lock up grief any more than the tide."

"With respect, I don't even have grief. I don't know if my parents are dead or alive. What I mean by closure is more a start than the end. I'd like to be free to *start* grieving." Camille reached for her glass, but it held only red-stained ice.

"Happy hour is about to close, sir," said a woman's soft voice in the dark.

"Two more."

Across the bay, an outdoor concert started up, sending scrambled melodies over the water. Screaming girls sounded like seagulls.

"Bloody K-pop." Ed leaned forward into the light. Behind his head, a Ferris wheel changed its colors. "How can I help?"

"You didn't happen to know them? Patricia and Magnus Kemble, lived at Tanglin Green, two kids?"

"Afraid not."

Camille gave a one-shoulder shrug. Long shot.

"I left Singapore toward the end of '99. About this time of year, actually." He paused to recall dates. Camille could have told him: his employment pass was canceled on October 31 and he exited the country on November 2. "Must have been October, November, something like that 'cause I met my first wife—Josie's mother—at some awful Christmas party in London." And Josie was born in 2000? Fast mover.

"I hoped there might have been some overlap between your business and theirs—yachts and planes?"

"I didn't get into aircraft until later. No, I was a trader then. Didn't end well." He toasted her with his fresh drink. "I went bankrupt. Hence my departure from Singapore. Between me and you and the gatepost, my current wife is not aware of that fact, and I'd rather she didn't learn about it anytime soon."

"Your secret's safe with me."

"It's not a secret. I just haven't told her the details. It's a matter of trust."

"Trust?" She broke a leaf off the bushy stem of celery.

"You came to Singapore for a job, right? You're independent. But my wife gave up everything to follow me. Home, friends, social life. Would she have taken a punt on some ex-bankrupt? Don't think so. Especially because—well, it's a long story—but *her* father went bankrupt in a public scandal when she was a girl."

That explains the media intrusion, Camille thought.

"So she craves stability. But my business was solid and everyone loves Singapore. We hadn't known each other long, but"—Camille noted again his unseemly haste—"I needed her to trust me."

Lying to gain trust. She could feel her mind cruising away on a tangent of Edward Bonham's personal intrigue. All the questions she wanted to ask about her parents had gone up in the air like ticker tape. Ed's glass was empty again. She slid her untouched Bloody Mary forward into the lamplight.

"You sure?" he asked, fingers ready to dispose of the greenery.

"Go ahead." The celery was flung into the darkness. "To get back to my parents. I'm trying to explore their networks. This happened pre-Facebook, so it's hard." She saw the corners of Ed's mouth rise, the tips of his canines emerge, and she realized how young she sounded, how naive. "Everything got cleared from their house by the landlord— address books, Christmas cards, business files—any record of their lives, basically." Fresh screams from the concert. Neon strands of light webbed the bay. "I was thinking that maybe there were places where expats hung out back then? Where long-termers might remember them?"

Ed blew out his cheeks. "Have you checked the clubs? There's a British Club, Dutch Club, Tanglin—loads of them—American Club. And I assume you've tried the yacht club?" He mirrored her nodding. "Hang on"—he leaned forward into the light—"your parents weren't known at the yacht club?"

Camille shook her head.

"Don't you think that's strange?" Ed said. "For people in the yacht business?"

Down below, the painted prow of a wooden bumboat bobbed alongside the floating boardwalk, out of sync with its rise and fall.

"I do have a theory." Camille watched three stocky men in black suits choose the right moment to jump to shore. The lit points of their cigarettes danced like fireflies. "I think my parents didn't tell us everything."

Ed laughed soft and low. "Parents do that. It's called parenting."

"What I mean is, I think they had another source of income."

He drained the last of the drink, his eyes luminous, fixed on hers. "Such as?"

The movement of the waitresses in the dark brought to mind a shadow from the past: the slim figure of her mother, framed in Camille's bedroom doorway at the house in Tanglin Green, summoned by her daughter's cries in the night. Pale and weary, forcing kindness, she switched on the light and exposed Camille's recurring fears for what they were—ideas in dark corners. A peck on the forehead. *There's nothing there.* And now Camille was crying out to this man about her parents' secrets. With a spotlight trained on her grand theory, it felt like the monster under her bed: insubstantial and faintly silly. She couldn't bring herself to say "spies."

"Nothing criminal," she said at last. "There's no evidence of that, anyway."

"Good. You don't want to get mixed up with crime in Singapore."

"I should have shown you this straight away." She rummaged in her bag for the Filofax and opened it to the photo of her parents in the *kopitiam.* Ed used the torchlight from his phone to inspect the image. He handed the picture back.

"And your parents were called?"

"Patricia and Magnus."

"It was a long time ago . . ." He hesitated as though he might say more. The bar, the boats, the neon lights, all receded.

"What was?"

"I don't recall those names." He switched off his phone and it became too dark to read his face. She waited, but he didn't say any more. On the waterfront, tourists moved in a syncopated dance along the quay. Everyone in motion. Ed would move on too if she didn't get her questions in first.

"How is your family recovering, after the incident with your helper?"

"Incident? That's a delicate way to refer to a suicide."

"It's a delicate subject."

Ed leaned into the light and his eyes were stone. "It's brutal."

"Awmi's death was particularly violent."

"At least she didn't chuck herself off the balcony, I suppose. The whole condo didn't have to witness her, sitting on the edge while she made up her mind. Kids watching, wondering what it'd look like if she jumped. And then finding out. Suicide is fucking inconsiderate."

His strength of feeling startled Camille, and it made her wonder what happened to his first wife, but she tried to focus, to steer him now that he was in motion.

"Did the police suggest any motive? I'm curious because—"

"You volunteer for HELP. Josie told me. Don't look so surprised: I travel, but I'm still her father. We talk. It's another reason I wanted to meet tonight, actually." He pushed his drink aside, and Camille noticed his shoulders brace as he started talking about his daughter. His voice like a dart, sharpened into a warning. "I think it's a bit much, you turning up at her school like that."

Camille took a gulp of water. "I'm sorry if I overstepped the mark. There's been a spate of suicides. Helpers from Burma are especially vulnerable."

"I wouldn't know much about that. And nor would Josie."

Ed made a scribble sign in the air to the waitress. Camille was losing him.

"She mentioned that your helper asked for money? Was it for loan sharks? I only ask because debt is one of the most common reasons we hear for suicide—"

"You can't apply logic to the decisions people make. She came to me with a problem, and I gave her a solution. She had money. She had options. The choice she made next was inexplicable. I don't want my family publicly humiliated because of her decision." When he leaned forward to sign the drinks chit, the half-light picked out the first white hairs at the peaks of his cheekbones. He handed it off to the waitress and smiled at Camille, but now it was less flashbulb, more tea light, the warmth flickering. "I don't mean to sound cruel. I'm tired."

"HELP isn't planning to publicize the case at the moment."

For a long moment, they held eye contact. She felt a warmth on her thigh and looked down to see his hand. She watched seconds tick by on his wristwatch. When she didn't return eye contact, he peeled his fingers from her skin. "You look like you need another drink." He fished in a pocket for a note and laid the tip under one of the glasses. "Happy hour's finished. Do you fancy going somewhere less classy?"

She did fancy another drink. She fancied the cold fire of a Bloody Mary, the promise of hard liquor once she'd thrown aside the embellishments. With a twist in her belly, she realized she fancied his hand back on her knee.

"I need to get home."

"Who's waiting for you at home, Camille?"

"I'm not a big drinker."

Ed stood up out of the light. "Then I'll love you and leave you."

She got up too. "If you remember anything, would you let me know?"

"About what? Your parents or our helper?"

"Both. Either. I don't mind."

He gave a low laugh and bent to shake her hand. She smelled him then, a woody tang that carried another solid blow of recognition. A familiarity that bordered on presumptuousness, burning the tip of her tongue like the Bloody Mary.

"Thanks, Teddy," she whispered into his ear. Her words were swept away by a scream from the K-pop crowd, and she wondered if they had really come out of her mouth, if he had heard. But he froze, and they were nose to nose for a moment, his eyes narrowed. Camille used her height disadvantage to duck under his arm and down the dark path to the steps. She didn't look back even after the throng swallowed her up and carried her along the Singapore River.

Chapter 20

Amanda labored through her morning laps, weighed down by worries: Laureline Mackenzie's parents must be in Tokyo now, perhaps staying at the Grand Hyatt, a hotel conveniently close to the club where their daughter was last seen. She flipped up to tread water, distracted by a figure crouched in the flower bed—a gaunt woman with hands covering her face as though she were counting to ten and everyone should hide.

Amanda glanced around for Ed, but he was farther down the pool, his strokes barely visible on the surface. She hauled herself from the water and tied a towel around her waist as she walked across the grass. She'd never seen the woman before, but that was no surprise: the Attica was made up of three towers that housed one thousand apartments. A town flipped on its side.

"I searched the whole island, but he is here all the time." The woman grasped Amanda's bicep and switched into a barrage of French. Amanda peered between the heliconia leaves and saw what she thought was a cushion with the stuffing pulled out, before she recognized it as an animal.

"Is that your dog?" Amanda said.

"It is awful. We complain many times about the pest control. So much poison. He is not the first."

Amanda watched Raja, their concierge, striding toward them, out of place beside the pool in his three-piece suit. She didn't envy him the heat as the woman turned on him. Her distress ricocheted off the blank faces of the towers. Amanda lingered until Ed sprang from the pool. "Good," he said, when she told him in whispers. "That poodle shits on the path every morning. And she leaves it. Wouldn't surprise me if the management poisoned her dog."

Amanda ushered Ed toward the lift. "It wasn't the dog's fault."

"Madam?"

Amanda turned to see Raja approaching.

"I'm going for a shower. Early meeting." The lift whisked Ed away.

Raja looked composed despite his roasting. "There is a delivery for you, madam. In the management office."

"I'll pop down and pick it up later."

"You need to take it now. It is from the police." Raja said the last word with very wide eyes. Amanda followed him to the office. As soon as she was through the door, the indomitable woman who managed the condo pointed her Biro at a huge box: "Take it." Amanda signed for the parcel and opened it right up. She recognized Awmi's clothes, the pretty necklace she wore on Sundays.

"What am I going to do with all this?" she wondered out loud. Even though "all this" was a pathetic sum total of a human life. The manager flapped her hands in a shooing motion. Maybe she was superstitious about having a dead person's things in her office. Amanda hefted the box against her chest and wrestled it out through the door.

In the apartment, water crashed in Ed's bathroom. Amanda shifted the box through the kitchen and onto the rear balcony. She dropped it on the bare mattress of the maid's room. It was bulky but not heavy. She could find Awmi's home address from the agency and send it to Burma. That would be the right thing to do: closure for the family. She could hide some cash inside, compensation. *Or maybe they would see it as blood money?*

She opened the cardboard flaps again. On top was a collection of metallic nail polishes, which she'd bought Awmi as a birthday gift. A framed family photo. Her mobile phone. A ziplock bag of medicine.

Amanda fingered the pills through the plastic. The shiny strips looked like contraceptives. Meek little Awmi. So innocent. Turned out Amanda was the naive one. In any case, the pills hadn't worked. The gold strips went into the trash: Awmi's family didn't need to see them. Then a jar of paracetamol that was almost empty. And a piece of paper, which she took out and unfolded. It was a letter from the Singapore Police Force titled "Evidence Withheld": two bottles of the medication clonazepam in the name of Edward Bonham. It listed the details of the prescribing doctors, who were both in Manila. Amanda slipped the letter into her pocket. Why did Ed have this drug, clonazepam? Why were the bottles in Awmi's room—did she steal them and try to overdose? Is that why the police hadn't returned the medication—they needed it for tests? She closed the door once more on the secrets of her helper's bedroom.

Ed was in the kitchen, eating breakfast while looking down on the ships. The indignant cry of a koel bird pealed through the canyons of the towers, hollering its own name to exhaustion. Amanda wondered if she should write him a letter about everything she'd found in recent days: the condoms, the photo from the strip club, the illicit pictures of women, and now the drugs found in their helper's bedroom. It would be easier if she could get the facts straight on paper. But then he'd have time to come up with excuses. It would annoy him, the implication that she'd been snooping, gathering evidence. He would seize on that to divert the argument from his huge misdemeanor to her small one. *Well,* she'd tell him, *you've been traveling more and more, being distant and evasive, and we interact as though you're an exhibit behind glass. I watch you, but I can't reach you. Now you want a break from trying for a baby. It makes me wonder if there's something you're not telling me.* And she hadn't been wrong, had she? As soon as she started looking, she'd found something. And kept finding things—now there was this drug . . . What was clonazepam even for?

Fuck him. It was time to confront him, deliver the evidence in a sucker punch and watch his reaction.

Amanda pushed open the door, and Ed's spoon clattered into his bowl. "Christ, you scared me," he said.

"We need to talk."

"Too right we do. Do you know about this?" He spun a letter across the counter. Amanda saw a Ministry of Manpower heading and picked it up. It was addressed to them both.

> *Re: Death of Foreign Domestic Worker*
> *Further to confirmation from the Coroner that the FDW was pregnant at time of death, the MOM has been in receipt of evidence that the FDW was underage while employed by Mrs. Amanda Bonham—*

She looked up to see Ed's lips pursed so hard they were white-tipped. "I didn't know about this."

"Just read it."

She scanned the letter. The pressure group HELP had compiled evidence—original school reports, interviews with close family members—that indicated Awmi was around eighteen years old now, and only sixteen when she'd first arrived from Burma. While the onus was on maid agencies to comply with Singapore's regulation that maids should be over the age of twenty-three, it was felt that in light of her pregnancy and the extremely young age of the girl, the employer had not taken due care. The MOM had fined them $5,000—the total of a security bond paid when Awmi arrived—and barred them from further employment of a maid. Amanda slid onto one of the barstools and wondered if it was the seat or herself who wobbled.

"You had one job to do, Amanda. One job."

"But . . ." She threw a hand in the air as though tossing salt over her shoulder for luck. "I don't know anything about this."

"Exactly. The only responsibility you had in this whole life of luxury was the person who did all the housework for you. And you didn't check her paperwork. You didn't check the reputation of the agency." He dropped his bowl and spoon in the sink with a crash that sent slops from the dirty dishes down the front of his trousers. "Did you even talk to her? Surely you could tell the difference between a sixteen-year-old and a twenty-three-year-old?"

"She did look young, but don't they all?"

"What are you saying, Amanda? *They all look the same?*"

"Don't be sanctimonious. I meant young people in general—Josie looks older than seventeen when she's done up. And what about you? Couldn't you tell? It sounds like you were a lot closer to Awmi than I was!"

"What does that mean?"

"She came to you, didn't she, when she was pregnant? Why was that, Ed?"

"I told you. She was convinced you'd send her home, because you'd be jealous—"

"Maybe with good reason!"

"Don't be bloody ridiculous. And how did HELP know Awmi was underage? Why were they digging in the first place?"

"Ask your daughter—she's the one who spilled the beans to Camille Kemble."

Ed snatched up a tea towel and wiped at the slops on his thigh. "This place is a disgrace." He flung open the door under the sink and hauled out cleaning products. "Is it too much to expect a bit of loyalty?" A fire extinguisher toppled onto the tiles with a clang.

"Josie didn't know the significance of what she said—"

"She knew *exactly*, because she told me that she'd tried to tell you that Awmi was underage and you refused to listen. She was pissed off and went running to the first person who showed her any attention." Ed brandished a cleaning spray like a pistol. "It's like her mother all over again." He threw the bottle into the sink and picked up the fire extinguisher, turning it between his hands. "No fucking loyalty." He raised the fire extinguisher over his head, turning this way and that, squinting as though trying to glimpse rationality behind a swaying curtain of rage.

"Ed?"

He looked Amanda up and down, before turning to face the window. His arms levered back behind his neck and he slammed the red canister into the glass. It landed in the sink, and before the broken china had settled, he was gone. Amanda waited until she heard elevator cables rattling. She stood up from where she cowered behind the counter and walked to the window, placing her palm over the jagged star that marked the point of impact. If she listened hard enough, she could hear the wind's song through the shattered eye.

Chapter 21

Coffee shop jazz jangled Amanda's nerves, the clatter of cymbals too similar to the sound of metal shattering glass. She tried to calm herself by watching a ship slide into the darkness. But someone, somewhere was whistling. Unlucky, her mother said; sailors believed it challenged the wind to whip up a storm. She hoped her mother had moored for night.

Ed had texted to say he needed to work late again, this time a call to Europe, and Josie had gone to the library. The enormity of the apartment dwarfed Amanda. She tried switching on the radio to fill the space, but the local announcers warned of traffic in exotic parts of the island that were foreign to her—Tuas and Sembawang and Pasir Ris—making her feel more isolated than ever. So she had fled the condo to tackle her own tasks in the coffee shop by the waterfront.

She resumed copying from the family calendar that was normally pinned to the fridge: Ed's work trips that year. He'd been in Tokyo when the Australian hostess, Laureline Mackenzie, disappeared. He'd been in Orchard Towers when the photo of the man with the stripper was taken. Like her body craving caffeine that only made her shake, she couldn't stop looking for more.

Since January, Ed had been away thirty times to twelve different cities. The most popular destinations were Manila, Zurich, and China. He traveled to meet clients, sometimes flew aircraft for buyers to test-drive, and, when the deal was done, delivered the plane. People with that kind of money expected Ed to go to them.

She wrote a list of cities Ed had visited down the left-hand side of a sheet of paper. That was column one. In column two, she wrote dates of travel. Where she had further details, she added them in column three: hotels, commercial flight numbers, girlie drinks he'd ordered at the bar. She drew a long line down the page to designate column four. Under this heading, alongside his most recent trip to Tokyo, she wrote "LAURELINE MACKENZIE."

On the table, Amanda's phone buzzed. A text from Mostess at book club. *Molly,* she corrected herself. *Her name is Molly.* She swiped to read. Hey! Just checking to see if you went back to the clinic. Hope all well, M.

Amanda tapped "Reply" and hesitated. It was kind of Molly to remember. Her insides bubbled with the need to talk, worries and fears racing each other to the surface where they burst wetly in the air. What could she say? *I'm checking to see if my husband is a pervert before I have his baby?* She tapped the name of the missing woman with a fingertip—*or worse than a pervert.* She could hardly tell Molly the truth. At best, she'd scare her away. At worst, sharing her suspicions would make them real.

Didn't go to the clinic. Hoping to get Ed on side first! *Prayer Hands Emoji*

A response came right back: Stay strong! Let's get coffee *Coffee Mug Emoji*

Amanda replied in the affirmative. Her phone buzzed again and this time it was Ed: on his way home. She replied that she was out shopping, back soon. *I mustn't start acting weird.*

In the Google search, she typed "Zurich." From her list of girlie drinks that Ed had bought, she entered the date on the receipt for the Aperol. Exactly one month before Laureline Mackenzie disappeared in Tokyo. A pattern? She dug her lacquer-hard nails into her palms and then released them, hit "Search." She scrolled past German-language reports until she came to a story on a website for English-speaking expats in Switzerland.

*Murder has not been ruled out in the case of an
18-year-old exotic dancer from Brazil who died of
an overdose from a date-rape drug in the luxurious
Pfannenstiel Grand Hotel.*

The dates matched, but Amanda knew from his receipts that Ed
had stayed in a different hotel; she typed its name into an online map.
Again, the two pins lay side by side. The hotels shared a bergstation, a
funicular railway that brought guests up the hill from the city center.
She flicked through the photos on her phone until she found the receipt
for a Bloody Mary and an Aperol. On the night a Brazilian stripper
died at the Pfannenstiel Grand Hotel, Ed had purchased two drinks in
its lobby bar.

It can't be possible, she thought, *for Ed to do something like that. I would
know. If he was capable of killing. I would know.* She took a slug of coffee
and found it was cold. *Violence would leave a trace. I'd get a glimpse of it
beneath his surface, surely?* She stared through a wall of glass. Humidity
twisted streetlights into stars. Behind the window, air con fooled her skin
into making goose bumps. *I can't even trust my own sense of hot and cold.*

Rubbing her palm with the thumb of the other hand, she felt faint
scratches from the punctured window in her kitchen. Recalled the look
Ed had given her when he'd held the fire extinguisher aloft, looking
for something to break. His face like a mask. Why would someone
collect pictures of women—broken pieces of women? The photos on
the hidden phone had the same froideur as his demeanor when she'd
caught him looking for the device on the balcony, pretending it was his
passport that had gone missing. He had detachment down to an art.

She wrote carefully on her piece of paper, in column four next to
Zurich: "Brazilian dancer / hotel / 18." And she went back up the column to the information beside Laureline Mackenzie in Tokyo to add
the number eighteen.

Both aged eighteen.

She drew two circles around the number. She watched as a drip of coffee touched her note paper and blotted, curling up the corner as though it were burning.

Eighteen. Josie turned eighteen soon. She thought of the countdown on her blog. Amanda picked up her phone and went to the site. The timer showed ten days. She clicked and saw a new line drawing, a pair of high heels, one standing upright, one on its side.

In the future: Ten Days Until D-Day
In the past: Thirteen Days That Made Me Me
Post 3 of 13: Holiday Romance

It's dark outside the taverna. The night smells of wild herbs and clapped-out cars. We're supposed to stay away from the road, but Madison, who is older, wants to say goodbye to the beach. She says it's too dark to take photos so I leave my camera behind.

The sea is sprinkled with silver coins turning heads or tails. All around us, tiny lights flash—bing!—as though there are fairies in the olive trees. Madison says they're not fairies, they're fireflies. I'm going to tell Teddy all about the fairies when we get home. Madison asks why I call him Teddy and not Daddy, and I say that everyone has a daddy but only I have a Teddy, and she says that's stupid and I say she's stupid. I leave her behind in the olive grove, but she runs after me and grabs my arm because she's afraid of the dark. When we reach the road, the coach is pulling up to take us to the airport. We squint our eyes in the headlights and the dust. I feel bad for the fairies, flying around in that dust. The coach stops with a big sigh.

Madison points her eyes toward the steps of the taverna. All the grown-ups are there, saying goodbye to the fat cook and the tall waiter with the smile. Madison abandons me then, darting out of the darkness into the headlights, where she shouts to her mummy that it's time to go. The adults come down the steps into the car park; if they see me running across the road now, I'll get told off for going to the beach. So I slip behind the coach, which is parked against some bushes, making a sort-of alley that leads to the taverna. The engine starts up with a shudder. I squeeze alongside the coach and I'm almost there when the tall waiter steps in front of me, pulling a woman behind him. She stumbles and giggles. The side of the coach throbs as I crouch into the space behind the tire.

Their bodies block the light. I can see their feet. The man's scuffed shoes face the coach. Hers, in high heels, lift off the ground, scratching against his legs. It doesn't seem like they'll notice me, so I crawl out and scoot between the gnarly trunks of the bushes and onto the steps of the taverna, where I find our suitcase and wait for her there.

The woman pressed between the coach and the waiter is my mummy. But she is not Mummy now. She is wearing high heels and her hair is red from the coach lights. My camera is hanging off the handle of the suitcase. I pick it up and snap a photo—one flash, bing! like the fairies—so I can show Teddy how happy she looks once we get home.

Chapter 22

All the way home from the coffee shop, Amanda wondered if Josie's blog was a confession. A child working through guilt for alerting her father to her mother's infidelity. Because what then? What did Ed do when he saw his wife in the red light, pressed against another man? She thought of the photo on Josie's nightstand. Her mother smiling, hair flailing, indifferent to the wind and the fact that she planned to kill herself that very day. *Indifferent,* Amanda thought, *or innocent?*

Everyone—including the authorities—had concluded that her death was a suicide. But what if she looked happy because she was happy? What if she had no plans to die that day?

The lift arrived at the apartment with a soft chime, a gong sounding through the empty halls of a palace as though trying to wake Sleeping Beauty. Amanda shook her head once as she got out of the elevator, wired from too much coffee.

In the blood-red kitchen, voices. Female. A stabbing yelp that could be laughter or tears. Ed's bass reply. Josie's figure passed the doorway. Someone else was there too—Willow?

Slipping her shoes off, Amanda tucked them under her arm, then darted down the corridor in the opposite direction, past her Chinese pots. All her secrets. And now she knew that Ed also had hiding places: the helper's room where she'd found the phone. Could there be more?

Through ripples of light, past Chairman Mao pixelated in fingernails, she went to Ed's dressing room. His closet stood open. She got
down on her knees and pressed her hands inside each shoe, right into
the toes. Then she stood and faced his suits. She went through the
pockets, ran her fingers along lapels and hems. Finally, a holdall on the
top shelf, his sports bag. She found squash balls, muscle rub, nothing
incriminating. She stopped, staring and thinking, until the automatic
light went out and she stood in the dark.

*Another night sleeping alongside him, stiff and cold like I'm inside a
glass coffin.* She went to the doorway, slammed on the light. Hidden
behind the door was a short rail to hang dry cleaning for the maid. Ed's
suit crumpled from travel. Amanda ran her hand down the sleeve, feeling heavy winter wool. Not a fabric suited to tropical Singapore. Her
fingers slipped into the inside pocket. Nothing. She ran both hands up
and down its full length, front and back. She stopped. There was a thin,
hard patch somewhere inside the breast.

She opened the jacket, revealing amber-colored lining. There was a
bump the size and shape of a credit card. Fingering the inside pocket,
she found a slit in the silk, its edge starting to fray. Inside: a plastic card.
She held it in the light and, for a stomach-shrinking moment, thought
it was her mother's key card from the library ship, the one she'd locked
in her safety-deposit box. *How could that be here?* But she turned it and
saw a logo. The Pfannenstiel Grand Hotel. Her heart double-thumped.

Amanda closed the jacket and fastened the buttons. Then she
opened them again. How had she found it? *Would he know she'd been
here?* She smoothed the wool, clicked off the light. At the door, she
heard voices overlapping in the kitchen, Ed's bass tone creeping through
the apartment like low fog. She held the card by the corners. The
Pfannenstiel Grand Hotel. Where the exotic dancer died. But Ed had
not stayed there; he had a bill from the neighboring Dolder Grand. So
why would he have a key to another hotel? She turned the room card
between her fingertips.

If he'd been involved in a woman's death, why keep an incriminating item?

Killers keep trophies, don't they? Certain types of killers. *Serial killers.*

A popping cork jolted her into motion. She moved down the hallway to a tea caddy marked with a double happiness symbol, a traditional wedding gift. She dropped the key card inside. As she turned toward the voices, her vision rippled. Outside the huge windows, the ships were blinking points of light, like fireflies. *Fairies.*

The kitchen door slid aside, and Josie marched out. When she saw Amanda, her hand flew to her chest. "You scared the crap out of me!" She recovered and set off toward her room, trailed by a sniveling Willow. "Dad needs you, there's stuff going down. Willow's staying tonight. That was so freaky . . ."

"Amanda?" Ed appeared in the doorway. "Erin is here." The tone of his voice intended some meaning that Amanda missed. She couldn't take her eyes from his hand, as cool gray as the metal doorframe it encircled. His index finger was bandaged—presumably from the fire extinguisher—but he tapped it twice, businesslike, on the glass door. "Are you with us? Could use you in here." He turned away, leaving fingerprints on the brushed steel.

Erin sat at the counter, her neurotically thin fingers gripping the stem of a wineglass. Ed poured Amanda a drink and handed it to her with a "you're gonna need this" expression. When he turned to fuss at the sink, she stared at his shoulder blades shifting beneath linen, until Erin's voice dragged her attention away.

"It came to a head today. Chuck me out when you need to."

When she didn't attempt to fill Amanda in, Ed wrung the dishcloth. His arms folded over his chest and his shoulders slid to his ears. "Arnault left."

Erin's eyes flashed up. "It was mutual."

Amanda slid onto a barstool. She took a sip of wine and held it in a pool on her tongue. If she was careful, she could let it dribble slowly down her throat without even swallowing. She did this several times while Erin was speaking.

"We'd agreed a while ago to cohabit until Willow finishes her schooling. Another year, and then all three are at university. But he's filed for divorce. He's going to fuck me over. He'll say anything to get me out of Singapore."

"How can he get you out of Singapore?" Ed asked.

Amanda and Erin gave the same involuntary scoff, and the kitchen bristled for a moment as the universe scored an invisible dividing line between the sexes.

"We *trailing spouses* live on thin ice, Ed, which cracks a little more each day, like our tired, out-of-date faces." Erin drained her wine, her profile gleaming as light bounced off Botox-thickened skin.

Ed raised his eyebrows and his glass.

"As soon as a divorce is finalized," Amanda explained, "Arnault could revoke her Dependant's Pass." This was a common thread on SOWs. "Then Erin would have thirty days to get a job with an Employment Pass or leave Singapore."

"And I'm a trained actress, Ed. A fucking *actress*. Past forty. How many jobs are open to me, do you think? Executive jobs with an EP?"

Ed turned his chin from side to side.

"And the worst-case scenario is Arnault continues to sponsor the children to stay in Singapore but not me. I have to leave, but I can't take the children home without his permission. Because of the Hague Convention. So, in his ideal world, he gets rid of me, keeps the kids, and probably shacks up with a younger model." Erin unfolded a tea towel to find an unsullied corner to press to her eyes. "With my luck, he'll find an actual fucking model."

"A lot of models are quite ugly," said Ed.

Erin clawed across the counter to reach the bottle. "Says the man with a wife ten years younger than himself. And totally hot."

"I'm five years younger!" Amanda protested, but Erin waved the comment away with one hand, sloshing red wine.

"I'm sure Josie's mother was relieved to hear that."

Ed stepped forward and placed his glass on the counter without making a sound. Amanda watched Erin's eyes flit over Ed's face, which had set as hard as the surface. Erin pulled herself up in her chair and brushed her hair back. A physical retreat.

Finally, Ed's lips softened enough to speak. "Josie's mother died. When Josie was fourteen. She hates talking about it. I met Amanda shortly afterward. A little too soon for Josie, but that's how it happened." He gathered up the empties and took them to the sink. "I think we've had enough for tonight."

Water crashed into steel as Amanda escorted Erin to the lift. The women waited in the chill stream of air con. Amanda couldn't select one thing to say from the clamor inside her head, so she focused instead on the *scritch scritch* of Erin's fingernails as they clawed the inside of an elbow that was raw with eczema. The rhythm steadied Amanda, and by the time the mirrored doors of the lift slid back, her brain had zeroed in on the thought that bothered her most: *Willow.*

Willow shouldn't be near Ed. Amanda grasped Erin's elbow, and she staggered slightly. "Take Willow home," she whispered. The crashing water in the kitchen stopped abruptly, as though the apartment had taken a sharp intake of breath. Erin's expression moved through several options and settled on conspiracy.

"Is it Ed? I know he can be . . . inappropriate."

"Inappropriate how?" She could feel brittle flakes of eczema under her thumb.

"He's chivalrous—until you displease him. Let's just say it's a pattern I've come to recognize. Someone who functions at the extremes."

The photo of Josie's mother came to mind, and Amanda wondered if her infidelity had sent Ed to the extreme. Or even over the edge.

"Are you safe, Amanda? Is Josie?" Erin's voice brought her back; the image replaced by wolfish eyes too close, too hungry, too triumphant.

"It's nothing like that!" She managed a half laugh. "I just think you and Willow should be together tonight."

Erin scanned Amanda's face, as though the truth were written between the lines. *Interesting,* Amanda thought, *that she's chosen to erase her own.*

"I'm upstairs if you need to talk." Erin marched off to Josie's room and rapped on the door. "Or if you need somewhere to run." A moment later she swept past with her daughter. Nothing more was said, and with a soft gong the mirrored doors closed.

Chapter 23

Collin held Camille at arm's length and turned full circle while standing on the bed, showing her via Skype the extent of his new apartment. She cooed over the view of Kowloon Bay but complained that the sofa didn't look like it folded out to a spare bed.

"It doesn't," said Collin, "and it's too small even for your short arse."

"I'll sleep in your whirlpool tub."

"Funny. You can have the bed. I'll sleep standing up in the shower."

"It's swanky, though. Great view."

"There's the *Aqua Luna.*" He held the phone up so she could see the glowing red sails of a wooden junk cutting through the neon-lit waters. "Wave," he said, and she did. He turned the phone back to himself. "How's Singapore?"

"Good. You should visit."

"I've been loads of times. When are you coming to see me? It's embarrassing you've never been to Hong Kong. How do you keep face in the expat crowd?"

"I don't try to. The expat crowd is . . . too tense. Self-satisfied, but at the same time terrified they'll have the rug pulled. They make me think of ants."

"Welcome to my world. When the rug gets pulled, they come running to HR." Collin shifted position, sending Camille hurtling out the window to the skyline and then back to his face. His hairline had started to recede, and she realized with a jolt that her brother was around the same age their father had been when he first emigrated to Asia.

"What do you think Mum and Dad would make of us, Col? Sellouts, aren't we? Corporate meal ticket for you, civil servitude for me."

Collin got up off the bed. She watched his chest and heard the click of the kettle being switched on. His face reappeared, lips pursed.

"What are you on about?" he said.

"Nothing. I went to Tanglin Green."

"Again?"

"Why not?"

"Stop wallowing, Cami."

In the background, the kettle rumbled to boiling point.

"I met this bloke," she said. "He lived in Singapore in the '90s, and I showed him a photo of Mum and Dad. He said he didn't recognize them, but I could tell he did." She raised her voice over Collin's scoff. "He said, 'I don't recall their names.' Isn't that a weird way to say it: 'I don't recall their names'? Like he wanted me to read between the lines."

"A mystery within a mystery."

"Right!"

Collin shook his head and stared out the window, his profile backlit by foreign lights. "I knew this Singapore move was a shit idea. You're going to start obsessing again, aren't you?"

"I can find out what happened to them."

"You won't. And it'll consume you like it did before. I'm trying so hard to stay dry, but this conversation is enough to drive me to drink."

She watched her brother pour boiling water onto instant noodles.

"Ed picked up on this one thing," she said. "I told him I'd been to the yacht club, right?"

"Who the hell is Ed?"

"The bloke I met."

"The weird one?"

"He's not weird. He's a hotshot businessman. Sells private aircraft. Bit of a silver fox."

"So you fancy him?"

"I think he might have been having it off with his helper."

"Massive eye roll."

"And then she killed herself."

"Doesn't say much for his sexual prowess."

"It's not funny! She was vulnerable."

Collin apologized.

"Just listen, Col. Ed said—"

"Ed, Ed, Ed!"

"Stop!" Camille laughed despite herself. "Edward Bonham said it was weird that no one remembered Mum and Dad at the yacht club. That *is* weird, right? Considering the business they were in?"

Collin pushed a pair of disposable chopsticks through the plastic wrapper, snapped them apart. "After fifteen years? Not really."

"If they'd been well-known, people would remember. It's a tight-knit community. So what if . . . they weren't well-known. What if the yacht business was a cover?"

Collin grunted through his noodles, but Camille plowed on.

"Today I called the port authority and requested the historical paperwork for their yacht. All the old float plans and outward clearances have been computerized. And I went through the original Interpol paperwork when I got home, and those documents were never included in their file, so either the police didn't request them or they disregarded them. And this is what I'm thinking: If their yacht *didn't* have outward clearances from Singapore, then that's interesting. Because how can you run a yacht charter without sailing anywhere? But if I find that Mum and Dad *did* sail from Singapore on the day they disappeared, then I can make the same information request at ports in Malaysia and Thailand and track their route."

"You won't find records at the other ports—"

"They didn't sink. It doesn't make sense. It's a busy shipping lane. They would have been seen."

"Yachts go down fast."

"Let's not discuss that theory again."

"It's not a theory, it's the only explanation that makes sense. More sense than your 'espionage' one. They disappeared. Their yacht disappeared. Unless they sailed all the way to the Bermuda Triangle . . ."

Camille made a gesture in front of the camera as though she could swipe him off the screen like an unattractive Tinder profile.

"Cami—"

"Their business is the key. Which has been my point for years."

"When we were kids, we pretended they were spies."

"Right!"

"When we were kids, Camille!"

She watched her brother get up and shrug on a denim jacket.

"Don't hang up," she said.

"I'm meeting someone."

"At midnight?"

"I got a match. I'm young, footloose, and fancy-free. I can meet people whenever I want"—his eyes loomed large on the screen—"and so can you." Collin lunged to throw the noodle pot into the trash can, sending her into another spin.

"Haven't you wondered why you're living in a shoebox with a sea view?" she said.

"What's your point?"

"You can't let them go either."

"There's nothing to let go. They've gone. And anyway, what does it matter?"

"It's who we are!"

"No, *we are* who we are." Collin went to the window and turned the phone so that her screen filled with dazzling lights. "Look at this city. Look. Every one of those lights is a living thing. Our parents disappeared and, yes, our childhood disappeared with them. And it's sad that we don't have a mum to tell us how cute we were and what kind of cake we had on our birthday. But that's in the past, and here in the present, we're alive. So get up, Cami, go out"—the phone swung back to his face again, his eyes so much like hers, and his voice softened— "and live a little."

There was silence while Camille swallowed something that stuck in her throat like undercooked noodles. Other young people lived for flirtation, dalliances, broken hearts. But having your heart broken—well, that assumed it was intact in the first place.

"I called him Teddy."

"What?"

"The Ed bloke. I recognize him, but I can't place it. And when I said goodbye, I called him Teddy."

"Maybe you want to cuddle up with Teddy?"

"It was subconscious. It meant something."

She watched her brother walk out the front door, his white teeth turning gray under the Chinese strip lights beside the lift.

"Seriously, Col, do you remember anything about the name Teddy? From Tanglin Green?"

"I'm going now. Teddy was your bear, a soft toy. We each had a bear and so little imagination that we called both of them Teddy."

Collin lit a fuse in Camille's mind and it caught. She remembered. Not the bear, she couldn't picture him at all, but the feeling of holding Teddy by his legs, as fat as a baby's, while she played in the garden.

"Good night, Cami."

"Good night, Col."

The screen went dark and she felt limp with loneliness, as flaccid as overstretched elastic, and she didn't have the strength to reach out to anyone. It was for the best; look what happened last time—she'd ended up embarrassing herself in front of her boss. Thank goodness he'd been professional enough to turn down her offer of a drink; she felt too weightless to withstand even a flurry of romance. Even if he seemed decent, past experience told her that men were as predictable as the Kowloon lights. They switched off by morning.

Chapter 24

Amanda sat cross-legged on cold marble in front of the window, scooping hummus directly from the tub with two fingers. The horizon was a dusky slash that bled into the ocean. Legions of clouds approached. At thirty stories, you could look the storm right in the eye.

She knew she should have eaten before opening a bottle of wine, but she'd needed a glass before Josie got home from the library, Dutch courage for the talk she had spent the day rehearsing. It was time to ask Josie about her father and perhaps swallow unpalatable answers. Josie wouldn't welcome the confrontation, but it was in her best interests. *One day, she'll understand.* Amanda said it out loud. It tripped off the tongue, the kind of thing a mother might say.

That morning, after Ed packed yet another bag, she'd gone to the gym and hit the treadmill, running like she was scared. *Ed thinks I don't take responsibility. Well, I'll be responsible for finding out what he's up to.* She spent the day cataloguing everything she knew. She laid out the pieces of her suspicion. Putting together a jigsaw without knowing what picture might emerge. Maybe Josie could click the puzzle into place? So Amanda warmed herself up for the talk with one glass of red. And Josie didn't come home. Half a bottle later, she still wasn't home.

She'd gone to meet Willow after spending the day at the library, so maybe they'd decided to see a movie? *It's not late, there's no safety issue.*

But Josie always checked in, and besides, Amanda had built herself up for this talk and wanted to get it over and done with.

Avoiding the wine bottle, she padded through the apartment to the bedroom, where she sat in an armchair. In the half-light, the luminous hands on Ed's bedside clock pointed out to sea. She thought of the timer on Josie's website and pulled out her phone. Today's post was illustrated with the grinning face of a pumpkin.

In the future: Nine Days Until D-Day
In the past: Thirteen Days That Made Me Me
Post 4 of 13: Remember, Remember the Fifth of November

The Guy is creepy. The straw inside his clothes makes his body look broken, and the head we made from an old football keeps falling off. He looked okay in the daytime, but now it's dark, the circle I drew for his laughing mouth is screaming as if he's seen what's coming. Teddy gets him on top of the bonfire in our back garden and all the mummies cheer.

Mrs. Traynor from the flat upstairs hands out sugar-free sticky apples, which are gross, and when I go inside to the bathroom, I dump mine in the bin. When I get back outside, Teddy has lit the bonfire and the flames jump into the night, making a noise like breaking glass. The Guy catches fire and his face melts. We light sparklers and Teddy takes my wrist and writes the word *Jo-Jo* on the darkness. Then we hear screaming. It's Mrs. Traynor.

"She probably saw her toffee apples in the bin," says Teddy.

But it's not that. She's pointing to the big tree that stands in the next-door garden but hangs over ours. "The branches are going to catch!" she shouts. Teddy tells her it's too wet to burn, but she's running inside. "It'll set fire to my flat!" Teddy gets the bucket of sand he prepared earlier, and the other daddies help him sprinkle some on the bonfire until the flames stop being so overexcited. He sprinkles a little bit on my head in case I get overexcited.

Close to the fire, my face is burning but my back is chilled by the night air. Teddy tells me to close my eyes. "Feels like you're two different people," he says. "Or in two places at once—a cold place and a hot place." When I open my eyes, Mrs. Traynor is back, tugging Teddy by the sleeve. He looks up at the tree. "Not that," she says. Her mouth looks like the Guy's did before we burned him. "They're having a side party upstairs." Teddy looks at the window of the flat above ours. The reflection of golden sparks makes it seem like it's burning. Mrs. Traynor tells me to stay in the garden. I write the numbers one to ten in the sky with a sparkler before I follow. Into the kitchen, out through the living room to the front door of our flat, which is flung open to the communal hallway. They must all be upstairs because that's where the shouting is coming from. And that's where I saw my mother going earlier when I came inside to throw away the lollipop.

Mrs. Traynor is saying bad words. There's one I haven't heard before, but I like the sound of: *slag.* I whisper the word until Teddy hammers down the stairs and spins me around by the shoulders, saying, "Outside!" He throws a bucket of sand on the bonfire and stands on the kitchen step to announce to the people in the garden that it's been wonderful but it's school tomorrow so we'd better call it a night.

When they've gone, I can make out, high in the sky, the colors of fireworks from the display at the park. It's too far away to hear the bangs and cracks over the sound of Mrs. Traynor screaming at Mr. Traynor upstairs. "Get out!" she screams. There's thundering on the stairs.

"Are Mrs. Traynor and Mr. Traynor getting a divorce?" I ask, but Teddy pushes me aside and runs out of the kitchen. I walk into the living room and sit on the arm of the sofa, where I can see into the hallway. Teddy holds Mr. Traynor by the shoulders as though they're going to hug, but then rocks his head forward and knocks him on the nose. Mrs. Traynor gallops down the stairs and pushes Teddy into our flat. He slams the door and punches it. He's breathing like a bull. He rubs his punching fist with the other palm.

When Teddy turns and sees me, he groans, so I say it's all right. "It's not, Jo-Jo Sparrow. It's not. Can you go to your bedroom? Can you stay inside, whatever you hear?"

I ask if I can play my computer game and he says I can. He goes into their bedroom and I go

to mine. When I hear him shouting, "Where are
you hiding, Mrs. fucking Bonham?" I put on my
headphones.

At bedtime, Teddy reads me a story. Afterward,
he tells me she's gone away, but not to worry. "She
ruined that family's life," he says, when he tucks me
in for the night. "I'll not let her ruin ours."

Amanda checked the date on her watch: fifth of November. She
tucked her feet up and rested her cheek on a cushion. This account of
Josie's childhood made her feel quite normal for the first time in her
life. Yes, her parents had their issues, eccentricities afforded by privilege,
but she could see now that they'd kept the worst of it behind closed
doors. Maybe that's what made Laura so remote: a habit of keeping it
inside. Ed and Josie's mother, though, acted out the whole soap opera
with Josie in the front row. But—Amanda shifted to fling her legs over
the side of the chair—this provided common ground between herself
and Josie, their shared experience of tempestuous parents. She settled
to thinking of how she could allude to what she knew without letting
on that she'd peeked at the blog.

When she woke, the framed sky was as dark as the screen of her
phone. It was almost eleven. No messages. Her feet burned with pins
and needles. She checked Josie's bedroom, but it was undisturbed, and
there was no sign of her in the rest of the apartment. She tried her number
again and it rang out. Ed wouldn't land in Zurich until morning so
she couldn't call him.

Now it's a safety issue. She got her laptop and navigated to iCloud
and Find My iPhone. She waited for their devices to load, her mind as
blurry as the spinning wheel on the screen. Josie never stayed out late
without letting someone know. She could imagine her laconic tone:
"Yeah, well, I don't need the drama, do I? I'm kind of over the rebel-
lious stage."

The Find My iPhone list appeared with Amanda's device at the top. It hadn't found Josie's or Ed's. Was that because their phones were switched off? Panic prickled her edges, like a match head running over the striker and throwing up tiny sparks. Late as it was, she'd have to call Erin.

Amanda dialed the number, and it connected on the first ring. "What?"

Amanda was caught wrong-footed by the tone, but she identified herself.

"Didn't bother to read the screen," Erin said. "I thought it was him."

"Arnault?"

"I've been trying to reach him all night. What time is it?"

"It's after eleven. Sorry to call so late, but have you seen Willow and Josie?"

"I thought they're with you? Ed's away, right?"

There was a scratch on the line, and Amanda pictured Erin clawing her own elbows. "I haven't heard from Josie since this morning."

"They must've gone to the movies. Or a friend's place. You know what they're like."

"I feel responsible, especially with Ed away."

"They'll be fine—it's Singapore. I've got to go, call coming in. It might be him."

"Okay, thanks, Erin, please let me know if—" But the line cut.

Erin was right. It was Singapore—safe little Singapore. But low crime didn't mean no crime. And what if she'd been in an accident? The hospital only had Ed's contact number, and he was on a flight to Europe . . .

She snatched up her security pass and took the lift to the swimming pool. The humid air carried threads of spiderweb that stuck to Amanda's lips as she hurried past empty sun loungers. Apart from skittish geckos, the deck was empty. She followed the orchid path around the side of the tower toward the lobby, marching up to the security desk, where a guard rose to greet her with a purposeful, "Yes, ma'am?" But she hadn't seen the girls either, and she walked Amanda back to the lift, pressed the button for the thirtieth floor, and said she would buzz if she had any news.

Home again. Amanda checked her watch and found she'd been outside for less than five minutes. And yet the space had changed. Maybe it was just the contrast with the humid night, but the apartment felt sterile and chilled, as white as a meat locker.

"Josie?" she called out. Then, quieter, she didn't know why: "Awmi?"

When there was no reply, Amanda tried Josie's number again, but it went to voice mail. She slapped her phone against the palm of her hand. *I should call the police.* But what if Josie was safe and sound at the cinema with her phone switched off? Maybe the police wouldn't consider her "missing" yet? And what if they came to the apartment to find Amanda three Merlots down, as thickheaded as she'd been the last time they came?

According to Ed, Josie had hundreds of Facebook friends, but of course they didn't post contact numbers. In any case, who would pick up at this time of night? After fruitless searching, she found herself on SOWs. Tonight they needed a champagne brunch, a chess tutor, a recipe for buttermilk. The hive mind buzzed.

It's a community. There are women dying to help. It's what they live for.

She typed in the box and hit "Send" before she could change her mind: My 17-year-old stepdaughter went out with a friend and hasn't come home. The friend is also not home. Her mum isn't too worried, but it's unlike my stepdaughter not to let me know where she is. Her father's on a flight to Europe. I don't want to overreact but I'm thinking of calling the police. Any advice?

Within seconds the comments section was bubbling with typing women.

<u>Jennifer Moran</u> *I hope your child is OK!*

<u>Fionna Stone</u> *This happened to me—I called the police and they gave my daughter a really HARD TIME!!!*

<u>Allison Ghosh</u> *Do you follow her on social media? Maybe see if she's checked in anywhere? Just a thought . . .*

<u>Nina James</u> *A 17-year-old on Facebook! Mine would rather shave her head live on Snapchat!*

<u>Allison Ghosh</u> *I didn't specify Facebook. I meant any social media.*

<u>Nina James</u> *OK, yeah, but "check in" is totally FB— we're so ancient LOL!*

<u>Allison Ghosh</u> *I think it is possible to use "check in" generically.*

<u>Tara Hussein</u> *Try to stay on topic, ladies. Amanda— what about other friends or parents? Do you have a class list from school with their contacts? I can help you ring round some people?*

<u>Jennifer Moran</u> *I'm happy to drive to her favorite haunts and look for her?*

Amanda went through and liked all their messages—irritating and touching ones alike—unsure what to say in reply. The class list was a good idea; Josie must have one. But where? Then a private message pinged on Amanda's phone.

Molly: Just saw your message on SOWs. Is she home yet? X

Amanda typed back in the negative.

Molly: Oh, no. Poor you. Do you have a number for her friend?

Amanda: I'm going to call her mother now and ask for it.

Erin's line was engaged. *Bloody Arnault.* Amanda tapped a quick text asking for Willow's number. Then she went back to Facebook. She clicked onto Josie's page—no updates—and navigated to Willow's—no updates—and sent them both private messages.

Then she replied to Molly.

Amanda: So how long do I leave it before calling the police?

Molly: My kids are so young—I don't have these issues! Is the other girl's mother not worried?

Amanda: She's going through some marital problems—not sure she's got her eye on the ball TBH.

Molly: Oh dear . . .

Amanda: I'm sure Josie just lost track of time.

Molly: Better safe than sorry . . .

Amanda: You think I should call the police?

Molly: Is this out of character?

Amanda: It really is! But then she's been upset recently bc our helper died.

Molly: OMG! When did that happen?

Amanda: Last week. She killed herself. Josie was upset. We all were. So, I don't know. Could mean she's just acting out . . . Or it could mean she's vulnerable and I should be more worried . . .

Molly: That's awful! Can't believe you didn't say something at book club!

Amanda watched the cursor blinking. Why hadn't she told the women at book club? Why hadn't she spoken about it to anyone? It was true she'd been distracted by all this worry over Ed. *But is that all?*

Molly: You still there?

The cursor blinked. Why? Why? Why?

Amanda: I was caught up in the fertility thing.

She waited for a reply, but none was forthcoming. Molly's instincts were good. Deniability wasn't plausible.

Amanda: Obviously, I feel guilty.

Molly: But why?

Amanda: She was a young girl, in my house, and I didn't protect her . . .

Molly: What from?

Amanda: I don't know. That's the point. I never really got to know her.

Molly: How long was she with you?

Amanda: Almost two years.

Molly: I'm not surprised your stepdaughter's playing up. She must be in shock.

Amanda: I feel like she's going off the rails.

Molly: Because of the helper?

Amanda: Maybe there's something else.

Molly: Such as?

The cursor blinked again: Why? Why? Why?
Maybe because her father has a side so dark I never spotted it lurking in his shadows.

Amanda: I don't want to overreact, but I think I should call the police.

The phone buzzed in her hand—Willow's number from Erin. She dialed. While she waited to connect, she wondered if her mother had fretted over her when she was a teenager. It didn't seem likely. Amanda had given up teenage rebellion quite easily; it would have taken a huge effort to top her mother's infamy.

The phone started to ring. And kept ringing. She hit redial a couple of times, and finally decided she had no choice but to call the police. After she'd explained her story and answered the officer's questions, he rang off. Amanda sat on the hard sofa to wait.

She was woken by the buzz of a hornet. First light, as thin and gray as tin. The buzz sounded again, and Amanda realized it was her phone. She pushed herself up and grimaced at her garlicky breath.

"Mrs. Bonham?" The female voice on the line sounded weary.

"Yes, speaking?"

The woman introduced herself, but Amanda didn't catch the name. Just her title—sergeant—and the fact that she was calling from the central police post.

"Is this about Josie?"

"Yes, ma'am. You can collect her from the station now, please."

"From the station?"

"Yes, ma'am. We are ready to release her."

"Is she okay? Has she been arrested?"

"She's fine, ma'am."

"Then . . . why is she there? Why didn't anyone call me?"

"We are calling you, ma'am. There is no problem. You can collect her now, please."

"But—"

And the phone went dead.

Amanda called for a taxi while she changed into a clean top and got down to the lobby just as it pulled up. At such an early hour, they cruised to the police station. As she paid the taxi and got out, another cab pulled up. Erin. A third delivered Arnault. Erin was on her phone. "But the girl is a minor," she was saying, "how can you question a child without a guardian? Her parents have rights!"

"Actually, we don't," Arnault said.

"We don't what?" Amanda asked.

"Have rights. The police can question a minor without an adult present." He shrugged. "Law of the land."

Before she could think how to respond, the doors of the police station opened. Willow came racing out, down the steps, and into her mother's arms. Josie walked behind, taking the steps in her own time. A third girl emerged. Unlike Josie and Willow, who were crumpled after the long night, this one was pristine. Her silky hair skimmed over brisk curves down to her waist.

"That's Mae," said Josie, when she reached Amanda. "She's in the year above."

Mae bounced down the steps, straight into Arnault's embrace. He rocked back to lift her off the ground, her chopstick legs dangling from black shorts whose edges were frayed like the pubic hairs she'd barely had time to grow.

"What the actual fuck?" Erin looked to her fellow women one by one for validation—Willow, then Amanda, then Josie—before turning to confront her husband. "Seriously, Arnault? Right under our noses?"

Arnault turned Mae by the shoulders into a waiting cab, which drove off into a blushing sunrise.

Chapter 25

Enclosed in the elevator at the Attica, Amanda pressed her thumb to the console, but nothing happened. "It's broken," Erin said, waving her security tag over the panel. The lift ascended with a tremble, and the women stood in silence until Amanda and Josie got out at their apartment.

Josie flicked her considerable fringe from her face. Smeared kohl eyeliner made her look both waiflike and world-weary, badass and beaten. Without any prompting, Josie launched into her defense: she and Willow had gone to a party at the house of a boy—Rafferty—whose parents were away. "I fell asleep, and the others left me to go watch a movie in the den. I woke up to the police hammering at the door." The officers had driven past earlier in the evening when a neighbor complained, but they considered it was just kids in the pool. That neighbor was always complaining. "But when an *ang moh* called at midnight to report her stepdaughter missing," Josie said, "they smelled blood."

"I was worried." Amanda felt a spark of indignation. "And the police were doing their job."

"They were determined to nail us."

"They didn't have to try too hard, did they? They'll press charges against Rafferty for the weed." Amanda winced internally at the word *weed*, which she had used perfectly naturally once upon a time, but now sounded stiff with age. "You're lucky to get away with a warning."

"They had nothing on me. I wasn't in the den. They went through my phone, but as soon as they saw I don't communicate with Rafferty—I literally don't have his number—they lost interest."

"Isn't he Willow's boyfriend?"

Josie shrugged one shoulder as if this was a matter of such triviality it deserved no words.

"Is there anything else I should know?" Amanda asked.

Josie isolated a rebel strand of curly hair from her dark halo and pulled it straight in front of her eyes. Tugged it out. "It would be better if Dad didn't find out."

"He's going to find out. And he's your father, he should know."

"It would be better for both of us if he didn't."

Amanda kept quiet, creating space for Josie to fill. The truth was here if she could only locate the strand amid the mass of silence and pluck it out: What kind of man is Ed?

Josie's eyes skittered, and for a moment it seemed she would speak. But then she muttered that she was tired.

"Are you scared, Josie?" Amanda heard herself say.

Josie wrapped the hair around her fingertip until the skin whitened. "I always win him around."

"And how do you do that?"

A laugh caught in her throat, a strangely adult sound of resignation that Amanda felt sad to hear coming from a child. "Lifetime of practice." And that shoulder roll again, as though the consequences were starting to weigh heavily.

"He's going to find out, one way or another." Amanda was pleased for once that he was traveling. It allowed time for things to calm down before he saw Josie. "I guess we can hold off until he's home. I'll explain it wasn't your fault."

"My fault?" said Josie, and she gave that laugh again. "It's *you* he's going to be mad with."

"Me?"

"You know what you did, don't you? When you called the police?" She was walking toward her room with Amanda rolling along behind her like a dropped marble.

"What did I do?"

"You ruined that family's life."

Josie's door slammed, but her words circled Amanda along with the scent of rotting jasmine. An echo from Josie's blog: her mother had *ruined that family's life*. She'd angered her husband and then she'd died. The coroner recorded a verdict of suicide, but what was that except a best guess? A stranger couldn't know what was in a dead woman's mind. Or her husband's. Amanda didn't know, and she shared his bed.

She lay down on the sofa. Ed would land in Zurich and call when he picked up her frantic messages. The impotence that came with distance would anger him. She'd have to tell him something. A partial truth. Snippets from the evening zipped past, like moments on repeat. Molly saying, "Better safe than sorry." The police sergeant: "There is no problem, ma'am." Josie: "It's you he's going to be mad with." And Erin: "Seriously, right under our noses?" This final scene played again and again. *Right under our noses?*

Erin knew about Mae. Otherwise, she would have said something like, "What are you doing with that girl?" But she hadn't been surprised, only annoyed that he was showing her up in public. *Right under our noses.*

What a hypocrite. Amanda punched a cushion into place. Erin was only concerned about keeping it quiet long enough to get out of the country with her dignity intact. Never mind poor Mae—and Willow! And now that Josie was pissed off with Amanda, it would be harder to have their talk. And Ed would come back like a Fury; the wind was still whistling through the kitchen window from his last fury. He'd ask why she hadn't had the glass replaced; the apartment was going to wrack and ruin.

But what's the point in carrying out repairs when a demolition is in progress?

Amanda wrestled with her limbs until she got comfortable. It felt like seconds later that her phone rang, but the room glared in the morning light. She pressed the mobile to her ear.

"Have you heard?" Erin's voice lilted with the same glee as when she'd pronounced Ed an abuser. Given their similar circumstances, Amanda thought there should be fellow feeling between the trailing spouses: flailing spouses. But, instead, they could be two passengers in an aircraft that was plummeting to the ground, and they'd just noticed there was only one parachute.

"Have I heard what?"

"About the photos?"

Amanda's hesitation was enough.

"I'm on my way down," Erin said.

Amanda slipped into clothes and pulled a brush through her hair. Josie's room was empty, but she answered Amanda's text right away: I'm down by the pool. Amanda peered from the living room window and picked out a sliver of a girl lying on her distinctive beach towel. When the lift chimed, Erin marched into the kitchen and accepted a glass of water. "You might want a stiff drink when you see this." She laid her device on the counter and spun it around so Amanda could see. "Willow saw this today. The photo was posted anonymously."

Amanda picked up the phone. The photo showed a girl tangled around a boy on a bed. She had one hand up to shield her face and a knee raised in defense, but there was no mistaking the identity—it was Josie.

"Taken at the party?" Amanda said.

"There are more."

Then a photo taken from a different angle: Josie lying across the bed with both legs over the side, the boy hunched between her knees. Where the first image might indicate fooling around, this one was graphic and unequivocal. Amanda shut down the phone and spun it back to Erin.

"Where were they posted?" she asked.

"On the chat forum that Josie set up herself."

"The one on the dark web?"

"Not anymore. She moved it. It's just on a normal . . . hosting . . . I don't know . . . site."

"So the whole school might have seen them?"

"The forum has been active in the past few hours, yes."

Amanda got her own phone, tapped in the website—Sexteen—and found the offending post. She scrolled past the photos and read a handful of comments—but when she felt the hot nausea of carsickness, she shut off her device.

"She's going to be mortified. Do we know who the boy is?"

"I'm not sure you've quite grasped the worst of it." Erin placed one fingertip on her phone and slid it back across the countertop to Amanda. "Look at the boys."

Amanda hadn't noticed much beyond Josie. She scrolled back to the first shot of the girl wrapped around a fair-haired boy, their skin honey-eyed by lamplight. And then that lurid picture when he was between her knees . . . except—she glanced up at Erin's sardonic face—the boy kneeling between Josie's legs had dark hair. Two different boys.

"Now do you want something stronger?" Erin asked.

Oddly, she heard in her head a snatch of a song Josie often played: "Stronger Than Me." Amanda knew she should be the stronger one, just as Amy Winehouse said, because she'd been on this earth longer than Josie. And she understood why a girl would do this to herself. She'd been there, mired in the belief that she had one thing to offer, one thing in her control, one thing that would get attention. She even had the photos in her safety-deposit box to prove it. The inviting warmth of a man's spotlight was all too tempting for someone outside in the cold, the way she'd felt after her parents' scandal. Trying to gauge her value, she had sold herself cheap. And now she heard Josie's voice: *I always win him around.*

"Are you going to tell Ed?" Erin asked.

"Can I speak to Willow?"

Erin snapped upright. "Willow wants to take a break from Josie. She finds her . . . a negative influence."

"But Rafferty is Willow's boyfriend. It was his party—"

"That boy in the picture, the blond one? That's Rafferty." Erin slid off the barstool and drained her glass before heading to the lift. "Maybe I'm jaundiced by my own messed-up marriage, but if you want an explanation for Josie's behavior, I'd suggest looking closer to home. Promiscuity—lack of self-respect—is a classic sign of abuse. I know it's hard to imagine you could be living with someone who's capable of such a thing, but look at Arnault. I did not see that coming."

"I'm sorry about Arnault."

"It's okay. I'm going to destroy him." Erin's fingers tore at an eczema patch, a prominent wristbone straining through her skin as though a tiny bald head were trapped inside. "He'll be working to pay me off until he's bones." The lift doors closed.

Amanda's phone rang, sending a jolt through her insides.

"Why didn't you tell me?" Ed's voice was a small, hard vibration of air, an arrowhead coming her way.

"I left you messages—"

"You didn't mention drugs and arrests. Fuck, Amanda!"

She hesitated, hearing incongruous cowbells and yodeling—the quaint soundtrack of the Zurich airport sky train that she remembered from their last ski trip. This time it didn't make her smile. "I wanted to tell you in person, when you called. How do you know?"

"Josie, obviously. We don't keep secrets in this family."

"She asked me not to say anything!"

"I knew something was up as soon as I heard her voice. She told me everything."

Everything? How much of everything?

"What were you thinking, calling the police?" Ed said.

"She went missing. What else was I supposed to do?"

"She's not a baby."

"And nor is she an adult. She could have been preyed on by some man—"

"What?"

Amanda started telling him about the happy couple—Arnault and Mae—but Ed interrupted: "Where is she now?"

"At the pool. I'm sure she's got her phone if you want to call."

"Just checking she is where she says she is. I have to see a client this morning, but I'm heading straight back."

Amanda closed her eyes. It used to be that Ed cutting his business trip short was a pleasure; the moment he stepped out of the lift felt like that magical hour around dusk, when the tropical air nuzzled her skin and good times were about to roll. But now his presence seemed more like the midday sun: harsh, unrelenting, volatile. She didn't know where she wanted him—at home, where he wasn't a danger to women in hotels, or away, where he wasn't a danger to Josie. *Or myself.* Bad things had happened to the last woman who got between Ed and his daughter.

"It's the first rule of living in someone else's country," Ed said. "You never get a fair deal from the police."

He would be home soon. She couldn't avoid him much longer. She put Ed on speaker and made placatory noises while finding her overnight bag. She packed for three days. Added outfits for Josie too. Then transferred cash from the belly of the ginger jar into the zippered pocket of the bag. She thought of her frozen embryos. She could feel them jostling in their tubes, too full of energy to rest, like puppies in a pet shop pawing the glass. She heard their little mewls and yaps.

"Are you there, Amanda? Are you even listening?"

"I'm here. I'm listening." She zipped up the bag just as the bedroom door swung open and Josie marched in.

"Is that him? I've been trying to call." Josie took the phone from her hands. "I just heard that Raff's father got a call from the headmaster. The police are pressing charges. Possession with intent to supply. Mandatory custodial sentence. So they've gone—the whole family."

"Gone where?" asked Amanda.

"To England. Packed their bags overnight and got the first flight out of Singapore."

No one spoke. The phone broadcast sounds from far away. Train doors giving exaggerated sighs as they had to open and close yet again. Ed's voice was a low rumble: "Now do you get it?" Amanda assumed he was speaking to her. As did Josie, who dropped the phone on the bed and left the room. "Fuck, Amanda. You ruined that family's life."

Chapter 26

Camille's hand shook as she reached for the mouse to put her computer to sleep. She didn't want anyone in the press office to read the screen over her shoulder; this Reuters News report needed to stay off their radar for a few more minutes. "But you must retract the quote, Ruth," she said into the phone, keeping her voice low but steady; whispering would only attract attention. When Ruth demurred in her little-girl tone, Camille felt her own growing harder. "Because it's not true, that's why. The quote is inaccurate and damaging. And we were *off the record*." When the journalist continued to object, Camille could think of nothing else to do except slam down the phone. So she did that. Then she stood outside Josh's office door and hauled in a deep breath. She had to tell him. Better he found out from her than someone else. She rapped three times.

"Wait!" Josh shouted from inside. "Unless it's Camille, in which case, get in here."

He already knows.

Camille went inside and closed the door. She sat on a red nylon chair at his desk, flinching when he thumped the coffee machine. It gurgled and he hit it again. He used language she never expected to hear from a diplomat, then went to the window, rubbing a coffee capsule against his thigh as though he might absorb caffeine that way.

"Ruth Chin," Josh said at last. "Reuters News Agency." His voice could have cooled the midday sun.

"I spoke to her last week."

"The *Straits Times* just called. They want a statement in response to a story Reuters published a few minutes ago, in which the British High Commission *demands* that the Singapore government upholds UK standards of human rights for maids. Direct quotes coming from this office." Josh hurled the coffee capsule across the room. Camille heard it bounce off the office door. "This is a storm of shit. A tropical typhoon of brown stuff. I have to brief the high commissioner in five minutes. In turn, he has been summoned to meet the foreign minister. Tell me that Ruth Chin plucked this quote out of the air and we can demand a retraction."

"I just called her, and she says no retraction."

"I'll deal with her editor," he said sharply. "Tell me it had nothing to do with your involvement with HELP."

"I gave her general quotes about foreign influence in domestic affairs before I knew she was working on this story. At the same time, she asked me for a contact at HELP and I put her in touch with the lawyer—"

"You spoke to Ruth Chin about HELP?"

"Off the record—"

"No such thing as off the record."

Camille pressed her lips together. Josh retrieved the coffee capsule, which he slotted into the machine, then stroked a flashing button. This time, the machine didn't dare defy him.

"You promised me," he said, watching brown stuff fill his cup. "I made it quite clear that your activities at HELP are incompatible with this job. But you used this thing with Ruth Chin to push your own agenda—"

"She misquoted—"

Josh held up one flat hand, and Camille fell silent. "Go home."

"I'll call Ruth again—"

"You're suspended until further notice. Go home."

"We were off the record. She has to honor that—"

"There is no honor, Camille." Josh took his cup. "No honor at all." The phone on his desk rang and he swore. "It's the high commissioner. Go on: out." She scurried from his office to a soundtrack of her boss groveling. "We'll have to ride this one out, sir," he was saying. "Even if I could get a retraction, which I doubt, we have to consider that it might draw more attention to the story . . ."

In the bathroom, Camille shut herself in a cubicle and gave up. She'd humiliated herself, her boss, and the high commissioner. It took a lot of pressure to make her cry, but when the tears fell they were as heavy as diamonds. Camille caught every one in her hands. Then she lowered the toilet lid and sat down.

With a wad of toilet paper pressed to her eyes, she considered how she'd run and run--she'd run seven thousand miles to Singapore—but the past followed like a mugger, sneaking along, ready to pounce when she least expected it. Camille had gone from obsessing about her parents to obsessing about helpers.

She left the cubicle, splashed her face, and went back to her desk. She addressed an email to Sharmila Menon and the board at HELP, apologizing for the short notice but informing them that she had to stop volunteering with immediate effect. Hit "Send." Then she forwarded the same email separately to Josh to show him she'd resolved the conflict of interest.

As she handed in her security pass to the receptionist, she looked back over her shoulder to see the pressroom through the glass wall. It was time to sort herself out, get her head straight so she could do her job properly. She'd have one last go at resolving what happened to her parents; she'd track down the paperwork on their yacht and approach Edward Bonham once more. Somehow, he was part of the puzzle. If she applied enough pressure, he'd crack and she might be able to work out from his broken edges where he slotted into the picture.

Chapter 27

In the future: Eight Days Until D-Day
In the past: Thirteen Days That Made Me Me
Post 5 of 13: Loop-the-Loop

I've got the Cessna on long finals toward JFK when the doorbell rings. Teddy shouts at me to answer it, but there's a 747 coming up behind me—which is stupid, air traffic control would never order that—and when I try to make a steep bank out of the stack the joystick gets too sensitive in the side wind and I start pitching. The doorbell rings again and I hear a key turning in the lock. I stand up, hit pause.

Teddy's bedroom door opens and he comes out, textbook in hand. He's got air law and meteorology exams tomorrow, that means rules-for-planes and the weather. He looks at the front door and at me and back at the front door. A woman comes in and stops in the hallway. She doesn't say hello, but she walks forward and stands her suitcase beside the coatrack. She's wearing clothes they sell at Camden market. She looks at me and starts to

Jo Furniss

cry, not making any noise, just like her eyes are overflowing.

Teddy turns away and rests his forehead on the doorframe.

"You've shot up, Josie," she says.

I don't know what I'm supposed to say. Teddy might be angry if I'm nice. Or if I'm not. Out of the corner of my eye, the computer goes onto screen saver; a ball bounces from side to side, trying to squeeze itself into a corner.

My mother is not well, that's why she went away. She looks fine now, though, apart from the crying. Her hair is as thick and dark as mine. Or mine is like hers. Now I know why Teddy made me cut it. He said it was because he didn't know how to tie it back, that we had to make adjustments for not having a mother. Teddy comes over. He takes the joystick from my hand and puts it on the coffee table. His hands gather up my shoulders and he bends to whisper in my ear. "Say hello, Jo-Jo Sparrow."

So I walk forward a step and she rushes in, her patchwork trousers snapping between her knees, and hugs me so tight I can hardly breathe. She takes a long sniff, as though she has a cold, and I realize she's smelling me. When she lets go, I wobble on the spot. Something has dug into my chest, and I see her long necklace, with a pendant shaped like a scorpion. There's an angry red dent in my skin, as though I've been stung.

"You could have phoned," Teddy is saying.

"It's my house."

"After all this time . . . think of the child."

"My lawyer says I shouldn't let myself be pushed out of the family home. It can be used against me."

"Your *lawyer*?" Teddy turns around and slaps the joystick off the coffee table onto the sofa. Then he turns back to me and does the shoulder thing again. "Can you play in your room, Jo-Jo Sparrow? I need to speak to her."

"But I'm on long finals."

He smiles with his nice teeth. "Just half an hour. Then we'll land somewhere tricky. Tibet."

"Saba!"

"Dicing with death, you are. All right, Saba. I need to sort this out first, okay?"

I go to my bedroom, close the door, and then let it open an inch.

"Josie, close the door."

I close the door. Then I jump onto the bed, climb out the front window, run around the side of the house, and hunker down underneath the living room window, which is wide open.

"You're fucking kidding me." Teddy's voice. "No contact for a year and then *custody*?"

"I'm not supposed to discuss details with you. My lawyer said."

"Let me get this straight—your lawyer thinks you should move back into my home—"

"It's our house."

"The house currently occupied by your estranged husband and abandoned daughter—"

"I never abandoned her—"

"Maybe you should have told her that. So, your lawyer wants you to move back into *this* house, with me, but we're not allowed to discuss what's happened? Where you've been? Who you've been with? Josie had her birthday and Christmas without you, with no idea where you were—"

"I sent postcards."

"Yes, the postcards—very dramatic . . . We read them over breakfast, when I was getting her ready for school each day."

"How is school?"

"Just fuck off."

There's a crash, a splintering crunch, that sounds like a plate or a mug smashing. Then it goes quiet. Maybe they're looking for the dustpan and brush? I should tell them it's under the sink. I wonder where they're standing. Is Teddy pulling his hair like he does when he gets angry? Saying "fuck off" means he's angry. I get onto my knees in the flower bed and inch upward.

"Where are you going to sleep? We only have two bedrooms," Teddy says.

"I'll move in with Josie," my mother says.

"She can come in with me."

"She's too old to sleep in a bed with her father."

"Don't you dare insinuate—"

"I'll sleep on the sofa then."

The paint on the windowsill splinters under my fingertips as I pull myself up to peep inside. Teddy sits slumped on a chair at the dining table, his thumbs sticking through his hair like goat horns. My mother comes to stand at the window. She lowers her eyes and sees me, crouching in the roses. Her mouth smiles. She reaches through the window and pulls me to my feet, hugs my head to her belly. She smells strange, foreign, like one of her postcards; touched by other people's fingers. When Teddy sees me peeking around her stomach, he makes a droning noise in the back of his throat, like the little Cessna fighting the wind on its long finals.

Amanda stood on the back balcony, phone in one hand and a cigarette in the other. Once upon a time—in her London life—she allowed herself one a night. Back when she thought she knew stress. Now, she gulped the first hit to her core—almost whooping into the night with the rush of it—and found herself taking drag after drag until she flicked the butt into the darkness in an arc of orange sparks.

There was a part of her—she had to admit—that wanted to eavesdrop on Ed's relationship with his first wife. He never mentioned her, except in curt confirmation of the facts. As clinical as a surgeon reporting the condition of a patient. *My wife died.* Emotion so deeply buried, it had compacted to coal that fueled Amanda's curiosity.

If she confronted Josie about the blog, she might stop writing it, and Amanda would lose these insights. There was a new drawing today. A goat, so intricately shaded it looked alive. Josie promised eight more installments about "Teddy." Just over a week until Amanda knew what Ed had done to his wife, the mother of his child. Amanda stroked the goat's horned head with a fingertip.

She looked up from the screen and let out a startled scream—a figure in the doorway—her cigarette packet slapped to the tiles. Ed stepped over the threshold from the kitchen with an advance that pushed her back against the parapet. He caught her by the biceps.

"Did you know about the photos?" His eyes and teeth were white in the darkness.

"She didn't want me to tell you—"

"You knew?" Spittle flew.

"Yes, but—"

"How dare you!" Ed leaned against her, and the edge of the parapet slid from Amanda's shoulder blades to beneath her ribs. She teetered for a moment before he loosened his grip. Her feet found the tiles as he stepped back, kicking her cigarette packet aside.

"You stink," he said. "I never married a smoker. Or a liar."

"Did Josie tell you?" she asked.

"Erin. In the lobby. My fucking neighbor told me there are photos of my daughter all over the Internet—"

"I was going to tell you as soon as you got home—"

"Where is she?"

"She went to the library."

"You let her go out?"

"What do you mean 'let her'? I have no authority. And you're the one who lets her do whatever she wants. Do you want me to mother her or not mother her? I have no idea what you want."

"Sometimes, Amanda, I don't want any of it!" And he was gone.

Amanda peeled her back off the parapet and picked up her crushed cigarettes. *He was angry,* she told herself, *he wouldn't have let me fall.* But there was a thin line—so thin it was invisible—between falling and not falling.

Chapter 28

Camille made her way through Chinatown's night market toward a *kopitiam* she wanted to visit. Her thumb flicked the phone ringer. Was it too late to call Edward Bonham? She'd been trying him all day; he must be flying. Busy, unlike Camille, who was dangerously underemployed after being sent home by Josh.

At the old-time café, she got herself a green tea and a seat. From her Filofax, she pulled out the photo of her parents. The doorway was key—the alignment of arch and pillar. This was not the place. She slipped the photo away and sipped her bitter drink. Then she picked up her phone and dialed before she could change her mind.

As soon as Edward Bonham spoke, his clipped speech told Camille he was drunk.

"Where are you?" he said.

She hesitated. "Chinatown. I'm on my way home soon. I wanted to ask you—"

"I wanted to ask you something too. But tell me, where's home?"

"River Valley."

"I'm on Mount Faber. I can see all the way to the ships. Lovely night for a walk."

"I can imagine."

"Don't imagine. You should see it for yourself. Did you know some plants release perfume at night?"

"I didn't know that." Camille smiled behind her hand. A long pause was filled with the noisy fervor of nighttime insects. She added: "Watch out for snakes."

"Why did you call me Teddy?"

Camille shifted in her seat. "Slip of the tongue."

"Why don't you come for a walk and tell me?"

A walk? At night? Was he serious?

"Are you there, Cami?"

Her brother called her Cami. The familiar name flaked away a layer of intimacy like cheap varnish.

"Walking in the park at night doesn't sound safe." She glanced up and saw an old lady at the neighboring table, watching her with open interest. "I saw a cobra the other day." She was babbling now. "Jumped right over it."

"I'll look after you."

She adjusted the phone closer to her mouth. Under the marble table, her feet pressed onto the tiles, gaining purchase. "I'm heading home," she said.

"You could stop off on the way."

"It's not on the way."

There was a long pause during which she wondered if Ed was really worried about her calling him Teddy or if—

"I can come to Chinatown," he said. "There are places we could meet."

Ah, she thought, wondering when Edward Bonham had pegged her as a woman who might be interested in a dangerous liaison. "No, thanks."

"I won't ask again. But if you ever want to—"

"Good night, Ed."

Camille ended the call and snatched up her drink, shouldering her way into the crowd. It must have been the first time he unleashed his smile, when he startled her into taking a moment too long to reply, a moment during which her eyes slid to his shoulders, and she could almost feel them bunching beneath her palms. Edward Bonham was the kind of man who missed nothing that might be to his advantage. He had slipped that moment into his pocket for later. He was patient, she had to give him that. And confident. He'd derailed her from what she wanted to ask: if he had really recognized her parents; if they had met before.

She wondered if this kind of invite worked in business hotels, if that's where he honed his skills. And she considered what a hookup in the park would entail. She drained the iced tea, chilling herself with every gulp and every thought of what Ed planned to do to her in the dark of the forest.

Chapter 29

Interpol. Amanda struggled to remember the name but then grasped it like a mosquito in the air. *International crime is investigated by Interpol.* Unlike Ed, who never suffered jet lag, she was wading through treacle after losing last night to Josie's antics. Ed and Josie were finally home, tired from either reading or whisky. But Amanda couldn't bring herself to lie next to her husband. Not even after he apologized for the "scene"—as he called it—on the balcony.

Instead, she went to the balcony, the night air bloated by a downpour. The glare from the skyline turned low clouds red and yellow, like a highway at a standstill, blurred taillights in the rain. She'd read an article claiming that air con was heating up the island and, like the apocryphal frogs in hot water, everyone was boiling without complaint. Was that what had happened to her too? Like a domestic abuse victim, she had accepted the incremental advances of Ed's bad behavior? It would explain why she'd become so inert. That and the fact she had nowhere else to go. A nasty voice teased as though she were her own playground bully: *No one would miss you.* Unlike Laureline Mackenzie, whose family went looking for her in Tokyo, no one would notice that Amanda Bonham was gone.

She let her self-pity burn off and rubbed her upper arms, still tender from where Ed had grabbed her, here on this balcony, the place where another woman had died. A woman who had Ed's pills in her room, who might have been pregnant with his child.

Enough.

Amanda went back to the chill of the kitchen and let the glass door slam. Her bag was packed and ready to go. But running away was also a risk; abusive men don't let women leave. And Josie would be left alone. Their embryos would die. She had to stay until she knew for sure what Ed had done. Who he really was.

So, Interpol. *International crime is investigated by Interpol.*

She got her laptop. Opened their website. Terrorism. Cybercrime. Drug trafficking. On the top right of the page was a link to Missing Persons. There on the front page: Laureline Mackenzie. Amanda read the facts she already knew by heart. Below the headline were thumbnail pictures of hundreds of other people. She clicked through to the search page, selected "female" and an age range of 17–20. Search: 159 results. Eighteen pages of lost women. If she called Interpol with a handful of suspicions, what would they say? *We're drowning in lost women; come back with evidence.* Or maybe it would be like calling the police when Josie went missing, and she only brought down a whole heap of trouble.

Interpol sought a woman in Jamaica, aged eighteen. A woman in Chile, aged eighteen. What was it about eighteen? Laureline Mackenzie and the Brazilian dancer had both been eighteen. She picked another page. More women in Jamaica; Ed never went there, thank goodness. Why didn't the authorities do something about their missing women? Or had they grown used to it too, like frogs in hot water? And then she had it, the thought bubbling up from her mind: Awmi's real age was eighteen.

Amanda's spine bristled as though someone was behind her. Ed was in bed, asleep, but she felt his darkness enter the room. The attacks she'd read about online were remote events in exotic locations. But Awmi had been here. Amanda had found her ruined body.

Her feet made kissing noises on the marble as she walked to their bedroom. Ed was dead still. Even defenseless and prone, he looked forceful. His limbs bronze against white sheets. She watched his skin writhe with perpetually moving shadows thrown by the tide. The death of Awmi—if Amanda were to add her name to the list—meant that Ed had brought his violence home like herpes from a hooker. Amanda had detached her husband from the other Ed who existed abroad. But they were one and the same.

Ed, whose wife died. Whose helper died. Whose visits to foreign cities coincided with more deaths. Whose daughter was taking a slow swan dive. Whose second wife was nursing bruises and questioning if it was safer to stay or go. Who knew she ought to report her suspicions to the police . . .

But what would happen then? Would the Singapore police arrest him? Or wash their hands of it and deport him? How long before they ejected her and Josie—their residency dependent on his work permit?

She hugged her goose-bumped shoulders. The marble floor felt cold even though the air outside shimmered with heat. Everything in Singapore felt artificial, fake, a distortion of nature. She returned through the massive lounge, where long windows that didn't open kept her trapped: outside while inside. She threw herself onto the sultry balcony, where heat beat around her like a pulse. It was uncomfortable, but it was real. She curled onto Awmi's bare mattress, a hint of bleach acrid in her throat, and finally slept . . .

. . . Badly. A mosquito found her at dawn. She clapped it between her palms and drew the hollow victory of her own blood. Cold pricks rose up around her ankles like echoes of its last laugh. The hair around her forehead crackled with dried sweat as she pushed her torso up from the sagging bed. A mirror over the sink showed a face so puffed up by humidity it looked like a pink frog. Amanda let herself into the kitchen and watched the sky, awash with watery clouds like soapsuds sluicing the deck of a ship. Way below, the blue envelope of the swimming pool opened up like an invitation, and she felt a pull to freedom. She put her flat palm on the smashed glass and found it as cool as water.

"Don't jump." Ed was behind her. "Mozzie bit your face." Amanda raised her hand to the spot, like covering an exposed breast. "You're up early," he said, pouring milk into a cereal bowl from a great height without spilling a drop.

"Couldn't sleep."

Ed watched her from across the kitchen while he ate. "You look a bit . . . puffy."

"I don't feel good."

"And you're quiet."

She shrugged.

"Are you pissed off with me? About Josie? Or the window? Or the balcony? Or am I under suspicion because what's-his-name, Arnault, is dicking about with a schoolgirl? Have you had one of those dreams where I'm shitting in your best shoes?"

Amanda felt her arms fold, then realized how defensive she looked and unfolded them. She looked out the window for a long moment, and when she looked back at Ed, he said, "You are pissed off with me."

"You seem to think this is funny."

"None of it's funny." He got up and clattered his bowl and spoon into the sink. "I feel like we're in free fall." He came and stood in front of her, spreading his legs on either side of hers and gathering her torso into his arms. He pressed his face against her lank hair and spoke right into her ear. "We're not like Willow's parents, Amanda. Their problems are not our problems. I know I'm away a lot, and it takes a leap of faith to trust each other, but it's worth it, isn't it, for what we've got?" He levered himself back so that she was at arm's length and locked eyes. His intensity made hers water. "Me and you. And Josie. Don't cry, for Christ's sake, I'm telling you I love you here."

Amanda looked down at his feet bracketing hers. Questions burned inside her throat. She couldn't hold them in. Something had to come out. Anything.

"Do you go to strip clubs?" Her throat contracted around the last word, trying to swallow it back.

"What?" His hands were on her upper arms again, paining her subterranean bruises.

"There was this photo posted on Facebook the other day—"

"Not Singapore Overseas Witches." Ed turned away to the counter, snatching up his key fob.

"There was a photo of a bloke dancing with a stripper. Someone's husband. It got me thinking . . . I'd rather know if you go to that kind of place, then there's no misunderstanding if someone spots you and—"

"You women! You're like the Taliban morality squad."

"That's—"

"It's not. Whatever you're going to say, it's not justified. It's shit. Sometimes my clients want to go out. They're spoiled, rich bastards—99 percent men—who flash their cash. If there's one thing these people teach me, it's that money does not buy taste. They want to drink whisky in the Four Floors."

"Is that a club?"

"Four Floors of Whores. You know it—Orchard Towers—we went there once."

Orchard Towers. *Four Floors of Whores.* She forgot people called it that.

"I bloody hate the place." Ed's face twisted as though his words made a bad smell. "All these women swarming me as if I'm a wallet made of meat. It's . . . degrading."

"So why do you go?"

"Where do you think all this comes from?" He threw up his arms like a worshipper. "This is what it takes. A bit of sacrifice. From both of us." His arms slapped back down to his sides.

"I wasn't accusing you."

"Yes." Ed took three strides across the white floor and kissed her, crushing her lips against her teeth. "You were." He strode out into the lounge without looking back. "And for fuck's sake, call the management office and get them to replace that broken window before it shatters and tears you to pieces."

She washed the breakfast things, feeling the world's dank morning breath through the hole pierced in the window. With soapy hands, she chased ants across the work surfaces until she lifted the coffee machine and found a writhing mass of them underneath. Her phone buzzed with Ed's number. She took a breath and picked up.

"Hey."

"I booked us a last-minute trip. Let's get Josie out of Singapore and give us some time together."

"Doesn't she have school?"

"She's suspended until Friday. But exams finished today and there'll be a party, and I want her out of that scene. So I got us a lovely suite at Cuti Island, overlooking the South China Sea. Just us. No strippers. Car coming at four. All right?"

What could she say? "All right."

"Thank fuck for that."

Chapter 30

Amanda stood on the end of a wooden jetty, two hours' drive into Malaysia, its planks shifting under the weight of passengers as they boarded the last launch of the day. A sea breeze pawed her skirt. Diesel on the water made greasy rainbows.

"Coming?" The plank bucked as Ed arrived with a weekend bag in each hand. "Josie left her book in the car. I sent her back for it." He slid one hand around Amanda's hips. "Hoping we can snatch some romantic time."

Amanda raised a hand to block the sun from her eyes as she looked into his face. "Josie's struggling. You need time together."

"She's all right now; she's away from those boys."

"It started before that party. The suspension from school—"

"That was nonsense."

"She's either locked in her room or at the library. I know what it feels like to be alone—"

"She's coming." Ed smiled down the jetty as his daughter ran toward them, her little weight sending the structure into a precarious dance.

"We're about to crumble into the sea." Josie grinned behind cat-eye sunglasses. Ed gave Amanda a significant glance: *She doesn't seem to be struggling.*

"Then let's get off this jetty and onto the boat." He took Amanda's shoulder and turned her toward the launch.

"Yeah, let's get going," Josie said, "so I can be a gooseberry all weekend."

Ed pinched Josie's bottom as she walked past. "Goose for a gooseberry!"

The jetty pitched Amanda forward. That pinch was a rare moment of physical contact between Ed and his daughter. They didn't cuddle or kiss good night or hold hands. In the kitchen they took opposite routes around the island counter, like two figures in a cuckoo clock who emerge daily to dance. Was it weird that father and daughter never touched? She thought of Erin's insinuations. Could such an absence be evidence of something else being present?

The launch chugged out of the harbor. The Malaysian rain forest hung in a long, brooding fringe—like Josie's bangs—that flopped up the coastline as far as the eye could see. Singapore was tucked around one corner, out of sight but not out of mind. They reached open water, and the driver gunned the engine so they skittered across the flat sea. Soon, an island arose, a green mass of trees and a pale curve of beach. Finally, another wooden jetty belonging to the resort, in better repair than the one at the government-run port.

"Welcome to Cuti Island!"

Children stampeded ashore. Several men in batik uniforms jumped down to relieve them of their luggage. Ed threw his shoes onto the pile of bags and said, "I don't intend to wear them again for the next two days."

Josie pulled off her Converses. "Race you to the beach!" They clattered along the pier and jumped onto the sand. Amanda gathered the last of their belongings, allowed the captain to hold her elbow as she stepped onto the jetty, and followed a plump receptionist who inquired after her crossing, her car journey, her credit card. She was led away to take care of formalities, feeling like the mother of two kids playing in the sand while the sun went down.

Amanda woke the next morning to find herself alone. The ceiling fan lumbered around with a whine that in the night had sounded like a baby's cry. Ed had been restless too; in the darkest hour, he flung his arm onto her neck so that she jerked away and slid to the floor. She'd stayed down on the gnarled floorboards, ear pressed to a gap through which she could hear the ocean. Instead of relaxing her, the seawater moved in surreptitious rushes, and she imagined it eroding their stilts until the whole lofty house fell.

When Ed settled, she'd curled fetal on the mattress. At some point, she slept. Now, the sun was high. Wrapping herself in the sheet, she saw a double kayak slide past the window with Ed and Josie paddling in sync.

Their breakfast was being picked over by mynah birds. As she poured coffee, the kayak thumped the stilts. Ed and Josie climbed onto the deck and shook themselves off like puppies.

Ed sat, and the birds scattered. "Happy?"

"Feels like a different world to Singapore."

"It used to take people time to travel. Three months sailing from London to Singapore. Time to adjust." Ed sipped coffee, watching fishermen putter past the reef. "Nowadays, we step through a door from one reality to another—summer to winter, east to west, the wardrobe to Narnia. Our bodies can take it, but the mind . . ."

Amanda held her cup to her lips, breath rippling the surface as she watched Ed's profile against the crisp ocean. He might have been addressing the horizon for all he seemed aware of their presence.

"Every time I fly," he went on, "I feel like I leave part of myself behind. A shadow that carries on living my normal life."

"That's creepy," Josie said.

He spun on his seat to face her. "The view made me poetic. This is fucking paradise. Isn't it, Jo-Jo?"

"It's fucking paradise." She wrapped a towel around her and tucked in the end. "Is there Wi-Fi?"

"Over by the bar." Ed picked up a croissant and pointed the sharp end along the beach. "But the villa's refreshingly unplugged. So we can talk instead."

Josie reached for her phone and ostentatiously switched it off. "Should we be poetic, like . . . I am the eye of the hurricane, moving in silence, hidden amid the distraction of the storm? Or however it goes."

"I'd rather talk about your birthday." Ed followed this statement with a long draft of coffee, pleased with the effect of his drama as Josie bounced in her chair.

"You'll be eighteen," Amanda said, her voice as hollow as the kayak bumping in the waves.

"If you're thinking about my birthday already, you must be planning something big."

Ed picked a lychee and ripped the spikes apart to extract its gonad-shaped core. He popped it into his mouth and said around its bulk, "It's secret. Amanda doesn't know."

"Will she be there?" Josie glanced between them.

"It's something you and I have to do alone."

"In Singapore?"

"I'll take you to my special place."

"Is it dangerous?"

"It's worth the risk. You'll be free from this earthly realm."

"Sinister . . ." Josie scrunched up her shoulders. "Please tell me it's scuba diving?"

"Not down. Up." Ed split the red flesh of another lychee. "To the heavens."

"What is it?" She pulled her legs up to her chest and rocked on the chair.

He spat a seed on the deck and rolled his eyes. "Come on, Josie. I've been looking forward to this moment. Try to keep up. It's something you've been asking for. Our guilty pleasure since you were little."

Josie's feet slammed onto the planks as she clutched the table.

"Something I've been practicing a lot recently . . ." he prompted.

"Flying? You're giving me flying lessons?" Josie threw herself back in her chair. "What do you think about that, Amanda?" She looked triumphant.

"I think"—Amanda watched Ed hold slippery fruit between his teeth—"your father has been plotting meticulously for some time."

"True." He spoke out of one side of his mouth, staring out to sea again. "I've tested a few locations, and Zurich is perfection. We'll do it there." He pointed to a distant aircraft scratching a white line across the sky. "I feel like a priest before a baptism. It'll be exhilarating."

Wooden footsteps sounded, and two waiters in batik uniforms arrived. "Clear for you?" They indicated the breakfast things.

Ed got up and dived from the terrace into the sea. "You coming?" he called out when he surfaced, water quivering in his hair. Josie threw down her napkin and went after him. Amanda picked up a silver dome and placed it over her breakfast plate.

"You don't like?" The waiter's eyebrows crossed in concern over her untouched egg.

"It's gone cold." She picked up a drinks coaster, flicking the edge of the cardboard just like she'd done earlier that week to the hotel key card from Zurich that she found hidden in Ed's suit.

Chapter 31

Neuroscience is a detective story, Camille read on her smartphone while hanging on to a leather strap on the bus. *As we try to regain memories, we look for clues to uncover the background to a case.* Except it wasn't a "case." It was her life, her childhood. The more she could glean from the primary source of her own memory, the more she could get out of Edward Bonham.

She scanned the article until she got to a part about childhood amnesia. The phrase "parenting style" caught her eye. *While "pragmatic" mothers focus on instructions that help a child perform a task, "elaborative" mothers construct narratives around childhood experiences.* She wondered what kind of mother hers had been, although she might as well wonder about Lani because she'd spent so much time with the helper. *Research shows that an "elaborative" style results in enhanced long-term recall of detailed memories.* The article didn't state what happened when any style of parenting stopped at the age of ten.

Blank condo windows blurred past until Camille pressed the red button to request her stop. The bus released her into midday air as stodgy as muffin dough. She hurried along the pavement past the British High Commission, stepping into the road where rain trees burst through the concrete. Along the side street that led to Tanglin Green, the sun stabbed down. She wrestled free a giant leaf of a taro plant and held it over her head like a parasol. She and Collin had loved hiding under these plants; elephant ears, Lani called them. *You see,* Camille thought, *memories are there if I can catch them.*

She chased other moments around her mind. A garden party when she drank gin by mistake, an older girl who didn't want to play, a nest of baby cobras that someone took away to release in the forest. She drew in a sharp breath, as though one of the snakes had turned on her; no one rescued cobras. They must have been slaughtered. Here was another invisible layer between herself and the truth: childhood ignorance.

She was too unreliable a witness to shed light on what had happened to her parents. And yet a sputtering light bulb was all she had to go by.

That, and Edward Bonham.

The problem was, Camille thought as she flung aside the jungle umbrella when she reached Tanglin Green, she didn't trust Edward Bonham. And she didn't trust herself around Edward Bonham.

At the compound gates, a thin gruel of sweat trickled down her spine. She closed her eyes. Smell, she'd read, was the best trigger for memories. Fish out a smell and it should come with a memory attached, like a dancing minnow on a line.

Camille breathed. She smelled traffic fumes and the drainage channel. She drew Singapore in deeper. Pool chemicals, rain-soaked earth, *roti prata.* Smells flitted through her mind in a zoetrope of sensation, but she might as well be illiterate because she didn't have the words to describe the effect—to describe her own life. When she opened her eyes again, they were wet.

At the gateway, she stopped before the barrier. An elderly man in uniform got to his feet in the guardhouse and came out.

"Good morning, miss. Are you visiting?" His eyes were very bright.

"Good morning, uncle. May I ask how long you have worked here?"

"I been here one year, miss."

Camille looked over the red barrier to where the neat-edged tarmac ran between the houses to a stand of rain forest beyond.

"Can I help you with something?" There was a slight edge of impatience in his voice now. He was an old man forced into the midday sun. "Visiting a friend, is it?"

If Camille could get inside and walk around, she knew she would recognize her house. "She lives in this block to the left . . ."

"Okay, you find her. Just go." The guard turned his bent back and pressed a button inside the hut to raise the barrier even though she could easily walk around it. With the guard's eyes on her back, she strode down the road and veered confidently off to the left. Once out of sight of the gatehouse, she stopped. Road noise receded behind the mass of trees. The houses were built around a kind of village green, which boasted a communal swimming pool. That was new. In the middle of the school day the pool lay undisturbed, swimming only with clouds. Forest cicadas greeted her with a squee of delight.

The new pool disoriented her, but she knew her childhood home had backed onto the rain forest, which put it on the other side of the green. She walked quickly under the covered walkway, not wanting to be approached by residents. The houses were the same as ever. She could feel the cool metal of the window latch in her palm, wrenching it open to yell at Collin. She knew instinctively that it was possible to drop from a bedroom window onto the corrugated iron roof of the covered walkway and shin down the pillar to the ground. And then she knew that her house must be at the end of the row: the only place where the walkway ran directly beneath a bedroom window. So there it was. Her old home. Lani should be crouched on the stoop, waiting to pick up the schoolbag that Camille would fling aside in her haste to beat Collin to the fresh gingerbread biscuits cooling in the kitchen. How they'd taken Lani for granted! Her patience with their impatience, her sweet nature, her affection.

Camille drew another sharp breath. But, of course, Lani had been doing a job. Like the memory of the cobras, Camille readjusted to an adult point of view. She didn't doubt that her nanny's warmth had been genuine, but maybe Lani needed hugs in lieu of cuddling her own children. Perhaps the attachment to Camille and Collin was compensation for raising her own family via the money she sent home. Maybe her devotion reassured her that she wasn't a bad mother.

Bold with adrenaline, Camille walked up to an open window and peeked into the living room. This had been her home, and she still felt a kind of ownership. Birthday parties and sleepovers. Family dinners and film nights. Plaiting her mother's hair while her father threw a Frisbee with Collin.

Something like that. She scratched a prickle of sweat on the back of her neck; she'd thought that once she was here, seeing it with her own eyes, there'd be a gush of memories. All she got was a trickle.

She pushed herself away from the window and followed the concrete walkway to the rear of the gardens. A chain-link fence, swamped by creepers, divided the homes from the rain forest.

The garden behind her old house was smaller than she remembered. The land seemed to shift under her feet, shrugging off its childhood dimensions and resizing to adult scale. The two images—now and then—overlapped in her mind. She remembered columns of ants churning up rivers of loose soil like valleys seen from the sky; seedpods that rooted with supernatural speed; bold macaques that Lani kept from the kitchen with well-aimed ice cubes; and stiff grass that left Camille scratching herself bloody even while she planned her next adventure.

A sharp rustle snatched Camille's attention to the forest. A jungle fowl flapped onto the fence, its iridescent tail gleaming. There'd been no fence when she lived here. In fact, she recalled, they'd trespassed into the rain forest so often there was a rough pathway into the trees. They'd always wanted a tree house but only managed a lean-to that her mother feared would harbor snakes. They'd tortured her with their wandering. She'd worried about the swimming pool too. Ah, yes! There'd been a swimming pool. Right in the garden. Aboveground, with a wooden deck built around it—and that's where they found the nest of cobras!

Camille walked closer to the fence as though she could sneak up on the memory and spy it in its native habitat. She remembered a garden party. Voices laughing and beer cans fizzing. Smoke from the grill. Sausages spurting fat when she stuck in her fork and ketchup licked off her chin. Heat that boiled over inside her body. She'd wanted to swim, but her mother didn't like her to swim alone. *Even great swimmers can get a bang on the head!*

"But I'm hot!" Camille's indignation was feverish.

"Call Collin."

"He's with his friend. It's not fair, I don't have anyone to play with. I'm going in!"

"You need someone to watch you."

"I'll watch the pool"—a man's voice.

From her vantage point by the fence, the scene played out; *then* overlaid onto *now* like the shadow puppets that had decorated her childhood bedroom.

"You don't have to do that," Mother told the man. "Cami can wait."

"I might dip my feet." He laughed. "I'm roasting."

Mother dug a beer from the cooler and pressed it into the man's hand while she bent and whispered into Camille's ear: *No splashing, no screaming, five minutes only. He's here to talk with Daddy.* Then Camille was free to grab her savior's arm and drag him in her wake, her mother and the other women cheering—for him, Camille saw now through her adult filter, not for the excited girl but for the handsome man who was sweet with children. What woman doesn't cheer for that?

She let go only when she was sure he wouldn't change his mind, and then she raced up the steps, smashed through the safety gate, and leaped into the simmering air. They say anticipation is already happiness, but her relief as she was swallowed up by the water exceeded all expectation. She stayed at the bottom, the sun's rays skittering like fireflies over her skin, until the man's feet appeared, dark and wiggling, making her laugh out wobbly bubbles that she chased to the surface.

She hadn't meant to splash him. She heard her mother's voice again quite clearly as she leaned over the garden fence, peering into her childhood. "No splashing!" But the refreshing water had filled her with voltage, and she rocketed to the surface, triggering a curling wave. She watched, useless to stop it, as the wave rolled around the rim of the pool, gathering size and pace until it washed over the man's trousers, his shirt, even splashing his face.

He had smiled and told her not to cry, but all these years later her skin burned again with shame and panic because she had soaked the guest who came to speak to Daddy. She remembered the rough towel in her hand, his wet hair between her fingers as she scrubbed him, the sound of his laughing protest. And she remembered his face emerging from the cloth: damp, ruffled, but smiling—thank goodness, smiling. She remembered his eyes as he promised not to tell her mother. She remembered his face. Edward Bonham's smiling face.

Chapter 32

"Is that a Sea Breeze?" Amanda pointed at Josie's drink, wedged into the sand beside her rattan mat. Amanda settled onto a sun lounger, and Josie closed her laptop.

"Dad said I could." Josie picked pineapple off the rim of the glass and sucked it into her mouth with a soft pop.

"Vodka in the middle of the afternoon. You'll be asleep by dinnertime."

"Surprised you're not on the frozen margaritas yourself." Josie waved her hand along the beach bar to indicate that everyone else was getting tipsy.

"I've already got a headache."

Josie squirmed around in a crackle of snapping fibers. "You're not pregnant, are you?"

"No! God, no."

Josie turned back to the sea, pulling her gleaming white baseball cap down to touch the top of her glasses. She licked the corners of her lips in her feline way and said, "You'd make a good mother."

"I hope I get the chance." As soon as the words left her mouth, Amanda wanted to bury them in the sand. Was she supposed to have said that she considered herself a mother already—a stepmother to Josie? Or would that be overstepping the mark?

"You're not distracted like those mothers who have stuff going on." Josie's voice was nonchalant, but her lips remained parted, eyeteeth showing. She dug at the cuticle of one thumbnail with the other. "I don't suppose Dad's keen."

"What makes you say that?"

"Well . . ." She scooped up white sand and let it run from her fist like an hourglass. "I guess he had enough with me. Being a handful."

"He's never described you like that—"

"He had to look after me when she had her breakdown. And then after she died."

Amanda waited, but Josie was silent. "He wanted to look after you; he's your father."

"It was hard for him. Everyone wondering why his wife killed herself, what drove her to it. As though someone else must have climbed into the driver's seat and taken over her controls. Which is stupid because then it would be murder, right, not suicide?" Josie sucked pineapple bits through her straw. "He gave up a lot for me. So maybe that's why he's not sure about having another child."

Amanda reached for her own drink and drained it, her mouth as dry as sand. *Since when is he "not sure" about having a child?* Stopping fertility treatment was temporary—that was what he said—until she recovered from the miscarriage and he got back on an even keel at work. He said he wanted kids. He knew she wanted kids. People don't just change their minds about that. *Has he been keeping his true feelings from Josie or from me?*

"I remember this one woman at my mother's funeral." Josie cleared her throat. "She kept saying, 'I just can't see it.' No one else dared mention the s-word—suicide—but she stared out the window the whole time, saying over and over, 'I just can't see it,' as though scientists had discovered a new color in the rainbow." Josie got to her feet, hands on hips, scanning the beach. "I suppose if you do have a baby, I could help look after it. Pay it back."

Amanda sat up on her sun bed. "There's nothing to pay back. And it's a moot point because I'm not pregnant."

"You're not too old. Where *is* he?"

"He went to get snorkels."

"Over there." Josie pointed to Ed, who was leaning against a lone palm tree with a pile of flippers at his feet. He seemed rapt by a group of teenage girls playing volleyball in tiny bikinis. Amanda remembered the illicit thrill of sun and eyes hot on her bare skin; the girls were flaunting themselves and enjoying the attention. *But Ed's staring right at them. One of their dads will notice and thump him.*

Josie watched too, pulling the sleeves of her modest rash vest. "I'm going for a swim." She ran across hot sand into the crystal water.

After the girls scored a noisy point, with much high-fiving and readjusting of bikini bottoms, Ed seemed to come around. He stood upright, one hand steadying himself on the tree, glancing up and down the beach, and gathered his snorkeling equipment. Amanda found her book and opened it somewhere in the middle before Ed reached her.

"Good match?" she asked.

"What is?"

"The volleyball."

He glanced over his shoulder and half smiled. "Too hot for all that." His face looked ashy despite a flush of sunburn across his cheekbones.

"Maybe you should cool off?"

Ed looked down at her. "What?"

"Cool off. Maybe you should."

"Where's Jo-Jo Sparrow?"

Amanda dropped the book into her lap. "Are you all right, Ed?" He was pale and rubbing at his elbow.

"Hot, isn't it? I had a bit of a head rush, slipped on some water by the bar. And Bernardo's kicking off about paperwork for the jet. Says it can't wait." He threw his mobile phone onto the lounger and hauled the plastic mask onto his face. The snorkel flapped foolishly as he glanced around. "Where's Josie?"

"In the water."

He nodded once and set off, high-stepping as Josie had done on the hot sand.

Amanda watched Josie swim in to meet her father. They kneeled in the shadows, baby waves pushing them together and apart as he adjusted her mask. There was some disagreement over the life jacket; Josie waved it away, Ed shrugged his on and clipped it shut. Finally, they pushed off into the shallows and two spumes of spray marked their progress to a dark patch of reef.

Amanda motioned to a passing waiter, and when she looked back, the sea was flat and empty. A low drone signaled the arrival of a dive boat. A flash of yellow flipper on the reef: Josie diving. She tried to recall the exact words of their conversation a few minutes before, but the lines were as slippery as the ones in her book. Something about Josie being a burden, wanting to pay it back. She recognized the lone-child guilt, but she was surprised by the weight of the millstone that Josie carried. A low rumble of male laughter at the bar, and in her head Amanda heard Ed say: *You owe me.* Could Josie's guilt be coming from him? Was that something he'd told her? *You owe me.* Was that how he might justify . . . abuse?

Why did that word make her shudder when she suspected him of so much more? A pattern of attacks on eighteen-year-old women, in preparation for whatever he had planned for his own daughter as soon as she was of age. As soon as Amanda knew, she became responsible. And that was one thing Ed was right about: she didn't like responsibility.

She looked at Josie's laptop. Had she been writing? Posting on her blog? Amanda picked up her own device. The website loaded in her browser. Timer: six more days. A new image: a hand-drawn GIF of a stick girl pushing against a window frame until it broke apart, and she fell out. The scribbled lines blurred to a frenzy as the girl plummeted. It was disturbing. Amanda tapped the GIF to make it stop repeating the image over and over, and it connected her to a new page.

Preamble

A sapling rises
When timber bequeaths the light;
Cultivating fruit

For his sour relish.
Your voice in the rain, crying
"Leave her to ripen."

In the future: Six Days Until D-Day (oops, lost a
day—stupid island Wi-Fi!)
In the past: Thirteen Days That Made Me Me
Post 6 of 13: Winners and Losers

The slightest breeze stirs the cotton bunting across
the starting line. All the parents sigh with relief.
Mothers who are not in the race slump beside
the running track, fanning themselves with wilted
napkins. The school nurse arrives with a fresh supply of oranges. I inch my toes onto the white line.
Even the chalk is melting. Crouched low to tie a
lace, I see ants crawling in the grass. The sound
of cheering children recedes, as do the parents'
shouts of encouragement and teachers' booming
instructions. I steady myself by focusing on Teddy,
a hundred yards away at the finishing line. He gives
us a thumbs-up.

To my left, Lillian and her bovine mother pose
no competition. On the far side, Clement points
to his eyes with two fingers and turns them on me
while his mother adjusts her sports bra. I imagine

he's an ant who will be squashed when I start running. The next pair aren't even on their marks. And
in the lane directly to my right, my mother's blin-
dingly white trainers, looking like they've just come
out of the shoebox.

I shift my gaze to Teddy on the finishing line.

Mr. Cox walks behind us and pokes his finger
between our ankles, tugging the lace that binds
our middle legs together. "Nice and tight," he
says. "Put your arms around each other." But when
I try to slide my hand around her waist, his hand
is already there. She looks back over her shoulder
and giggles. "You're a dead cert," he says. Then
Mr. Cox leaps away onto his step and holds the pop
gun aloft. The crowd goes still.

"Last race, ladies and gentlemen," Mr. Cox
shouts. "The one we've all been waiting for. Bigger than the Wimbledon final."

"At least the women here get equal pay," says
the bovine mother.

"What—nothing?" says Clement's mum. The
mothers cackle like crows.

"The final!" Mr. Cox bellows, to a few listless
whoops. "Of the St. Dymphna's Sports Day mother-
and-child three-legged dash!"

My calves harden. The rings on my mother's
left hand dig into my rib as she pulls me close.

"This is ours for the taking, Josie." I glance
up at her. She's wearing the huge sunglasses that
Teddy said make her look like a praying mantis.
Her wrinkles spread out from behind the lenses as
though her face has been smashed by a cricket ball.

She calls them laughter lines, though she says it in the voice that means she's speaking in opposites.

"Feet behind the starting line, please."

Her white trainer jolts back an inch, leaving a smear of chalk and ants.

"On your marks—get set—go!"

Our conjoined leg lurches forward and our bodies bump together, my head bouncing off her left breast. She lifts me with her arm and our outside legs scissor forward, then the middle leg strides out again.

"That's it! One, two; inside leg, outside leg." Her voice is as bubbly as pop. "One, two. One, two." We get into rhythm. There are shouts of laughter—someone has fallen—but we are galloping along. Teddy is bent over, clapping his hands, and I can see his mouth shouting, "Come on," even though I can't hear his voice. Two heads bob along behind her elbow on the far side, but we're a stride ahead and Teddy is coming up fast.

"One, two," I shout and we're across the line and Teddy catches me as I fall and she comes down with me because we're tied together.

"You won!" Teddy grabs my shoulders and joggles them up and down. Mr. Cox appears through the crowd and says, "Medals." Mum pulls at the cloth that's cutting into my ankle now, but when it won't come loose because it has pulled into a knot, Teddy gets a Swiss Army knife from his pocket and slices through the fabric. Mum follows Mr. Cox to the podium, which is really just a plastic box with a scarlet cloth over it.

"Come on, Teddy," I try to pull him up.

"Well done, Jo-Jo Sparrow."

"Come and see me get my medal."

"I have to go. The traffic to the airport will be bad."

"You're not going to Saba, are you?"

Teddy laughs. "No, just Schiphol. Easy landing. Nothing to worry about."

"I don't want you to go!"

"I'll bring you a present from the airport."

"You're back in time for the weekend?"

"Of course. I wouldn't miss our weekend. I've made a plan. We're going to run away together."

"On a plane?"

Teddy laughs again. "To the circus!"

I'd seen signs for the circus. "Cool," I say, and don't tell him it's too young for me.

"It's a grown-up circus," he says.

"Can we run away on a plane another day?"

"We'll be together soon enough. Kiss for Daddy."

Teddy squeezes me and makes a bear noise. I watch him walk across the school field in his pilot uniform, making other mums' heads turn like sunflowers following the sun.

Amanda scrolled back to the poem. Her eyes lingered on "his sour relish," until a thump to her right snatched her attention. She'd thought it was a falling coconut, but someone was running. A man had jumped from the bar onto the beach, heading for the water. A glass shattered as another man pursued. They reached the sea and waded in with their clothes on. Amanda stood. The atmosphere had flicked with a switch.

"Oh my God!" A fluty voice from the bar, hitting a shrill note.

The dive boat roared to life, pulling Amanda's focus to the water. She started across the hot sand. Clothed men were wrestling something in the water. Not wrestling—carrying. As her feet sunk into wet sand at the water's edge, the dive boat blocked her view. A hand on Amanda's shoulder made her head whip around.

"Is it your daughter? And husband?" The receptionist's eyes were round with shock. Amanda looked down to see that she'd grasped him around the forearms, her hands as pale as the sand in the shallows.

"Josie wasn't wearing a life jacket."

The sharp nose of the boat beached, and too many people clamored to help. Amanda stayed put, ankle-deep in sand and sinking. Josie was on the swim team. She went to the pool every day, diving, freestyle. How could she drown? How was that possible in a few minutes? In calm water, alongside her father.

Her father. Surely he hadn't hurt her? Surely not. *Right under our noses.* The phrase rang around her head like a birdcall from the rain forest.

The crowd parted. A flash of yellow flippers. Held in Josie's hands as she waded to shore.

"Josie!" Amanda wrenched her feet from the sand.

Through the crowd came an ungainly procession: the two rescuers, struggling under the dead weight of a man. As they carried him up the beach, Ed's limp hand brushed Amanda's. He disappeared beneath a cairn of bodies that bent to attend to him. Josie folded under her own weight and plopped down in the shallows. Amanda knelt and took her shoulders.

"What happened?"

"She saved his life, that's what!" Gruff Australian accent from the boat. "He'd be a goner if she hadn't spotted him."

Amanda tugged at Josie's arm, and when she couldn't get her to her feet, she left her bobbing in the water beside the boat. She ran to join the group around Ed. The receptionist tried to turn her away, but she pushed past and fell onto the hot sand beside a young Singaporean, a hotel guest, the one who'd first gone running to help. He glanced at her while pumping Ed's chest.

"What's happening?" she asked.

"I'm a doctor." He gave a tight smile that may have been a grimace of effort. A man kneeling on the opposite side of Ed bent forward to breathe into his mouth. The doctor nodded at his mate and said, "He's a vet." He carried on pumping in a steady beat.

"Will you save him?" Her voice came out as though she too were drowning. The doctor glanced up at the receptionist and said something in Malay. Amanda didn't understand the words, but the tone was unmistakable. *Get her out of here.* The receptionist bent toward her, but she shrugged his fingers away and sat on her heels to give them space.

The sky seemed to have been sliced down the middle, the blue side menaced by a mass of storm clouds. It was like this in the tropics: changes too rapid to predict.

There was a crunch of sand, and Josie kneeled beside Amanda.

"You shouldn't watch this, Josie."

"I have to."

"Swap!" The vet picked up the beat while the doctor used his T-shirt to wipe sweat from his face. "How long was he under?"

"Not long," Josie said. "He pointed out a baby shark, and I dived. When I came up, he was floating facedown and his snorkel was gone."

"So you took a breath, dived down, and came straight back to him?"

"Yes."

"One dive only?"

"I couldn't see the shark, so I came back to ask him where."

The news seemed to galvanize the doctor into action while Amanda closed her eyes. She heard the thump of fists on ribs—hurting Ed in order to save him—and then the melody of waves grinding shells to dust. People would think she was praying for her husband's life. Instead, she thought of sand running through Josie's fingers like an hourglass. Was time running out or was time running in?

She opened her eyes to the divided sky. Thousands of feet overhead, an aircraft flew into the cauldron of clouds. She thought about Ed saying that we travel too fast, stepping through a door from one world to another. Amanda had stepped out of the place where she trusted him and believed their marriage was so sacred it should be immortalized with a baby into a new reality where he was a shadow, a dark force hanging over them like a malevolent cloud.

His hand curled meekly in the sand. She should hold it, squeeze him back to life, call his name. But instead she thought about where those fingers had been. This hand touching the faces of the women on Amanda's list, the ones whose demises coincided with Ed's business trips. That hand squeezing her arms as he pressed her against the parapet. Those hands on Josie. Maybe the universe had chosen to intervene? Maybe the hourglass was giving time back to Amanda, to Josie, to the women Ed was destined to meet on future business trips. Tragedies that would never happen if he died now, in the sand.

"Swap!" The doctor took over CPR.

"What's happening?" Amanda asked. If the universe wanted Ed out of the picture, why was it taking so long?

The vet rubbed the heels of his hands in his eyes. He couldn't look; he thought he had failed. The doctor continued pumping Ed's chest, arms shuddering now. Amanda reached a hand toward his exhausted shoulder but instead clutched his battered cap that had fallen into the sand. What would the doctor do if she told him to stop?

Would the universe really make Amanda choose?

A splash of warm sand across her thighs. A grunt and a wet retch.

"That's it, man, breathe!"

People cheered.

Amanda closed her eyes again.

Chapter 33

Amanda dodged the motorbikes that crisscrossed the petrol station. Why did Malaysia build everything out of concrete that sharpened the sunlight into arrows? Their driver had the hood up, refilling the screen wash at her insistence after driving blinded by a filthy windscreen. She felt his male resentment like a hot blade and gave him a wide berth as she went to look for her sunglasses in the open trunk.

Ed lay on the back seat, Josie trapped by his legs. They were an hour from the border to Singapore. Adventure was all very well, but not when you're having a heart attack or allergic reaction or whatever Ed denied was happening. Maybe it was a reaction to thinking him dead, but now she urgently wanted to get him to the hospital.

"I'm going to tell her if you don't." Josie's voice, a sharp hiss, carried over the seat. The driver turned on a tap of sizzling water, and Amanda missed whatever was said next. Tap off, and she could hear Ed. "I'd get no second chances." A motorbike screamed past. Then Ed again: "If we tell anyone, I'll have to stop and I don't intend to stop."

Amanda's hands went to her face, and her thumbs felt something behind her ears. The sunglasses were on her head. The driver got in and started the engine. Josie sat up straight and rubbernecked when she noticed Amanda standing at the open boot. "Oh, hey. Is there any water?" Amanda ripped a bottle out of the plastic wrapper and passed it over the seat. Josie snapped the seal and gave it to her father.

"Do you want to take a turn in the front?" Amanda asked. "Stretch your legs."

Josie's eyes flickered down to the seat where Ed lay out of sight. After a moment she said, "I'm okay." Amanda got in the passenger seat with a glance into the back, where Josie was slumped against the door, the seat belt pressed like a gag across her face.

They crawled across the causeway from Malaysia to Singapore, cars stretched in lines like forest ants. Amanda focused on the sea, a no-man's land between two worlds: fish farms, sampans, and tankers. Singapore rose like Shangri-La. Amanda was a chosen one, she could enter. But for how long? Imagine if Ed had drowned . . . Would Amanda have a month to leave the country—like Molly's friend, Melissa Something, whose husband died?

If I'm forced out of the country, what happens to my embryos?

What happens to Josie?

She started searching on her phone for the regulations concerning frozen embryos. Could she take them with her? Was that even possible? How many Prada bags would it cost? She searched for answers until they jerked to a halt—at the Attica instead of a hospital. Thirty minutes later, she stood before Chairman Mao while Ed packed another bag.

"You're leaving?"

"Don't start, Amanda."

"I thought you were going for a checkup?"

"Bernardo called. Says his buyer defaulted on the payment. I don't trust that little shit."

"Manila again?"

"I'll be back tomorrow night." Ed dumped one load of clothes from his case and replaced it with another. He went into his bathroom, and Amanda heard him rifling under the sink.

"What are you looking for?" she asked.

"A gun." A can of shaving cream rolled out into the bedroom.

"What?"

Ed strode out. "Kidding. Ha ha. I've got a headache. Feels like someone's stabbing my eyeballs with a pitchfork."

"And you're not going to the doctor, why?"

"Sarcasm is ugly, Amanda." He spun around to face her. "I'm trying to rescue my fucking business. Can't you read the writing on the wall? Or do you need it spelled out in pixelated fingernails?" He leaned over her shoulder and she flinched, but he only flicked part of Mao's cheek across the room. "I need this sale. Or our adventures in business class are going to come crashing down." He hauled the handle of the suitcase up with a definitive snap. "And I don't need to go to the doctor because I got dehydrated, that's all. Messing about on that bloody kayak. I'll buy some pills at the airport and I'll be fine."

"There's coconut water in the fridge."

"Coconut water? Right. Thanks for the sage advice."

His lips struck her somewhere on the chin as he went out the door. Amanda unpacked her belongings onto the bed like flotsam washed ashore. She pulled out a tattered baseball cap. A confetti of white sand sank into the rug. Her fingernail plucked the frayed embroidery of a Harvard logo. She hoped the hat hadn't been of sentimental value to the doctor whose intricate accent outlined a road map of an excellent education. As she scooped her hair into his cap, she pushed aside an image of him kicking around in the sand for a hat that must have disappeared while he was bringing a dead man back to life.

Amanda lay in bed, watching a cruise ship blaze toward the harbor like the circus coming to town. Her mother would be moored in a grubby port. For some reason, she pictured Laura like a pirate captain, writing by the light of a candle. *Ridiculous.* It was a modern ship. Satellite Internet and GPS. If she'd ever been invited on board, she might be able to picture the reality. She rolled away from the sea view, wishing she could switch off her mind—or those perpetual lights—and get some rest. The sleeping pills on Ed's nightstand were tempting . . . And that reminded her . . . She swung her legs from under the sheet and scrabbled in her bedside drawer for a folded piece of paper. In the hullabaloo that had followed the notification that Awmi had been underage, she had forgotten about the other letter—the one from the police about Ed's withheld medication. What had he been taking? Could it explain his episode at Cuti?

On the way to the kitchen, she listened at Josie's door, but all was quiet. She took the letter from the police into the maid's room and laid it aside while she searched systematically through the box, but there was nothing more than Awmi's personal belongings. Amanda sat on the bed and opened an Internet browser on her phone: the police had listed the confiscated meds as "clonazepam." *Used to treat convulsive disorders and panic attacks and/or anxiety.* She scanned the paragraphs about neurotransmitters and GABA receptors. *May result in addiction. An addict might score pills from doctors in different countries,* Amanda thought. *Commonly used as a recreational drug. A sudden withdrawal might explain his collapse at the beach. Also documented as a date-rape drug.*

Ah. Date-rape drug. A sting rose on the back of her calf, and she slapped the spot where she'd been bitten. The mosquito was already gone. Stealth hunter. Sneaking up and administering anesthetic before taking what it wants. The phone buzzed in her hand. Unknown number. She hesitated a moment and took the call.

"Is that Jacaranda?" The voice on the line was male but as high and tight as a flying bug. "Jacaranda Mitchell?"

It took Amanda a second to catch up. "Yes, this is . . . she . . . Jacaranda."

"I'm calling on behalf of my wife. She bought your so-called designer bag last week." The voice was slightly slurred, maybe drunk.

"You've ignored our emails so this is a courtesy before reporting the matter to the police."

"What emails? I'm sorry, but I've no idea what this is about." She walked rapidly into the living room and pulled her laptop open. "I've been away so I haven't been online."

"Well, if you had, you'd see that your cottage industry has been exposed. My wife wants her money back, and so do your other victims."

The laptop came to life, icons popping up. As soon as Facebook appeared, she went to SOWs. A post pinned to the top of the page had hundreds of comments. It accused her, or at least Jacaranda Mitchell, of selling a fake Prada bag.

"Don't compound it by lying. Or playing dumb. Return the money and we'll say no more. I don't want to get involved in a court case, but I will call the police if I have to."

Amanda opened Gmail in another tab and went to the in-box for Jacaranda Mitchell. "Can you give me a moment to read your emails? I have them open now."

He huffed as though that were an imposition in itself but stayed quiet.

Amanda opened the first email from her buyer. *I met you recently to buy your Prada bag and handed over $2,000 in cash. The following day, I took the bag to the store to arrange a professional clean, which they carried out. However, I got an email today from their workshop to say the bag is not original. You can see attached photos of the poor workmanship that shows it is not a real Prada—the stitching has a number of faults. I don't want to make accusations, but you claimed when you sold me the bag that you didn't have a receipt/proof of purchase because it was a gift from your husband. Whether you believe it to be authentic or not, I want a refund right away.*

"I see," Amanda said.

"So what are you going to do about it?"

"The bag is real. My husband bought it in Zurich."

"So he says—"

"Why would he lie?" It was a rhetorical question, but a dozen reasons popped up like targets at a duck shoot. *To shut me up. To keep me sweet. To relieve his guilt.* Underpinning them all, a painful truth: *because I'm easily bought.*

"Well, someone's lying. I just want my money back. And the other women do too."

"What other women?"

"The ones you've suckered on that Facebook page."

"I haven't suckered anyone."

The man, whose name she didn't even know, gave a nasty laugh. "True enough. You sucker yourselves with this designer bullshit." He rang off.

On Facebook, SOWs were revolting. Another of Jacaranda's buyers had taken a Hermès bag she had bought a month earlier to the shop and been told that it too was a suspected fake. Naturally, everyone who'd ever bought from Jacaranda was demanding pay back, proof or no proof. The self-proclaimed victims were smothered in a virtual group hug from a gleeful #squad of rubbernecking strangers: "Oh babes, that's awful," "Don't worry, doll, that bitch'll get her comeuppance," "So sorry, hon."

Babes. Doll. Hon.

The lingo conjured up fake friends with fake nails and fake smiles, slurping down drama like cheap Chardonnay. Amanda shut the laptop and slumped sideways on the sofa. She'd raised $7,000 by selling that Hermès bag—her engagement present—and spent it at the fertility clinic. If she had to return that money, plus the $2,000 for the Prada and the various shoes . . . Twelve thousand dollars at least. A week ago, she would have defended herself to the hilt. Yes, she'd deceived people about her name—she didn't want Singapore society knowing that Amanda Bonham flogged her husband's guilt gifts for cash—but that was all. It was a white lie. Nobody died. She thought the bags were as authentic as her crow's feet. But now she couldn't be so sure.

If she wasn't the liar, then maybe—once again—Ed was.

Chapter 34

Camille suggested meeting Joshua on the neutral ground of a *kopitiam*. She knew he liked the local brew. Josh ordered a breakfast of kaya toast and eggs, which arrived translucent and sat between them in a cup, two additional eyeballs that Camille could do without.

"I'm afraid the high commissioner hasn't made a decision on your job," he said. "Did you see the latest on Reuters?"

Camille was up-to-date. A group of Singaporean lawmakers had signed an open letter protesting what they called the BHC's neocolonial attitude. The row was escalating.

"I'm not here to beg for my job," Camille said. "I'm going to use the suspension time to get well."

"Are you sick?"

"In a way. I don't know what to call it. Maybe it's a kind of addiction or compulsion. At least, that's how I view it."

"Camille, I had no idea."

"Yes, you do. I get . . . obsessed with certain ideas."

Josh bobbed his head to one side.

"It came to a head this week, and I feel like I've surfaced from the murk. I'm seeing clearer than I have for a long time. It's all to do with my parents."

"It was a terrible thing to happen to a child," he said.

"It seems obvious now that I'm compelled to work for HELP—even to lose my job—because I feel guilty about our helper, who was sent away when my parents disappeared. I was never able to say goodbye to Lani or find out if she was okay. I didn't even know her full name."

"Camille . . ." Josh put down his fork.

She shrugged. "I'm only stating the facts. My point is, that's a surface issue. Working on the HELP campaign feels like I'm making a difference—"

"HELP does make a difference."

"But it's not the endgame. It distracts me from the deeper issue, which is the question mark over my parents. It's been fifteen years, and it consumes me now as much as it ever did. People might sneer at the idea of closure, but not knowing what happened . . . it's like living in a house with an empty space where the front door should be. You can't stop watching it, you can never settle, you can't go away and leave. If I can only close that door, I'll have . . . peace. So I think that's what I need to focus on. This open door brought me to Singapore. And I think it brought me to Edward Bonham."

"Bonham? Why him?"

"First time I saw him, a picture of him, I recognized him. And yesterday I finally placed it. He came to our house when I was a child. He knew my parents."

"You remember him from so long ago? You were how old?"

"About ten. Maybe younger. I don't know the exact date, obviously. But it was him."

Josh shook his head. "Memory is an unreliable source of information."

"I remember him. And he acts like he knows me—" Camille stopped. She'd been about to get into the late-night booty call. That part she intended to withhold from her boss.

"Forgive me for asking, but I assume you're not romantically involved with Mr. Bonham?"

"No." Even she heard the defensive edge to her honest denial.

"Because that would not be entirely appropriate."

"He must be fifteen years older than me!"

"That far over the hill? Let me assure you, men of the grand age of forty are not so ancient as to be considered saints. I apologize for the intrusive question, but I do have to clarify the nature of a liaison between an employee and a professional contact."

Josh folded his hands together on the table. Camille realized she had been told to spill the beans. It sometimes took her a few moments to translate diplomatese.

"While I was getting the paperwork together for the Bonham case," she said, "I noticed that Ed had been in Singapore at the same time as my parents and, so I thought, working in a similar industry. I asked if he would help me to find them."

"You're hoping to find them?"

"I'm always hoping to find them."

Her honesty flapped around like an injured bird. It startled them both. Camille gave a small shrug as if to say "there it is."

"And did Bonham know your parents?"

"He looked at their photo and said he didn't recall their names."

"Is that a no?"

"That's what I've been asking myself."

Josh pulled his face into a downward smile and regarded the ceiling for a moment.

"You have a steely streak, Camille, that I underestimated." He dabbed his lips with a paper napkin even though he'd pushed the runny eggs aside and forgotten about them. "I knew Edward Bonham back in the day. I knew more about him than I wanted to."

Camille remained perched on her chair, as still as a bird over water, resisting the urge to let off a volley of questions.

"He was involved in some dodgy businesses, and, quite frankly, it would have been my pleasure to see him kicked out of Singapore and out of our hair. Happily, his professional demise came about through natural causes."

"He told me he went bankrupt."

"He told you that?"

"But he hasn't told his wife, apparently."

"Not surprised. Expensive woman."

"I knew there was a whiff about him," she said.

"He appears to be legitimate now—aircraft brokerage is a thriving industry, a lot of money to be made—but I would advise against getting into bed with him, which I mean in a purely euphemistic sense. First your parents and now the dead helper—he has a way of drawing people into his drama. Women seem particularly susceptible to his stage presence."

She wasn't about to make any promises to Josh, so she diverted the conversation to float plans for her parents' yacht. As soon as the documents came through, she would seek matching documents in the relevant countries—the most likely being Malaysia, Thailand, or even Burma.

"Burma?" asked Josh.

"It could be anywhere in Southeast Asia. But those are the places they mentioned when I was a kid. They loved Burma."

"Burma was a tough patch in the '90s. International sanctions. It's a land of opportunity now, but only because it was a no-go zone for so long. Of course, there were tourists who wanted to visit even though tour companies boycotted Burma. It was considered unethical by some, but your parents might have been willing to cash in on that market."

Camille felt a slow slide inside herself, as though her shadow had stood up of its own accord and started to walk away. It was the part of her that still believed the fanciful explanation she'd concocted for her parents' activities: a derring-do tale of spies on the South China Sea, which Collin dismissed as childish. The shadow pulled from her side with a final tug and slipped out the door like a chastened girl. Maybe her parents had simply kept their business under the radar to avoid any backlash.

She reached into her bag and drew out her Filofax. She flipped open the pages, soft from time, and extracted the photo from the plastic cover. She laid it on the table and slid it forward with one fingertip.

Josh accepted it in the same way. "Your parents?"

"Patricia and Magnus Kemble. This is the picture I showed Ed. He recognized them, I'm sure he did, but he said he didn't know their names."

Josh tapped the image. "Maybe he recognized the place." He spun the photo around to face her. "That's the most famous bar in Burma. The Raffles Club in Yangon. It's always been a popular hangout for diplomats, journalists, and the more intrepid kind of businessman. Nowadays it's been taken over by tourists, since the country opened up."

"It's a coffee shop in Singapore."

"It does look like a *kopitiam* with the marble-top tables." He rapped his knuckles on their own and then pointed to the arched doorway in the picture. "But that's the RC. I've been many times. And see the poster in Burmese script?"

She took the picture from his hand. "I thought that was Tamil."

"Burmese. And that"—he tapped the doorway again, the shadow of a temple outside—"that's part of the Shwedagon Paya."

Even Camille, who had never visited Burma, knew Yangon's iconic site.

"Last time I saw Edward Bonham was in Yangon." Josh picked up his runny eggs and broke the yolks.

"What was he doing there? And how come you know the place so well?"

"I did a stint there as part of my training, and I went back and forth quite regularly until they put a communications manager in country. As for Edward Bonham, he said he was a paper trader. Impenetrable business, I couldn't get to the bottom of it, and I couldn't work out the connection with Burma. But I spotted him in the FCC once. Bonham was there with a couple. British accents. The three of them drew attention to themselves."

"He does like a drink."

"Quite the opposite. Burma was—is—one of those places where the expat crowd is usually male, behaving like they've died and gone to Saigon in the '50s. They drink too much, get leery, pick up a girl, piss in the street, and fly home the next day, leaving trouble behind. So long as the girl isn't the daughter of an army general, you're all right. By contrast, Edward Bonham and this couple were sober, composed—tense. They were waiting for something."

"Are you saying my parents were the couple?"

"As I said, memory is an unreliable source, so I can't be sure. But I do remember Bonham because I was already aware of him. Suspicious, frankly."

"Was he a spy?"

The spoon came to rest in the egg cup. "It was a good place for people to disappear. In my experience, a majority of people who disappear want to disappear."

"Did the UK have spies in Burma?" she pressed.

"I should imagine so, yes. But I've told you all I know." Josh downed his coffee. "We can put Edward Bonham and, judging by this photo, your parents in Yangon. I don't know what they were doing, but I'm damn sure it wasn't handing out free pencils to schoolchildren. Nor do I think they were secret agents who got thrown to the wolves."

She picked up the photo and slid it back into the Filofax. "When did you see Edward Bonham?"

"Must have been 1999. I left Yangon in September of that year—"

"Just before my parents disappeared."

"Leaving aside espionage to focus on the facts, this is the salient point: if Edward Bonham says he doesn't know your parents, I would suggest that Edward Bonham is a liar."

Chapter 35

Amanda was taking a shortcut through Marks and Spencer to the taxi stand, when she heard a familiar voice: "If I can deliver books to girls in Burma, you'd think you could supply knickers to Singapore."

She watched her mother at the customer service counter. The assistant hammered at a keyboard as though it might activate a trapdoor. "We have your size available at other stores, ma'am—"

Laura stamped her foot—literally stamped her foot: "But the customer is at *this* store. Oh, forget it." She strode off toward the café and sat at a small table. Amanda slid into the seat opposite.

"Mother. Fancy seeing you here."

"Oh. Amanda." Laura planted her carpetbag on a spare chair. "I do hope I haven't upset you."

"By omitting to tell me you're in town? And yet we bump into each other anyway, just by chance. It's almost as though there's a special connection between mother and daughter."

"Amanda . . ."

"And you even have time for lunch."

"I'm sorry I couldn't stay last time. And I'm sorry I didn't call this time."

A waitress offered white menus, held open like doves' wings. Amanda folded hers onto the table. She couldn't remember a single occasion when Laura had apologized for anything. "Are you okay, Mother?"

Laura's blue eyes flicked up. For the first time, Amanda thought she looked old. Her mascaraed lashes protruded like fir trees caught in a landslide. One eye, Amanda noticed, drooped more than the other, introducing a new asymmetry that robbed her mother of beauty more effectively than seventy years had ever managed to do.

Laura looked away to the waitress and ordered a salad and black coffee. Amanda muttered, "Same," and then said to her mother, "Has something happened?"

"I can't stay for long, I'm afraid. I've an appointment."

"At the doctor?"

"Neurologist."

"What for?"

Laura flapped her hand as though the question were a mosquito. "I may have suffered a cerebrovascular accident."

Amanda glanced at the drooping eye again. "A stroke?"

"Yes."

"On the boat?"

"We were in port. Near Yangon. I slipped and fell on deck, and they took me to the local doctor, who decided it was a stroke and all hell let loose. The insurance wants me to check it out at one of their authorized clinics, you know what they're like. There was a flight to Singapore, so I'll tick their boxes and get back to work tomorrow."

"I'll come with you to the neurologist."

"You're busy—"

"I'm not."

"Then why aren't you busy?" Laura gave the table a swipe. "You're a grown woman. What do you do with your time?"

Amanda leaned back to allow the waitress to deliver their coffee and fuss with the cups until Laura said, "That's fine, thank you," and then, "I said they're fine." The girl scurried away. "I worry about you, Amanda."

"You've never worried about me. You outsourced me."

"I was working. Working mothers aren't a new phenomenon, whatever the media might suggest. You're not out of the ordinary. Mothers of my generation weren't held hostage by their offspring like women are today. But it doesn't mean you were abandoned. You always had the greatest care, and it was—what do they call it now, "parenting style"?—our *parenting style* to encourage independence. You were just more resistant to that than most."

"I see."

"And you know what they say about being over the age of thirty?"

"What do they say?"

"You have to stop blaming your parents."

"Let me get this straight: you had a brush with mortality, so you decided to come here and put me right before it's too late?"

"No, I came here to find out how badly my brain is damaged."

"It seems quite sharp to me."

Laura laughed, a fragile tinkling like wineglasses crowded precariously on a tray. She picked up her coffee cup but put it down again without drinking. "Don't know why they serve it so hot. It's scalding."

"Sorry for snapping," said Amanda.

"And I'm sorry too. I planned to phone you after the appointment—*I did*—to see if you could meet later. You know I hate fuss."

"You could let me help you. I know you don't think I'm capable of much, but at the very least I could arrange a taxi."

"I think you're very capable. Your teachers always said you were gifted, when you worked. But capability is a muscle that wastes away if you don't use it. And I've never seen you use it. This world you live in now—all the trappings—it's . . . making you weak."

"You sound like Ed. He says I want independence but don't want responsibility."

"So he's more than just a pretty face. How is Edward? In the country?"

"Nope."

"I see."

The waitress arrived with two salads. Laura dragged a fork through hers as though checking for booby traps. Amanda speared a baby beetroot. "I'm having problems with Ed. And Josie. It's all a bit of a nightmare, to be honest."

"This is all lettuce." Laura pushed her food away. "I'm probably not the best person to advise. I'm predisposed to think the worst about what men get up to in anonymous hotels."

"In Ed's case, you might be surprised."

"They're like dogs; they run around chasing their balls. All the panting and slavering—"

Amanda snorted. "There's nothing wrong with your brain, Mother."

"That's what I told the insurance company. What about the girl? Is she still not going to school?"

"She was picked up by the police at a party where a boy had drugs. That got blamed on me—"

"How's that?"

"I called the police when Josie didn't come home."

"Sounds reasonable."

"Thank you! It was reasonable. What else was I supposed to do, sit back and do nothing? I know I've only been in Josie's life for three years, but I've really tried with her. It's been tough because she's hard to fathom, tightly wound somehow, like . . ." Amanda made a swirling motion with her fingertips.

"Lace."

"Exactly. I'm frightened to start picking for fear of unraveling her altogether."

"Losing her mother so young must have affected her."

"So you do listen . . ."

"I do."

Amanda steepled her hands over her mouth. They were trembling. "I've been wondering . . . about the nature of the relationship between Ed and Josie."

"Ah."

"Yes."

"Well, that would affect her self-esteem. And even if she's lived with it for a long time—kept it hidden—sooner or later cracks would appear."

"But how can I be sure? No point asking either of them. I won't get an honest answer."

"No. If there's one thing I know from experiencing sexual abuse . . ." Laura made slow jazz hands in reply to Amanda's shocked face. "It was a long time ago. Let's just say London had a different cultural landscape in the '70s. Consent was a form you signed with a false name at the abortion clinic. And I never did that either, before you ask. What I'm saying is, when you're not shown any respect . . . it changes how you look in the mirror."

Amanda tried her coffee cup and found her hands steady enough to drink. Then she said, "I wonder what Josie sees?"

"That's what you need to find out."

"There's more, actually. This is going to sound a bit dramatic. But I think Ed is . . ." Amanda tried, but she couldn't say it. All that she wanted to vocalize—her suspicions—pushed and strained like marauders at the gate. Overwhelming. She couldn't let them in. Nor could she burden Laura, not with her mother's bottom lip fluttering with another tic of time. *And,* she thought, *how do we come back from this if I'm wrong? How do I face my mother next time she cruises into town? Just say, that time I believed my husband was a killer—misunderstanding. And, good news, I'm pregnant with his baby! Yes, the guy I thought was capable of murder, isn't that a hoot!*

"Unfaithful, I suppose?" Laura said at last.

"Spectacularly so."

"Oh, darling. You're not the first and you won't be the last."

"There's a pattern of . . . women. Of course, I don't have proof, and if I confront him without evidence, the only one who will lose out is me, because I stay in Singapore by Ed's grace and favor. And if I leave Josie behind. Alone . . ."

"You're not a fool, Amanda. And you've always been willing to see the good in people. I remember your father walking out once, when I confronted him over one of the girls in the office. And you ran down the street in your nightgown to drag him home." She planted both elbows on the table. "Trust your instincts. Find the evidence. As I did with your father and the fraud. His fall damaged the whole family, but it was like a sickness; I cut off a limb to save the body."

"I don't know how to find proof."

"Oh, I think you do."

"What do you mean?"

"You're more resourceful than you give yourself credit for." Laura signaled for the waitress.

"Why do you say that?"

The girl arrived with the bill in a leather sleeve, and Laura handed over a note and waved away the change. "I have to visit the ladies' before we walk to the hospital."

"Why did you say that?"

Laura gathered her carpetbag onto her lap. "I would have given you my engagement ring one day, so I don't really care that you stole it. But taking my key card for the *Guanyin* was, quite honestly, a bloody nuisance." She slid out from the bench and put her hand on Amanda's shoulder as she brushed past. "Put that energy to good use, Amanda, before it burns you up. Maybe you could call a taxi? I'm not up to the walk in this heat."

Amanda flushed as though they'd already stepped into the sunlight.

"But no fussing, do you hear?" Laura strode off toward the restrooms. "And I have to be at the airport by five."

Later, Laura had her boarding pass printed and no luggage to check in, so they walked straight to passport control.

"Can I visit the ship sometime?"

"The cabins are tiny."

"I don't mind."

Laura pulled her daughter into a hug that consisted of bumping breastbones.

"Of course you can visit. Get yourself sorted out first. We're leaving for Bangladesh in the morning, should be interesting. You could join us in Dhaka when you're ready?"

Amanda nodded.

"You have more strength than you imagine." Laura moved toward the security officer, brandishing her boarding pass.

"Mother?"

"I must go—"

"Do you hate Dad?"

"I don't like him. But for some reason I keep loving him."

"Do you regret having a child with someone you don't like?"

Laura came back and placed a cool palm on Amanda's cheek. "You're a consolation, never a regret." She replaced her hand with an equally cool kiss. "And anyway, you can make the most of regrets. They're a marvelous incentive to change. Thank you for coming with me today, to put my mind at rest."

"I'm glad you're okay."

Amanda thought about her mother's regrets all the way back to the Attica. She imagined how she must have spent months gathering proof of her father's financial irregularities, which included siphoning off funds from charitable organizations. How she must have known that public opprobrium would rain down—that her name would be stained along with her husband's—and she must have foreseen the loss the family would suffer: home, security, status. But she did it anyway. And she did it alone.

For the next two hours, Amanda went methodically through the apartment. Every drawer, every inch of wardrobe, even Josie's underwear drawer. She went back over two years' worth of business trips and looked for corresponding cases of women missing or killed, raising a few more question marks. The facts were organized in her mind, but she still hadn't found anything that counted as evidence. She had the key card from the Pfannenstiel Hotel in Zurich, but that was circumstantial. There was one last place she hadn't searched. A set of keys in a drawer in the bureau had a spare for Ed's downtown office. Amanda called a taxi.

Traffic backed up in the evening rush hour as they passed Raffles Hotel, lit up like a wedding cake. She directed the driver to let her out; she'd move faster on foot. Cutting through the tropical courtyard, she reached North Bridge Road and strode between angry brake lights toward the Central Library—Josie's favorite haunt—using the landmark to orient herself to a side street where Ed's office was located. A night guard barely registered her as she slipped through the automatic doors. She took the lift and followed the dimly lit corridor. She tried two keys before the third slipped into the lock with no resistance.

She let the door click behind her. Strip lights blinked on like a drunk person waking up. The office was simple but stylish, a cross between a psychiatry practice and a top-end car showroom. Two tan leather sofas faced each other across a table laden with monochrome photography books. On the wall beside this arrangement was a huge print of the picture Amanda had found on the phone in the maid's room: a blue sky broken by the dark blur of a propeller. She pulled on a pair of latex cleaning gloves and lifted the frame to peer behind, as though it might hide a safe. When the wall was blank, she felt slightly ridiculous. *It's not* The Pink Panther, she thought.

On the opposite side of the room stood a simple trestle table with an iMac and an Eames chair, also in tan leather. Amanda nudged the mouse and the computer came to life. She tried variations on his password until the screen cleared. She was drawn to Photos. She double-clicked and software whirred to life, taking its time to load. As she squinted her eyes, the flower icon turned into an aircraft propeller. Then fragments of women filled the screen—images from the hidden phone. The lips and skin and pores of other faces. She swallowed a rock that had appeared in her throat. She recognized one of these women.

The small tattoo on an expanse of skin; a lavender-colored flower that made Amanda think of orchids by the pool. She clicked Get Info to find the date of the photo, then checked her list: it matched her notes for Laureline Mackenzie. On the missing girl's Facebook page, she found an image that had been used in the media: a gang of schoolgirls with arms thrown high to reveal matching graduation tattoos.

Amanda moved the arrow to the toolbar and shut down the computer.

She was wrong.

The tattoo wasn't a Singaporean orchid. It was an Australian one. Like her friends—and like the photos on Ed's computer and the ones he'd hidden in their helper's room—Laureline Mackenzie had tucked under her arm a Cooktown orchid, the national emblem of her home state of Queensland.

Chapter 36

Amanda flailed on the cross-trainer until she was light-headed with a vertiginous sense that she might dive through the window into the morning sun and land in a flower bed, surrounded by orchids. She caught her breath on the hard sofa, her bottom leaving a heart-shaped stain, then she went for water. The wrist monitor showed her heart still racing. She needed money, her own money, the profit from her London house. She could ask Ed to authorize a transfer. *And put him on full alert.* No, as her mother pointed out, she was capable of taking what she wanted.

Using online banking, she checked the maximum ATM withdrawal amount for her account: $3,000. With Ed out of the country, she could get away with it for a few days and pay off the buyers of her bags. Or buy flights for her and Josie; screw those grasping women, she needed to look after herself now. She navigated to their joint account. Her thumb went to her lips, and she tugged at a hangnail, leaving a fuchsia rip. The balance had fallen by half a million dollars. She refreshed the page. It was true. Half a million dollars had disappeared from their account. She tapped to see the statement: the money had been transferred the previous day to a numbered account. Offshore. Unidentified.

She slapped the laptop shut. Her body prickled with adrenaline. She paced by the lift until it arrived, and then she enjoyed its thrilling free fall. *Half a million dollars.* Along the path to the swimming pool, she slapped away the orchids' slack pink mouths. *How could he do that?* She wanted to sink underwater until her lungs screamed and spots appeared before her eyes.

"Madam!"

She had marched past a man in a suit before she registered him as Raja.

"You cannot swim!"

At the deep end, a worker with a long pole poked at a mass floating in the water.

"What is that?"

"It's another dog, madam."

"Dead?" It was such a stupid question that Raja didn't answer.

Amanda trailed chlorine back to the apartment. Josie watched the activity at the pool from the kitchen.

"Whose dog is that?" Amanda said. "They're going to be devastated."

"It's a Bernese." Josie turned away. "Gets walked by a maid three times a day. The pest-control people should be more careful." Amanda watched her count ten grapes into a bowl. She filled a glass with steaming hot water and squeezed in lemon juice, before downing the cloudy liquid in one gulp.

"Good for the digestion," Josie said, through contorted lips.

"What are you struggling to digest? That handful of grapes?"

Josie picked up the bowl and made to leave.

"I'm sorry, don't run off." Amanda watched her climb onto a high stool, and then got herself a glass and pressed the lemon for the last of its juice, topping it up with hot water. "The trick is to do it on an empty stomach. Then follow it five minutes later with a shot of espresso. Goes through you like an enema."

"Spoken like a pro."

"Being thin was considered one of my achievements back in the day."

"What were the others?" Josie bothered a grape with her front teeth.

"Being rich. Being popular. Being engaged to other rich and popular people."

"How many times?"

"Engaged? Not that many. The proposals dried up after my parents lost their money."

Josie spat a seed into the bowl. "Weren't they really rich, though?"

"We thought so, but it was mostly on paper. They made a show of being philanthropic when that was in vogue. Set up a charitable foundation. I met Bono. Then my father was done for fraud and I went off the rails."

"How?"

Amanda sipped at the sour water as she considered the nights she couldn't remember and the ones she'd rather forget. Even though she'd been older than her stepdaughter at the time, her exploits now seemed tame compared to Josie's. "I subconsciously forced my parents to look after me." She clattered ice cubes into her glass. "The partying dried up along with the money. I spent my trust fund on a house when I realized my father was dipping into that too."

Josie put her hand to her bowl of grapes but found there were none left.

"I don't know why I'm talking about this," Amanda said. "I don't expect anyone to feel sorry for me. I was given more than most kids get in a lifetime. Except"—she looked in the cupboard for a mug, but it was empty, and when she opened the dishwasher she closed it again on the smell—"except I'd been sent to a school where they taught deportment and polo and they held balls where boys wore white tie and talked about their handicaps, so I wasn't qualified for real life. They bred a poodle and then expected me to be a—" Her hand flapped around in the air, grasping for a conclusion.

"Pit bull?"

"And now I sound like a spoiled cow. Which I was. Am." Amanda closed her eyes for a second and tried to regroup. She'd been rattled by the sight of that poor creature in the pool.

"Your parents were caught up in their own drama," Josie said. "Mine were the same."

Josie never mentioned her mother. A chink opened between them, a shard of light.

"We're both only children, aren't we?" Amanda nudged.

"Parents say they should stay together for the kids. But mine tore each other apart. I tried to get them to stop, act as the go-between, but I couldn't. They literally tore each other *to pieces*."

"It wasn't your fault."

"But they were fighting because of me, weren't they? Neither of them would leave because they wouldn't leave me."

"You can't blame yourself for that—"

"I trapped them in misery. If they hadn't had me, they could have walked away. And my mother would still be alive. So it is, it is my fault."

Amanda was stunned by the logic.

"But you're different," Josie went on, looking at the distant ships. "You don't have to stay. You could walk away at any time."

Amanda moved around to stand at the end of the counter, putting herself in Josie's eyeline.

"But I don't want to walk away from you," she said.

Josie got off her stool and walked past Amanda—their arms almost brushed—to reach the sink and rinse her bowl.

"You should, you know," Josie said. "You should go."

"Why?"

She laid the crockery on the draining board, then her face lightened as she pointed through the glass. "The cockatoos are here." Amanda followed her gaze to see white flashes between palm fronds. Without the raucous squabbling that accompanied the flock, it was like glimpsing angels.

"You know they're not indigenous to Singapore?" said Josie. "Just pets who escaped. So why do they hang around where people might catch them? It's like they've got Stockholm syndrome."

"Maybe they're laughing at us? All that screeching could be laughter."

Josie shook her head briskly. "They're scared. In their heart, they know they're pets."

"Are you okay, Josie?" Amanda asked. "You can tell me anything. I'm not a sweet innocent. You won't frighten me away." Once again, she had an urge to lay a reassuring hand on the girl, but her hand hovered as though trying to work out if an electric fence was switched on. There was always a tension, an invisible force field that prevented her from reaching Josie. She turned away and laid both hands flat on the cold window, on either side of the hole that Ed had smashed. She spoke instead to Josie's reflection. "If someone is hurting you—anyone at all—you can tell me. Even if it's your father. Even if it's Ed." When Josie's gaze didn't budge from the birds below, Amanda forced herself to stop staring, to look away and give her space. There was a long silence. Amanda steeled herself; clearly, she had to ask her straight out. *Has Ed ever touched you? Inappropriately?*

When the cockatoos swept out of sight, Amanda turned back to the kitchen, but Josie was gone.

Chapter 37

When Collin returned Camille's Skype call, he was framed in an Instagram-worthy shot, lying on sand with a sunset bleeding into the sea.

"Tough life then?" Camille said.

"We hiked to Tai Long Wan. What's up? I had missed calls."

"Who's we?"

"A new friend."

"The one from Tinder?"

"Turns out we have mutual friends from work. Small world."

"Are you in love?"

"It's our third date, and shut up. She's right here." He turned the phone to show a woman with hair the same color as her Ray-Ban lenses, smooth and shiny, so long it covered her bikini top. "I'm hardly listening to your conversation at all," she said in an international-school accent. "You guys carry on."

"Camille, this is Sao Lai. Sao Lai, this is my nosy sister, Camille."

Both women said, "Pleased to meet you."

"So why all the calls?" Collin said.

"I need you to come to Yangon."

"Oh God . . ."

"I got the outward clearances and float plans from the port authority. They sailed to Yangon three times in the months before they disappeared."

"And what does that prove?"

"Edward Bonham was in Yangon as well."

"How do you know that?"

"My boss told me. He'd been keeping tabs on Bonham in Singapore, and then Bonham surfaced in Yangon too."

"That doesn't make Bonham sound like someone you should trust."

"I know. That's why you've got to come and help me."

"I'm not going to Yangon to look for ghosts."

"But my boss—"

"Isn't your boss going to fire you if you act any crazier?"

"It's not crazy—"

"It is!" Collin's outburst sent Camille's view of the sunset flying. When the phone settled again, she saw that Sao Lai had laid a comforting hand on her brother's forearm. She heard him apologize and promise to be back in a few minutes. He got up and strode down the beach. He had a look on his face like an end-of-their-tether parent taking a child for a time-out. "Camille, I don't know what to say anymore. What do you think you're going to find in Yangon? It makes no sense."

"It makes sense to me."

"I don't want to hear any more about it. It upsets me, don't you get that?"

"You pretend not to care, but you do."

"Of course I care! I let it eat me up for years, just like you. But I don't want to waste my life. Before I know it, I'll be thirty, and you know what they say about turning thirty?"

"You have to stop blaming your parents."

"Exactly. So I've let it go. I quit the booze. I've got an interview that could mean a serious promotion. Like, life-changing. And this woman"—he glanced back down the beach—"you know how they say you just *know* when something's right?"

Camille's smile dragged tears into her eyes.

He shrugged at the quaintness of it.

"I understand," she said.

"That's a relief. I thought you were melting down."

"No, I get it. Because that's how I feel too. I just *know*."

Collin swore under his breath and looked out to sea.

"This Yangon connection . . . I feel like I'm on a conveyor belt, you know what I mean? It's showing the way, and I just have to do the legwork. Everything—the paperwork from the port authority, Edward Bonham, the information from my boss—all of it leads to Yangon. I'm going to Yangon, whether you help me or not."

There was a long silence, during which she heard the hiss of waves as they drowned in the sand.

"Good luck, Cami."

"Is that it?"

"Yes."

"Then . . . enjoy your date." She saw a final few seconds of sky before Collin ended the call. She let the phone idle in her hands until the screen went dark. The paperwork from the port authority was laid out in chronological piles, which she gathered up and slid inside a manila folder. She took this to the filing cabinet. Her fingers continued to another section where she'd collated reams of documents relating to helpers. She plucked out her notes on Awmi. The printout of the photo she'd taken of the pill bottles belonging to Edward Bonham slipped onto the floor, and she retrieved it.

Maybe she was crazy. Chasing secrets and lies. Maybe she should do as Collin had done—get counseling and lock the whole issue behind a door. But she'd tried that before, and it worked for a while, until the handle started rattling, like a scene in a low-budget horror movie. No, she was different from Collin. *Same same but different*, as they say in

Singapore. She'd tried shutting it down; now she would try another tack: confronting it head-on.

She closed the filing cabinet and went back to her phone. Collin wasn't the only one with work opportunities. Earlier that day, Sharmila had emailed an intriguing offer: the chance to work as a paralegal, preparing cases involving foreign domestic workers for the International Labour Organization. It was tempting, especially with her BHC job in jeopardy, but Camille sent a polite refusal. Like Collin, she was on the mend. She'd promised to concentrate on her job and she would. This suspension had turned out to be a moment of serendipity, time she needed to sort her head out.

And Collin had been right about another thing: she had no idea who to contact once she got to Yangon. She needed help, and her only option was Edward Bonham.

Chapter 38

Amanda watched a bat pluck the taut surface of the pool, making the night lights ripple. *That's me,* she thought, *even my lightest touch makes waves.* Her instinct was to get out of Singapore, away from Ed. But she didn't have the right to take Josie out of the country; she wasn't a legal guardian. At best, leaving would create a delay while Ed searched for them. At worst, Amanda could be blocked from Josie's life, and then who would watch her back?

In Josie's victimized state of mind, who knew if she would even agree to leave? Her comment about Stockholm syndrome had been directed at Amanda—a plea to *save yourself.* Or maybe Josie was self-aware enough to recognize that she was the victim: *You could free me, like the birds, but I'll still be Daddy's pet.* Amanda's fingers trailed the lids of the Chinese pots that kept her secrets, making them chatter, but she kept going to the office at the end of the corridor.

A yoga ball demarcated a corner that Amanda had once claimed. She rolled the ball across to sit in front of the filing cabinet. All their expenses went through Ed's company, which was just as well because the cost of living in Singapore drowned her in zeros—a year's rent cost a quarter of a million dollars, Josie's school fees another thirty thousand, then health insurance, life insurance, travel insurance. The figures were like a tide that swept her away to an island of her own inadequacy. Staying in Singapore without Ed's financial support was not an option.

If he were to be arrested and his assets frozen, she wouldn't be able to keep her head above water, never mind keep Josie afloat too. All this documentation proved was that Amanda was literally worth more dead. But that wouldn't help either of them.

So she and Josie had to go to the UK. With the proceeds from her London house, she could find them somewhere to live. But she needed that money, and not in dribs and drabs from the ATM. Their banking file was thin—Ed kept everything online; at least he cared for the environment—but she found a security device marked with a logo of a turtle standing on the letters CIIB. A Google search identified the Cayman Islands International Bank. Amanda went to the website and tried to log in using the number on the dongle. *Error: the username or password does not correspond to our records.* She bounced the device on her palm. She could confront Ed with it. It wasn't like the dongle was hidden under the floorboards; it was right there in the filing cabinet.

Did he assume she took no interest in their financial affairs? That she was too passive to catch him out? She dropped the device inside the folder, trying to remember the last time she'd opened it. The drawer grated in its runner. She'd been so complacent. Her dependence on Ed had crept up in degrees like a person losing fitness, each lazy decision insignificant in itself but amassing to weaken her. Let Ed sign the paperwork, let Ed take care of bills, let Ed earn the Employment Pass. Let Ed be in sole charge of Josie. Women had thrown themselves under horses to gain the freedom that Amanda dodged as though it were a clod of earth kicked up by hooves.

She caught herself rocking on the rubber ball, moving with a raw energy concentrated in her thighs. She felt like running, just getting up and going right out the window, anything to be in motion. But instead she forced herself to take control. Ed was right; independence didn't come for free.

The filing cabinet opened with a creak. There was one final document, a brown envelope containing papers. Amanda extracted a life insurance statement, a corporate policy taken out by Ed's company. It was dated to the time they arrived in Singapore, covering them both, and it was still current. In the event of her death, it would pay out $50,000. She wasn't worth as much as she believed. Not even dead.

Ed was worth considerably more: almost a million dollars. But Amanda's attention was caught by an asterisk: *bonus due to Death in Service*. She flipped to that entry. She read it twice to make sure she understood. If Ed should die of natural, criminal, or accidental causes while acting on behalf of the company, his policy was subject to a bonus payment of $2 million. She rocked back and forth on the yoga ball. So, if Ed died on a business trip—death in service—she and Josie would be free.

Her thoughts drifted back to Cuti Island, Ed lying stricken on the sand and her wondering if it might be better if he were gone. *Dead,* she forced herself to be blunt, if he were *dead*. If he was doing what she thought—to Josie and to those other women—of course he had to be stopped. She remembered her breathlessness as he'd rested on a knife-edge in the sand—as though her slightest exhalation might send him one way or the other—and the salt in her mouth. She wiped her eyes and found that the taste of salt was real. How could she think these things? For months, all she could focus on was creating new life with Ed, and now . . . what was she doing, thinking about his death? She refiled his insurance policy and held the drawer so it closed without a whisper.

As she left the office, Josie emerged from her room. Her hair was scraped back under a chunky headband. A shapeless top with long sleeves covered the tips of her fingers. Spotlights in the hallway picked out downy growth on her shins, her knees like an old man's chin. Amanda recalled a conversation, less than a year earlier, when she sent Josie to find a pair of shorts that fully covered her small buttocks so they could attend a brunch at Raffles without causing the elderly waiters to spill their mimosas. Nagging a teenage girl to show less flesh had felt vaguely satisfying, as though she were following a script from a television sitcom. *I sound just like a mum!* But this chaste, meek, puritanical Josie left her speechless.

"Won't you be hot in long sleeves?" Amanda managed to ask.

"Air con. I'm going to Starbucks."

"It's late already. Aren't you back in school tomorrow?"

"It doesn't matter. Dad called me earlier. Says he's made alternative plans."

"Plans for what?"

"School, I guess." Josie sang a few bars of an Amy Winehouse song about how her father says she's fine but stopped before the chorus and pressed the button for the lift. "Anyway, it's an emergency—I'm meeting Willow."

"I thought she wasn't allowed to see you?"

"Didn't you hear? Erin's gone mental. She called the police about Arnault, but Mae's over the age of consent. So she booked herself and Willow onto a flight back to South Africa last night, but when they got to Changi the airline wouldn't let them board without a letter from Arnault permitting them to leave the country. But in the meantime, Mae's parents found out about the affair because Erin told the school, and Mae's dad came to the Attica last night, and security wouldn't let him in, so he trashed the orchids and the police arrested him, so now Mae's dad's in the shit and he might get deported."

"They won't deport him over trashed orchids."

"Criminal damage." Josie shrugged as though stranger things had happened.

"It won't come to that—"

But a wave of her laptop case ended the conversation, and the lift doors closed.

Why does she need her laptop to meet Willow?

Amanda took out her phone and navigated to Josie's blog. The countdown ticked away. The screen reloaded to a line drawing of a Janus face, looking both ways at once, one eye open and one closed. She hesitated, as though the image might bite, and tapped again.

In the future: Four Days Until D-Day
In the past: Thirteen Days That Made Me Me
Post 7 of 13: The Week She Died

I'm in my favorite hiding place—pretending to be asleep on the back seat of the car. On the days they're talking to each other, they make jokes about it: *That girl could sleep anywhere.* I just keep my eyes closed and listen.

Today we're going to the hospital. They're not talking, and the radio isn't even on. I let my eyelids flutter and see that she's staring out of her side window. In the rearview mirror I can see Teddy's forehead frowning. The air is so tight, it's like being inside a balloon.

Teddy's hand goes to the mirror and he tugs it down, checking on me. I stop fluttering and keep my eyes closed. We stop in traffic and the car goes even quieter without the tires shushing on the wet road. Even through my eyelids, I see the glow of Christmas lights in the high street. She says they go up earlier every year; it's only November!

He ignores her for a while and then says: "Who are we seeing?"

"A consultant gynecologist. Private. They don't do prenatal paternity tests on the NHS."

"I don't suppose many people have pathologically unfaithful wives."

"You're not testing the baby, you're testing me."

"Let's not—"

"No, let's. Let's rake it up again, Edward, because we like doing that, don't we?"

"We went through it last night. Let's do the test and end the conversation."

"The test could cause a miscarriage."

"It's a tiny risk, like one in a hundred."

"It's a significant risk. I read about it on the Internet. And that's not even the point."

"What is the point, my love? That we haven't fucked in months, so how can it be mine?"

The thought of them doing it. Now I wish I was asleep. Chloe reckons she did it behind the cricket pavilion with a fifth-former from the boy's school. But it's obvious he only likes her because she goes with anyone who buys her a Coke from the vending machine.

I hear the indicator ticking and Teddy asks which building we need, so we must be at the hospital. The car stops, and it's dead quiet.

"We're early," he says.

She doesn't reply.

"Don't do your hurt act."

"What do you expect, Edward? First you make me go through this awful test, which could kill the baby, and then you don't even remember sleeping with me? I'm still your wife! And you don't remember?" She gulps as though she could suck the words back inside. Her face is hidden by a thick scarf of dark hair. "It's the drink, you know it is. God knows, you don't touch me often, but when you're pissed you might roll on for a few minutes. I take what I can get."

"You always have."

"Stop it. We've been through it. There hasn't been anyone else since—"

"Since the last time?"

"Since I came home. The baby is yours."

"If it isn't—" Teddy rips the keys out of the ignition and gets out.

"It is!"

He slams his door and then opens the one next to me. His weight on the seat, a knee beside my belly, as he rolls me into his arms. There's a smell of oranges as he reaches to click off my seat belt. I stay asleep. He places his palm on my shoulder, ready to shake me awake. His voice is low, almost a growl, and I think of that dog that chewed Chloe's face under the slide. The one they put down. "Do you hear me, woman? If that baby isn't mine, you're a goner."

Amanda shifted her focus from the screen. The windows of the surrounding apartments reflected the pool so that the whole condo appeared to be drowning. She wondered if every pane hid a scandal, secrets held by the likes of Ed and Arnault, whose status shored up their male egos until they regarded themselves as kings of the world—immune to natural morality by dint of privilege—while wives like Amanda and Erin, mere *trailing spouses* shipped between continents like the cameos once carried by colonialists, as unraveled as mad women in the attic.

In her blogs, Josie never referred to her mother by name. Maybe Ed had poisoned Josie against her, reducing the woman to an anonymous figure of contempt. But as Josie matured, her point of view would shift. Maybe these stories were a way for her to separate versions of the truth: her recollection versus her father's? Perhaps memories emerged year on year, like fossils from a cliff. The photo beside Josie's bed, taken on the day of her mother's suicide, showed them bundled up in coats. November would be about right. The timer could mark the anniversary of her mother's death. It wasn't the sort of thing you wrote on a kitchen calendar.

Once again, Amanda had a vertiginous urge to jump. She spun away from the window, past the coffee table, where she clipped a corner of her laptop and swooped to catch it. But her foot snagged the rug, and she slammed into the Chinese display cabinet, landing on her knees.

It groaned and tipped forward, sending her ginger jars sliding to the front edge of the shelves, their shifting weight rocking the unit back until it smashed against the wall. Amanda gripped her screaming knee with one hand as her pots settled with a long rattle—except for one, a diminutive blue-and-white ginger jar, the only genuine antique of the lot, which she kept out of harm's way on the highest shelf where even she couldn't reach it easily enough to store her secrets. As she watched, the jar built enough momentum to tip forward over the lip and turn a single graceful arc, lid flying clear, hitting the marble to burst into fragments.

As the sound bounced away around the apartment, her hand went to her face and she pulled a splinter from her cheek. On her fingertip, a fragment as thin as an insect stinger was tipped with her blood. She flicked it away. Another broken shard lay beside her foot, and she reached to pluck it up, intrigued by a red splash of lacquer. She turned it once in her fingertips and dropped it again. It wasn't porcelain, it was a fingernail. A fake fingernail.

Just beyond was another one, only this fingernail was painted coral with a contrasting yellow tip. Amanda sifted through the remains of the urn.

She found five acrylic fingernails, which she laid out like a ghost hand. The one in place of the pinkie finger was bronze, the color of Awmi's favorite nail polish from the set Amanda had bought her. She turned over the lid of the pot, which had broken cleanly into two halves; hidden underneath was a tiny ziplock bag containing another fingernail.

This one looked different from the others. She peeled open the plastic and tipped the nail onto her palm and brought it to eye level, letting the spotlights play over a yellowing tip and ragged edges. And the curved inner surface that was still webbed with thin coils of skin where it had been torn from the extremity of a human hand.

Chapter 39

Camille sidestepped along the arrivals concourse until her reflection on the glass overlapped Ed's flesh-and-blood figure behind the barrier. His head snapped up, as though he could feel the weight of her imprint on his back. Unbuttoning his suit jacket with one hand and swinging a carry-on with the other, he strode past passengers herding around the luggage carousel. A bank of customs officials flanked the sliding doors to the exit, and he gave a friendly nod as he swept past. One of the younger officers, her painted face framed by a hijab, giggled when he saluted her. Camille wondered what it was about pilots that gave them more swagger than, say, bus drivers.

He weaved through the blockade of families and friends, past drivers holding white boards with corporate names in block type, and out of the crowd toward the indoor taxi queue. Camille trotted alongside to match his stride.

"Hello, Ed."

He swung his case into the other hand and carried on walking. "Camille. What a coincidence."

"Not really. I've waited for three flights to come in."

"I told you I'd call as soon as I got back from Manila." He stopped behind a line of people with trolleys.

"I'm sorry to doorstep you, but things are moving on," she said.

"In which direction?"

"Toward Burma."

Ed ran his hand over his face. He looked exhausted, with nicotine-stain bags under his eyes. Or, she noted, he might have the remains of a black eye. He hadn't shaved and his sideburns were coming through gray. As though he knew she was weighing him—and finding that he came up short—he fastened his jacket. Then he peered down at her and pulled one of his sparkling smiles.

"Maybe we should plan a little trip, you and me?" he said. "A mini break in Yangon. I did a lot of business in Burma once, still have contacts." He beckoned her to keep up as the line went forward.

"Wouldn't your wife mind?"

"If she knew, I think it's very likely she would mind, yes."

Camille bobbed her eyebrows.

"Although I could tell my wife that I agreed to take you to Yangon in return for you getting HELP off our backs." The queue moved forward again.

"I resigned."

"I'm sure you could find a way. They got us banned from having another helper, so maybe that's enough punishment for the time being."

They were close to the exit now, and Camille felt a hot blast every time a taxi pulled up and the doors opened.

"You don't seem very surprised," she said.

"By what? You turning up at the airport? You've got previous . . ."

"No, by Burma. It's almost as though you knew my parents had been there."

"I told you, I don't know a Patricia and Magnus Kemble."

"So what name were the people in the photograph using when you met them in the Raffles Club in 1999? And what did you call them when you came to our house in Tanglin Green?"

Ed's smile suggested that he wanted to ruffle the top of her hair.

"I'll make a deal with you, Camille. Don't pull stunts like this. In return, I'll take you to Yangon tomorrow and get a name for the couple in that photo."

Camille's heart skipped, and when Ed advanced to the front of the queue, she was unable to move her legs. The doors opened and humid air tarred her skin. "Sentosa," he said to the attendant. He turned back to Camille with his arms spread, and for a moment she thought he might kiss her. Instead, he scooped her shoulder into one hand and flicked her hair away from the opposite ear to whisper into it.

"If you're worried about traveling with me, you can rest assured that your honor is safe. My daughter isn't much younger than you, and woe betide the man who forced himself on her." He pulled back to his full height, and once again there was a foot of air between them. She couldn't imagine this man acting as a father, especially to a vulnerable girl. "Are we on? Shall I set it up?"

"We're on."

A cab pulled up, and Ed gave Camille a salute of farewell and triumph, a ringmaster taking his leave of the circus.

Chapter 40

Ed's presence in the apartment squeezed Amanda into a girdle of tension. He was already into the booze and a rage. Beside the big window, with ships' lights on her back, she stood poised like a dancer who knew she couldn't put a foot wrong or she'd get hurt.

"If you'd been more careful, Amanda, we wouldn't be here in the first place, would we?"

He sloshed vodka into tomato juice and ground a layer of pepper, the same color as the faint cloud he had above one cheekbone, as though a black eye was fading. When she'd pointed it out, he shook her off. Another little injury explained away. A bump, a scrape, a trip. And yet she knew Ed wasn't a clumsy man. Random drinking injuries perhaps; could he be drinking more—even more—when he was away? Or something else. Someone else. A slap, a kick, a scratch. *Defensive wounds?* His bruise looked worse in the swelling orange glow, and she tried to stay focused on the argument.

"You let me think those designer bags were authentic," she said. However much she tried to hold back—avoid goading him—indignation pushed words out of her mouth.

"They were!" Ed took a swig and spat a pepper flake from his bottom lip. "Well, that last one wasn't, maybe the last two. But the others were kosher. And if you can't tell an original from a fake, then who gives a shit?"

"The people who paid me."

"Is this how you kill time, Amanda? Is this where the money goes?"

"You buy the presents, not me!"

The haze highlighted the torsion of Ed's bare shoulders as he lifted the glass. *Just a few weeks ago,* Amanda thought, *I would have slipped my hands around him. He might have dribbled Bloody Mary into my open mouth, undressed me in front of the window, making jokes about the baby names we could choose if we conceived beside water: "Skipper," he'd say; "Blue," I'd say; "Bob," he'd laugh.* Where had that Ed gone? This apartment—the soporific lights and the climate control and the lullaby motion of the boats—had lulled her into a waking dream.

Maybe nothing had changed. Maybe she had woken up.

For all that she was alert now, though, the nightmare logic remained, and she couldn't stop herself from trailing Ed into the living room; before she could think of self-preservation, she was kneeling on the sofa. The air-conditioning made a rhythmic ticking, the sound of fingernails tapping glass. She thought of the Chinese pots, where she had replaced the smashed ginger jar with a cheap doppelgänger. Five false nails, literally a handful, shrouded in tissue. A human fingernail, torn off. What would it take for him to add another one—was it more likely if she stayed or if she fled? *Because he won't let me go, especially if I take his daughter. That's not how these stories end.*

"Ed, the bank balance," she said to his back.

"I moved half a million. I need it to tide over the business. Nothing to worry about."

"It's hard not to worry. All my profit was in that account."

"All *your* profit?" Ed glanced over his shoulder, the razor-sharp angles of his profile blazing. "It's yours now, is it? What's mine is yours, and what's yours is yours too?"

Her cheeks burned as bright as the ships.

"It's been years since you sold your house, Amanda." He came toward her, the ocean lilting behind him like a stage curtain, lights flaring and dying. "What do you imagine you've been living on?" He leaned over the back of the sofa, stretching around her to grab a handful of her trim backside. "This? Do you have any idea how much our life costs? How much of your profits are left, do you think, after living like this for three years?" He released her and rested his glass on the back of the sofa, cold sweat soaking the wool.

"I can't work in Singapore."

"Expats find work all the time. They get an LOC." He took a long drink. "You don't know what that is, do you?" He rocked back on his heels, his lip curled enough to show an eyetooth. She wondered if he might hit her. It would force her into motion, like a push into a cold swimming pool. "Letter of Consent," he whispered. "Consent to work. Should a person choose to do so." He drained his drink, strolled over to the wastepaper basket, dandled the glass for a second, and hurled it down. Amanda felt a sparkle of shock, as though glass dust were tumbling through her veins.

Ed ran his hands from chin to hairline. "Got to keep face, haven't I? I've been wearing this game face for so long I can't remember what I really look like. Remember that *Bian Lian* dancer with the masks?" He glanced over at her.

"The Man with Fifteen Faces."

"My mask of sanity." He leaned a shoulder against the window, head tilted to touch the glass. "Thought I was on a roll. Throwing sixes. And I'd go out with a bang instead of just . . ." He laughed harshly. "And now I'm mixing my metaphors." He fixed his gaze on her. "What game are we playing, Mrs. Bonham?"

"I don't know, Ed."

"Come on, have a stab. You play games, don't you?"

"Solitaire?"

"That's you, solitaire. Buckaroo—that's me—I'm that donkey in Buckaroo. Stuff gets piled on my back, and if I can't bear the weight, it's game over. All the pieces go flying. So I have to bear the weight, don't I? I can't just kick it off, because I'm the man. I'm the provider—I hunt—and the women gather, and once upon a time, you gathered nuts and berries, something useful, but now you gather fucking handbags. And"—Ed strode across the room to grab a ginger jar from the shelf. He bounced it once in his hand like a choice piece of fruit—"pots." He spread his fingers wide to let it fall. "We don't chase our dinner now, but it's still okay for me to do all the running because men *want* to prove themselves—that's what they say, isn't it?—it's in our *nature*, we feel emasculated if we don't provide. We're *empowered* by working all the hours God sends, and you're *empowered* by fucking handbags."

Ed bent double, and she thought he might throw up, but instead he scrabbled the shards of pottery into a pile, as though marking a tiny grave. He came back to the window and folded himself onto the edge of the carpet, his head tipped back, eyes closed.

She'd found Ed in this pose at the New Year's Eve party in Switzerland where they first met. After they devoured each other's words for hours—stripping themselves to the bone—he excused himself to go phone his teenage daughter to say good night. His departure left Amanda lonely amid friends, too exhilarated to be weighed down by their boorishness. Toward midnight, she fled to the den, where Ed was folded up under the window, as attractive and enigmatic as a piece of origami. She smelled loneliness like the spring flowers curled beneath the snow outside. He lifted his head as though he could smell hers too. After they walked to his hotel under fireworks rising from the dark valley, he pushed her onto the balcony to see her naked in the cold.

Amanda had been drawn to his darkness. It gave her somewhere to hide. And now that she had plunged to its depths, was it unfair to be surprised? She hauled her legs from the sofa and went to him, as she had in Switzerland, sliding down the glass to sit beside him.

"Is this all Josie's got to look forward to?" he said.

"What do you mean?"

"You have hopes when your kid is born. Hopes for them, but also for *yourself*. You think it's going to get better, as though each generation is an upgrade. You think you'll be a fantastic parent—better than all the other dickheads—and your kid will turn out awesome because you'll pull yourself together and be a role model and because, in the end, you've got the fucking Bonham genes. Superior stock! Or you convince yourself it's all about nurture, right? You think that if you remove all the obstacles that held you back—all the failures you've convinced yourself are someone else's fault: your parents, your luck, your wife—then that kid will rule the world. And it's so disappointing, the way it turns out. Because however much you try—and I really tried, Amanda, I was on my own and I really tried . . ." He grabbed her hand out of the air, and she felt her lips peel apart at the tears in his eyes. "But however much you try, society gets hold of them and changes them, and however much you knock sense into their heads, they come out the same entitled, lazy, messed-up version of yourself. And it's that moment when you look at your kid and you look at yourself and you realize that you're both so fucking"—Ed banged the back of his head once, hard, against the glass—"average."

"She's far from average. She's smart and—"

"She was suspended from school. She's got no friends."

"She loves music. Cold Sister—"

"Only to please me. And I don't even like the band much myself. She latched on to it . . ."

Amanda felt a spark of anger. A reignition. "She's not a doll or an experiment, Ed. And she's not your plaything."

"She's turning into her mother." He patted the back of Amanda's hand and placed it on her knee before pushing himself to stand, wavering with the lights. "She's a slut. That's the truth of it. She's a slut like her fucking useless mother. And I have to put a stop to it."

Chapter 41

While Amanda took her morning shower, Ed left for the airport again. A potential lifeline, he said, for the business. His absence felt like loosening a belt, although the shush of air con still echoed his verdict on his own daughter: *She's a slut*. Amanda held a towel tight around her chest, hands clamped as if in prayer. She picked up his scribbled note from the bed: "No clean shirts!" His dirty linen could wait. Her phone was on charge by the window, and she looked out to sea while it fired up to reveal angry messages from SOWs, still on about bag-gate. Another mess that could wait.

She deleted texts until she reached one from Molly:

Hey, has your Facebook account been hacked? People are saying the profile of this Jacaranda woman selling fake designer bags looks exactly like yours, but you've been identity-frauded. Right?

Amanda hesitated. The secret festered like an ant nest under the coffee machine. Maybe explaining to someone would flush it out into the light. Surely Molly would be sympathetic if she knew Amanda wanted money for fertility treatment?

Can we meet for coffee? It's all a bit of a nightmare.

Molly's reply came right away: So have you been hacked?

Amanda: It's complicated. Can I explain over coffee?

Molly: Have you been hacked?

Amanda: No.

Molly: Are you saying this Jacaranda woman is you?

Amanda: It's a long story. I had no idea the bags were fake.

Molly: But why?!

Amanda: I needed money for fertility treatment.

Molly: I don't mean why you need money. I mean why would you lie to us?

Amanda: I didn't lie! I thought the bags were real.

Molly: You lied about who you are—the fake name! OMG are you the other one too? Annaliese Del Rey?

Amanda sat on the bed. She used the sheet to wipe her eyes.

Amanda: I didn't want everyone to know. I didn't want Ed to know.

Molly: You don't want people to know you're stealing from them—duh!

Amanda: I'll refund everyone.

Molly's profile displayed *typing* for a long time. Outside, a vast cruise ship eased into dock at the pace of a glacier. The horn gave a long moan, a collective sigh on behalf of the passengers at that view, this heat. The phone pinged.

> Molly: That's not the point. We're a community—SOWs and the book club—the only real community expat wives have when they're far from home. Some of my friends bought your stuff. You've ripped off your own, Amanda. That's low.

> Amanda: I'm sorry. Can you please keep it to yourself while I make it right?

> Molly: You're asking me to lie for you?

> Amanda: Just don't say anything until I've sorted it out. Please.

There was no reply. Amanda got off the bed and walked through to the kitchen. She needed tea. Cereal. Anything to fill the hollow in her stomach. She hoped there was milk in the fridge, although it would have had to be put there by fairies. The phone pinged.

> I'm sorry, but we're not close enough for me to lie on your behalf. I don't want to feel complicit in this. I'm not going to broadcast your identity, but I think it best if you keep a low profile and don't come to book club. The others are feeling less sympathetic than I am. You might want to avoid SOWs too! I hope you get this sorted and find a better way forward with your fertility treatment. Molly.

Amanda deleted the whole conversation. She went to the fridge—no milk. Bananas stewing in their own juices. *Thank God I didn't tell her about Ed and Josie.* The door closed with a slam, and she thought of Josie's blog. It seemed to represent everything Amanda felt in the last two weeks—kept in the dark with only her fears for company. *What was that timer counting down to?*

She marched along the hallway. In lieu of the contaminated pool, Josie had gone to the gym. Her bedroom had its usual seamy tinge, and Amanda gathered damp towels off the rug. The photo of Josie's mother was in place beside the bed. She picked it up and looked into the woman's eyes, wondering what she'd been thinking on the day she supposedly killed herself, leaving behind her greatest gift—her child. She squinted to see if anything was written on the Polaroid print. The white space was hidden by cardboard, making the photo into a neat square. She looked closer and saw a tiny fleck of blue; the top of a scribble? *A scribble of a girl . . .*

Amanda turned the frame, an expensive one with tiny screws in the back. On Josie's desk, she found a metal nail file and used it to open the frame. She lifted away the wooden backing, cardboard, and finally the Polaroid. When she turned the picture, a flurry of air-conditioning chilled her neck, as though it were coming from the scene in her hands. Mother and daughter—so alike—pummeled by the elements. And beneath the picture, in the white space, a handwritten note: "Beachy Head, 13 November."

It made sense. Beachy Head: a notorious suicide spot. And 13 November: three days from now, a bleak anniversary marked by a bereaved child. She returned the photo to the frame and left it beside Josie's bed. Of course, she must be fascinated with her mother's suicide. If Ed's unwillingness to deal with his daughter's current issues was anything to go by, she'd never been given a chance to talk, to grieve. Until she found the dark corners of the Internet.

Amanda opened the blog on her phone. A new post was illustrated with a black-and-white GIF of Amy Winehouse giving a double thumbs-up as she left a room, above the caption "They only miss you when you're gone."

In the future: Three Days Until D-Day
In the past: Thirteen Days That Made Me Me
Post 8 of 13: Hospital

When the doctor comes in, I'm lying across the plastic seats in the waiting room, listening to Teddy's ancient Walkman. I only had time to throw a cardigan over my pajamas before we came to the hospital, and I see the doctor's eyes flick over my vest top. As the singer says on Teddy's cassette, I was the first one in my class to grow breasts. The doctor looks too young to know Pulp. I'm lucky to have Teddy teaching me grown-up stuff.

"Josie Bonham?" The doctor sits in a chair by turning it around with its back to me and straddling it. Like a cowboy.

"Are you a doctor?"

"Yes, I've been looking after your mum since she came in. You can see her if you like."

"Is she going to live?"

"Of course! She'll be fine, and so will the baby."

I fold my arms and feel my boobs press together.

"What's your name?"

"Dr. Khan. I'm your mother's gynecologist. Luckily, I was on call tonight, so I got here in time to meet her ambulance. Do you understand what happened, Josie?"

"Where's my dad?"

"I thought he would be here with you, actually. Do you know when he'll be back?"

I shake my head.

"He seemed upset earlier, so . . ." Dr. Khan looks around as though Teddy might be hiding behind the window blinds.

"He thinks the baby's not his, so . . ."

For a moment, I think Dr. Khan is going to say something important. But then he slaps both hands on his thighs and says, "I'll catch up with him later then. Do you want to come and see your mum?"

"Do you smoke?" I say.

"Nasty habit," he says.

"Yeah, but do you?"

That makes him laugh. "I do actually. Surprising how many doctors smoke."

"Can I have one? It's been a tough night."

"I'm not giving a cigarette to a fifteen-year-old."

I can't help smiling, even though that shows my braces.

"You're not even fifteen, are you? God, I'm old." He spins the chair under the table and when his pager trills, he clicks it off without looking. His thumb stays hooked in his jeans, a cowboy again. "Your mother won't be discharged until morning, so after you visit her you can go home."

I walk under his nose to the door. "Who's going to take me home tonight?"

He comes around behind my back, reaching to open the door like a gentleman. I put my hand around his wrist, and the touch makes my stomach knot. The softness of his skin over the hardness of the muscle. His sinews twist out of my grip, and he steps back.

"I'm sure you're feeling upset after everything that's happened today," he says. "We should find your father now." He's holding his wrist in the other hand as though I burned him.

The pager chirps again, disturbing us, and I reach toward his waistband to switch it off.

"Stop. That's not appropriate behavior between a child and an adult. In fact, I think we should open this door now." He steps quickly around me, pulls open the waiting room door, and goes outside. Along the corridor, I see Teddy walk up to the nurses' station, where one of the blue dresses takes his empty coffee cup and fluffs up her white hair.

"My dad's coming," I say, and Dr. Khan glances over his shoulder. "Are you going to tell him what just happened?"

The pager goes off again, and Dr. Khan crushes it in his hand. His eyes are soft and hard at the same time, like his wrist, like my insides as I wonder if he will tell Teddy and what Teddy will do if he does. But the doctor shakes his head. "If you need to talk, Josie, about . . . whatever's troubling you, I can recommend someone. She's a great therapist, you can tell her anything."

"What's going on?" Teddy arrives and stands behind me. His hands land on my shoulders and slide down my bare arms to enclose my wrists. Dr. Khan pushes his own hands deep into his pockets.

"It seems likely the amniocentesis prompted some bleeding—"

"The paternity test?"

"—but it's stopped now and the baby's heartbeat is steady. Your wife has been admitted for observation so you can go home and get some sleep. Unless, Josie, you'd prefer to stay with your mother? I could make arrangements—"

"We're going home," says Teddy. "We're on holiday tomorrow."

"Your wife needs rest, Mr. Bonham. Please be careful."

Teddy sends me toward the sliding doors with a little push. "If Mrs. Bonham knew how to be careful, Dr. Khan, we wouldn't be here in the first place, would we?"

Chapter 42

Amanda watched Josie from the doorway of her room. Her wet hair made her seem smaller than usual, and Amanda couldn't shake the image of the young girl from the blog, trapped between warring parents in the sterile atmosphere of a hospital. Even after her workout, Josie bristled with pent-up energy, rocking side to side on her swivel chair, an espresso cup nesting in her hands.

An overnight bag lay open on the bed. "Why are you packing?" Amanda asked.

"Going to Willow's for a sleepover."

"I thought she wasn't allowed to see you?"

"I don't think Erin cares anymore." Josie flickered a hand. "They're leaving any day now."

"What about school?"

"Dad says not to bother." She pushed herself into a full spin, as restless as a toddler. "I'm not going back because of Switzerland."

"I don't understand. What about Switzerland?"

"The new school? Zurich?" Josie stopped herself abruptly by catching her feet against the wheels. She opened a drawer, took out a sheaf of papers, and handed the top sheet to Amanda. The heavy paper was embossed with the logo of the Institut Zugerberg: a boarding school for girls in the Swiss tradition. The letter confirmed that Josie had a place to start.

"When did this happen?"

"We talked about it after the suspension. But when the photos were posted online . . . He doesn't want me going to a school where everyone saw me getting fucked."

Amanda winced at her bluntness.

Josie shrugged. "He says it's a better education."

"The schools in Singapore are excellent."

"Didn't he tell you?" Josie's voice took on a cold edge that Amanda hadn't heard since she first met Ed. Josie had grounds to be angry, that was certain, but not to take it out on Amanda. She had always dealt with Josie's hostility by letting her comments slide off like ice cubes and resolved to do the same now.

"Do you want to go to this school, Josie?"

"Dad says he's in Zurich every few weeks. We can spend weekends together. There's an airstrip, and he knows someone who knows someone, so I'll learn to fly."

"But do you want to go?"

"Not really." Josie spun her chair again, dark hair snapping around her head. Amanda recalled the beach at Cuti Island and Josie offering to help with a new baby. Was she going along with this plan because she felt she had to make room? Or was she too scared to say no? "You don't have to go, Josie. I'll talk to your dad when he gets back from Manila."

Josie rolled her eyes. "He's in Burma."

Amanda looked at the coffee in Josie's hands and ached for a shot. Something to wake her up. "What about your friends?" Even as she said it, she thought, *What friends?*

Josie shrugged again. "Willow will be gone soon. That's expat life: everybody leaves. This sleepover might be the last time I see her."

"I'm sorry, Josie. Say goodbye from me."

"And the others will miss me when I'm gone, right?"

Amanda pictured Amy Winehouse's frail figure in a doorway. They both stood in silence. The conversation flitted away like a bat.

"Can I keep this?" Amanda said. There was a phone number on the school letter; she would call later, once Switzerland woke up, to check if Josie really had a place. If it was true that Ed planned to send her away. She left the room thinking that if he'd done all this to take Josie to the mountains for long weekends, his reasons could be far from natural. She reached her wall of ginger jars, and instead of comforting her, their prissy arrangement was annoying. How ironic that she collected empty vessels, curated versions of herself: pretty, flimsy, hollow.

It was time to ask Josie about Ed. Straight out. The girl had opened up about school, so maybe she was ready to talk. But how to say it? *Just start and see where it goes.* She forced herself back toward Josie's door. Even if Josie denied it or refused to answer, she would be able to read something in her reaction. She had to ask her outright. Now. The door was ajar—

A loud trill rang through the apartment. The iPhone lay dormant in Amanda's hand, but the trill repeated. Must be the other phone, the house phone. It never rang. Amanda went into the living area and scrabbled around beside the TV for the handset.

"Hello?"

The line was dense with wind noise, as though she'd been pitched into the air along with the signal. Slowly it solidified into a voice: male, accented, Asian.

"Ah . . . Mr. Bonham? Edward Bonham?" Ed-*Ward* Bon-*Ham.*

"No, this is his wife. Can I help you?"

"Ma'am, I'm looking for a Mr. Ed-ward Bon-ham?" An American lilt told her the voice was Filipino.

"He's not here. Can I ask who's calling?"

"Do you know where I might find him, ma'am?"

"He's traveling. Is this Bernardo?"

"Bernardo? No, ma'am. I don't know a Bernardo. Does Mr. Bon-ham have a cell phone number?"

"No." Amanda winced. No idea why she felt the need to lie, and such a ridiculous lie at that.

"Mr. Bon-ham doesn't have a cell phone?" A ripple of amusement.

"Yes, I mean, of course he does, but—" The man's voice was robotic, like he was programmed, and she knew instinctively that he wasn't someone she could charm. He seemed to reach down the line and catch her around the throat. "What I mean to say is, he's not available on his mobile now. He's on a flight. But I can get a message to him if you tell me who's calling."

A small sigh, maybe only a shift in the ether. "This is the police, ma'am. In Manila. We would like to speak to Mr. Ed-ward Bon-ham."

Amanda's heart trilled like another phone ringing. "What's it about?"

"I am not at liberty to discuss, ma'am. But if Mr. Bon-ham—"

"Was it another woman?"

The line creaked and groaned with a sound like a weighty person sitting down in a wooden chair. For long seconds, Amanda listened to other noises too, distant voices or scratches of white sound, and wondered if they were interference or whether the policeman had put his hand over the mouthpiece to speak to someone in the background.

"Hello?"

"His number please, ma'am."

Amanda reeled off the number from memory. The officer thanked her, and the line went dead. She placed the handset back in its stand, its charging light turning red.

She went to her laptop. A Google search for "woman, death, Manila" revealed so many hits she knew she had to narrow it down. She strode through to Ed's bathroom, fishing in the wastebasket for receipts, finding a thick envelope. She pulled the papers out and checked the dates; yes, they were from his trip to Manila earlier this week. The envelope itself was embossed with a logo for the Makati Plaza Hotel. That was all she needed to know. She jogged back to her laptop and put the hotel's name into an advanced Google search, refining the dates to the past three days. There was one hit on a local news site.

Police suspect foul play in death of bar girl

The brief story detailed how a hostess was seen leaving the bar of the Makati Plaza Hotel with a Caucasian man, hours before her body was found in a dumpster behind the building. The woman, eighteen years old, was the daughter of a nightclub singer, which was the main focus of the piece. The police were linking the death to a number of previous assaults near the hotel. Amanda recalled Ed describing his plan for Josie's birthday when they sat on the deck at Cuti Island: *I've been practicing a lot recently . . . I've tested a few locations.*

She double-clicked a grainy photo so that it filled the screen. A pair of stockinged legs sprawled in a spotlight cast by a streetlamp. The photo had a staged quality, like a still from a film noir. But as the image clarified, Amanda felt she was standing there in the alley, inhaling the viscous stink of grease blasting from the kitchen, her eyes adjusting until she made out the figure of a girl, tiny and broken, framed by the light and the aura of her spread-eagled hair. Amanda's thoughts went to Josie's photo, the one of her and her mother, their hair tangled in the wind.

Her head spun with vertigo. *I have to know if he is doing these things.* She could be in space, in a vacuum, unable to get oxygen, literally drowning in nothing. Because she had so much evidence and yet nothing of substance. So many puzzle pieces, but she still couldn't put Ed in the picture. However hard she looked, she couldn't make him out. *I can't see it,* she thought. *I can't see Ed, my Ed, murdering a woman.*

Tears came then, with a gulp like a baby's first breath. How many other women had deluded themselves? How many wives of serial killers refused to face the truth until it crept up to their doorstep in the form of police officer's footsteps? She had a simple choice: be an enabler or fight for the truth—whatever the personal cost—like her mother once did. *But I have to be sure. I have to see it to believe it.* She laid her fingers onto the image of the dead woman on the screen as though feeling for a pulse.

Chapter 43

Out of the corner of her eye, Camille noted that the man sprawled on a barstool—the only other guest in the Raffles Club of Yangon—was subjecting her to a detailed visual analysis. This was exactly why she hated bars, this feeling of being a skinny heifer at a cattle sale, inspected and found wanting. The barman polished coffee cups and watched the scene with interest but no allegiance. Late-morning sunlight gave the street outside the arched doorway the same washed-out tone as the photo of her parents, taken in this very spot fifteen years earlier.

Ed was late; maybe his flight had been delayed? Camille checked her phone before she remembered she had no roaming service. Cell phones weren't banned in Burma, not anymore. But the Wi-Fi flowed like treacle through a tissue.

A woman entered, a walking posy of flowers, and the man who'd been watching Camille slid to her side, calling to the barman for coffee to go. Camille felt a warm flush of shame. Maybe he had just been wondering why the white woman looked in such a state? She used a napkin to dab the shine off her nose and was just considering lipstick when Ed arrived, eating up the bar in his long stride. His hand wiped his face, like a showman changing his expression from happy to sad. Or sad to happy.

"Morning, Cami." Ed waved at the barman. "Americano. What would you like?"

She tilted her glass to indicate the iced coffee. "So, have you heard from your contact?"

"Straight to business. He should be here soon. I just hope—" Whatever he hoped for was interrupted by a waiter with a squat glass of water. "I just hope you're not disappointed."

"Whatever happens, I appreciate you coming here."

"Least I could do."

"Well, it's not really, is it?" She plucked the straw from her drink and used it to emphasize her point. "The least would have been giving me a phone number scribbled on a piece of paper. Or calling ahead to set up a meeting. But instead you jump on a plane to a dodgy country—"

"Burma's all right." He toasted Burma.

"You know what I mean. You don't have to be here."

"I do have to be here, as it happens. The people I know don't talk to strangers."

"Who are they?"

"Doesn't matter."

"How do you know them?"

"Previous life. I don't really want to elaborate any more than I have to."

"Don't you think I have a right to know?"

"Not really, no. Unless you're looking for problems. Are you looking for problems, Camille?"

She held his stare while the waiter placed a coffee between them and scuttled away.

"Ed, look, I don't want to compromise you. But I do want to find out what happened to my parents. And if I know how they were involved with these people, how you were involved, I'll be better placed to get the information I need."

"Knowledge is not always power. Sometimes it's a millstone around your neck." Over Ed's shoulder, the barman rattled peanuts into a bowl. Ed turned his chair so he could see the doorway.

"All right then, let me tell you what I know," she said, "and you can correct me if I'm wrong."

Ed produced a bottle of pills, unscrewed the cap, and palmed two into his mouth. Camille tried to glimpse the label, but he slipped it back in his pocket. She picked up her drink and sheltered it in her lap. "I assume we're meeting a government contact from the 1990s. My boss confirmed that you and my parents were in Burma at that time, during the old regime, the military junta. Of course, Burma was closed then and heavily sanctioned by the West, so when my parents got picked up, the British authorities had little or no influence." She took her straw and jabbed it rapidly between the ice cubes, glancing at Ed's face as she said, "A tourism business would have been a good cover for spies."

"Spies?" Ed's eyes left the door and fixed on her.

"Joshua MacAlpine was watching you. Said your activities were suspicious."

"You think we were spies?" Ed's softened tone was too much. His hand rose and fell, as though he wanted to pat her arm but thought better of it. She felt like an angry child tempted to dissolve into the open arms of a forgiving parent.

"Weren't you?" she whispered.

"I wasn't a spy, Camille." Ed downed his coffee and checked his phone. "He should be here by now. Fucking useless Wi-Fi. We need to go to the hotel and find out if he left a message."

"You don't think my parents were spies?"

Ed looked over to the bar and made a scribble sign in the air. "I didn't really know them, not personally. And I never heard anything about espionage. Yes, I want the bill, that's the universal sign for 'bring me the bill.' What do you think I want, your fucking autograph?"

The solid ground under Camille's feet crumpled and fell away. Josh had all but denied her romantic idea of espionage, but she had clung to the notion, convinced that her simple faith in her parents' goodness could make it true. She had always thought of herself as a rationalist, but instead she'd proved to be an idealist; like everyone who lives inside an echo chamber, she only listened to what she wanted to hear.

"Are you coming?" Ed swung a rucksack over his shoulder.

Camille teetered on the edge. The rules she had made—never be alone with Ed, stay in public places, don't take risks—seemed juvenile now. It was time to be a realist.

"If my parents weren't spies, Ed, why *did* you meet them in Burma?"

He let out a sharp breath. "I thought we were on the same page here." He did the face wipe again, but this time sad remained sad. "If you really need to know, Camille, your parents were in the same shitty business as me. Drug trafficking. Me and your parents, we weren't spies—we were drug mules."

Chapter 44

The a-scribble-of-a-girl website had become an obsession for Amanda, a compulsive tic. She had read today's post already—Teddy separating little Josie from her sick mother, just as he now planned to remove her from Singapore—but she couldn't resist checking her phone again, even while navigating a busy street. Jostled by pedestrians, she squinted at the countdown clock: 00 days, 13 hours, 34 minutes.

Where had the time gone? Only this morning the clock had said three days. How could the timer skip so far ahead?

Thirteen hours.

She felt a tingle of rage in her fingers: What was Josie playing at? Thirteen hours took her to the early hours of tomorrow morning. If Josie was counting down to the anniversary of her mother's death on November 13, why jump to tomorrow morning? And what would happen to the remaining blog posts? She'd expected five more installments until she knew what happened between Ed and his dead wife. Would she ever find out now?

She caught a glimpse of herself in a shop window. A shapeless dress added a size to her frame, and harsh lipstick added years to her age—a disguise of sorts. For good measure, she had pulled on a baseball cap and sunglasses. Molly's words rang in her head: *You might want to keep a low profile.* An understatement. Amanda wanted the ground to swallow her up, but she'd settle for not being recognized by any SOWs on home turf.

This area was her hunting ground, where she had plied her trade: this branch of Starbucks, this cute bakery, this café overlooking the water. She had soiled her own backyard. But now that she had what she'd come for—the only item of value she had left: the engagement ring from the safety-deposit box—she could scuttle home and hide.

The promenade beside the water was mostly deserted in the heat of the day, and she hurried to the taxi stand, her sunglasses sliding down her sweaty nose. But as she passed an alfresco café, ducking for a moment's relief into a fine mist of water sprayed over the sidewalk, she heard a voice she recognized: "I must be honest, ma'am, I'm an ex-con, ma'am." The octopus-tattoo guy hawking smiley-face key rings. He launched into a monologue aimed at two tourists nursing iced coffees. Amanda veered into the seating area and took an empty table.

Any day now, Ed would spirit Josie away—the admissions officer at the Institut Zugerberg in Zurich had confirmed there was a place reserved for Josie. What then? Amanda couldn't wait for the blog to show her the real Ed; she needed to go looking for him.

A shadow slid across the sun, and the ex-con aimed his spiel at Amanda.

"I'm selling these high-quality products, ma'am, to achieve my goal of an honest life."

She held up her palm. "Don't want a bloody key ring."

"It's only ten dollars, ma'am."

"That's criminal!"

"It's a lot to me, ma'am." The man's head and shoulders twitched in the body language spoken by recovering drug addicts the world over.

"I'm going to call the manager." She picked up her bag as though he might snatch it. His eyes flared, and he lumbered away along the sunbaked waterfront with his face turned from the yachts that nodded like canting clergy at his disgrace. Amanda left the café and trailed him at a distance. To be sure about Ed's activities—enough to hand him in and give up everything she had in the process—she needed to get close enough to see for herself. She could be in Burma by tonight, but she had to go incognito—she didn't want to get implicated alongside him—and that would take more than a shapeless dress and sunglasses.

The man stomped on, head down under bent shoulders, and eventually turned into an underpass. Amanda scurried forward to catch up. Her eyes adjusted halfway down the stairs, and she realized he was waiting at the bottom, eyes squinted as she descended toward him. He put the key rings against the concrete wall, as though signaling that they both knew this encounter did not involve smiley faces.

"I had to make you leave," she said. "I can't speak to you in public."

The man rolled his head to one side.

"I need something."

A flicker of his eyebrows and twitch of a shoulder showed that his temporary stillness was passing, as though he could only hold the pose for a short time.

"I'll pay you more than key rings."

"What you need?"

"I need to know you're trustworthy. Properly trustworthy, I mean. Not this 'faith in my honesty' shit."

"I've gone straight."

"But you know people?"

His eyes flickered to the top of the stairs, where Amanda saw a CCTV camera. She reached down and fingered a smiley-face key ring. Plucking one from the board, she handed him a ten-dollar note. "Let's walk." The key rings chattered, but she didn't talk until they reached a maintenance stairwell, its door ajar. Inside, he settled. The intrigue calmed his agitation like the hair of the dog to a drunk.

"I need a passport," she said.

"Do I look like an embassy?"

Amanda held out a fan of banknotes, fresh from the ATM. A crisp tang of hope filled the air. "I need a special kind of passport," she said, and the guy put down his board. "One that doesn't have my name in it."

Chapter 45

Ed's hotel room was a sea of overvarnished wood. Muslin drapes framed the french windows. He threw the shutters open to reveal an ornate Juliet balcony, then sat by his laptop with bars of sunlight lining his back. "Help yourself to a drink." The curtains began to sway limply against the breeze.

Drugs.

It made sense. Smuggled on and off her parents' yacht in the trash or wrapped inside the sails, maybe even hidden in the luggage of guests. She could imagine a dozen ways they would have been able to bring packages ashore. She could see them smiling as they sluiced down the deck. Then the sunbaked image whited out.

Drug runners, traffickers, criminals.

Her parents.

"What if they'd been caught?" she asked. "What would have happened to me and Collin?"

Ed didn't turn around. "Maybe they didn't have any other option."

"Getting a job is another option. Something decent."

"You wanted to dig up the past."

Camille shifted in her seat. She was parched but didn't want to drink his bottled water, just in case—she hadn't forgotten the bottles of clonazepam. "Does your wife know you were a drug trafficker?"

His unkempt hair shook. Camille saw the vulnerable place where
the smooth skin of his neck slid inside his shirt. She wondered what
would happen if she reached out and stroked him there, which of the
Edward Bonhams would respond: the father, the husband, the man who
carried date-rape drugs? And which version of Camille would touch
him: daughter, lover, an impetuous someone she could feel lurking
under her own skin? She watched a pulse beat in his throat.

"And your daughter? Does she know?"

"Oh, shit!" Ed jumped up from his laptop, hand clamped to his
nose. He swore again as he turned, blood dripping between his fingers.
Camille snatched a towel from the bathroom and told him to tip his
head back. It was awkward on the high-backed chairs, so she pushed
him to the bed. He lay flat and blood ran down the sides of his chin and
over his nape onto the white sheets. She pressed the towel to his face,
an archipelago of red islands rising to its surface. She left him holding
the cloth and fetched a bath towel. She mopped his face and scrubbed
at the sheets beneath his head.

"Don't worry about the mess," he kept saying. But she did worry.
The blood kept coming. She soaked one corner of the towel with water
from a bottle and wiped his face. He closed his eyes, lips pressed tightly
together as though he was humiliated by her attentions. After a while,
his nose stopped bleeding. But he stayed down. Camille stayed next
to him.

"Can you get me a drink?" he said.

"Water?"

"Yuck."

She got a whisky out of the minibar and poured it over two ice
cubes. Ed pulled a pillow under his head, palming blood onto the cotton, and propped himself up to drink.

"I've never seen a nose bleed that much," she said.

"It happens."

"How often?"

"Too often." Ed swirled his scotch in a figure eight, creating a storm in a glass. "I may have developed epilepsy."

"At your age?"

"It can happen even to an old guy like me. I've had dizzy spells over the years, migraines. Easy to ignore. I thought it was stress, a hangover, lack of sleep. Didn't recognize them as symptoms. Until I had an actual seizure, what they call a grand mal. Like you see in movies, fitting, drooling, the works. So it looks more and more like I have epilepsy."

"You *think*? Don't you know?"

"No formal diagnosis."

"Why not?"

"You can't get epilepsy in my business."

Camille drew back from him. "You're a pilot . . ."

"And if I report it to some well-meaning doctor in Singapore, he'll have to pass it on to the authorities. They'll stop me flying."

"You've been flying planes even though you have seizures?"

"I don't take passengers. Well, only my fucking useless partner, Bernardo, and no one would miss him."

"But that's crazy. What if you have a seizure in the air?"

"I haven't had one for ages. A few slips and falls. Minor injuries: black eyes, nosebleeds. Nothing serious—until last week on the beach. But I'd missed my medication for a few days; the police confiscated the lot, and I couldn't get more until I saw my friendly doctor in Manila, so . . ." He waved his hand to indicate it was irrelevant, but his eyes flicked to hers and away again. "I can control the seizures with medication."

"Clonazepam doesn't mix with alcohol. You shouldn't be drinking."

Ed's whisky glass stopped in front of his mouth. "How do you know I take clonazepam?"

"You took something in the bar, right in front of me. And the police found bottles of it in your helper's room when she died. I thought maybe they were—" She stopped.

"What?"

"Clonazepam can be used as a date-rape drug."

"Jesus! With all due respect, I don't need to rape anyone."

"Rape isn't about need. It's about power."

"Needing that kind of power is a sign of weakness, as far as I'm concerned. No, the medication is for seizures. Our maid hid them in her room so Amanda wouldn't find out. I paid her to keep quiet."

"Why don't you just tell Amanda?"

"Because"—Ed adjusted himself on the pillow again, smearing more blood—"because my business is going to fail when I lose my license, and there's nothing I can do to stop it. And we're all dependent on the business. Not just the income but the school fees, our apartment, our health care, even the right to stay in Singapore. We live in this bubble and I'm about to pop it." He drained his glass, losing most of the scotch down his chin, where it spread the blood onto the sheets. His head dropped back onto the sullied pillow.

"Maybe she deserves to know."

"And maybe she deserves not to be dropped on her arse by a man she trusted with her whole life. It's not easy letting someone down." He held his drink out, nudging Camille off the bed toward the minibar. She refilled the glass, which he accepted, and he patted the sheet for her to sit. "My wife worries that she's dependent on me, but she has no idea how dependent I am on her."

"Because you love her?"

"But does she love me enough to be the wife of a failure?"

"For better or for worse?"

He gave a grunt of laughter. "In my experience, wives prefer better."

"You're very cynical."

"You know what they say: when a cynic smells flowers, he looks around for a coffin."

"It's intellectually lazy," Camille said.

"It's experience."

"It's a cop-out. It means you don't have to bother trying."

He rolled up into a sitting position. "Your youthful optimism is delightful, but you're the one being intellectually lazy."

"Why's that?"

"Because you're ignoring the fact that you don't know what the fuck you're talking about."

She got up and went to the window, wrenching the window wide open, its latch scraping in a well-worn groove.

"When is your contact going to arrive?" she said.

"I'm waiting for his call. Be patient."

Outside, it was unnaturally quiet. Car horns were once banned in Yangon, and Camille wondered how long people went on obeying the rules out of habit. She heard Ed move off the bed and stand behind her. Her eyes stayed on the street, but the tiny hairs on her nape rose toward him like coral on the tide.

"I remember you," she said. "You came to our house once, to a party in the garden."

Ed didn't say anything, so she turned, the muslin curtain slipping over her arm as soft as a bedsheet. She took a step backward so she could study his face, the ornate railing of the balcony a hard line against her back.

"I remember you too," he said. "You nearly drowned me."

"It was just a splash."

Ed squinted. "How much do you remember?"

"I was in the pool. You put your feet in—"

"You soaked me."

"And I remember thinking Mum would be angry. And I would have to tell her what I'd done . . ."

"And the bear? Do you remember the bear?"

"Oh yes! You brought us teddy bears. Even though we were too old for them."

"Single bloke. I had no idea what to buy for kids."

"I really liked it." Camille saw again a handsome bear, its silky fur and chubby thighs, and a scarf around its neck. She remembered how it was so perfect she couldn't believe it was for her—wouldn't even let herself wish for it, because she couldn't stand the disappointment—so instead of saying thank you, she handed it back to the guest, Daddy's work friend, and felt silly when everyone cooed. She loved that bear at first sight. "Teddy brought a teddy. We thought that was hilarious."

Ed smiled, and Camille realized again how beautiful he could look. "No one's called me Teddy for years."

"Was it your code name?" said Camille.

He laughed. "You've watched too much TV. Everyone called me Teddy back then; it was a nickname."

"And now?"

"Just Ed. I came home from Singapore and changed my ways. I wanted to distance myself from that boy who made childish decisions. So I went back to Edward. Ed. And my wife hated the name Teddy. It drove her crazy later when Josie picked it up again."

"But in my garden you were still Teddy."

"That party was the death of Teddy. Do you remember what happened after you drowned me?"

She turned her back on him, and the balcony pressed into her stomach. He slid sideways onto the narrow ledge beside her, his hand encircling her wrist as though they might jump. She smelled a hint of woody orange, from either Ed or the gardens, and closed her eyes as she leaned a shoulder into his chest.

"What do you remember, Camille?"

The water refreshing me like cool voltage. But after she soaked their guest, the shame burned her up. She ran toward the patio—calling out that she was sorry—but her mother was gone. She followed voices through the house. With her hand on the cold metal latch of the window frame, she edged it open until she could make out words from the road out front.

"We have a warrant, Mr. Kemble."

The police officers—two of them, with two more beside patrol cars on the drive—waited while her father inspected the paperwork. Her mother appeared in the doorway, ushering Collin toward the back garden with a football in one hand and a teddy bear in the other. "Quickly, Cami," her mother ordered, and she followed.

In the back garden, her mother spun her by the wrist so that Camille folded in a curtsy onto the blanket. Her mother snatched the teddy and flipped him onto his tummy on the tartan wool. A zip along his furry back ripped open, making Camille wince, and mother wiggled a white package inside. She zipped the bear up and pressed it into Cami's hands, and repeated the same with Collin's teddy. "Sit. Stay. Do not say a word to the police," her mother ordered. "You're having a teddy bears' picnic. Understand?"

"Yes, mummy."

"Look natural." Their mother whirled into the house. Teddy stood alone on the patio. His eyes moved between Cami and Collin—he looked upset—and she felt a jolt in her tummy; they weren't doing what Mother told them. They weren't looking natural.

"Come on, Col," she said. And she started singing "Teddy Bears' Picnic" in a wavering voice.

"You're in for a big surprise," said Collin.

She looked up at Teddy and saw his eyes wet with tears. She had to try harder. She sang as Teddy strode past them, down the path into the woods, where he vanished between the trees.

Camille released her hands from the metal balcony of the Oriental Hotel. "We played teddy bears' picnic until the police left," she said. Sharp slivers of lead paint were embedded in her skin.

"I couldn't watch," Ed said.

"It must have been terrifying. You know what happens to drug smugglers in Singapore."

"It wasn't that. I was too cocky or nihilistic to think about consequences. But I couldn't watch your parents do that to their children. They behaved more like addicts than dealers; there was nothing they wouldn't do. It was—" He released her wrist. "It woke me up."

"They hid drugs inside our teddy bears?"

"I started to wonder what else they might be capable of. Would they use you two as mules once you were old enough? Or force you to swallow packages?"

"My parents never hurt us."

"I'm relieved to hear that. I felt guilty about leaving you. That stayed with me for a long time. I shouldn't have left two kids to fend for themselves with parents who weren't responsible. Later, when Josie came along, I—" Ed went to the bedside table and downed the dregs of the whisky before coming back to the balcony. "I guess they sent you to boarding school after that. Maybe it was a wake-up call for them too."

"So what happened after your . . . epiphany?" Her voice sounded as spiky as the lead paint on her hands.

"That's what it felt like when I stood in that rain forest with the sun throwing down spears through the trees. The cicadas stopped, and all I could hear was your teddy bears' bloody picnic. I knew drugs ruined lives. That there were junkie mothers. Broken homes. Innocent people killed by dealers. That I was the seed that rooted these problems. But out of sight is out of mind, right? And I really was a cocky little shit. But standing in the rain forest, with your voice and those pointing fingers of sunlight, I had a fucking epiphany. That's the exact right word for it."

"So you stopped being Teddy?"

"I did. Well, almost. Until Josie picked up the name. Infuriated her mother."

"What happened to her?"

"Different set of problems. Depression she struggled with for years. It got worse after Josie arrived. It consumed her. I tried to keep Josie away from the worst of it, but . . . I often thought of your parents during that time. Guess I understood them a little better. Parenting is easy until you have kids." His hands landed softly on her shoulders for a moment and then slid the length of her arms to her wrists. Camille turned to face him, a foot of dying sunlight between them. His face blushed with watery blood. If he were to lean down a few inches, he might kiss her on the forehead.

"Do you cheat on your wife?"

He released her wrists. "It would be simple enough, the amount of traveling I do. Women approach me quite often in hotel bars, we have a drink, and they *talk*. Maybe it's the darkness or the booze, but I've heard it all—secrets, disappointments, affairs. It's more intimate than a hookup in some ways. I'm like a priest."

"And then what?"

"I say good night."

"After all that flirting?"

"Not flirting—listening. But it's true, once or twice a woman has been angry or even tearful because she assumed I would hit on her sooner or later—because that's what men do, isn't it, given half a chance? It's such a cliché."

"Some clichés exist for a reason. So what do you get out of it?"

"Business travel is boring. People think it's glamorous, but it's boring and lonely. So sometimes I talk. When I feel like it. I never get to be honest at home. Not without causing aftershocks that might hit the next day or in a month's time. But talking in a bar with a woman I hardly know who just wants to hear the truth—it feels like freedom."

"I bet you don't tell your wife."

"No, I don't."

"Because you're emotionally unfaithful. Which is a little socio-pathic, to be honest."

"There's no betrayal. No ulterior motives. No power play."

Camille reached out and wiped a shadow of blood from his chin. It was odd, she thought, but despite being alone in a hotel room in a strange country with a man she barely knew who was covered in blood, she felt quite safe with Ed. The air between them was crystal clear. He caught her wrist and tucked it around his back. His other hand pressed her brow, so that her face turned sideways against his chest.

"You won't get angry or tearful if I don't seduce you?"

"No, I'm okay," she said.

"Let's stay like this for a while then. Unless you want to order room service?"

"I'm not hungry."

Her breathing steadied as her muscles softened to his shape. They stood on the balcony with the muslin curtains swaying like the thin membranes of a cocoon, the lights and sounds of domestic life far away on the street below.

Chapter 46

The painted fingernails of the check-in girl picked through the dog-eared pages of Amanda's fake passport. Not Amanda: Elizabeth Arina Skye.

Pleased to meet you. My name's Liz.

Hey, call me Lizzy!

How do you do? Eliza.

Hi there, I'm Beth.

Amanda checked her watch—she'd made the evening flight by the skin of her teeth—and saw her hand trembling. The check-in girl inspected a visa for Mongolia, a country Elizabeth Arina Skye had visited for three weeks the previous year. Amanda had googled Mongolia in the taxi on the way to the airport in case she was questioned. Ulaanbaatar: coldest capital city in the world. Intrepid traveler, this Elizabeth Arina Skye. What would she do in this situation? How would she steady her nerves? Lizzy Skye would brazen it out. Amanda felt herself pull up taller, her hips loosen inside her skinny black jeans. Lizzy Skye only wears black. She goes on holiday to Mongolia. *If I can channel Lizzy Skye, I might get through this.* Changi Airport was the perfect place to adopt a new identity. It never seemed real anyway. The passengers were too artful, posed; their diversity was too exact. It was like being inside one of those computer-generated images of a future hotel development. *So,* Amanda decided, *Elizabeth Arina Skye can do this.*

Two policemen in blue-black uniforms strolled past with their hands resting on automatic weapons. She stiffened again. Lizzy Skye would never have fallen into this mess. The passport lay open on the check-in desk, spread-eagled beneath a keyboard that pressed down like an officer's knee in its spine. The woman tapped a lacquered nail on a key. The two policemen turned at the end of the row and sauntered back.

"Ms. Elizabeth?" The painted lips were speaking to her.

"Yes."

"Sorry for the delay, ma'am. It says in our system that you are a gold privilege member?"

Amanda made a sound that might be taken for affirmation.

Is there a photo on the system? Has she seen that it can't be me—

"I have upgraded you, ma'am. Here is your boarding pass. Have a nice flight."

When Amanda finally sat in seat 1A, she closed her eyes. Her heart clattered around her chest cavity like a bird sucked into an aircraft engine. She knew she would be able to do nothing more than sit, holding herself together, for the short flight to Burma.

None of the signs were in English. Burmese appeared to be a collection of circles, like an ancient depiction of waves. They took her mind to her mother. She reached for her phone and remembered with a jolt that she shouldn't use it; her location would show up on the phone records. *Stupid.* She double-checked that she'd left it switched off after the plane; but didn't people in movies take the battery out? *How can you take the battery out of an iPhone?*

The taxi sputtered to a halt outside the Oriental. The hotel looked romantic with its long shuttered windows and muslin curtains drifting in the breeze. After changing into harem pants at the airport, Amanda blended in with the backpackers sweating on the street. Even inside the hushed foyer, pods of tourists lingered to photograph the colonial splendor as a cover for enjoying free air-conditioning. Amanda could have been one of them right up to the moment she went to the reception desk and checked in to a river-view suite.

While a man tapped her details into the computer and prepared her room key, she folded a note into a thin column and tucked it inside her fist. Like a conjurer, she flicked her fingers forward, and the money appeared. She closed it inside her grip again and laid the hand on the reception desk. "I have a business meeting with a guest later," she told the receptionist. "I wonder if you could tell me his room number? It's Mr. Edward Bonham."

"Oh, Mr. Edward!" The receptionist laughed. The antics of Mr. Edward were obviously well celebrated among the staff of the Oriental. "Mr. Edward went out." He held out her room card on two palms like a blessing. "With his wife."

"His wife?" Amanda forced her arms to move and her mouth to smile. "I've never met Mr. Bonham's wife. What's she like?"

"At first I thought she is his daughter"—the receptionist giggled behind his hand to signal he meant no offense—"but no, he said she is his missus. Pretty. And shy. Like that famous actress in the film. The little one."

Amanda tried to think of shy little actresses but decided she didn't want to pin down exactly which famous beauty Ed's missus—had the receptionist misheard "mistress"?—most resembled. "Right. Good to know. And if you could tell me his room number . . ." She conjured the folded note from her fist.

But the receptionist was already tapping on his keyboard. "Room 513, ma'am." He glanced down, confused, at the money. Amanda also looked at the note as though surprised by its appearance. "For the bell-boy. Where is he?" The receptionist summoned an ancient porter, who picked up Amanda's half-empty backpack without comment. Inside the gilded lift, he pressed the button for floor five, and Amanda's stomach jolted in time with the elderly cables. She and Ed were on the same floor. That could be useful, but it also increased the risk of him seeing her. Maybe she should complain about her room, kick up a fuss, insist on a higher floor? She'd already asked too many questions. Better to stay under the radar.

"This is it, ma'am," said the porter, as the elevator doors slid back. She walked into a sleepy corridor. Nothing moved, not even the air, not even her breath as she passed 513. Her room was a few doors farther down. The porter took an age to fumble the card into the slot— Amanda eyed the lift, willing it not to open and deliver Ed into the corridor—until a green light flashed, and she pushed past the old man into a darkened room. While she held out the folded money, he fussed over every individual light switch. When he finally left, she fell onto chilled white linen, her hair mussing up an arrangement of orchid petals, her hot skin soothed by the cool stream of a fan. But any tranquility was broken by stabbing thoughts. *What now? If Ed already has a woman lined up, what do I do to stop him?*

She took her phone out of her bag and almost switched it on before she remembered: Amanda Bonham must stay at home in Singapore; she has turned in for the night. The only flaw in the plan was Josie. The farewell sleepover at Willow's would keep her out of the apartment all night, so long as she didn't bail out and come home. If Josie reported Amanda missing . . . It made her nervous that she couldn't check on Josie.

She rolled off the bed and picked up her key card. There was a business center. Ed had a laptop, so he wouldn't be there. She slipped into the corridor, her fingertips easing the door into its frame, as though Ed were a sleeping monster who might stir. She headed away from the lift, following the fire escape plan on the back of her door, and found the stairwell. A few minutes later, she was in a windowless room, where an ancient PC fired up with a loud complaint. Once online, she hesitated over Facebook; might it show her location? Instead, she decided to check Josie's website. The countdown timer showed 00 days, 02 hours, and 55 minutes remaining.

Amanda checked her watch; that would take her to around midnight. But then she noticed the blog had a new post. Until now, Josie had published only one a day. Like the timer itself, she had changed tempo, speeded up. The latest drawing was a nest, a bowl of thorns, with a single egg inside. The diary entry was titled "The Day She Died." Amanda clicked and the page reloaded.

In the future: It's D-Day, so nothing

In the past: As events in the present have overtaken those of the past (is that logically possible?!), I must cut to the chase and reduce to ten posts the Days That Made Me Me. So this is the penultimate. Ten is a nice round number. Though it doesn't sound as ominous, does it?

Post 9 of 10: The Day She Died

We're almost at the top of the cliff when she stops. She wants Teddy to take our photo. She's giddy on pregnancy hormones.

"Get closer to the edge." Teddy ushers us off the path, and the roar of waves swarms up the cliff. The wind flings spray into my face. The sea is the color of dishwater. She pulls me back from the cliff top by my hood.

The lady in the visitors' center warned us that cliffs can crumble after rain. There could be a landslide. A slump. People don't often die, she said, but sheep do. Stupid creatures sleep on the edge, and the ground falls out from under them.

"Don't close your eyes, Jo-Jo Sparrow. Smile." Teddy bobs up and down to get a good shot.

Our hair is whipping about and gets so tangled we don't know which hair belongs to whom. We're still fighting for control of our hair when Teddy takes the shot. The picture spits out the front of the camera as his phone rings. I smile at the famous guitar riff from our favorite band, Cold Sister, which he just uploaded. He shoves the Polaroid into my hands and turns his back to the wind to take the call. We carry on until we're at the top. The cliff juts out high over the beach almost to a point, the shape of my tongue if I stick it right out. I go to the tip of the land and stick my tongue out and taste salt.

"Get back, Josie. If there's a gust of wind, it'll take you right over!"

"Or the land could collapse," I say. Coming back from the edge, my legs feel numb at the thought of falling, as though I'm already weightless. She takes my hand between her warm palms and rubs my fingers so they tingle with blood.

"I'm going to try harder this time, Josie." She looks down into the dishwater. "You're going to see a big difference with this child, and I hope that doesn't make you jealous. I feel so guilty sometimes that I had to go away—"

"You were sick."

"I was. I was really sick."

The wind punches her in the small of the back, and her hair flies up. She is smoothing it down when Teddy arrives, finished with his phone call. He grabs her shoulder and spins her around to face him, sending her dark hair flying again.

"That was the doctor," he says. "But you already know, don't you?"

She wipes wet strands of hair that are stuck to her lips.

"Go down to the pub, Jo-Jo, where it's warm." Teddy hands me a fiver. He doesn't take his eyes off her wet face. "Wait for us there. I need to speak to your mother."

I take the money, but it convulses in the wind and flies from my hand. The note skitters through the air and snags on a withered bush a few meters away, and I run to snatch it back, but then hunker down behind the dense knot of gorse, hidden by its yellow flowers. Teddy has his back to me, but his voice booms like falling rocks, as loud and rough as the waves hitting the base of the cliff.

"Why did you put us through it if you knew? I told you I wouldn't do it again."

She backs away, and her foot slips on the wet grass, her thick, dark hair covering her face so I can't see her expression. Teddy moves forward, stepping after her, off the grass onto the desiccated earth that juts out from the land.

"I'm sorry, Ed. I thought the baby was yours. Honestly, I was sure. I was only with him the once. I was drunk."

"How could you do this to me? And to your child—your living child?" Teddy remembers me now and glances over his shoulder, checking I have gone down the hill to the pub. The path twists out of sight, and I am hidden by the winter flowers. His hands close around her upper arms when he turns back to her. Her toes scramble for purchase on the barren ground, sending flurries of dirt over

295

the edge, arcing through the air where they will dissolve in the water below.

"What am I going to tell Josie?" he says.

I stand up behind the bush. Her eyes flicker from his intent gaze. She calls my name, a warning or a plea, I can't tell. He shakes her closer to the lip of the land. The wind inflates her hood, a red sphere against the dank sky, and her face is streaked with tears and snot. It reminds me of a photograph of myself when I was a toddler, snapped after I'd picked up a lollipop from the grass and found it stuck all over with ants.

"Go on then!" Wet fronds of hair, as dark as seaweed, slash her face. "You've always wanted her for yourself."

He twists her wrist so she bends over backward. His other fist is under her chin, hair surging through his fingers, her whole body heaving beneath him.

"I gave you everything," Teddy shouts. "All you ever gave me is"—he turns his face for a moment to spit out a piece of long hair that is stuck to his mouth—"sloppy seconds. Why are you such a slut?" Her head snaps backward into the cold air. Their bodies are pressed together. Beneath their feet, the bony roots of long-dead plants are all that bind the earth to the land. Cracks run through the soil, and I think of a broken fingernail that has ripped too close to the skin, no way to save it once the first crack appears. The best you can do is tear it off and hope it doesn't bleed. Their feet dance in the dirt as they push each other over the cracks toward the end of the earth.

Chapter 47

Under a brisk fan, turned up high to relieve the late-night crowd at the Raffles Club, Ed ordered beer while Camille concentrated on clinging to the arms of her barstool. He mustn't see that she was falling: a broken shard of glass, tumbling through the air, by turns shiny and dark. She vibrated with nervous energy, like a struck bell, and wished for the calm she'd felt on the balcony earlier, when Ed held her until she relaxed and then gently let her go to sit alone on the sofa while they waited for their contact to call.

"We need to talk," he said, offering her a bowl of peanuts.

"No aftershocks." She managed a smile but refused the nibbles.

"I mean we need to talk about my contact." He rubbed a hand over his face. "There's a few things you need to know."

"Okay . . ."

"The fact is, I'm here for self-serving reasons. I need money, and this is a job."

"What kind of job?"

"A delivery. I'm a delivery boy."

She picked up a water glass in two hands and felt ice slide down her throat.

"And you're the package, Camille."

Under the stool, she slid her foot between the handles of her bag and pulled it toward her. As long as she had her passport and money, she could run. Just get a taxi to the airport and go.

Ed's phone beeped, and he turned toward the arched doorway, the street outside flooded with golden light from the pagoda opposite. "He's here. I'm sorry I couldn't say more in advance and make it less of a shock. But it wasn't my place to tell you. It should come from him."

"Who?" She watched a tall figure step through the archway, an outline that transformed when it was halfway across the bar from a stranger into someone she once knew as well as she knew herself. She felt herself slither off the barstool and land as softly as a tiger.

Despite the unfamiliarity of a limp arm that swung at his side, Camille recognized his posture, his fleet glances to size up the room. Ed stood too, an honor guard between her and the new arrival. She laughed, a yelping scoff of disbelief. "This isn't happening," she said, "this is a sick joke." She stepped backward, and the barstool shifted with a sharp bark.

"Camille?" His right arm hung useless, the palm forced around so that it was open to her.

If the body was broken and baffling, the voice was unmistakably that of her father. She closed her eyes and heard water lapping against a hull, the cries of seabirds mingling with her gleeful shouts as she and Collin jumped from the prow into a crisp ocean. Saltwater blurred her vision. She snapped her eyes open and, for the first time in fifteen years, felt her father's gaze. Except she remembered his eyes as blue and now they were dirty ice.

"Where have you been?" she asked.

"In prison."

His appearance was a shock—he had suffered, that was obvious—but it was the look in his eyes that appalled her. His detachment, his reserve. His uncertainty. The father she remembered was suave and sophisticated. With a patter and a smile that came easily. This wasn't the same man, even if he inhabited the same damaged body.

He raised his good arm to her face.

"Don't touch me." Her voice was muted behind clenched teeth.

Her father's fingers dropped. "It's me, Camille."

"I know it's you. Don't touch me again."

"We should have gone somewhere private." He looked around as he said this, casting out blame on a line. "But Teddy said you didn't trust him—"

"I was right not to trust him," she said.

"He did me a favor. He owes me."

"I owe you nothing." Ed's voice was low. "I was long gone when you got arrested."

"Then you did it for money, Teddy. You'll get your drug deal and buy your way out of whatever mess you've got yourself into. Shame I couldn't buy my way out of nearly fifteen years in prison."

"Did you just get out?" Camille asked.

"Last year."

"Last year?" She caught the whine in her voice, hearing again the little girl who got told off for interrupting adult conversations with her childish inquiries. But now a spark of anger told her she wouldn't wait for permission; she didn't have to be seen and not heard anymore. She had a right to answers. "Why didn't you contact me? Or Collin? He's in—"

"Hong Kong. I thought you were better off not knowing." He pointed at his withered arm. "Every day I was inside, your memory kept me alive. Even when they hurt me, I thought of you two, free and happy, and it kept me going."

Camille pressed her palms against her skull, harder and harder, trying to stop herself from flying apart into a million pieces. Over the years, she'd added to the real memories of her father a little color, a little definition, a little delusion. She had redrawn him to her liking. Now, faced with the real man, she recognized her caricature for what it was; like the clients who wanted an archetypal Englishman, she had painted him into the role of a perfect father. But the person standing before her had put his family at risk, had left his kids to fend for themselves, had failed to contact her for a year. Still, he expected sympathy.

The lazy fan above their heads agitated their shadows. A hard laugh escaped her, a bitter shot to douse the tears. If Magnus Kemble knew his daughter at all, he would recognize that she did feel pity for him, but in the manner of a parent watching a child who can't fasten his pants. "I've been looking for you for fifteen years," she said, her voice calmer than she felt. "I didn't know if you were dead or alive. That's torture. That's solitary confinement. Dreaming up ever more ludicrous fantasies until everyone thinks I'm as naive as a child. It's a torment, living in hope. You could have stopped it at any time, written me a letter, made one phone call."

He raised his hand to scratch an eyebrow with a thumbnail, a nervous tic that Collin shared. There was no wedding ring.

"Where is she?" Camille whispered. "Is she in prison? Is that why you're still in Burma—are you waiting for her to get out?"

He scrubbed at his martyred eyes. "She died a month after we were arrested. Dengue, they said. They didn't tell me for years. I took all this"—he waved to indicate his injuries—"thinking I was protecting her. But she'd been dead all along. That's why I didn't contact you before. Better not knowing. Better without me."

"Better for you, maybe. Better to take the easy way out." She thought of her mother saying she was the schmuck who had to muck out the boat. She recalled her whirling skirt as she zipped drugs into her children's teddy bears. "She always did your dirty work. I bet you don't have a clue how to survive without her."

"I don't," he said, simply. "This is all I know—this world, this business."

"Is that why you got in contact now? You think I might be of use to you? That I can help you because I work at the British High Commission?"

"Like I said before, this was Teddy's idea. And when he came to me, I decided it was time you knew what happened to your mother."

Camille turned away, pressing her thumbs into her eyeballs to compose herself as her anger dropped away, the final veil of dignity behind which she tried to hide. She was fully exposed and couldn't fight the tears anymore. A hand squeezed her shoulder. Ed.

"I'm going to leave you now," he said. "Give you some privacy."

She looked up at a diluted version of his face. "There will be aftershocks."

"You promised not to get angry or tearful."

"Only if you didn't seduce me. Turns out there's more than one way to fuck someone."

"I thought I was giving you what you wanted."

Magnus Kemble stepped between them to slap Ed on the back. "I'm grateful, even if Camille isn't so sure. We'll be in touch."

"The deal is on?"

"Consider yourself on standby."

"This is a one-time thing. One consignment. I need the money by Friday. And then I'm never setting foot in fucking Burma ever again."

"Myanmar, Teddy. It's a different country now. New name, new rules."

"Same old merchandise. Same old faces."

"You seem happy to take the same old cash."

"You think I'm here for my health?" Ed gestured at the man's mangled arm as he walked away. "If you need me, I'm at the hotel. That whisky won't drink itself." He dropped a pile of soft notes onto the table before striding out the arched door into the temple lights.

Chapter 48

Amanda tasted the musty lipstick, pushing it around her mouth like Ed's whisky-heavy tongue. She rubbed her lips together and pulled them back to reveal bloodied canines. The effect gave her a shudder. Of what, she thought? Fear? Excitement? Certainly adrenaline. The woman in the mirror was a force to be reckoned with. *Call me Lizzy Skye.*

She cracked the bedroom door and peeped down the corridor. Empty. She propped it open with a shoe and skittered along to the lift lobby, where a console table held a blue-and-white vase of orchids and a telephone. She pressed 1 for housekeeping and requested a turndown service for room 513. *Right away, ma'am.* She scooted back to her room.

No one stirred during the five minutes it took for a maid to arrive pushing a cart loaded with toiletries. Amanda used her hand mirror to watch the corridor. The maid tapped at room 513, waited a few seconds, and then used a card on a lanyard to unlock the door. Amanda mentally crossed off one option; she wouldn't be able to steal an entry card from the cart.

Plan B.

She waited until the maid was inside and then walked along to the room, handbag under one arm.

"Excuse me," Amanda said as she ducked inside.

"I'm sorry, ma'am."

"Could you leave me, please?" she said, all breezy white privilege. "I need to lie down. Sunstroke." The maid backed out and closed the door. Amanda pressed her hands and forehead against the wood, watching through the peephole the distorted image of the woman pushing the trolley toward the lift. She glanced into the bathroom, which smelled of citrus. On the marble unit beside the sink stood a bottle of clonazepam.

This has to end. Now.

Amanda went to the main room. The long windows were wide open, and the noise from the street below was as discordant as her heartbeat. The room was a crime scene. Blood everywhere—smeared across sheets, soaked into towels, a distinct handprint on one pillow. How could Ed be capable of such violence? And whoever he'd hurt like this—so much blood—how did he get her out of the hotel, past the receptionist who'd said the couple left together, who must have seen her with his own eyes?

Maybe this was just the start, and Ed planned to finish it later? But why would a woman return for more of this horror? She thought of the clonazepam in the bathroom. A sedative to make her compliant?

She'd seen enough. She had to stop it. At least save one more victim from him.

She gathered all the bottled water she could find, dropping an empty in the bin. The cheap wafer-thin bottles, Amanda knew, meant the lid could be pulled off without breaking the plastic seal. She did this now with one bottle, holding it away from her body so the spillage was soaked up by the rug. She opened several bottles and left them beside the bed.

In the bathroom, she tipped a handful of clonazepam pills into the toothbrush mug. How many would be enough to slow him down? She tipped in a few more. Then she let the tap run until the water was steaming. She poured a dribble over the pills and left them to soften into mush. With a teaspoon, she got a good dose of clonazepam into each water bottle, shaking them to dissolve. She wiped the bottles clean with a flannel, placing one next to the bed, on the left: Ed's side. One beside his toothbrush at the sink. One more on the console. Good. Maybe that would do it. A dose of his own medicine. Then she could work out what to do next.

But something bothered her. Ed wasn't a big fan of water.

She looked around the room and spotted a black leather tray on the coffee table. It held a heavy glass and small ice bucket. And a small bottle of Japanese whisky, sealed with a cork. She unfolded a sheet of headed notepaper from the tray: *Dear Mr. Bonham, The Management would like to thank you for your patronage of our hotel. Please enjoy this gift with our compliments, from all the staff at the Oriental.* Amanda added the remainder of the clonazepam to the whisky and swirled it around before arranging the bottle on the tray.

Whisky or water. Choose your poison.

In the lobby, Amanda positioned herself behind a huge display of white lilies, hidden from sight but close enough to overhear the reception desk, where visitors came to complain about trivial matters in a persistent drone like mosquitoes. The cloying smell of the wilting flowers made her sneeze, and she fished in her handbag for a tissue, which came away smeared red like Ed's bedsheets. Without using a mirror, she replenished her lipstick. The lobby hummed with activity, bodies moving along set routes in the manner of ants. The motion formed a central circle of empty space, an expanse of marble like a theater in the round, onto which Ed strode.

Her stomach flipped at the sight of him. It was the same feeling she'd had when she first saw him at that party in the Alps, corralled by women. A lost soul who needed rescuing. *What a stupid fantasy,* she thought. *I'm the one who was waiting to be rescued.* All her blustering about independence. All her pride. Her resentment of the famous—infamous—Dependant's Pass. She'd always been ready to cast herself as damsel in distress. The victim who ran into the arms of the wolf. She and Ed relished their roles of predator and prey, the only two with reason to stray from the path.

Now, he commanded the stage, strolling toward reception—toward Amanda—while talking on the phone.

"Listen, Jo-Jo, I'll be there when you get home from the sleepover tomorrow. I'm catching the red-eye."

He listened. Eyes on the lilies, but unseeing.

"Jo-Jo—"

Nodding.

"Josie—"

Thumbs pressing into his eyes.

"We can talk about the new school later. I'm at the hotel, packing to leave."

He held the phone away from his mouth so Josie couldn't hear his exasperated sigh.

"I'm in my room, right now, packing. Where's Amanda?"

Listening.

"When you see her, tell her I love her."

A beat.

"I know you always tell her. And I love you too. Bye."

A beat.

"Bye."

Ed put the phone in his pocket and rolled his eyes at the receptionist, smiling.

"There was a woman asking for you, sir."

Amanda shrank deeper into her seat. Bloody hotel staff were too good.

"Was she young and beautiful?" Ed asked.

The receptionist laughed. "They are all beautiful, sir."

"True enough. Was it Camille?"

Amanda sat up higher. Camille Kemble? That little troublemaker.

The receptionist shook his head and tapped at the computer. "Ah, no, sir. It was a Mrs. . . . Miss Elizabeth Arina Skye."

"No idea who that is." Ed shrugged, unconcerned.

"And you had a message from Mr. Magnus—"

"Magnus Kemble?"

The receptionist's eyes flicked up. Amanda couldn't read the significance of the look: admiration or alarm? Both.

"It's okay; he won't come here, bringing your establishment into disrepute." Ed waggled his eyebrows to show he was joking, but as he turned away, the receptionist started whispering to a colleague. Amanda ignored them and watched Ed walk into the waiting maw of the lift. None of it made sense. Was Camille Kemble's blood spattered across the room? Ed had said he would do anything to stop her domestic worker campaign. *Pest control,* he called it that night at the restaurant. Or maybe he'd just taken a fancy to her, chosen her as his victim. But seeing him in action with the receptionist . . . he was the same as ever. The same cocky, charming Ed. She had expected to find him unrecognizable from the man she knew: a psychopath, hiding behind a mask. Instead, this felt like any holiday they'd ever taken; Amanda waiting in the lobby while he joshed with the staff. And what had he said to Josie on the phone? *If you see Amanda, tell her I love her.* And then: *I know you always tell her.*

Josie had never one single time passed on a message from Ed. Not once.

Amanda jolted, knocking one of the lilies, which released a shower of rusty pollen. As she pulled out her phone, she heard Ed's voice again. *I know you always tell her.* Although Amanda never felt she knew Josie, not really, she assumed Ed did. But if he didn't know his daughter—if he took her for an innocent despite all the evidence to the contrary— then who knew the real Josie?

The phone came to life, and Amanda thought, *Screw anonymity.* Self-preservation gave way to survival instinct. She had to know what

Josie was doing. For the first time in days, she felt sure about something: *This is all about Josie.*

00 days, 01 hour, 05 minutes.

And another new post. Her third in one day. A drawing of a bird, a sparrow. *Jo-Jo Sparrow*, Amanda thought. *Jo-Jo Fucking Sparrow*. She jabbed the delicate bird hard enough to knock it from the sky.

In the future: It's D-Day, so nothing.
In the past: Everything. Even the future.
Post 10 of 10: The Final Moment

Teddy and my mother tussle for long seconds on the bare earth of the cliff top. Then she bends toward the dishwater sea, almost pulling him over the edge, and he is forced to retreat. He rights himself while she stays down, staring into the waves. It looks to me as though an invisible person way down on the beach has her by a cord around the neck. Like she's a kite. Or a dog. She waits, cowering, a dog on a lead.

Something in Teddy returns, and he grabs her arms once more, this time pulling her back from the edge. He lifts and carries her, toes dragging two lines in the dirt, to the safety of the grass. They stand there, panting. When she finally raises her head and looks him in the face, he reaches out to her for the last time, but only to throw her to the ground. She sprawls under her mess of tangled hair, while he wipes his hand over his face. He is wet with sea spume; we all are. I can see that he wants to say something, but it hurts too much. He told me once that feelings cut you from the inside. We both hurt him, my mother and I, with our sharp feelings. He takes a step toward the cliff edge—I almost run to him—but then he stops and strides away down the hill. The buffeting wind covers the scramble of my feet as I skirt around the gorse bush so he doesn't see me hiding there.

As Teddy disappears around the bend in the path, she gets to her feet. I watch a peregrine falcon, fighting to hover in the wind. Its tail dips side to side, but it doesn't waver; it has spotted prey and only needs to wait for the right moment. Then it drops like a stone, its body tucked into the shape of a teardrop. I walk to where my mother is brushing her clothes clean of dirt and droppings.

"What did Teddy mean?" My voice startles her. "When he said *he wouldn't do it again*?"

She collects all the flailing strands of her hair and pulls up her hood, forcing them inside.

"Did he mean he wouldn't raise another man's child again?"

"Josie—"

"He's not my father."

"Josie—"

"When were you going to tell me?"

"He *is* your father. He adopted you at birth. He loves you." She looks at me slyly. "Sometimes I think too much."

I kick at the dirt, but we're too far back for it to go over the edge. "How can you love someone too much?" I ask. "Surely any amount is better than not enough."

"Jo-Jo—"

"Don't call me that."

"Josie, does he touch you?" She comes toward me and puts her hands on my wrists. Her fingers are hot. Her pulse is bouncing. She's getting a thrill out of this.

"Why are you asking me now?" I say.

Her eyes skate over mine.

"I've lived with him for ages," I say. "If you think he's a, whatever you're trying to suggest—pedo—why did you leave me with him?"

"Please answer the question, Josie. I've been too frightened to ask before. Because I didn't know what to do if you said yes. And I'm sorry for that. But after the way he was just then, pushing me toward the edge—you saw him—I know he's capable of anything. I didn't realize it before, but he is. And I'm here now. I can help you. So does he? Touch you?" She's squeezing my wrists in her hot hands.

"Don't be disgusting." I pull away from her. "He'd never hurt me." I walk onto the spit of land where it points to the sky.

"Come away from the edge, Josie, please."

"Are you going to keep this baby?"

Way down below, the ribs of a shipwrecked boat protrude from the murk. The tide must be going out. Rocks are emerging.

"Can we go home and talk? In the warm." Her voice shivers. *She's in shock,* I think. "It's such a long way down the hillside. I'm not sure I can make it."

"You'll get down. I'll help you."

She comes closer, standing beside me on the cliff top.

"I want to know about the baby. What you're going to do with it."

"Her. It's a girl."

We watch a gray wave race to shore. I brace myself for the impact, but it comes to nothing on the beach.

"I haven't told him yet," she says. "I'm hoping it might change his mind. Another little girl to love as much as he loves you."

The peregrine falcon spirals up the thermal, so close I could reach out and dash it from the air. I turn to face my mother. "He'll never love another girl as much as he loves me."

My words buffet her like the wind. She takes a step back, her foot brushing the last strands of grass that cling to the land.

I follow her to the edge. "Teddy doesn't want you." I jab her in the chest, and she puts her hands up to protect herself. "Turning up at our door because you're too stupid to take precautions. Even I know how to roll one on and I'm only fourteen. You're a drunk and a failure, and we won't clear up your mess again." Another jab as she turns, using her shoulder to shield herself. "He doesn't love you. And he won't love another man's child."

"He loves you, doesn't he?"

"Leave Teddy alone." I'm so close I could hug her.

"Oh, Teddy! Our blessed Teddy. Why do we have to call him by that stupid name?"

"You don't call him that," I say, as my hands find her hips. Her weight pushes back into my palms, giving me purchase. "He's my Teddy. And I won't share him with another little girl."

And I push.

So hard I almost go with her over the edge. But she's bigger than me, heavier. Her feet slide off the packed earth and plummet, but she doesn't fall clear of the land. Her body twists and her breasts slam onto the dirt; she gives a last huff as the wind is knocked from her, and her weight drags her slowly down as though her body is being sucked into quicksand and not falling through hundreds of meters of clear air. All ten fingers claw lines through the dirt until one hand finds a grip on an exposed root. Two fingernails cling on. The tips turn pink and then white. I hear her voice from below the ragged edge of the cliff, a rapid cry like a bird's mating call. Her hair must have jumped loose from her hood to spiral in the wind. It's so thick and dark. It swirls like seaweed caught in the tide. Like mine. Beautiful.

Her fingers crawl away across the bone-white root.

And then they are gone.

I reach down and pick up a fingernail, ripped off at the root. I tuck it carefully into that tiny pocket in the front of my jeans. The condom pocket. Then I start screaming and run down the hill to Teddy.

Chapter 49

A slender girl crossed the hotel lobby, making a beeline for the lifts. Thick, dark hair swirled in her wake. Amanda dropped behind the lilies. The elevator opened, and the girl vanished inside.

What was Josie doing in Yangon?

Amanda stared for a moment at the balletic movement of bodies across the foyer, as though performing for her. The blog—the countdown, the stories, the clues spooned out in bite-size morsels—had all been a performance. A confession. Aimed at whom, Amanda didn't know, but like a trail of candy, she had followed a merry dance, starting in a frosty London park, with Josie's hero confronting a dangerous dog, and ending on a cliff top where she claimed him for herself.

She killed her own mother.

What else is she capable of?

As the elevator light showed that Josie had reached the fifth floor, Amanda was running across the lobby to the closing doors of the second elevator, shouting for the occupants to hold the lift. Inside, she jabbed the button for the fifth floor, earning a tut from a couple of tourists behind her.

"It's an emergency," she hissed. "My husband's dying."

The door opened, and she glimpsed their startled faces as she left.

She skittered down the corridor toward room 513. The carpet swallowed her footfall, so she felt as inconsequential as a ghost. Nothing moved except air against her skin. Heavy wooden doors lined her route, a forbidding row of judges in dark cloaks. At room 513, she pressed her ear to the wood but heard only the rush of her own blood. Behind her, the lift chimed as it sank to the lobby.

Amanda hammered on the door. What did it matter if Ed saw her now? She had woven a tapestry of guilt, and she felt it unraveling beneath her nimble fingers. She knocked again. Inside, she heard an ugly rush of sound as the toilet flushed. And the door opened a crack.

"Ed?" She pushed the door back. He was on his knees. A dense smell hit Amanda in the face, and she put her hand up to cover her nose. Ed fell back into a fetal position.

She checked the empty corridor behind her and went inside, clicking the door shut.

"Ed? Is Josie here?"

He didn't try to ask questions—why was Amanda here, what was happening, why would Josie be in Yangon when she should be in Singapore? He didn't seem able to talk or even grasp that it was his wife who had come to his aid in a country thousands of miles from home. With Amanda's help, Ed made it to the bed. He curled away from her, his long body folded into a question mark. He lay still, too still.

On the bedside table, half a bottle of whisky remained. And an empty water bottle. *What have I done?* she thought. *Has the clonazepam made him so sick so quickly?* She needed to get help. The phone hung from its cradle; she put it to her ear and heard a sound like the sea. She tapped the receiver, but the line was dead. When she tugged the cord, it whipped up into the air, loose, severed from the wall.

The phone had been cut; someone else had been in the room. Amanda could feel Josie's presence, as if she might be on the other side of a two-way mirror, watching.

Ed groaned and tried to move, but this time it was too much; he heaved and sent bile across the bloody sheets. Amanda grabbed his phone from the bedside table, kneeling beside him to press the pad of his forefinger onto the button. The iPhone came to life. He'd missed three calls from Camille Kemble. Amanda didn't have time to wonder at the woman's role in events. She tapped in 999, then changed it to 911. What was the emergency number? She had no idea. And what would happen if she called the police? How would she explain these circumstances? Would they be able to save him? His breathing had turned to rapid panting. Would they arrest her? She was right here, red-handed. The maid had seen her trick her way into the room. There were sedatives in the water. She had traveled on a false passport. Ed heaved one more time, his whole body convulsing, but nothing came. There was nothing left.

Amanda found her way to the sofa beside the open window. A warm breeze stirred the muslin curtains, and she shivered in response. Her mother said a shiver was caused by someone walking over your grave. For a second, she wished for her mother; Laura would know what to do. But a presence in the room demanded attention. *There were three in this marriage,* Amanda thought, *but only two here. Where was the third? Where is Josie?*

With a whisper that brought Amanda to her feet, the interconnecting door opened. It took her a moment to notice the steak knife that Josie held in front of her crotch, the girl framed in the wall opposite the bed. Amanda ran to slam the door, but Josie blocked it with a shoulder, slipping into Ed's room and letting it click behind her.

"Give me his phone," she said. She released one hand to take the mobile from Amanda's limp grip. "Did you call an ambulance?"

"I didn't know the emergency number."

"Liar. You didn't want to get caught." Josie punched the PIN into Ed's phone with her thumb and checked for outgoing calls. Satisfied, she slipped the mobile into the back pocket of her jeans. Then she produced a white belt from a hotel bathrobe, pointed the knife at Amanda's hands, and, when she obediently held them out, bound her wrists. Josie went to sit on the right side of the bed. She stared at her father, biting a hangnail. When he bucked, gripped by a stomach spasm, she pressed both hands over her mouth.

"Teddy?" Josie said. After a beat, it became clear that her father wasn't able to answer, and she swallowed a gulp of air. "I didn't think it would be this bad." The serrated edge of the steak knife made ridges in the bedsheet as Josie shifted her weight, leaning close to his ear to whisper over and over, "I'm sorry."

Amanda kept the door within reach. "He's had an overdose." She waited for a reaction, but Josie sat back on her haunches, working her teeth against the hangnail of the thumb holding the blade. She would cut herself if she wasn't careful. Josie's habitual self-control—what Amanda had always taken as a cultured air of teenage nonchalance—had evaporated. She finally saw the real girl, her riot of mixed-up colors, fragmented like the picture of Chairman Mao she both loved and hated. Josie projected a coherent image, but up close she was an artful arrangement of broken pieces. The blog had revealed the blows that shattered her.

Amanda knew she couldn't stick her stepdaughter back together here and now, but maybe if she could reach her, she could do enough to make the center hold. Enough to get all of them safely out of this room . . .

She peeled herself off the wall and approached the bed. "Your father's really sick, Josie. We should call an ambulance. It'll be okay if we get him to the hospital. I'll take care of all the rest."

Again she didn't respond, so Amanda folded herself onto the edge of the mattress. "He's your father."

The girl rolled to her feet, knife wavering in her hand, and Amanda retreated to the wall. "Well, he's your husband, isn't he? And you're the one who poisoned him."

"It's only a sedative, but I think he's had too much."

"The postmortem is going to find him full of rat poison."

"It was clonazepam. His own medication."

315

Jo Furniss

"No. You stole poison from the pest-control people at the condo. You tested the dose on those poor dogs. This was premeditated." Josie scissored her arm so that the point of the blade was all Amanda could see. "You're a murderer. A barren depressive. Ed never loved you the way he loved me, and that sent you over the edge. Our bond, mine and his, was unbreakable. You're just another link in a chain of romantic mistakes. And when you realized that, you killed him."

Let her burn off steam, Amanda thought. *Don't react.* "We need to call an ambulance for your father."

"It's too late. You killed him. Because you were so deluded, you convinced yourself he was cheating and murdering women."

"How do you know about the women?"

"I know everything you do. Selling your gear. Your 'secret' identities." Josie made quote marks in the air, the knife emphasizing her irony. "Your bank accounts. Interpol. I'm everywhere. Your shadow."

"But how?"

Josie rolled her eyes to show she was indulging an out-of-touch stepmother. "You use the same password for everything. I mean *everything.* Even the bank, which is just stupid. I hacked you in five minutes." Beside her, Ed's body bucked, a violent thrash that almost sent her off the bed. "I thought he'd go to sleep." Josie stroked his streaming brow with shaking fingers. The knife hung by her side and Amanda wondered if she might grab her wrist, overpower the slight girl, shake or bite her hand until she dropped it. But with bound hands, it would be difficult . . .

"We need to get him to the hospital, Josie."

Ed groaned, and Josie shrugged one shoulder to shield herself, refusing to see what she'd done to her father. She chose to go on the offensive instead. "Wouldn't you prefer to hear about the murders your husband committed?"

The ghost enclosed Amanda in its embrace and squeezed air from her body.

316

"How many women did he hurt, Amanda?"

"Five. That I know about."

"That you *know about*?" Josie's nose wrinkled in disgust. "How many women did Ed hurt, Amanda?" She shifted the knife so the blade pointed backward in her grasp. A stabbing grip.

"I don't know."

"How many do you think?" Josie got to her feet.

"I don't know."

"Have a guess." She took a step closer.

Amanda's voice came out very quiet. "None."

"That's right. None. He didn't hurt a soul. I can't believe you doubted him, after all he's done for you. But you were very easy to convince. It's almost like you expected the worst, which isn't surprising, I guess, considering your own family. Are you interested in the technical details, the software that let me copy real news sites and post my own pages on the Internet? Once you picked the right keywords—it took you a while—up popped my stories. Now that's what I call fake news!"

"But Laureline Mackenzie was on Interpol; you couldn't fake that."

"Laureline Mackenzie was real. She gave me the idea. It was so weird that she disappeared when Teddy was *right there* in Tokyo. I thought to myself, What if he did it? What if he kills every time he goes away—different cities, different jurisdictions—how long could he get away with it? Ages, probably, because he's smart. Like me. Most of them aren't as smart as Teddy and me. Did you see the news this morning? Laureline Mackenzie was found in a guy's basement. He cut out her tattoo. I liked that orchid. I spent hours Photoshopping it onto pictures to load on Teddy's old phone."

Amanda's eyes closed for a beat. "And the other women?"

"Zurich was mine. And the alleyway in Manila. There were a couple of others you didn't even find. You don't question your sources, do you? You don't corroborate a story; we learned that at school. But you believe everything you read just because it's on the Internet. It's actually really antifeminist the way your mind works. You think that because the victims are strippers and hookers, nobody cares about them."

"But the police called about the one in Manila."

"Take a moment, Amanda, give yourself time to catch up . . ."

Josie had regained her swagger as soon as she turned her back on her father. "But that was a man's voice," Amanda said.

"Voice modulation software is child's play—literally, kids at my school use it to pull pranks on their friends."

Ed let out a low moan that sent a shudder through Josie's shoulders, and she went to him, tugging the pillow under his head, heavy-handed fussing like a child with a hamster. Whispering apologies. Amanda wanted to slap her fingers off his skin.

"What about Awmi?"

Josie wiped her hands over her face—the serrated blade barely missing her skin—in a gesture that mimicked Ed. "I don't want to talk about that now."

"Why not?"

"It's too much. On top of this." She gestured at her father. "I just feel . . . responsible."

"Did you trick her into drinking the bleach?"

"Of course not. How would that even be possible?" She rolled her eyes. "She was pregnant, and Teddy gave her the money for an abortion, but she couldn't go through with it. Said she was in love with one of the gardeners. He cut fresh jasmine for her every night when she walked with him. And the weird thing is, she didn't seem at all worried about the future, just said God would find a way. She was happy. This man was prepared to give up his job in Singapore and take her to his country. And I got kind of angry, you know, because she was *nothing*, really. She wasn't pretty or clever or accomplished like I am, and yet nobody feels like that for me. Teddy doesn't love me enough to give up everything to be with me—"

Amanda was about to jump in to say that Josie was loved, but she went on.

"So I told Awmi you'd send her home as soon as you found out about the baby—that you'd be angry because you can't have children—and she'd never see her boyfriend again." Josie's voice dropped to a whisper. "I told her she either had to have the abortion and lose the baby, or keep the baby and lose her lover."

"You told her that?"

"Maybe what I said had something to do with her decision?" Josie's hands were shaking so hard the knife wavered in her grasp, and Amanda had competing urges: grab them to stop the trembling or grab them to snatch the knife. "I'm sorry, but I was . . ."

"Jealous?"

"That's bad, isn't it? Jealous of a maid."

Amanda bit back a retort, not wanting to anger her. "It's a lot to carry on your conscience. Did you tell your dad?"

Josie scratched the tip of the blade along the sheet, snagging cotton threads as she went. When she looked up, her hands were still again. "I hate it when you don't understand. It's so frustrating."

Amanda held out both hands in a gesture inviting Josie to share.

"I spend every minute of every day trying to get Teddy to love me. I get top grades, I'm on the swim team, I'm into his music, but he doesn't care. So I take another tack; I start fucking up. I get suspended, I post sex pictures on the Internet—"

"You posted pictures of yourself?"

"Still, he doesn't care. He's more interested in that girl from the British High Commission. There's always another one waiting in the wings. I thought when I got rid of you—"

"Is that what all this is about? You've been trying to scare me off?"

"But you're tenacious, aren't you? A pit bull who won't let go. Either that or you're a doormat. I can't decide. What happened to Awmi was horrid, but it was useful for my purposes: it woke you up. And once you started peering into my cage, I fed you peanuts. All along, you thought you were my keeper, but really you were my monkey."

A prickle of anger stirred Amanda's insides. "Great line. Did you practice it in front of a mirror?" There was a grim satisfaction in seeing the teenager roll her eyes yet again, only with less conviction now and no snappy comeback. Amanda relished the moment as she might enjoy scratching an itch until it bled.

The muslin curtains swirled in the evening breeze. Amanda had the same urge to jump that she'd felt for weeks. Only now she knew what she was running from: not Ed but his daughter. Now Amanda understood why she'd never been able to touch the girl: not because she didn't have a maternal instinct, but because she did have a survival instinct. She'd sensed danger all along.

Holding her hands forward so that Josie could see she posed no threat, Amanda moved toward the open window. She couldn't jump—they were on the fifth floor—and she had to work out how to get Ed from the room. Maybe she could shout to someone in the street?

"All the evidence was fake, designed to make me leave, so you and Ed could be alone," she said.

"As fake as your handbags. Shout from the window if you want. No one will understand what you're saying." Josie gave a sardonic laugh. "Welcome to my world." She slid two fingers into the front pocket of her jeans to extract a tiny ziplock bag. "This is real, though." She tossed it at Amanda, who caught it against her chest. Inside was a yellowed relic.

Amanda stared at the shriveled nail under plastic. "Your mother's?"

Josie shrugged. "It's all she left me."

On the bed, Ed murmured, "Josie," which made Amanda shudder; but did she want to succor him or silence him? She couldn't do either while Josie stood over him with a knife, watching through luminous toddler eyes. *Finally, she has what she needs: our full attention.* She flicked the fingernail onto the bed, where it slipped between the sheets crumpled between Ed's legs.

"Is this because of your mother?"

"I can't even remember her name."

"I don't think that's true. On your website, you were counting down to the anniversary of her death."

"No, I was counting down to the day we were going to die. Me and Teddy. Like Romeo and Juliet. It would have been fitting to do it on my mother's anniversary, but when he came to Burma and you skipped off to follow him, I saw an opportunity. I reckon their policing is rubbish here. Makes it easier to blame on you. But after seeing Awmi . . . I'm not sure I can go through with the suicide part."

Josie reached over to soothe her father. While her back was turned, Amanda twisted her wrists against the belt that bound her hands. She had to keep Josie talking.

"He tried to do what's best for you, Josie. He's been a good father." Amanda gestured at Ed, fetal on the bed. "What has Teddy done to deserve this?"

"Don't call him Teddy. Only I call him Teddy. And he hurt me. Over and over again, he hurt me. So I needed to make it stop."

Amanda nodded, an idea flickering. And a nip of relief. She had detected something rotten in Ed; it wasn't all in her imagination. The girl sought revenge, the abused child turned abuser. How long had she suffered? On the bed, Ed kicked out with one leg.

"When did he start abusing you?" Amanda asked.

"You're being simplistic again. Teddy never touched me." Josie screwed the knife handle around in her grasp. "I thought those pictures would make him see what I'm capable of, now that I'm grown up. But instead he decided to send me away."

"You want him to see you in a sexual way? But you're his daughter."

"You read the blog: we're not blood. There was nothing to stop us. Even when he knew he could have me, that we could stay together, like we'd always wanted—once *she* was out of the way—he still resisted. Again, like Romeo and Juliet, it was only foolish social convention keeping us apart."

Amanda's relief burst into a physical stab of pain. Ed had done nothing wrong, and she had done nothing to defend him—so who was the guilty party now? Amanda leaned against the wall to keep herself upright. On the bed, Ed's muscles tensed and then released with a long sigh. The pain focused into a point as sharp as the tip of Josie's knife. Amanda was beyond caring. She went to him, the mattress sagging as she kneeled, and he rolled into her. She used the sheet to wipe bile from his chin. His eyes cracked open and widened when he saw her face.

"Mrs. Bonham." His voice was so rough that Amanda's throat burned in response.

"I'm sorry. I thought—"

"Watch out for Josie."

Amanda wiped her bound wrist over wet eyes. Unbelievable. He still thought she was the innocent one. After all the girl had done. *Watch out for Josie.* She stood with the knife turning in her fingers. *Watch out . . .* The ghost was back, its fingertips raising welts on her skin. *Watch out . . .* He didn't mean watch over his daughter; he meant beware of her. Amanda backed away from the bed. Unless she got out of this room, it looked likely that Josie would go for the full house and kill her stepmother too.

Chapter 50

Camille skittered across the lobby, chin up and eyes fixed on her destination. If she had to speak to anyone, she would cry, just dissolve into a stain on the marble. The elevator was closing. "Hold the lift!" Her voice came with the force of a death throe. The mirrored doors retreated. A few more steps and she almost slammed into the back of the elevator. She hit the button for the fifth floor.

When the doors opened again onto the stillness of the corridor, she hesitated to step out. She was desperate for a friendly face, a lifeline to reality. Then she would gather herself up and scurry back to Singapore with her tail between her legs. But the corridor was intimidating with its trick-eye pattern on the carpet. Beside her, a businessman sighed at his watch. Camille propelled herself into the rat run between doors, sure that the pupils of the peepholes followed her all the way.

Outside room 513, she raised her fist to knock but stopped when she heard voices. Female voices. She lowered her arm. Housekeeping? She heard a bark of laughter. Whatever Ed was up to now, it could wait; he'd brought her here, thrown her into this bizarre situation with no warning, and now he could deal with the fallout. She rapped hard on the door. The voices stopped. She rapped again. The faintest shadow behind the peephole told her she was being watched.

"Ed? It's Camille."

With a shush on the carpet, the door opened halfway. Despite the gloom, Camille recognized Amanda Bonham's immaculate feet inside expensive sandals. But she didn't recognize the ugly twist on the woman's face as she screamed at Camille to run. In Camille's second of hesitation, a knife appeared under Amanda's throat. The woman froze, her eyes swiveled toward the blade, and she staggered backward, hauled into the depths of the room. "Get inside or I'll cut her throat." The voice was female, young. "Bolt the door or I'll cut you."

Camille fixed the safety chain behind herself. Amanda fell heavily onto the sofa beside the french windows. She had her wrists tied. Beside her, Josie Bonham held a steak knife. The girl's eyes flicked to the bed, and Camille noticed Ed. He was wrapped up like a fist, shivering. For the first time, she registered the stench: vomit and whisky, cut through with something as sweet and acrid as bleach. Her eyes snapped back to the knife.

"Hello again." Josie swapped the blade into her left hand, so she could hold the right one out to shake. Camille slowly reached over the glass coffee table and felt the girl's fingers, as limp as asparagus.

"What's wrong with Ed?"

"Poisoned. By my stepmother. But Ed's going to stab her to death before he succumbs."

Amanda was brushing loose hair behind her ears, pulling herself together, her blue eyes fixed on Josie. She didn't look murderous; she looked terrified. Josie, for her part, possessed an unnatural calm, but the sheen of sweat on her face suggested it was a veneer, a carefully constructed front. Her eyes were slightly too wide, her breathing slightly too shallow. Camille thought of the cobra she'd seen on the boardwalk, ferocious with fear. The girl was also terrified.

Josie used the handle of the knife to scratch a strand of thick, dark hair from her brow. "You've fucked up my plan, Camille Kemble." She went to the bed and sat next to Ed, pressing two fingers to his neck, feeling for a pulse. Camille backed toward the door. "Stop or I'll stab you in the back. Why are you here?"

"Ed brought me to meet my father. But he's a drug dealer, a gangster. I—"

"I know that. I mean here in the hotel. Why did you come back?"

"I needed him."

Josie sprang from the bed and pointed the knife at Camille.

"What is it with women and my Teddy? Why do you all *need* him? What about me? What happens when I need him? I go to the back of the queue. It was supposed to be me and him, me and Teddy, Teddy and Jo-Jo Sparrow—that's what he said. He told me. He promised it would be me and him, for always, on our own. That's why I did it."

"Did what?"

"Killed *her*. So we could be together, Teddy and Jo-Jo Sparrow. And now—" Josie dropped onto the bed. Ed rolled but made no more noise, not even a groan. "There's always someone else. There will always be someone else. When it should be me and him."

Camille slid a foot toward the door. The girl had killed a woman. Her mother? The ground slid beneath her feet. Josie with a knife. Ed dying. Amanda as stiff as the Chinese vases decorating the room. And her own father a criminal. What would happen if Camille should be found here, beside the body of a known drug dealer? They'd think she was another limb of the family tree. She'd die like her mother in a Burmese prison.

She'd rather get a knife in the back. If she ran, she'd get through the door at least, head for the stairwell, scream. Or she could lock herself in the bathroom; it would take an army to break down these mahogany doors, and there might be an emergency phone beside the toilet. She took another step backward.

Behind her, a knock, three sharp raps. Camille flattened against the wall.

"Mr. Bonham?" the voice boomed. "This is the manager. A guest reported that someone on this floor is sick. Are you there, Mr. Bonham?"

"Help us!" Camille shouted, her voice becoming a croak as Josie's thin arm lashed her shoulders, twisting her around to hold the knife at her throat. She tried to shout again, but the pressure made her gag. She felt a hot surge of nausea that sent her head swimming, an instinct to bend forward to vomit fighting with a conflicting instinct to shrink from the knife.

"Mr. Bonham? I'm going to open the door."

The pressure on her throat eased a fraction, enough to breathe. There was an electronic click as a card slid into the lock. The mechanism released and the door slammed open, but caught on the chain. Camille gagged again as the blade drew her sinews into her spine. "Mr. Bonham?" The voice was louder now. It spoke rapidly in another language. "Stand back, please. We are coming in."

Camille heard a smash, but the door didn't move. Instead, shards of glass rained down. Not glass, she realized as she landed in the debris: china. She rolled to one side to see Amanda standing over a fallen Josie, the base of a smashed vase clamped between her bound hands. But the girl stumbled to her feet. Behind Camille, the door chain strained but didn't break. Amanda thrust a jagged shard at Josie, who knocked it easily from the awkward grasp as she lunged to snatch a clump of Amanda's hair and haul her like a cow caught by the nose ring through the french windows to the balcony.

"I don't see any other option, Teddy." Words directed at her father, who groaned and rolled toward the edge of the bed. Josie threw one long leg over the ornate balcony, straddling the railing on her tiptoes. She tugged Amanda forward until she too pivoted on the ironwork, hands trapped beneath her own body weight. "This is a family matter, Camille Kemble." Josie jutted her chin at the interconnecting door across the room. As though mesmerized, Camille pulled it open to reveal a mirror-image bedroom.

Behind her, the scrabbling of tools and overlapping voices in the corridor echoed the scramble of Amanda's leather sandals. The curtains that framed the teetering women swayed, beckoning Camille to help. She let go of the connecting door and lunged toward the balcony just as Amanda's feet left the floor. As she grabbed Amanda's hips, she heard a low groan from Ed, as he pushed himself from the bed and lumbered through the muslin to grab his wife by the arm and fling her aside.

A gunshot sounded—*no*, Camille thought, *not a gunshot*—the doorframe shuddering under a heavy blow from the hallway.

Framed by golden streetlights, Ed crushed Josie in his arms. Her knife, bloody now, bounced across the mahogany floor to where Amanda had fallen heavily onto bound hands. On the balcony, Ed faltered, disoriented. Another blow from the hallway obliterated Amanda's voice as she screamed his name.

Josie's arms wreathed her father's neck. "It's time," she said, and kicked off with her free leg, tipping the two of them over the railing into the warm tropical air.

The doorframe splintered.

A long scream echoed from below the balcony. Then silence again.

It was as though they were in the eye of the storm. A moment of respite before the security guards came through the door, before they were arrested, two foreign women charged with killing a father and child.

"Come on." Camille tried to haul Amanda to her feet. She instinctively ducked as the doorframe withstood another blow. One more and it must surely come in. She released Amanda and opened the connecting door—*fuck Mrs. Bonham, stay if she wants, it's her funeral*—but Amanda pushed herself up, dashing into the next room, Camille behind her, just as the main door slammed back against the wall.

"Mr. Bonham? My God!"

The voices in the room switched to Burmese and were shut out altogether as Camille closed the interconnecting door without so much as a click. She stared into the swirling grain of the wood. Behind her, the bed crunched under a woman's weight. Ed's wife sat with a picture frame in her hand. The room was decorated with Josie's childhood ephemera and photographs, a museum of herself.

"She was watching from in here," Amanda said. "I felt her as soon as I entered. Like I do at home. She's always been watching us."

"We have to get out of here."

"But I killed him," she whispered.

"If you plan on taking the blame, stay. But I'm leaving." They were sitting ducks. The police would question whoever stayed in this room. And when they saw photos of Josie strewn around, the same girl who fell from the balcony of the attached room . . .

Camille could not be found in this room. She went to the main door and cracked it an inch. Enough to peep down the corridor. Tools and broken wood were scattered over the carpet. Rapid voices next door. She had to move before more people arrived. Police, ambulance. She had to get out now. But she would need to pass the open door of room 513 to get to the lift; the other way was a dead end.

"There's a fire escape at the end of the corridor."

Camille jumped at the voice close to her ear. She looked up at the cool blonde who was handing her a way out. "Aren't you coming?"

"I should be dead too."

"You will be if you get done for murder in this country."

Amanda glanced at the framed photo of Josie and her mother, their dark hair entwined in the wind. She propped it on the table for the police to find.

Chapter 51

Neither woman spoke as they juddered along in the taxi, but every so often Camille saw Amanda raise a stringy tissue to her face to wipe away sweat and tears. Camille succumbed to the heat, tasting salt on her top lip. Faces slid by the window as busy sidewalks spilled pedestrians into the road. She wanted to scream at them to get out of their way. But she took a breath and forced calmness to fill her up like a balloon. Soon she'd be leaving this place. She could leave it all behind. Maybe.

At the drop-off point outside departures, she put a hand on her companion's arm. "Can you hold it together in there? We have to get out before the police come after you—"

"I'm on a false passport. It's South African. They won't connect me at the airport."

"How the hell did you get a fake—"

Amanda waved her out of the taxi. They walked to the terminal. One hour until the flight. The clock marked the passing minutes with a juddering hand. Camille thought of Ed's final movements. She had no idea what to say to Amanda, who had just seen her husband die. Her poise was fragile; she had no idea how long it might hold. While she waited in line at the ticket counter, she switched on her phone to a string of missed calls from an office number. How long would it take for news of a dead British national in Burma to reach the High Commission in Singapore? She redialed the missed call. A curt voice answered on the first ring.

"Camille." It was Josh.

"Did you call?"

"Once or twice. Where are you?"

"On holiday."

"Are you with Edward Bonham?"

Camille glanced at Amanda, who was mesmerized by a television screen showing BBC News with no sound.

"No."

"Good. We just got word from the British consul in Yangon that Mr. Bonham was found dead at the Oriental Hotel."

"Dead." He had to be—the room was on the fifth floor—but it sounded so cold in Josh's official tones. "What happened?"

Josh's voice became tinny as he explained the few details that were known. "And there was a young woman with Mr. Bonham. We believe it was the daughter, Josie."

Camille glanced over to check that Amanda was still placated by the television. "How is the daughter?"

"I'm afraid Josie Bonham is also dead. The police are thinking murder-suicide. Thing is, it's not clear who was the murder and who was the suicide. Edward Bonham had defensive knife wounds on his hands and was covered in vomit and God knows what else. The hotel manager claims there was another woman at the scene, but the police are not convinced. Descriptions of this second woman vary wildly. Tall, short. Aged twenty, aged forty. Blonde hair, red hair. They could only agree on the fact that she was Caucasian." The phone broadcast white noise. "Are you with me, Camille?"

"I'm confident the local police will get to the bottom of a simple murder-suicide."

"I'm sure that's true. You're heading back to Singapore now?"

"I'm at the airport."

"I spoke to the high commissioner. He's willing to bring you back onto the press team, though you'll have to go through another probationary period."

While she thought about it, the phone faded to black.

"Camille?"

"Thank you, Josh. I appreciate your efforts." After he rang off, she stared at the blank screen.

"They know?" Amanda's voice made her start. She handed Camille a paper cup of coffee.

"They'll be trying to contact you soon."

"But I'm not there. I can't go back, can I?" she said. "They're going to find out I was here. I've got no alibi. And the fact that I came on a false passport makes it look worse. They'll say I killed them both."

"What else can you do?"

Amanda didn't answer. She stirred her coffee with a spoon so slender it seemed like it ought to melt.

"We only came here to find my parents," Camille said. "Ed was helping me."

"Did you find them?"

"They're long gone." Camille hesitated. "I didn't sleep with your husband. To be honest, I would have if he'd tried, I felt so lost. But he said he didn't cheat."

Amanda held up one palm to make her stop. The queue moved forward, and Camille stepped into a space at the counter. "Two one-way tickets to Singapore." And then to Amanda: "I'll need your passport."

"I'm not going to Singapore. I just need to make a call." She dug into her pocket and came out with a few soft notes. "I won't need a passport. My mother knows who I am."

Camille gathered all the kyat from her purse and pressed it into Amanda's hands. "Take this. I'm sorry it's not more, but I can only get so much out of the ATM."

Amanda took one of the larger notes and handed the rest back. "This is all I need." She walked away to a phone kiosk.

Camille faced the counter. "One ticket to Singapore. Just one."

When Camille got to the gate, she watched figures moving inside the cockpit of the aircraft. The scene was lit by yellow floodlights that hit her tired eyes like handfuls of flung sand. The row of seats rocked slightly as someone sat next to her. She resisted the urge to tut; even with all the available space in the lounge, some guy had to crowd her. She hoped he wouldn't try to strike up a conversation—

"Good evening, Camille."

She turned to see Josh.

"What are you doing here?"

"Looking for my press team."

"But we just spoke—"

"There's this newfangled device called a mobile phone. When I couldn't reach you today, I tried your emergency contact—your brother—and he told me you'd come to Yangon. Thought I'd better see if you're okay. I'd just landed when I got the call about Bonham."

Camille pushed herself back into the cup of the seat and watched the activity on the tarmac for a few seconds before she spoke again. "Thank you for coming here for me, but I'm going to resign from the British High Commission. I'm sorry. I've been offered a job with Sharmila Menon as a paralegal working on human rights cases. I'm going to accept when I get back."

"You can take some time to think it over."

She shook her head. "I need to do something good with my life."

Josh's brow rose. "It seems to me that you have a lot of good in your life. A brother who cares for you, friends and colleagues who want you home safe. So much career potential. And at least one person who would like to make sure he has enough cash in his pocket next time to buy you a drink. Especially if you're no longer his employee." He tapped one finger on his chin, and the row of chairs stirred beneath Camille. "Plus, I've got something for you." He held out a Post-it note.

She read his elegant scrawl. Leilani Nullas. An address in Quezon City, near Manila.

"What is this?"

"I put in a request at the Ministry of Manpower. Via a contact. The last known address for a maid called Lani—I assume Lani is short for Leilani—who lived at Tanglin Green until 1999. It was a long time ago, but it might be worth a visit."

Camille pressed the Post-it note to her heart. She'd always kept a place in there for Lani. "Would you come with me, Josh?"

"Well, my son is coming to visit soon. Thought it was time we laid down some memories in Singapore. But after that, I'd be happy to offer consular assistance."

"Would you come as you?"

"Even happier to offer personal assistance."

She watched the pilots run through their final checks. "I met my father today. Or do you know that already?"

"He's alive?"

"And kicking. He's been here for fifteen years. In prison. How could that have happened? Without anyone at the BHC knowing?"

He shrugged. "We didn't have diplomatic relations with Burma fifteen years ago. But we would have known if one of our own was imprisoned. I can only assume he never traveled here on a British passport. And chose to keep himself under the radar. Didn't want to be found."

She thought back to her father saying that he wouldn't leave her mother here. Was he punishing himself, exiling himself out of guilt?

"Will you see your father again?"

"He's a drug dealer; he was setting Edward Bonham up with a shipment. Ed needs money to bail out his business. Or he did." The past tense stuck in her throat. "I don't think I'll see Magnus Kemble again, no. He's not my father, not the one I remember. We both had unrealistic expectations and found someone who didn't measure up."

"You could build a new relationship, perhaps?"

"The thing is, Josh, I loved my father. My real father. But I didn't like this man. And I don't want the reality to kill off my memory. For such a long time, the memory of my parents is all I've had."

"Maybe in time?"

"Never say never."

Josh nodded for a moment, and then said, "They say you have to stop blaming your parents when you reach thirty."

"Collin told me that too. So I've got a few years to go. But the fact is, the man I met today didn't value the bond between father and daughter. Even Edward Bonham understood that, for all his flaws. He was a good man, beneath all the bluster."

"I think you were a little in love with him, Camille."

"Father figure, maybe." She laughed, then flushed, realizing too late that Ed wasn't so much older than Josh. "He was a link to my parents. Simple as that. I know you hated Ed—"

"I saw nothing simple in Edward Bonham. He was damaged."

"We had that in common. But it seems to me you can be damaged and come out stronger, like Ed—he raised a child alone. Or you can be damaged and broken. Like Josie." A burst of crackle on the loudspeaker signaled an announcement that their flight was ready. Camille gathered her bag, ripping the zipper through metal teeth. "And whatever you say about him, at the end Ed was a gentleman."

Out of the corner of her eye, she saw Josh shift back in his seat. He stood up and folded his jacket with care.

"Camille, I've never in my life jumped on a plane because I was afraid for someone's safety. I'm glad I was wrong and you didn't need rescuing, but even so . . . I'm sorry you had to go to a man like Edward Bonham to feel respected."

"Not as sorry as he is."

Camille walked away to join the queue of passengers with boarding passes in hand. Josh stood in line behind her but had the grace to leave her to her thoughts. She wondered what her father would do now. If he might try to contact her again. If maybe, one day, he might stop blaming himself and come in from the cold.

Outside, the lights of Yangon burned behind black hills like a sacked city. Camille stepped forward to hand over her ticket, and Josh mirrored the movement. She watched their reflections stand together in the plate glass window, a whispered suggestion in the darkness. Shadows cast by tomorrow's sunrise.

Chapter 52

No phone, no ticket, no money. Even Amanda's stomach was empty. She showed a taxi driver the destination her mother had spelled out. Soon, wavering lights told her they had reached water. It would be a long drive downriver to a secluded port. She watched headlights from oncoming cars slide off her hot skin like cheap lotion.

In Singapore, there would be police lights sliding over the facade of the condo. Raja would be aghast. He would lead the police into the Bonhams' apartment, lingering in the doorway of the elevator, unsure where to stand while officers found Amanda in pieces: a passport here, a credit card there, a Dependant's Pass on the bedside table. What kind of picture would they construct from these scraps? And when they were done investigating and the flat was empty but for the dull chime of the retreating lift, would the Bonham ghosts creep out from the shadows? What had Ed once said? He always left a piece of himself behind. Tonight, he would put on one of his old bands and they would dance to "Chocolate Girl." He would strip off her silver wrapping while their reflections bled together in the glass.

Amanda let her fingers hang out the car window—open to the cool night air in lieu of air-conditioning—watching the world slide past as she had done while trapped behind the facade of the Attica. Josie's ghost must be there too; all along, she had been the heat on the other side of the pane making their vision waver. And she must be laughing—that girl's voice must be echoing around the void space of their rooms. Because she got what she wanted in the end; she got Ed, *Teddy*, all to herself.

A roadside pagoda in the shape of an urn made Amanda avert her eyes. Thoughts of Ed were too much. Her mind had been numbed by the blow. Right now, she sensed only his absence, but he was so often absent that the feeling was familiar. She thought of Ed on his travels, stepping from one reality into another too quickly to adjust. That was her now, lagging behind the truth. Sooner or later all the pieces would come together—the anger, the guilt, the sorrow—but right now the pain was a dim whisper, like the wind through the hole that he'd punched in the kitchen window, which would one day shatter and make the whole place howl.

The taxi arrived at the port, and Amanda walked into a sleepily lit building, past a man pushing a machine to buff already-gleaming tiles, and out to the water's edge. She crept along the dock until she found a dark corner where she could sit between tires tied to the concrete quay. She opened a bag of samosas she'd bought from a street vendor and gobbled them up. A stray dog with hanging nipples sidled up, and she threw her crumbs. Amanda tore the paper bag and made two origami shapes. *They could be boats,* she thought, *or little cribs.* Holding herself steady on a rope, she placed the cradles one by one into the water. They eddied for a while and moved out into the flow. Once they were out of reach, she sat back onto her haunches and then settled against the tire with the tide dropping away from her toes.

At some point, she slept, waking to a wispy sky the color of dry ice and the jingling harness of a horse and cart. The sound reminded her of the tiny vials of medication rattling in the fridge door and that took her to the frozen embryos, so far away but still calling to her. She looked for her cribs in the water, but they were long gone. Along the quay, the shouts of dockers preceded the birds to a morning chorus. A white ship had berthed, and she recognized the *Guanyin,* radiant against the gray water despite a century of service. On deck, Laura braced herself against the railing with arms as taut as sails while her crew juggled ropes around her. Amanda dragged her numb limbs beneath her body and summoned the strength to move along the dock, into the lee of the ship.

The gangplank buffeted concrete as her mother descended. The two women stopped a foot shy of each other. "So this is your boat," Amanda said. *"Guanyin."*

"Beautiful, isn't she? She's saved a lot of people."

A surge rose inside Amanda, a pressure that would only be relieved with tears. "I'm lucky you were nearby."

"Silly girl." Laura pulled Amanda to her shoulder. "Don't you realize I've always been nearby? Circling you at a distance. Like the moon." Arms closed around her shoulders, and she let herself turn to liquid.

"Ed died and it was my fault. I killed him."

"Goodness, I wish I'd been that brave with your father."

"Mother . . ."

"Well, don't be melodramatic. You didn't kill him. It was the girl. I knew there was something wrong with her."

"I knew it too. But I didn't listen to myself."

"It's hard to stand up for yourself when you're being undermined on all sides. Even I didn't help, talking about your father the way I did. That's what you get for being overemotional. Better to stay practical."

"I don't think I can—"

"You're suffering bereavement—and that will occur to its own unpredictable timetable—but we need to be practical and set a new course."

"I can't be practical. I can't even think straight. I keep seeing Ed with Josie touching his face. And I did nothing to protect him. I should have called the police—"

"Stop . . ."

"Would a jury convict me for what I did? The sedatives in the water?"

"The rat poison surely killed him."

"What if the sedatives made it worse. Is that conspiracy to murder?"

"Did you set out to kill him? Were you in collusion with her?"

"No. I wanted to catch him in the act and stop him from hurting any more women."

"Well, then."

"But there weren't any women!" Amanda pushed away from her mother and turned to the squalid water. "And I imagined him dead. Before. I thought the worst of him, and I decided that if it was true, we'd be better off with him dead. What sort of wife thinks that about her husband?"

"Oh, God, Amanda. Find me a woman who hasn't thought of killing her husband—but thoughts are not the same as actions. And you had more than enough provocation. You're not a perpetrator of this crime, you're a victim, a survivor. Josie would have killed you too."

"If we hadn't come to Burma, I think she might have done."

"So forgive yourself. Leave the guilt on this quayside with the rats and the trash. The grief will be coming with us, and that's quite enough to deal with. So now we do have to be practical. Are we going to Singapore?"

"That's the last place I should go. They might arrest me."

"Go in on the fake passport. I think you have something to collect?"

"I don't care about my things. They can clear the apartment. Dump it all. Even the things I kept in a safety-deposit box—all junk. Apart from this." Amanda rooted in her pocket and held out a ring, an antique emerald with a halo of diamonds. "I brought it in case I needed to sell it. But you should have it back. I'm sorry I stole from you."

Laura slid the engagement ring onto her finger, which Amanda saw was thinner, frailer than before. Old woman's hands. "So gaudy," Laura said. "Your father gave it to me to please his grandmother. We both disliked the ring—and the grandmother—but he did it out of

Jo Furniss

filial piety. She wrote him out of her will anyway. So much for doing the right thing. Shall we give it to someone? A random act of kindness?"

Amanda felt a tremor of a smile inside her, so slight it didn't show on the surface, but seismic nonetheless. It felt like hope.

"I do have something in Singapore I need to pick up," Amanda said.

Laura nodded, pleased. "Can you remove the embryos from the country?"

"I could make arrangements for that. Or, if I go when the time is right, I could transfer them and hope they stick."

"Let's do that then." Her mother clattered up the gangplank. "I think I'd make an excellent grandmother. I've grown up a lot since I had you."

Amanda lingered by the river. Little fish swam between plastic bags in the mushroom-colored murk. The air was warm and moist—nurturing conditions. She thought of the paper cribs she'd sent off, wondering if they'd made it yet to the insatiable ocean, how long it would take to cross the Andaman Sea and negotiate the Straits of Singapore. *Tell our babies I'm coming,* she begged the river. Her promises sprinkled into the water that would flow back to her embryos waiting in Singapore, frozen like spring flowers under the snow.

ACKNOWLEDGMENTS

Heartfelt thanks go to:

My inspiring agent, Danielle Egan-Miller, and her Browne & Miller colleagues, Clancey D'Isa and Mariana Fisher. My editors, Jodi Warshaw and Caitlin Alexander, for bringing order to chaos. In addition, Nicole Pomeroy and everyone at Lake Union Publishing who turned raw material into a novel, and Rachel Fudge and Erica Avedikian in the editorial team, and David Drummond for the gorgeous cover design. Also my fellow Lake Union authors for their wisdom, laughs, and virtual hugs.

Colleagues at the Singapore Writers Group, who enlightened early chapters during our critique meetings, and to Helle Sidelmann Norup, Paula Treick DeBoard, Emily Carpenter, and Alice Clark-Platts, who braved a messy first draft. Also to Stephanie Suga Chen, Jen Wei Ting, Justin Wan, and Damyanti Biswas for cultural orientation.

Susy Marriott and Tom Bromley at the Professional Writing Academy, whose short crime writing course spawned Camille Kemble.

Fellow author Captain Fatty Goodlander and his wife, Carolyn, who fed me lunch and sea gypsy anecdotes aboard their forty-three-foot ketch, *Ganesh*, while moored in Singapore.

The UK's Foreign and Commonwealth Office for their "British Nationals Overseas" online guidance, and for the many times our diplomatic service in various countries has helped this particular Brit abroad.

My depiction of the British High Commission of Singapore is vigorously (and no doubt hopelessly) fictionalized.

Robert and Linda Baigrie—parents of Arina Skye—donated a generous sum to have their daughter's name included in this novel during a charity auction at the 2017 Africa Society Ball in Singapore. Their donation went to the children's charity World Vision.

The people of Singapore: I'm sorry for relocating places and implying there are cobras lurking on every corner. I spent seven years living in your marvelous country, and I'm grateful for your hospitality. Especially the food. Roll a *popiah* for me. Also, the expat wives who shared advice and way too many personal details on rival Facebook forums.

All the Furnisses and Fosters who cheer me on. Especially Mark, who is an expat, a onetime pilot, and a frequent business traveler, but a less troublesome husband than Ed. And Lydia and Frank for handing out my books to strangers in shops.

Mae Nullas, whose professional and cheery running of our Singapore household gifted me time to write and enjoy my children. Also Karien van Ditzhuijzen from the Humanitarian Organization for Migration Economics (HOME), the NGO that inspired a pressure group I called HELP. I should make it clear that HELP and its methods are my creation, and any mistakes my own. A final nod goes to the "silent army" of migrant women who work in homes in Singapore and other countries; may they be treated with dignity and respect.

ABOUT THE AUTHOR

After spending a decade as a broadcast journalist for the BBC, Jo Furniss gave up the glamour of night shifts to become a freelance writer and serial expatriate. Originally from the United Kingdom, she spent seven years in Singapore and also lived in Switzerland and Cameroon.

As a journalist, Jo worked for numerous online outlets and magazines, including *Monocle* and the *Economist*. She has edited books for a Nobel laureate and the palace of the Sultan of Brunei. She has a Distinction in MA Professional Writing from Falmouth University.

Jo's debut novel, *All the Little Children*, was an Amazon Charts bestseller.

Connect with her via Facebook (/JoFurnissAuthor) and Twitter (@Jo_Furniss) or through her website, www.jofurniss.com.